Faith Hope and Love
Issues of Life

Diva Dorreen

ISBN: 978-0-9963612-2-4 (e)
ISBN: 978-0-9963612-3-1 (sc)

Dedication

I dedicate this book to those who dare to love themselves first.
SELF LOVE!

Diva Dorreen

CONTENTS

Acknowledgements

To my husband, Bernard, thanks for the many times I typed well past the time you were asleep.

Thanks to my sister-in-law, Kathy, who has been more encouraging than she knows.

Thanks to my sister Darlene, who had so many post-its sticking out of my book I thought it was a new flag.

My longtime friend and editor, Pamela Mc Neil, who reminded me that she is an educated Wellesley woman who could give me a proper edit. You are a lifesaver. Jessica Wright Tilles, from TWA, thank you for my final edit and critiques. They can only make me better the next book.

Thanks to my children, Trey and Samantha LA, who are doing their own *thang*. Thanks to my daughter, Tiffani, for being her own person, and Titus, for growing up so I can now do my thing. Cameron, continue to grow and spread your wings. Autumn, thank you for making me laugh. ☺ I love you all!

Prologue

The room was dim, but the circus -theme decor in the small mansion intrigued even him. It wasn't his first time, but he definitely didn't get the memo to come in his circus costume. Instead, he was dressed in dark leather pants and a Zorro mask.

Seated on the leather couch, with his strong thighs, muscular abs, and chest glistening from the oil he rubbed on earlier, his long arms stretched across the back of the couch invitingly. Many passed by, looking him over, taking in his defined physique, but he waved them off. He came to watch.

His sexual appetite was excited years ago, but tonight he only wanted a taste. The need to participate was dissipating. He was in love. There were many watchers, so he was not alone.

A woman wearing an acrobat costume swung from two rings that hung from the ceiling. He watched her flip around and around. Through her mask, he saw her eyes on him. Dismounting, she sashayed toward him. Then, front handspring, front handspring, and front walkover into a straddle until she hopped onto his lap into a full split.

He smiled.

"I haven't seen you in a while," she said, running her hands down his glistening chest to his private. "Where have you been?"

He continued to smile, but remained mute.

"I've been looking for you." She saw something vague in his demeanor.

"Why?"

"You left me wanting more last time."

Tilting his head to the side, he continued smiling. "I'm watching and you are blocking my view."

The young woman looked him over. His leather shorts, just long enough to cover his behind, sent a different message. She gripped his strong thighs, rubbed his muscular arms, and leaned in to kiss him, but his hand covered her mouth, blocking her from tasting the sweet nectar his soft lips promised.

"I'm only here to watch," he said, again. "And you know my rules. I don't kiss."

The woman pouted, and then smiled. Lifting up, she placed one leg behind her neck to show her flexibility smiling again, as though asking for his final answer. When he had not changed his mind she brought her leg down. Pushing up on his thighs, she swung her legs around, dismounting.

"That's too bad," she cooed, "I had new tricks to share."

Swinging her teardrop-shaped behind, the circus acrobat strutted away, making sure she gave him a show. Before she could reach the other side of the vast room, she was approached by a couple. Looking over her shoulder, she gave him one last opportunity to change his mind. He blew her a kiss and smiled.

Turning his attention elsewhere, he resumed his position.

Love is Patient and Kind

Caden had never buried a loved one. The weeks after India's service were harder than his breakup with Cuyler. He found himself not wanting to do anything except spend time with his toddler, Callia.

Surprised at how bright Callia was, when he arrived, it broke his heart to see her search behind him for India. A few times, she cried for no reason and he realized she was going through her own mourning. Those times he found the hardest. He knew she didn't understand and there was no way to explain it to her. Even he found himself reduced to tears during those times and Callia took care of him.

As his and India's intended wedding date approached, he found himself more secluded. He wanted the day to come and go. Once the day came and went, he believed he would no longer feel anxious.

Having received her wedding bouquet, he decided to visit her grave and leave it on that day. He asked the photographer to come to his house and take pictures of Callia and him as well. To some, it probably sounded morbid, but he had to do what he could to get through the heaviness that plagued him. That day would be the last day he would allow himself to mourn. He knew he would still feel sad, but he also knew this place he was in was not healthy. His life had to go on and he could hear India telling him the same.

He was a senior engineer in the firm now, and although excused from work until he was able to return, he knew it didn't mean forever. His projects were being run by Josh, the next in line for promotion. The partners suggested he clear his head and return once he had everything taken care of. They joked saying they didn't need any buildings falling.

At church, others looked at him with pity. Everyone tried to coddle him when he just wanted time to himself. It seemed there was an invisible wall between him and the single women at church. They appeared to want to approach him, but that invisible wall of sorrow and depression kept them at bay. Many tried to get to him through Callia, wanting to hold and play with her, but she would have no parts of any of them. He felt like the talk of the church.

The hardest time was at night when he was alone. Dreams of India often awakened him. When he reached for her, she was not there. This is when his mind raced, re-enacting the day of the tornado. Thoughts of different scenarios plagued him. What if he had taken her to dinner? She would not have been in La Plata. The what-ifs did not happen, leaving him to deal with what was.

Sometimes, he sat by the window, looking at the stars or lay in bed and watched them through the window. He used to believe when a person died they returned to the universe. He liked to believe India was out there, looking down on him, but then he became ashamed, wondering if she were angry as she watched him wallowing in self-pity, instead of going on about his life.

The eve of their wedding was especially difficult. Sitting by his window, he watched the moon tease him. It was a bright orange, indicating that the next day would be warmer than usual. It looked as though it was smiling at him.

"What are you smiling at?" he asked, then laughed for carrying on a fruitless conversation - with a moon.

The moon continued to smile at him. He imagined it was India smiling down on him, letting him know everything was going to be fine.

"I miss you so much, Indy. I wish you were here. I wish we had more time together. I'm sorry I wasn't there to protect you. Tomorrow is our wedding day. I have your bouquet and I will bring it with me when I come to see you. Callia and I are still taking our pictures tomorrow. I just wish you were here."

Passing clouds partially covered the moon, taking its smile with them.

Sighing, Caden leaned back in the chair. He needed to get some sleep. Closing his eyes, he tried, once again, to seek slumber. This time, sleep came.

Preston quietly climbed the stairs, trying not to awaken his girls. Callia heard him, as she called out to him from her crib. It was well past her bedtime, but Preston couldn't resist. He had not seen her all day.

Callia bounced and shook her crib when she saw him. He reached out for her and she reached out to him.

"Bonjour mon amour," he whispered, lifting her from her crib. "Hello, my love," he repeated in English.

"That only works on me." Cuyler stood in the doorway, smiling. The sheer gown he recently purchased revealed her nude, shapely body. Turning, she showed her backside and disappeared into the darkness of the hallway.

Preston kissed Callia and put her back in her crib. Rubbing her back, he told her, "Bonsoir precieux. *(Goodnight precious)*." Callia looked at him and smiled, indicating she understood. She fussed, as he tried to back out of the room. "Jusqu'a demain *(until tomorrow)*," he said, and left the room. He could hear her whimper a little, but she quieted down almost immediately.

"If I don't learn French, you two will be talking behind my back soon." Cuyler startled him when he turned the corner and entered the hall. "You know she has you wrapped around her finger?"

"Like mother like daughter."

They walked back to their room. Balloons that read CONGRATULATIONS hovered around their bed. Preston turned to Cuyler and smiled, knowing immediately what the balloons meant.

"When?" he asked, lifting her into his arms.

"In about twenty-eight weeks." She smiled.

"Thank you. Thank you. Thank you," he whispered, burying his face in her neck. Preston's mind raced to the finish line. He thought to call his dad, and then his mind went to his brothers. He didn't know whom to call first. Putting Cuyler down, he retrieved his phone from his pocket and immediately called his dad. He paced impatiently, waiting for him to answer.

"Pop!" he said, almost yelling into the phone. "You're about to have another grandchild!"

Cuyler watched as Preston phone hopped from one family member to another, giving each the news of the new arrival to come. After his calls, he turned his attention to her now lying on the bed with her legs in the air, wrapping the string of a balloon around them.

"That's how you got in that condition," he teased, easing between her opened thighs, as she enticed him. "I didn't believe I could be as happy as I am right now."

"Me, too," she responded, kissing him.

Preston stood to remove his suit, stripping off each piece, not caring where either article of clothing landed. Usually, he hung them as he undressed to keep them fresh to wear again, but this time he didn't care.

Cuyler watched with anticipation, anxious for the celebration to begin.

Preston woke to the sounds of Callia screaming and laughing. He loved waking to that sound. Rolling on to his back to the balloons still dancing in the air above his head, he smiled, remembering the two of them sharing the night before. He never tired of making love to Cuyler. Married for almost two years, they were having another blessing—a child.

Preston imagined what it would be and concluded he really didn't care as long as the child was healthy. *Another girl would be nice for Callia to grow with,* he thought, because, as Cuyler had pointed out, she had him wrapped around her finger. He heard Callia giggling, again, uncontrollably and decided to join the festivities.

As Preston walked to her room, he heard a familiar voice. It was Caden. He peeped into the room, trying not to disturb their moment. Callia's mouth was open, gasping for air, trying to breath and laugh. Caden was tickling her. Callia caught Preston out the corner of her eye and squealed for help.

"Bonjour Papa *(Hello Papa),*" she said to Preston through laughter.

"Bonjour precieux," he greeted. He walked across the room and shook Caden's hand. "Hey, man. What do you two have planned for the day?"

"We are going to put flowers on India's site, and then we are going to have pictures taken." Caden said.

Callia was Cuyler and Caden's daughter. Preston, though her step-father, had been a part of her life before she made her debut into the world. He was there at her birth and vowed to always be there for her.

It was hard to believe two years ago, he and Caden were rolling in Cuyler's living room floor, fighting for her love. Nor would anyone understand the bond formed through the love of a child and the death of a love one. It had only been a few months since India's death in the storm and through Callia two men, who should have been enemies, were friends – almost family.

The crazy triangle of friends, who were once lovers, had shared much in the passing months. They were living proof of how God could heal and turn people's hearts.

Watching Caden dress Callia in her flower girl dress, Preston remembered that today was supposed to have been Caden and India's wedding day. Preston's heart went out to him. He couldn't imagine life without Cuyler.

"You need me to help you get her dressed?"

"No, I've got her," Caden said, but his body language spoke otherwise, of which Preston noticed.

Preston went to Callia's dresser and pulled out her dress socks and shoes. "Is Cuyler still here?" he asked, wondering why she was not helping him get Callia together.

"She said she had to run to the office to get some files and she would see me when I brought Callia back."

Preston raised his brow. She did not tell him she was going to the office, which broke a rule they had set in place. He didn't realize he had stopped gathering Callia's things.

Caden watched Preston as he hesitated. "Everything okay?"

"Everything is fine," he lied.

Preston handed Caden the socks and shoes and excused himself. He went to his bedroom to call her. While waiting for an answer, he opened his closet to find a suit. He wasn't going to let Caden go through this day alone.

"Hey, sleepy head," Cuyler answered, "you're up."

"You didn't tell me you were going to the office today." He could not hide his irritation. He never liked the location of her office, but she insisted it be there for the convenience of her clients. The rules they established were to keep her safe, but most importantly to give him peace.

"I left a note on the bed."

There was a slight pause, as Preston searched the covers. "I'm sorry. I found it."

"I know what our agreement is," she reassured him.

"When will you be back?"

"I'm on my way now. Is Caden still there?"

"Yes and you need to be, too. He's heading to the burial site. Today is supposed to be their wedding day, so I don't think he should go alone. We should go with him."

"He will probably tell us not to come."

"That's why we're going to just show up. So come because he needs us."

This was why she married him. Preston was one of the most thoughtful people she knew. "I will make a few calls and be home soon."

She called Meagan and Candace and told them the plan. They said they would come. She also reached out to her sister, Tashia. She hoped she did not overstep, but whatever it took to cheer him up and get him out of his funk was worth a try.

When she arrived home, Cuyler quickly changed into the clothes Preston laid out for her and met him downstairs. He told her when she arrived that Caden and Callia were going to get their pictures taken first before going to the cemetery. She sent a group text to update everyone on his possible arrival.

A New Family

Caden arrived with Callia to the reception site. He had originally planned to do the pictures at his place until he learned he could not cancel his reservation at the venue.

The photographer had set up his gear in anticipation of their arrival. When Callia saw all the flowers and ribbons, she ran to them in excitement. Caden couldn't believe she was already eighteen months old. She screamed to Caden for him to come and look, as she attempted to eat one of the flowers.

"Callia, no!" he yelled, running toward her to remove the buds from her mouth. She quickly spat them out once she realized they did not taste as good as they looked.

The buds from the flowers ran down her chin and Caden wiped them off. "Are you hungry, baby girl?" he asked, wondering for the first time if she had breakfast. Callia just laughed at Caden and kissed his nose, as he often did her. "Come on. Let's get our picture taken. Okay?"

Caden lifted her in his arms. The photographer gave directions for the pictures. They took some in the garden, on the patio, and in a chair that was set up. After the session, he arranged to pick up the pictures in a few weeks and then he put sleepy Callia in her car seat. He needed to move on to his next destination.

The ride to the cemetery wasn't very long. He wished it were a little farther. He wasn't as ready as he thought to be back at the site. It had been months since her burial, but being there made all the feelings of that day rush back.

His throat tightened and the brim of his eyes burned from welling tears. Callia was now asleep, so he decided to take the time to pull himself together.

In the front seat were the vows he had written for India. He put the car in park and reached for the sheet of paper. He unfolded it and read over the words as though preparing for his wedding.

When I first met you, I was a mess and you let me know it

7

I was spiraling down and was so oblivious
When my tears would fall, you promised to love my pain away
I was surrounded by everything I needed, but had nothing I wanted
But you were there through my highs and lows, never asking for anything for yourself
You became my teacher, friend, and confident; my ride or die chick, never leaving me to stand alone
So, I let my heart take a chance to be loved by you and you never let me down
I came alive inside when I finally found my way
Love from you was so real, so true, so genuine
I was wise enough to know when a miracle unfolded
All my life I've waited for this day
You're my world, you're my life, you're my new beginning

The tears were freely flowing now and he was grateful Callia was asleep. Caden was oblivious to the people approaching his car until he heard the tapping on his window. He was too broken to look up and did not want to talk to anyone. Suddenly, his door opened. If alone he wouldn't have cared, but he had his baby with him, so he immediately became defensive.

Preston grabbed his arm in defense. Caden looked around at his newly created family who came to rescue him. Preston helped him from the car and embraced him. He held onto him until Caden pulled from his grasp. Cuyler had pulled the beautiful bouquet from the back seat and Tashia climbed in to sit with Callia.

With his arm around his shoulder, Preston led Caden to India's gravesite and the small group followed.

Cuyler handed him India's bouquet. He held it for a moment and then placed it in the stand in the ground made to hold flowers. He knew that by morning it would be gone, taken by another by passer.

Everyone stood in silence, waiting for Caden to lead the way in his plans for the visit, but he couldn't speak; too choked up to say anything. Looking down, he saw he still carried the vows he had written for their day in his hand and tried to start reading, but his throat was tight.

Cuyler took the paper from his hand and looked it over, but before she could begin reading, Preston began singing a song in the most beautiful voice she had heard from him. There wasn't a dry eye amongst them, including Preston's. Cuyler cleared her throat and read the vows. It was the first time she had a glimpse of what he shared with India.

They stood with Caden until he was ready to go.

"Good bye, India. I won't be back like this, because you're not here, you're here," he said, pointing to his heart. "I won't have to go far to be with you, because you will always be with me." After those last words, he turned and walked back to his car.

Callia was still asleep. Tashia climbed out of the back seat and embraced Caden. "It's going to get better. It doesn't feel like it will right now, but it will."

"Why don't you come back to the house, Caden?" Preston suggested.

"Maybe later. I have one more stop to make."

"Do you want company?" Cuyler asked.

"No," he answered, and then added, "I appreciate the offer. Thank you."

"Do you want us to take Callia?" Preston asked.

"No. She needs to come with me, but I will come by later." Caden nodded at Preston. "Thanks."

"No problem, Caden. We are here for you."

Once Preston was clear of the car, Caden pulled out slowly and headed for his last stop.

Congratulations

Auntie Khadada was expecting Caden and Callia's arrival. Although she saw Callia during the week, she looked forward to their visit together. She deliberately invited Caden over to take his mind off the day and what that day represented—loss and pain.

When she saw Caden in his tuxedo and a sleeping Callia in her flower girl dress, her heart sank. She took Callia to her bedroom. Gently, she undressed the sleeping toddler and covered her with a light blanket. It was beginning to get warmer outside, but there was still a slight chill in the air.

She kept Callia during the week. It was a shock when Cuyler asked her to be her babysitter, because she couldn't find a nannie, and Callia took to her so freely. She was ecstatic to keep her. Preston was relieved she finally trusted someone else with Callia. Khadada had formed a relationship with them and liked the couple.

When she returned to the living room, Caden was slouched on the couch with his head back on the pillows.

"How are you, son?" There was worry in her voice, not understanding why he was dressed in his tuxedo.

"Better."

"Why are you dressed in your tux?"

Caden looked down, forgetting what he was wearing. No wonder she looked mortified when she saw him at the door. "We took pictures since we already had the photographer and went to place India's bouquet on her grave."

Auntie Khadada looked somewhat relieved. "How did it go?"

Caden sighed and sat up. He felt he was being disrespectful by not looking at her and slouching. "It started out rocky, but a whole group of people showed their love by coming to be with us and it turned out rewarding."

Auntie put her hand on Caden's. "I'm glad you had a better day. I've been worried about you, but I can say you look a little more at ease."

"I think I needed to get by this day. When tomorrow comes, I believe I will feel even better. Today a friend told me it will get better and I believe her. She has lost someone very dear to her."

"Daddy," he heard Callia say when she entered the room. She was in her slip and socks. Her angelic face contorted as she yawned and stretched. "Auntie Dada," she said, making her way to the elderly woman and climbed into her lap. "Manger *(eat)*," she said to Aunt Khadada in French.

"Tell Preston if he's going to teach her another language I'm gonna need a translation book."

"You ready to eat Callia?"

Callia looked at her daddy with a blank stare and then she smiled and nodded.

"Oh. That's what that means, miss smarty pants," Auntie said, tickling her. "Well your food has been waiting for you since earlier, so come on and eat. Tell your daddy to come, too."

The three went to the kitchen to eat what she had prepared well in advance for them. They spent the remainder of the afternoon with Auntie.

When Caden reached Cuyler and Preston's home, Callia was asleep, again. He rang the doorbell and waited for someone to come and relieve him of her bag. Preston opened the door, but instantly took Callia. He took her to her room and tucked her under the covers.

When Preston returned downstairs, Caden was in the sunroom. He had changed his clothes from earlier, now wearing jeans, and a fitted shirt. He appeared to be lighter than earlier, and Preston was happy to see a smile when he saw him.

"Did you two have a good day?"

"Yes. I took her to see Auntie Khadada who sent you a message that she needs a translation book if you are going to teach her another language."

The two laughed.

"Cuyler and I will start Spanish next year," Preston informed him. "Callia is so bright. We don't want to waste one minute. She will have to learn so she can teach her brother or sister," he said, grinning. Acknowledgement inched across Caden's face, as he understood the meaning of Preston's statement. He reached out to Preston, giving him a hug and strong pat on his back. "Congratulations, man! I know you've been waiting for this moment for a while. What are you hoping for? A boy?"

"No, man, I'm hoping for healthy, but if I am allowed to choose, I hope for a girl so Callia will have a playmate and Cuyler will be willing to try again. I feel if it's a boy, she will shut me down, man."

Caden laughed at his strategy. Preston was always easy to talk to; he had really been there for him over the past months and Caden really appreciated him. "Man, I want to thank you for today. I don't know what I was thinking going there alone. If you had not come it could have been a bad scene, but it was something I had to do to put closure on some things."

"We are there for you, Caden. We are family now, thanks to Callia. That little joy has brought so many lives and hearts together."

"You might want to rethink that girl thing. I don't think she will give up her throne too readily."

Preston smiled, knowing what he said was true. Callia was fire. He believed there was a purpose for her and she had big things to accomplish one day.

Cuyler entered the sunroom with Callia in her arms. She must have heard you talking about her.

"Bonjour Papa," she said, yawning and reaching for Preston.

"Comment allez-vous *(How are you)*?" he asked. "Avez-vous eu une bonne journe *(Did you have a good day)*?"

"Oui *(yes)*," she answered.

"He asked her how was she and if she had a good day," Cuyler translated for Caden. "He asks her the same thing every day until she learns the phrases and answers, then he adds something else to it."

"I'm going to need a book, too," Caden teased. "I already told Preston, but I want to thank you as well for today. I wouldn't have made it through without you guys." He hugged Cuyler, as he had

Preston earlier. "Well I am going home to get my things together for work." Caden stood to leave.

"Stay for dinner," Preston offered.

"No. I'm not hungry. We ate at Auntie's. She shouldn't be hungry either," Caden said, pointing at Callia's belly." She laughed as though he tickled her.

The three walked him to the door. He turned to Cuyler. "I hear congratulations are in order."

Cuyler looked at Preston and smiled. "Thank you. Yes. It appears someone will have company in about seven months." She rubbed her belly." I guess Preston won't be jealous," she added and laughed.

They hugged goodbye and Caden was gone. Callia cried as she usually did whenever he left, but was fine within moments.

Preston put her down on the couch and became serious with Cuyler. "Now, sit with me and tell me about this case you are working on that took you to the office on a Saturday."

Cuyler hesitated because she knew Preston was not going to like the case. They talked often about which cases she should not touch. They had agreed she would not handle sex crimes. The previous firm that she finally left handed this case off to her. The client couldn't afford them, but she used to be them and charged much less.

Charged for a brutal rape, the man had an airtight alibi for the time frame the crime was committed. He was not from the hood, but she took some of these cases to help keep the doors open. Her old firm referred cases to her often, so she was doing well for herself.

"It's a guy who was referred from my old firm," she answered, avoiding the question, but she could feel his eyes waiting for an answer to his question. She sighed and turned to look him in the face. "He was accused of rape and—"

"We talked about this!" he said, objecting. "You need to forward him to someone else!"

"Why, Preston? The boy has an airtight alibi. He didn't do it!"

"Says the lawyer," he corrected. "I told you everyone who walks through your door is guilty! Isn't that what we agreed, Cuyler?" He asked much louder than he anticipated.

"Papa!" Callia cried.

Preston turned and saw her little face distorted, upset by his tone. He put out his hands and received her in his arms. "Desole! I'm sorry!" he said, calming her. Preston paced, rubbing Callia's back. He wanted to tell Cuyler not to take the case, but he knew it would only make her want it more.

The heat rose in him, as he felt the anger just below the surface. Callia was now calmed in his arms and was almost asleep, again.

"Damn, Cuyler!"

"Why can't you trust me?"

"It's not you I don't trust. I will always trust you, but don't ask me to trust anyone with my family!" He sat next to her on the couch, looking at her, never leaving her gaze. "Would you give up this case for me?"

"That's not fair, Preston! You know I would do anything for you, but don't make me go back on my word," she begged.

Leaning back, he closed his eyes. He didn't have a good feeling about this one and he couldn't shake it. He felt her snuggle close to him. Pulling her close he kissed her head. Callia was asleep, lying on his chest. They were his world. Dying and killing for them were one and the same for him.

This was her journey and he had to believe in her. The truth of the matter was he didn't trust her judgment. She believed people were good and he believed there was good in everyone, but more often than not people chose not to be good. They often chose the low rather than the high road. Cuyler always won her way with him, but this time he was selfish in the decision he knew she was waiting for.

"You are getting a gun and I expect you to carry it and learn to shoot it." Cuyler tried to protest, but Preston stood fast. "This is not up for discussion."

Cuyler quieted because she knew it would be a battle she would lose. She laid her head back on his shoulder, conceding to his decision.

Talking to the Moon

Caden pulled his last load of clothes from the dryer and took them to his room to fold. It took him a while to get back on track, but today was the first time he felt better. He thought the light in his heart would burn out, but the love and attention he received today gave him hope and the strength to move on.

After taking his shower, he lay awake in bed, looking at the sky through the window. The stars danced, calling to him as they did every night, drawing him to his chair at the window.

He sat, remembering when India picked it out. She said there was nowhere for her to sit and read when he slept at night and she was awake.

They went from store to store until she found the oversized monstrosity. It was almost large enough for the two of them to share. He found it to be comfortable as well and she often bullied him when he sat in it. He smiled, thinking of her.

Looking out his window, he found his faithful friend looking back at him. Caden laughed to himself. "So you're not smiling tonight?" he started. "Today was a better day. I can see things are going to get better. Today is the last day of my pity party. Tomorrow I will live again.

"I feel blessed I still have a job. They have really been good to me, so now is my turn to show them I was worth waiting for.

"Callia deserves her daddy back. Preston has been doing such a good job; I can't let him take my place. It's time for me to do my part, again. She's so smart, learning French. I need to get the lesson on disc and learn while driving. I can't have her speaking to Preston about me in another language.

"Monday, I meet Jacque for lunch. I hope I am able to forgive him soon, because my not forgiving him is taking too much energy. Life is short, so we need to figure this thing out. Help me to remember the boy he once was and maybe I can let go of his transgression against me. Cuyler forgave me so I should be able to forgive him, too.

"It's time to prep for the gala, again. I don't know how I will do it alone. Maybe my new family will help me get it done, but this is my passion. I know it will work out." Caden stopped wondering with whom he was having this conversation. Did it matter? Maybe he was going crazy.

For the first time in months, his eyes were heavy. He climbed into his bed, pulled the covers over his shoulders, and closed his eyes. Soon, he found sweet sleep.

Church was high. Caden felt free. He raised his hands in praise and felt cleansed. He cried. He shouted. He lay prostrate on the altar. He felt God was dealing with him and he let Him. He felt stronger than he had felt in a long time. He could feel the light in his chest burn bright, piercing the darkness that ate at him over the past weeks. He felt God's love and perfect strength pulling him back from the abyss he escaped in over the weeks and wrapped His arms around him, promising him he wouldn't have to go to that dark place again. He felt God's strength lift him to new heights. He still couldn't believe she was gone and believed she would never leave him, but she was gone and it was okay. Her love had lifted him to heights he would have never experienced had he never met her. He was a stronger person because of her. He understood love because of her, and knew he would be able to forgive his brother.

Preston and Cuyler were at his car after church. Preston carried Callia who shrieked when she saw Caden. He and Preston gave their customary hug and pat on the back, and Caden took Callia. They were going shopping and to eat together, so Preston could take Cuyler out. He was feeling tired and wished he could go back to his place to sleep, but any time he could spend with Callia was welcomed.

Callia was carrying her bunny book bag strapped to her back, containing all she needed for her outing.

"Don't forget she is potty training, so take her to the bathroom often," Cuyler reminded him.

He looked at Callia. "You better give me a five-minute warning or something."

"Good luck with that," Preston teased.

16

"I will have her home around eight, because tomorrow is my first day back," he reminded them, as he put Callia in her car seat.

"We will see you then," Preston promised and they all went their separate ways.

Pearl

Preston waited for Cuyler to prepare for their outing. He called to her a couple of times, expressing his impatience. "Cuyler, you're beautiful if you put on a potato sack and tie it around your waist. Come or we are going to be late."

"It would help if you tell me where we are going."

"That's why I laid your clothes out," he said, watching her come down the steps, wearing the fatigue pants and tie-dye shirt he put out for her, but she had a scarf tied around her head in gang style, and she wore combat boots and her stomach was out. Although pregnant, she was still sexy.

She walked to him with her head cocked to the side, smiling. "Is this what you had in mind?"

"No, but—"

She kissed him before he could finish his thought. She knew he didn't know he had chosen a midriff for her to wear. Turning, she walked away to reveal how low her pants were, deliberately swinging her hips with every step. She reached for the short jean jacket hanging on the coat rack by the door and entered the garage.

"She's going to get me killed today."

Traffic was light as it usually was on Sundays. The two headed for the Woodrow Wilson Bridge into Virginia. Cuyler was rubbing Preston's leg, not caring where they were going. She knew if he planned it, she would have fun.

"Stop," he told her, and she smiled at him. "Stop," he said, again, laughing at her diligence. "That's how you got in that condition, so keep your hands to yourself!"

Preston slowed and pulled into a rundown parking area with a dirty brick building that looked abandoned. Their location baffled Cuyler, but she was game.

Preston hopped out of the car and opened the trunk, pulling out a leather bag, before helping her out of the car. She walked with that curious look on her face he often saw on Callia's little face. When

Preston opened the door to the warehouse, Cuyler could hear muffled sounds of gunfire.

"Are you serious!" she said excitedly.

Preston didn't say anything. He continued to guide her through the building until they came to a check-in desk. There stood a stout man dressed in a tan T-shirt, fatigue pants, and boots. Cuyler muffled a smile. The man requested their identifications and gun permits. Cuyler handed him her license and Preston handed him all else. Cuyler looked at him in amazement, but didn't know why. He had been prepared since day one.

The man escorted them to a small private room. She opened the door to a small lightly lit room with one chair and three headsets hanging on a rack from the dingy wall. A man was already in the room and appeared to be waiting for them. Preston put the bag on the floor and pulled out two small leather cases. One was pink.

Cuyler almost couldn't contain herself. She reached to pick it up, but Preston held up one finger, indicating she needed to wait, as he often did when she became excited. Cuyler, at that moment, realized he did the same to Callia.

When he pulled the gun from its pouch, it resembled jewelry. It was beautiful. The handle was pearl swirled in pink. It was small and he chose it just for her. The instructor reviewed the gun with her, showing its parts. Cuyler just wanted him to shut up and hand it to her, but she remained patient and waited.

After the instructions, she learned how to load the gun, understanding she was getting closer to shooting. She loaded and unloaded the gun three times successfully. Now it was time to shoot.

Preston handed her a set of earphones, making sure they were snug. Standing behind her, he instructed her to relax against his chest and follow the instructions of the instructor. The first shot her hand jerked upward and the instructor told her what to do to correct the upward swing. She fired, again, this time hitting the outer black area of the silhouette. Steadying her hand, she fired, again, this time hitting the chest area.

Preston gave her thumbs up, letting her know she was doing well. He backed away from her, allowing her to stand on her own and she

19

shot, again. After adjusting a few times, she was back on her mark. When out of bullets, Preston took her gun and took his turn.

Cuyler watched the accuracy of his shooting and his lack of hesitation. He unloaded his clip into the same silhouette she shot into, his jaw slightly tensed. The lines of his body made the heat rise to her cheeks. She could feel herself become moist and was ready to leave. Preston saw the look on her face and winked. She mouthed the words *show off* and laughed.

They stayed for another hour taking turns and Preston introduced her to different stances and positons, exciting her with each touch. He showed her how to check the chamber and lock her gun before putting it away.

"Let's get something to eat before the boss comes home." Preston grabbed their bag and they headed to the car, but eating was not on her mind.

Caden sat on the Washington's steps, watching Callia chase a moth. She screamed each time she became close and thought she could get it and the moth would fly away, again. When he saw Preston's Cadillac pull into the circular driveway, he lifted Callia into his arms until they were parked.

Cuyler waited for Preston to open her door, before getting out of the car. When she stepped from the car, Caden wondered where they had gone, because they were dressed for battle. Seeing them together reminded him of his loneliness. He was eager to get back to work and to start busying himself on this fall's gala.

Cuyler, although in fatigues, looked as sexy as ever. No one would believe she was anyone's mother, but when she and Callia were together, you couldn't deny she was Callia's.

Preston and Caden shook hands and patted one another on the back. Caden bent to kiss Cuyler and the four walked into the house together.

"Sorry we were a little late," Preston offered.

"You guys look like you've been somewhere fun."

"Preston took me to the shooting range," Cuyler said, still excited about her venture.

Caden looked at Preston with a raised brow. "The shooting range?"

"Short story. I'll share later," Preston said, with both hands raised.

They walked into the house and one by one settled in the sunroom. Preston sat on the floor with Callia and she climbed over him backward and forward, laughing. He was amused at how she was so care free and happy. He imagined the new baby and her together and knew she would be ecstatic to have a playmate. Right now, each of them was her playmate.

"So why are you at the firing range?" Caden asked Preston.

"If Cuyler is going to be taking on cases dealing with some questionable characters, then I would like her to be able to protect herself."

Caden thought about it for a moment and thought it was a great idea. "Well she looks a little too excited about shooting," Caden joked. "I hope she isn't the one who will need a lawyer." The two laughed.

Caden gave a tired Callia a bath and dressed her in her pajamas. He played with her for a while and waited for her to say her goodnights. After putting her to bed, he said his goodbyes.

As Caden made his way home, he suddenly felt lonely again. It was during this time of day when things became difficult. There would be no one to welcome him or for him to share his events of the day with, except the moon.

His house was as he left it. He took the steps, two at a time, to his bedroom and prepared to take a shower, after which he would sit in India's chair and look for his old friend, the moon, for his nightly conversation. He had a lot to talk about tonight. Tomorrow was his first day back to work.

Tashia

Tashia sat in Zander's room and watched as he cleaned. The silence became unbearable, waiting for him to talk to her about the incident in school. Once again, he had gotten in trouble. She was at her wit's end. He had been late five times in the past month and had no explanation, because she dropped him off every day.

They recently had a blow up over aftercare. She knew he didn't want to go, but she didn't want them home alone and didn't know what else to do with him. Kids teased him because he was almost thirteen and still had a baby sitter.

"Why can't I play football?" He had asked the same question since he was nine.

"Because I have to work, Zander, and can't always get you there."

"You can get where you need to go!" The accusation in his voice bruised her heart. She saw her life in his, always the one in charge, the responsible one. He glared at her and she felt his hurt.

"Now that's not fair. Everything I do is for us all. The only place I've been is to school and work." He was no longer listening. He had shut her out. "Let me work on it, okay? I'll see what I can work out. But, you still have to do your part." She still got no answer. She attempted to kiss him goodnight, but he pulled away from her.

Slowly, she walked to his door and looked back to see he was no longer her baby. He was becoming a young man. She knew nothing about this subject. He had surpassed her level of expertise, but she did know hood and the signs were there.

When back in her bedroom, she cried. She didn't want him to fall in with the boys of their neighborhood. Zander was a good boy, and he was smart. If he went down that path, he would be a great criminal—just like his father.

Zander was a great help to her. He watched his siblings and was kind to them. He was going to be taller than his dad. His dad, Jesus, was Latino and stood five-ten. Already five-seven and looking her in the eye, he would soon test his limits further, she was sure of it. A change had to be made and soon. "God. I don't know what to do!"

Her phone rang. It was Caden.

Caden talked to the moon and discussed how to get past his loneliness. That was the most difficult part of his life right now. He wasn't open to bringing another woman into his life and everyone else was so busy. He wasn't ready to mentor the boys just yet, but wanted to do something. Zander was heavy on his heart. Cuyler used to say how she didn't want his surroundings to swallow him, which often happened when boys didn't have a strong, male role model in their lives. He didn't want that for Callia's cousin, either.

He looked at his watch. It was late, but he called Tashia anyway. The phone rang several times before she answered.

"Hello." Her voice sounded strained.

"Hey, Tashia! I hope I didn't wake you."

"No, I was just talking to Zander."

"I was just thinking about Zander. How is he?"

Tashia was silent. She didn't want to burden anyone with her issues, but she needed to talk to someone. Caden was family. "He's not doing too well. He's going through some growing pains."

Caden sat up. He knew what growing pains could become if not checked in Zander's environment. "What's going on?"

The pressures of her life weighed heavy on her. The emotions she had been holding in for so long were pressing to escape. She didn't want to let them out, because she didn't know how to put them back once they came, but came they did. Tashia cried. No one had ever asked about her kids. She felt relieved to have someone to talk to, but her emotions got the best of her and she couldn't pull herself together.

Her tears pulled at Caden's heart the same way her sister's did. "Take your time." Caden waited while she cried.

He remembered a different girl when he first met Cuyler. Tashia wanted to know who he was and why he wanted to see her sister. She asked him where his money came from, which he felt was an odd question, and where he was from. She was a tough girl; almost gangster. The woman he had seen over the past two years was much calmer and subdued, but she was struggling for her identity. For so long, she was Jesus' girl, then his baby's momma. Although she was no longer in that world, her address wouldn't let her leave. She was still a prisoner of her zip code.

"Would you rather meet with me tomorrow evening and we can talk?" he asked when he realized she was not going to gain her composure.

"Okay."

"Okay. Call me tomorrow and we will set up a time and place. Okay?"

"I'll call you tomorrow," she repeated, and then there was silence. "Caden?"

"I'm still here."

"Thank you." She hung up.

Tashia lay in her bed, hugging her pillow. How ironic it was that he called just when she needed someone to help her the most. Exhaustion overcame her. She needed help. He helped her sister. Maybe he could help her son.

She didn't know when she had fallen to sleep, but when she woke, she had a visitor. Solana was snuggled close to her, sleeping. Her angelic face always made Tashia smile. She was her little angel much like Cuyler was when they were younger. Although only two years apart, she was tasked with raising her sister at an early age. Solana was a good girl much like her auntie. She named her Solana, because she called Cuyler Sunshine as a child and hoped she would have the same fortune as her sister. She had hope for all her children.

Tashia never had much of a childhood. She guessed this was the curse of being the eldest. She did things no child should have had to do to take care of her family. When she was older, she learned to use her beauty to get what she wanted. She learned early that pretty was unpredictable, pretty was a curse, and pretty hurt.

Tashia tied up Solana's thick, curly hair to help get them prepared quicker in the mornings. She could hear the boys in the kitchen laughing. Tashia eased from under the covers and went to the kitchen to ensure they were doing what they were supposed to be doing.

Zane ran to his mother, hugging her around her waist. "Mommy," he said.

"You guys eat already?" she asked.

Zander wouldn't look at her. She went to him and kissed him on the cheek. This time he didn't push her away. He cut his eyes at her and went back to his task of making lunches.

"We already ate." Zane grabbed the fruit cups from the fridge and dropped them in the bags already set up on the counter.

The boys were such a contrast in looks. Zane had a different daddy. Tashia had him when she left Jesus to be with a man who claimed to love her and promised to take her from the only world she knew. Cuyler had just left and she thought maybe her luck had changed as well, but he turned out to be abusive and no different from the rest. Zander and Solana's dad came and got her one day when he heard she was being beaten. Not too long after, Zane's father was found dead in an alley outside of a club. They called it robbery, but she knew the truth. He was killed for mistreating her.

Jesus Santiago was his name and he loved Tashia. She loved him as well, but she knew to love Jesus was always to have connections to their hood and she wanted to break away. She also knew to be associated with him was an invitation to a short life. His was cut short in front of her. She only survived because his first in command shot the assailant before he could get to her in her hiding place. She missed him dearly, but that was the turning point in her life.

Zander was old enough to remember that life, and that frightened her. She knew he had the intelligence and creativity to do whatever he wanted, but only he could make that decision for his life. He was a leader.

Zander had not spoken. She knew he was hurting. She poured her morning coffee that he started for her, and watched him finish lunches. Slowly, she walked up behind him and hugged him tightly. Initially he protested, but she pulled him in tighter and stroked his curls. "I'm sorry, Zander." He stopped fighting and allowed her to love on him.

"What's wrong with Zander, Mommy?" Solana asked through sleepy eyes. She came to them and hugged him, too. "She didn't mean it, Zander," she said, not knowing why her mother was sorry.

Zander held onto his mother's arms wrapped around his. He knew he would bring her grief by the end of this day. He, himself, was saying sorry in advance. "I love you, Mom," he whispered and pulled away from her. He went to his bedroom to finish preparing for school.

Zander thought of his father. Many feared him, but he was no longer alive to protect him from the wannabes and gonnabes of the street. He was living in his father's legacy. People expected him to be everything his father was, and he was not. His father didn't want this life for him. He often told Zander he was going to college and make something of his life, but that money was gone. He knew his mother didn't have any of it; she worked too hard to have that kind of money put away. He didn't know what to do now.

Zane burst into the room. "Momma said come on!" Zane picked up his book bag.

Zander snatched him back and hugged him. "You make sure you always protect and take care of Solana, okay?"

A confused Zane pulled away from his brother. "Yeah okay."

"I mean it, Zane," he said, now looking his brother in the eyes. "I mean it," he repeated, barely audible.

"Okay yeah, but what about Momma?"

"Momma is a tough one. She just looks all soft." He thought of the night their dad was killed. His mother kicked one of the men and hit him in the head with a lamp when he burst into his bedroom. Zander was seven, but he still remembered and wondered if his brother remembered as well. Their mother took them and hid them in a room she called a safe room. He held one-year-old Solana in his lap and held onto five-year-old Zane. He never cried. He just kept looking at Zander for direction.

He heard his mother call for them and pushed Zane out the door. Solana was twirling in the middle of the living room. She was wearing the dress Aunt Cuyler bought her. "Zander do I look pretty," she asked, expecting her daily dose of admiration. He picked her up and smothered her with kisses until she begged him to stop.

Tashia looked at her children and felt blessed they had not been penetrated by their environment. "Let's go."

As they walked to the car, Zander received his usual "Hi, Zander," from the girls in the halls and on the street. He was a handsome boy. For the first time, she saw the fuzz growing on his top lip. Zander Santiago was definitely going to be one to reckon with.

She dropped Zander off first. He usually met his English teacher in the morning before school, because he was ahead of the rest of his class. He was abnormally quiet this morning. She would have to make some changes in their lives before she lost him.

"Momma, Zander acting strange today," Zane informed her.

"Strange how?"

"He told me to make sure I looked after Solana and made me promise." Zane looked for an explanation from his mother. What he got was a blank look.

"I'll talk to him later," she assured him, but in truth, she was frightened. She didn't want to frighten him, too. She couldn't call out, but she needed to pick him up after school. She could feel it in her spirit.

When she arrived to Zane and Solana's school, she didn't get out. She wiped the tears away and instructed Zane, "You're a big boy now, Zane. I need you to take your sister to her class for me, okay?" she asked calmly.

"Okay." He looked closely at his mother, sensing a change in her mood.

"It's okay, Zane. I will see you this afternoon. Okay?"

"Okay. Come on, Solana," he told his sister, taking her hand as Zander would. "They're gonna think you are a star today. You look beautiful." He walked Solana into the entrance of the school.

Tashia dialed Caden's cell. No answer. She called his office, and learned he was in meetings all morning. She left a message for him to call her when he had a break.

Tashia sat in front of her job, debating. She decided to call Preston.

The phone rang several times before he answered, but by this time, she had worked herself up. "Preston! Are you busy?"

Tashia's voice was so strained he didn't recognize it. "No, I'm not busy." He looked at the caller ID.

"I think Zander is in trouble," she cried.

"What kind of trouble?"

"He's been acting real strange and distant lately. Last night he was rude to me and he's never rude. I thought maybe it was the testosterone kicking in and dismissed it, but this morning he made his brother promise he would always look out for Solana. I'm afraid their pressuring him. He's of age." She was hysterical.

"Where is he now?"

"In school."

"Are we still listed on his emergency list?" Preston was thinking. He could pick him up from school and then what? There would be tomorrow and the day after.

"Yes."

"I will pick him up today and talk with him. We will figure something out," he promised. "Go to work and calm down. I'll keep you posted."

Tashia felt better, but she knew she had to get him out. They couldn't have her son. She went to work devising a plan for her family.

Caden had a lot of catching up to do at work. Everyone welcomed him back and he met with his boss most of the morning. Apparently, one of the project managers fouled up a project and he wanted him to fix it. Brad caught him up on what had transpired thus far. They talked about his circumstances and mental capacity. He explained he had his good and bad days, but the good were beginning to outweigh the bad.

Caden was setting up his office. His secretary came in to give him a message. It was from Tashia. He remembered a teary Tashia the night before and called her back immediately.

The phone went straight to voice mail, so he left a message. "Call me back."

"Hey. Are you all settled in?" It was Denise, his co-worker. She walked into the room before he could invite her. She probably felt the way was clear for her now with Cuyler married and India deceased, he rationalized, but even she couldn't be so tacky, he thought.

"I'm getting settled and about to go to another meeting to get caught up on this project."

"Aww. I thought maybe you would like to grab a bite."

"No. I'm not hungry." He didn't feel like Denise and all her charades yet.

"Well, maybe another day." She hesitated. "I'm sorry for your loss," she added and left.

Caden sat in his chair, wondering what to do next. He had another hour before his meeting and nothing to review yet. He looked at the picture of India, Callia, and him on his desk. "Woman, I wish you were here now. I don't want to date any of these chicken heads and I have no patience for nonsense."

His cell phone interrupted him. It was Tashia.

"Hey, Shia," he answered. "I tried to call you, but the call went to voice mail."

"I know. We really don't have good reception in the hospital."

"What time do you want to meet?"

"Preston is going to pick Zander up from school. Zane said Zander told him to take care of Solana. He sounded like he may not be back. You didn't answer so I called Preston, because I didn't know what to do."

She sounded scared and she had every right to be. It sounded like the hood was recruiting him. How far they would go to get him depended on how badly they wanted him, but Zander had to be the one to steadfast. No one else could do it.

"What time is he picking him up?"

"Before school is out, is all I know."

"I'll call him and get the details," he told her. "We are family, Tashia. We are there for you. Let us take care of this. Okay?"

"Okay. Thank you, again," she said through tears.

Zander couldn't concentrate. He found himself looking at the clock most of the day. Although he had until school was out, each minute counted, because he still did not have a plan.

At lunch, he couldn't eat. Big butt Brenda sat beside him. She made small talk, but he didn't hear her. Any other time he would have been shy and stumbling, because she was built like a grown woman. Instead, he excused himself and asked if he could use the bathroom.

Zander looked across the field through the bathroom window. He could disappear through the woods and not come back, but that wouldn't work because whatever he did affected Zane as well. He wondered what his dad would have done. What would he tell him to do? He couldn't stay hidden in the bathroom. He had to go back or he would get into trouble. Again.

When Zander entered the cafeteria, the teacher on duty called him to the front, and sent him to the office. His uncle was there to pick him up for his doctor's appointment.

Zander went to the office, not knowing what was going on. When he opened the door, his Uncle Preston was there.

"Hey, man, you ready to go? Your mom couldn't pick you up for your appointment so she sent me." Preston smiled.

Zander ran to his locker, grabbed his things, and quickly returned to the office where Preston waited. Once outside Zander saw a car filled with familiar faces—his Uncle Caden and Anthony—and felt a feeling of relief come over him. When he got into the car, they were all ready to talk.

"Hey, Zander," Caden said, shaking his hand.

"Come on and let's talk this out," Anthony said, motioning for him to get into the car.

Preston climbed in and the entourage drove away from the school grounds. Preston pulled into the first available parking lot and parked. One at a time, they asked Zander questions.

"Tell us what's going on," Preston encouraged.

Zander fell silent. He didn't know what to say.

"We can't help you unless you talk to us, Zander." Preston wanted him to understand they were there to help and not to punish him.

"When did they start approaching you?" Anthony asked.

"About a year ago. They started calling me little Jesus. Then they told me it was almost time for me to be initiated in the family. I didn't understand because my father told me he didn't want me to be a part of a gang. He said it wasn't for me. I didn't pay them any attention, but in the last month, they have been coming down on me. They told me I had until today to make a decision."

"Or what?" Caden asked.

Zander thought about the question. They didn't give him an ultimatum. They only said today was the day. He guessed they expected him to join. "They didn't give me one."

"That's good," Caden said.

"They expect him to join," Anthony said, amused by the conversation thus far. He once belonged to a gang until it no longer served his needs and he left. He remembered it was not an easy thing to do. Their biggest fear was him going to another gang and divulging their secrets, or, in his case, losing someone who instilled fear in others.

The men turned their attention to Anthony. He was grinning at them. Anthony turned to Zander. "Are you scared, boy?" he asked with a grin on his lips.

"Yes!"

"What are you afraid of? The gang? What they may do? What is your biggest fear?"

Zander pondered his question. He thought of the night they came for his father: The night his mother protected him because his father was dead. He thought about Zane and sweet Solana. "I don't want to end up dead like my father and leave my family unprotected," he finally answered. "I'm not afraid of the gang. I grew up in the gang with my dad."

"*Good*," Anthony Cooed. "Use that as your strength and stand your ground."

"Stand his ground!" Caden hollered.

Anthony ignored him, as he had Zander's attention. "Only you can fight this battle, Zander. Only you. Your momma can't help you with this, but I think you already knew that. You have to stand your ground. Remember whose boy you are. You are Jesus' boy. That alone stands for something. You let them know if they don't come for you and your family you won't come for them!" Anthony's gaze didn't waiver. He could see Zanders shoulders get high and his head lift. He saw his chest swell with pride as he remembered his father.

"*Yessss*. You feel it, don't you? You feel the inner strength you already had within you."

Zander *could* feel it. He wasn't afraid anymore. He could feel the strength rise in him as though his father was there with him. It was strange, but he didn't care what they did. He only knew they couldn't have his life. With renewed strength, he was ready to go and meet them. He was ready to tell them *no!*

"I'm ready!" he said, now angry; there were probably others who didn't want to be part of the gang either.

"You're going to get him killed!" Caden protested.

"Are you going to be with him always?" Anthony asked, turning slowly to look at him. He didn't like Caden. He was a pussy to him. *No wonder he lost Cuyler to his brother.*

Zander turned to Caden. "I'm not stupid uncle. I know what they can do, but they haven't threatened me yet. If I stand up to them today they will threaten me before they hurt me."

"Good, boy." Anthony liked Zander. He was a smart boy and caught on quickly. He pointed to his head. "Smart, boy! Now, let's review your meeting and what you will say."

They reviewed the meeting with him and Anthony gave him the signs to look for if he were in danger. He was ready.

The men let him out where he directed. School was out and they would expect him to come through this way. He said he would meet them at his home.

Zander walked down the street, but now his head and shoulders were high and he felt strong. He knew what could happen and he didn't care. He would fight for his freedom. He didn't know if he could fight—he never had to—but Anthony told him a fight began in his head not with his fist. Anthony also told him there was no shame in retreating. *"Live to fight another day,"* he had said.

When Zander reached the meeting corner, the guys were already there. They smiled as he approached. Zander was not smiling. He walked until he could see up and down both streets.

"I'm here," he said.

"Welcome to the fold, man," the boy with the old cut on his face said, patting his back.

"I didn't come to join. I came to tell you I'm the wrong man."

The members looked around at each other, bewildered.

Scar stepped up to Zander and Zander sized him up. Although small, he was pretty tone, which told Zander he was in good shape. He could not underestimate him if he started anything. "Then why did you come?" he asked, still grinning.

"I didn't want to be rude and miss our appointment. I said I would be here and I'm here, but this ain't my gig."

"So what is your gig?"

"I'm just gonna do me."

"What makes you think you have a choice?"

Zander looked at his stance. He wasn't threatening him. He was giving him lip service. He didn't want any parts of Zander. He was probably afraid Zander would eventually take his place.

Zander leaned into Scar and whispered, "You know they want to groom me for your job because of my dad. I don't have no beef with you and I don't want the job.

"You seem to be doing a good job with these guys and they follow you. I grew up in this life and I'm not interested. Let's not start something here. I am my father's child. If you start something I will finish it," Zander said with a force he didn't know he possessed. Maybe he was his father's child and he never had to put it to test. "Tell me you have to check with the higher ups and you will see what they want to do with me. When I walk away, call me a punk bitch, and tell them I will make the group weak. Tell them I am nothing like my father and you don't need me," Zander instructed.

"You bitch ass," Scar said, pushing Zander away from him. At first Zander didn't know if he was doing as he instructed or if something was about to jump off. "We don't want you as a part of our group. Jesus would be embarrassed you were his son. Get the hell out of here." Scar pushed him away and stared him down in challenge.

Zander resisted a smile. So, Scar didn't want him in the gang. He did fear his position with these boys if Zander joined. Slowly, Zander turned and headed for his home. He accomplished what he came for. He may be called a few names here and there, but that was tolerable for his freedom.

When he turned the corner, the entourage that came to rescue him today was all there, standing outside the car. Caden came to him and hugged him, but Anthony and Preston stood back. When he reached them, he told them everything that happened. He was ready to go inside and see his family.

Tashia paced the floor, waiting for word. She couldn't focus at work so she was sent home. Although she realized it was probably better to have stayed. The time she had on her hands was more than she could bear.

Zander was so much like his dad. Jesus was a man of means. He did what was necessary. He understood his circumstances and used what he had to make things happen. He was intelligent and fearless, which made him dangerous. He was strong and sensitive, which made her love him.

What he had here in the states was much more than his family in El Salvador. His mother shared the stories of twelve people living in a one-room shack. She told her how she and her husband saved over the years to escape their circumstances. During their dangerous journey, they were shot at and hunted, but they prevailed and made it into the country.

After their rocky start, they were able to secure a home for their family and Jesus' dad, Pablo, was doing well in his job, but his father was hurt while working and, because he was illegal, couldn't get any help so Jesus became responsible for his house at thirteen. He turned to the streets.

She met him when she was just twelve and he was fourteen. He would tease her when she passed by him. He called her endearing names and ran to open the door for her when she got home from school. He was her crush.

By the time she was fourteen, they were dating. The boys no longer catcalled when she passed by and no one hit on her as they did before. Cuyler became off limits as well and they never wanted for anything.

Jesus protected her and Cuyler like Zander protected his siblings. Zander was a take-charge boy. Her boy was becoming a man, forced to make grown-up decisions at an early age.

She missed Jesus and she thought about him in that moment. She wished he was there for their son. He would know what to do. He shielded her from a lot of things. He told her he would tell her what she needed to know. She knew the night he was killed that they were coming and refused to leave him as he had asked. He knew someone was stalking his territory and eventually would come for him. Truth was she felt safer with him than without.

She was glad she stayed. She held him in her arms while he died. He was not alone. He told her to get his children out of that hellhole. He told her where he had money for her and the kids, but someone else heard as well. When she went to retrieve the money, there was no heritage for his children.

His blood poured through the gunshot wounds he had sustained and Tashia sat in the warm pool of wetness, massaging his face. "Don't cry for me, Tashia. I knew this day would come. I just wanted to keep you and the kids safe."

He told her he was cold and didn't have much longer. In his last moments, he poured out his heart, professing his love for her. He fell in love with her when she was ten, but didn't have the nerve to speak to her until that day when she was walking into her building. He said he waited for her every day after and put word out that she was off limits. He told her when she left him he thought he would die. He couldn't eat or sleep, but he understood why she left. His infidelity was too much for her to tolerate. When he heard she was being mistreated he knew he had to come get her. He put her in that situation and he had to fix it. He said he loved her over and over and to take care of his children. Zane was never to know he was not his. If he learned from the streets, she was to tell him no differently. He wanted his kids to know he loved them and he was sorry he wouldn't be there for them.

She cried, thinking of that night. With her face in her hands, she felt strong arms encircle and embrace her. She looked up and it was Zander, with his dad's hazel eyes looking at her. Tashia stood and grabbed her son. He was home! He was safe.

"Shhhh," he told her. "Don't cry, Momma, I'm fine. I didn't want you to be worried and I knew you would be." But she couldn't stop crying, because she thought she had lost him to the streets.

Zander pulled away from her and went to the men who helped him find his inner strength through all of this. Her eyes followed him and she covered her mouth when she saw them standing there together.

"Thank you," she said through new tears. They came for her son and she would never forget. For the first time in a long time, she didn't feel alone. "Thank you," she said twice more to make sure they each knew she appreciated them.

"We need to get together and talk, Tashia," Preston told her. "We will leave so you two can talk." He looked at Zander and nodded.

Caden walked to her and gave her a hug. "Call if you need anything."

Anthony watched him closely. "Pussy," he mumbled under his breath and walked out the door.

Preston chuckled at his brother realizing he liked Tashia and followed him out.

Two-Fifty an Hour

Cuyler walked out of her office, with her client, and was surprised to see Preston sitting in the lounge. She smiled as she walked her client to the office door and told him to call her secretary with any new information.

She leaned up against the door, turning her attention to Preston. "I have a four o'clock appointment. What are you doing here?"

"Can I get a kiss or a hug? Something?" He smiled that broad smile that had captivated her heart years ago.

She went to him and pulled him into her office. She didn't want her client to walk through the door and see them.

"Oh, I get more than a kiss?" Preston joked, as she closed the door.

"You are so bad," she answered. "I don't want my client to walk through the door thinking I give 'happy endings'," she joked back and kissed him passionately. He lifted her to the desk, pressing close for her to feel his condition. "Damn," she whispered in his ear.

"Can't Robin hold your visitor for a few minutes?" he moaned in her ear.

"She could, but you have never been a few minutes," she moaned "except our wedding night."

"Awww. Cuyler that was one time. You are going to let that one time outweigh all the good times?" he teased, as he unbuttoned her shirt exposing her new breasts. "I wonder how you can keep these after the baby?" he mused, and buried his head between them.

"Preston I have a four o'clock. Quit it!" she said, giggling like a schoolgirl, but he continued to undress her. "You are going to be disappointed when you cannot finish!"

"Oh, I am going to finish," he promised her, as he unzipped her skirt. When she stood to protest, it fell to the floor. He locked his thumbs in her tights and pulled them down with her lace panties. "Ummm," he moaned in her ear before he nibbled it. He heard her breath draw in as he stuck two fingers into her wetness and gently played there.

"Damn you, Preston," she moaned and stuck her tongue in his ear, igniting him. She reached for his belt and undid it followed by his pants. They dropped around his ankles. She pulled his boxers over his round, hard behind and they joined the rest of his clothes. "Take me," she whispered.

"I got you." He lifted her. His strong arms carried her as they rode together. Occasionally he lifted to adjust her. Gripping her behind, he dug his fingers into her flesh, pushing deeper. It reminded him of their first time.

Cuyler rubbed his freshly trimmed head as if shinning it. She inhaled his cologne. "You smell so good," she said, nestling her nose in his neck, gently kissing him there.

Preston walked her back to her desk, pushing everything out the way. Some things fell to the floor.

"Shhh. My four o'clock may be outside," she whispered.

Preston laid her back on the desk, mounting her, still riding. "I am your four o'clock appointment," he revealed. "Robin is gone. Now relax," he whispered. He raised her legs in the air and took longer strokes, driving deeper until he found that spot way in the back that seemed to send her. Before she could get too high, he stopped, and messaged her breast, which had grown, before resuming. She trembled through the excitement, moving her hair stuck to her wet face. He pushed it out of her way, knowing it annoyed her.

"How is your meeting?" He was whispering in Spanish in her ear. Listening to her breathing, he picked up the pace and she began to moan.

"Te quiero *(I want you)*, Preston."

"Tienes, todo de mi," he said, letting her know she had all of him.

Cuyler's mouth fell open. She held her breath and arched her back, again, gripping his strong thighs. Slowly, she laid back and rested. Preston's hand rested on her pregnant belly. She shifted slightly.

"You okay?" Preston rubbed her stomach gently.

"Um-hm."

"Let me help you up." Preston helped Cuyler up slowly and dressed her. He continued to caress and kiss her as he put her clothes back together. She was looking at him, smiling.

"I charge two-fifty an hour for first-time customers, Mr. Washington, and you are nearing your hour."

"Only two dollars and fifty cents?"

"You know better."

Preston chuckled as he pulled his pants up, but she pulled them back down, gripped his behind, and pulled him close. She covered his lips with hers. "I said your hour is *almost* up. I can't help but love the way we make love," she whispered. "Do you need some time to regroup or do you think you can hit it again?" she teased him, rubbing his taunt stomach.

"Are you trash talking me, Mrs. Washington?" Preston smiled broadly. "I think I hear a challenge somewhere in there."

"Then let's go."

Uncle Anthony

A nthony stood outside Tashia's door, waiting for someone to answer.

"Who is it?" he heard her ask.

"Anthony."

Tashia opened the door, stunned to see Anthony at her place. He stood, looking indifferent to being there.

"Hey, Anthony. What brings you here?" she asked, with her head cocked to the side.

Anthony felt he might have made a mistake. She almost seemed annoyed he was there and she had not invited him in. "I came back to see if Zander had any concerns or questions."

"I'm sorry. Come in." She opened the door wider to allow him to enter. Tashia watched as he entered. He always seemed standoffish when she was around him. This was the most she had ever heard him speak.

He entered and stood in the middle of the room, waiting for direction. He was slightly taller than his brother and a little slimmer. He sported a baldhead, mustache, and goatee. Where Preston had slightly slanted eyes, Anthony's were large as though observing all of his surroundings. He was a handsome man with a mischievous smile. Most would have found him to be scary, but Tashia saw something else just below the surface.

"You may have a seat, Anthony." She gestured to the couch. "Zander! You have company," she yelled to the back of the apartment.

"Yeah, Mom," Zander answered, running into the room. He saw Anthony and became excited. "Hey, Uncle Anthony!"

"Hey, young man. I wanted to come by to see if everything was irie, and make sure you didn't have anything you needed to talk about."

"No. I'm good for now. I may need to ask more questions later, but today was great! I thought I was going to be scared, but I wasn't.

Like you said, this is my life and if I don't take charge of it someone else will."

"Were you scared?" Anthony asked.

"A little, but not much. Once I started talking it didn't matter," he answered pensively.

Anthony was proud of him. He liked that he didn't want anyone to step in for him. He wanted to handle things himself. He wanted to mentor him and help him through this difficult journey.

He watched his mother who stood in the kitchen doorway. She was not as beautiful as her sister Cuyler, but she was a beauty. She was curvier than her sister and bronze. Where Cuyler had a playful look, she was always serious. Anthony thought she was very sexy and part of her sexiness was her edginess.

"Well I'm going to go, but I also wanted to ask your mom if you and Zane could join our music club. It is an after-school program where the kids come each day to learn to play various musical instruments. There is no charge for the after school. Preston and I pay the rent on the building." He was now looking at Tashia.

Zander turned and looked at his mother, waiting for an answer. She was contemplating his offer, thinking it would be a great idea for the boys. She would rather have them do something constructive and not just sit at the center, waiting for her. The center wasn't that bad, but Zander had definitely outgrown it.

"Where is this place?" she asked, smiling at the options that had come through for her sons in just one day.

"They will have to catch the bus, but it is a fifteen-minute bus ride. If needed, I can pick them up on most days, but on some days my partner comes later so I have to be there when the kids start coming." He watched her as she evaluated his offer.

"Let me think it over and I will get back to you in a couple of days," she said, finally. "What time does the center close?"

"Six-thirty."

Tashia still was not sure. She knew Preston, but knew little about his brother. She watched as he evaluated her. She knew men. Anthony Laurent was there for Zander, but he was there for her, too, and she was not sure how she felt about that.

"Have you eaten, Anthony?" Not waiting for his answer, she entered the kitchen.

"I'm good, but thank you."

Tashia stayed in the kitchen, while he talked to Zander. Once she was finished, she gave Zander instructions. "Make sure you lock the door behind Anthony and your bedtime is at ten. Good night, Anthony, and thanks, again, for today."

"Goodnight. I won't keep him long."

Tashia checked on her other children before going to her bedroom. She needed a shower, but somehow felt naked with Anthony in her place. After stripping out her clothes, she looked at herself in the mirror. She didn't look bad for a mother of three. She was almost thirty-one years old, but her body didn't look it. She had no stretch marks and she was still tight. Her breasts could stand some work, but they didn't look bad.

She let down the bun pinned on top her head. Unlike Cuyler's, her hair was very curly. Her tight spirals dropped to the middle of her back. They framed her face, which was narrow, and her large eyes peeped through the curls.

For a moment, she allowed her guard to drop and thought about Anthony. He was definitely her type, but she might have been reading more into the visit than its intent. Besides, she didn't want a distraction from her kids. She had been ignored for years and all her spare time belonged to them, which was about to get smaller.

She lay on her bed and made the call she was dreading, but it was necessary. She had to secure her part-time in order to prepare for their exodus. After the call, she went to the bathroom to take her shower.

Anthony Laurent

C aden sat in his chair. He felt he slept better after talking to the moon. He knew people would think he was crazy if he told them he did that every night, but in truth, he knew he was talking to God.

"Thank you for your direction. Tashia really needed us today and I'm glad we were there for her. I didn't know You spoke that plainly. Work was good. I am really blessed to work for this company because another may not have been so patient with me. Tomorrow is a big day so I really need to focus in these meetings, so if You could help me with that I would appreciate it.

"I still miss India a lot, especially because I need to get started with this gala. If you have any ideas, I would like to hear them. Soon! Thanks for helping me to sleep at night. I have had the best sleep lately. Pastor told me to ask for sweet sleep and I got it.

"I don't believe I thanked you for Callia. I was angry when I first found out, but I don't know what I was thinking. She has been the biggest blessing. Keep my new family safe and continue to help me forgive my brother. Thank you. Amen."

Caden slid under his covers and the phone rang. It was Tashia.

"Hey! Everything all right?"

"Yes everything is good. I have a question for you."

"Okay."

"Anthony came by to talk to Zander and he asked if the boys could take part in his afternoon music school. Is he cool people?"

"That's funny."

"What's so funny?"

"He said he was full to capacity. He must be making an exception with your boys. His after-school program is great and those kids can really play. There are many trying to get into the program, so if he offered I would jump on it," Caden suggested.

"Okay. I think I will," she said. "Thanks, again, for today. You guys came through in a big way."

"No problem, Tashia. You have to let us know what's going on. Use us."

"I may take you up on that. I just took a part-time job so I can get us into another place by the end of the year."

"Use me. I have plenty of time on my hands."

"Thanks and goodnight." She would definitely be taking her family up on their offer if she were going to get her children out of the neighborhood. She had one more person to call and thank.

Preston silenced his ringing phone before it woke Cuyler.

"Hello," he answered.

"Hey, Preston! I just wanted to call and say thank you, again, for today. You gave me my boy back. Zander is back, again."

"That's great," he half whispered.

"Did I awake you?"

"No. Cuyler is sleep and she has court tomorrow, so I was trying not to wake her. I was doing some work, so I was awake."

"Oh, Anthony came by to see Zander, and he wants the boys to be a part of his after-school program."

Preston smiled, thinking about the way his brother looked at her. "That would be great for them. He runs a great, no-nonsense program to keep kids off the street."

"That's what Caden was saying. Okay. I will let you get back to your work. Goodnight. "

Preston smiled, again, thinking about his brother. He hoped he wouldn't take too long to say something to her. His brother was slow on the move and the least talkative of the brothers. Smiling, he shook his head. Reaching for the lamp, he turned it off and snuggled close to Cuyler.

"Quit, Preston, you're hot."

"I know," he teased.

Anthony knew she would call. He didn't answer the phone because he was busy, but he would call her back if Myra didn't take too long.

He returned his attention to the beauty riding him. He watched her face contort each time she came down. He knew it was all an act, but she got the job done better than most he had. She knew what he liked and she went straight for it, but now he was disinterested.

Lifting her from his lap, he stood and picked up his pants that were neatly lying across the back of the chair. Reaching into his wallet, he pulled out a couple of bills and threw them on the desk.

Myra looked at him, hurt; he was so cavalier in the way he paid her. "Oh, so you can't put it in my hand? You're going to just throw it on the desk like I was some common whore?"

Anthony looked at her, amazed she made the analogy. "But you are."

An angry, now dressed, Myra snatched her money from the desk. "I may be a whore, but I'm not common." She waited for a response, but when she received none she stormed from the office.

A playful smile crossed Anthony's face. He knew she liked him and she was exclusively his, but she was still a whore to him. He had a strange appetite and she satisfied his desires, but tonight he could no longer think of her; his mind was on Tashia Davidson.

He decided to call her in the morning instead. After dressing, he left the little room that now smelled of sex. He had work to do.

The club was quiet tonight. It was Monday, so he expected as much. He had to talk to his manager who was in the process of recruiting new employees and weeding out those who didn't want to work. He was trying to upscale the club from its former reputation. Although he had only been there a year, the change was evident.

Anthony walked through the club giving orders as he went. He headed to the bar to check the stock for the night. He could see everyone was on point and he could relax.

Myra walked past him and didn't speak. He laughed to himself. She went to the other side of the bar not to be near him. Anthony laughed, again, shaking his head.

He was a businessman first and couldn't have her affecting his money for the night, so he made his way to her. He kissed her neck and whispered in her ear, "You are what you believe you are and no one else should be able to tell you differently. If I say you are a queen and you still feel like a whore then you are a whore." He could feel her tension slowly leave her demeanor. "I apologize," he told her, as he reached around her front and grabbed between her thighs. "Enjoy your night." He left her to contemplate what he told her.

Anthony found his manager, Snow, in the back, getting the girls organized. Anthony sat down when he entered the dressing room. No one paid attention to him as they continued to dress, or undress, for the night.

Snow, who gained his name from his albino appearance, was there when Anthony purchased the club over a year ago. Anthony saw how well the girls responded to him and decided to keep him. It proved to be a good decision on Anthony's part because he did his job well.

"We need to talk, Snow," Anthony informed him.

"About?" The tall albino stood, overemphasizing his femininity and placing his hands on his hips.

"Staffing. Have you taken care of the list of people I gave you?" Anthony asked, referring to the people who potentially could be fired.

"Most. A few have not been here since our conversation and one may have made a decision by default," Snow answered, going back to what he was doing. "Trina didn't come in for the second day so I have termed her. I will send her a notice by certified mail tomorrow."

"What are you doing about replacing her?"

"She has already been replaced. I have a new girl starting on Friday."

Anthony raised an eyebrow. He was happy that Snow was being proactive. He was his biggest asset right now. "Okay. I will be in my office if you need me, but I believe I need you more than you me. Good job," Anthony told him before leaving. "Do well tonight ladies," he added over his shoulder.

"Bye, Anthony!" they sang in unison.

Once back in his office, he looked over his schedule. It was filling up quickly and agreeing to get the boys was probably more than he could handle, but it had to work. Anthony pulled out a small notebook from his drawer and began writing down his schedule.

Family

C uyler was in the office when Preston came downstairs. He peeped in. "What are you doing?"
"I'm looking at the private investigator's report on a case," she answered, never looking up.

Preston walked to her desk and sat next to her paperwork. "I need your attention for a moment," he said, grabbing her hands.

"Preston! I really need to—"

"This will take a moment of your time." His calmness always got her attention.

Cuyler put the papers on the desk and gave Preston her full attention. "Your sister reached out to me Monday concerning Zander," he started, raising his hand to stop the questions he knew she had. "Zander is fine. He is a smart and strong boy, but I'm concerned about Tashia. We need to reach out to her more and even get the kids when we don't have plans to give her a break. She never gets a break.

"She was very overwhelmed and actually felt she had no one to go to. She felt she was burdening us. So, I would like to plan a vacation with the kids as soon as school is out. Okay?"

"I think that's a great idea. I will try and make sure I have nothing planned for a week or two and we will make that happen."

"Okay. That was it. Back to work and I will see you this evening. I have Callia and will drop her off this morning."

"Thank you." She sighed.

"Stop stressing. You will do well today." Preston left to prepare Callia to leave.

Within minutes, she ran into the room and kissed her mother. "Bye, Mommy," she said, running out of the room as quickly as she had entered.

Cuyler returned to the report. Something did not add up, but she could not figure out what it was. She flipped backward and forward in the notes and became frustrated, but she had to go.

Grabbing her briefcase, she made her way to the garage.

SSSHHIA

Friday came much quicker than Tashia expected. The kids were going to Cuyler and Preston's for the weekend. Preston was taking them dirt biking on one of his empty properties. She packed a small bag to take to work with her.

"Mom! I'm going to be late for tutoring!" Zander yelled from the living room.

Tashia walked into the room, ready. "Let's go." The day was going to be long, but at least she did not have to get up too early in the morning. "Does everyone have their duffle bags? I will drop them off to Preston today and he will pick you up from school, Solana. Uncle Anthony will bring you two from the center and drop you off at Cuyler and Preston's."

"You told us ten times, Mom, let's go!" Zander was irritated.

Tashia thought he was a bit anxious. He was always big about timeliness, but he never was pushy about getting there. The group left to begin their day.

At the end of her shift, Tashia hurried to the parking garage to gather the kids' bags for a waiting Preston. As she walked to her car, she became nervous about her evening, but she quickly put the thought out of her head. This was a necessity.

The lounge looked as it did when she left. She heard there was a new owner and thought some things would have been updated, but assumed he cared no more than the previous owner. Her old friends welcomed Tashia warmly. They bombarded her with questions concerning the kids and her life. The new employees were not as welcoming, but she expected as much. Their world was competitive.

A skinny, mousy girl showed Tashia to her spot. She sat in the chair and examined herself in the mirror. She still looked like the same girl who worked here almost three years ago. Unzipping her bag, she began unpacking its contents and preparing for the evening.

"I think you have about an hour."

Tashia looked at the mousy girl. There were a few murmurs and eye cutting, but no one said anything directly to her. To go on last could be a blessing or curse. In this instance, it was a curse; these men did not know her and the ones who did would not know she was there. Now she understood why she received the cool reception.

By the time they came for her, she was ready. There was also time to close her eyes for a few minutes. Stilettos on, she picked up her coat, ready to dance.

Looking in the mirror, she saw her reflection. No one would ever believe she was the mother of three. Why was she doing this to herself? Removing the heart locket she received from her children, she placed it on the shelf as if she were leaving herself there in order to do what she had to do.

The walk to the stage was long. She got looks and stares. The other girls performed in what appeared to be undergarments, but Tashia was always classy when she danced, which set her apart from the rest of the girls. When she danced at the lounge before, she had many regulars who only came the night she performed.

Now at the edge of the curtain, she waited for her music to cue and to be announced. Snow approached her and kissed her on the cheek. "You are the best at this. Go get 'em!"

Her music cued, and the announcer introduced her. "Returning to the stage after she heard there has been none like her, get your tens and twenties together, gentlemen, because she doesn't take ones, still the queen at Hot Topics we give you, SSSHHHIAAAA!" the announcer hissed with emphasis.

Tashia strutted like a runway model, stopping on beat and swinging her hair. When the music picked up, again, she walked to the first pole and straddled it, swinging, legs extended straight out as she dropped, stopping just before she hit the floor. She had their attention now. The attendees knew they were in for a treat. Standing, she untied her belt and snatched off her coat, exposing her lace corset and garter.

She grabbed the pole from behind and slid down with her legs extended, stopping on every beat of the song. Just before reaching the floor, she swung her thighs back, gripping the pole between them and extending her arms forward, catching herself with just her thighs.

Stepping on the stage, she walked seductively to the front pole and swung until she was in a split on the floor with her back to the crowd. She was in front of her moneymen now, so it was time to work. She swung her front leg to meet the back and pulled up into a handstand, using the pole to support her. Lowering her legs on the pole, she allowed her thighs to grip either side, once again, pulling her upper body up until she was extended and upright. The crowd went wild. The money began to come quicker. The women who frequented the club to meet men began throwing money on stage as well. Once her set was over, Tashia strutted offstage the same way she came on. She picked up her coat from the floor as she passed it, and tied her sash before strutting and ascending the steps.

"And that was SSShhhiiaaaaaa," the announcer said, again, and the house was still going crazy. The stage girl brought her money. Tashia tipped the girl and went back to the dressing room. She needed to change and leave. She never waited until the end because of the groupies. The other dancers, old and new, praised her dance routine.

After she was dressed and about to go, one of the guards told her the new owner wanted to meet with her for a few minutes to introduce himself.

"Can I do it another night, Greg? I am really tired."

"He does not talk much, so it should be quick."

Tashia dropped her bag and grabbed her purse to go meet the 'new' owner. To her, they were all the same. They tried to feel the dancers out to see if they could get more out of them than what they came to do. She would have to set him straight and let him know there would be no 'happy endings' from her.

She knocked on the door and waited for the invite. She never knew what she would see at a place like Hot Topics, so it was best to wait for the invite.

"Come in."

When Tashia entered, the owner had his back to her. *How rude,* she thought. "You wanted to meet me?"

"Come in and have a seat," he directed. When he turned in his chair, Tashia thought she would faint.

Anthony was in his office doing payroll when Snow came to let him know the new girl would be up in five minutes. Since he was trying to change the image of the club, he wanted to see her himself. It would be better to cut someone on her first day than try to fix things later. "I'll be right there, Snow." Anthony put everything back into his safe and headed to the bar.

The room was packed. Anthony pushed past the groups of people to get to the bar where he could stand and see freely. There were men and woman ordering and picking up drinks. His barmaids had their hands full, trying to get drinks served fast enough to keep up with demand. He enjoyed nights like tonight. It meant the club was making money.

Myra smiled. "You came to help? I told you I need help back here on the weekends!" she reminded him, yelling through the noise.

"We're working on it, Myra. I got you covered."

Anthony began taking orders along with Myra. Soon the bar began to clear. The deejay was announcing the new girl. He looked up to see she was fully dressed in what looked like a trench coat. She high stepped across the platform, stopped, and swung her ponytail. She looked seductively at the audience and strutted to the first pole on the back part of the stage, playing to the side crowd. Gripping the pole, she slid down with her legs straight out in front of her. She had his attention. Myra noticed, too.

Anthony stopped serving and watched the new dancer. This is what he needed to upscale the club. She was phenomenal. She was sexy. She was classy. Yet there was something familiar about her. He looked a little closer.

"She's good," Myra said, now standing next to Anthony.

"What was her name, again?"

"SSSSHHHHIIAAAA!" Myra said, imitating the deejay.

Anthony looked closer when she was bent back, teasing the audience. "No way!"

"You know her?"

Anthony didn't answer her. It wasn't her business who he knew. He stepped closer to the stage and found a seat to watch. He knew she was hot, but he never knew she was this hot.

Tashia was a professional to the end when she picked up her coat and walked off the stage. Even when she left the stage, the money was still coming. Anthony sent word to Snow that he needed to meet with her in his office.

Myra watched Anthony in amazement. She didn't like his reaction. Never before had he taken notice of any of the dancers. He often stayed in his office and when not in his office he helped at the bar, but never before had any captured his attention. "I wonder what's gotten into him. He never took notice to anyone before."

"He just asked Snow to bring her to his office." The barmaid knew she was pushing Myra's buttons. Every employee in the club knew Myra was obsessed with Anthony. She got the reaction she was looking for and smiled.

Myra could feel the heat rise in her face and wished she hadn't said anything. They were jealous of her. She went to ask him, again, if he knew the new dancer, but Anthony told her to stay in her lane. Who was this girl? She watched as he walked through the crowd and back to his office. She went back to the bar.

"Don't worry about her. You know no one ever holds his attention long," the same barmaid reminded her. "Just like he doin' you now, he will be doing her later."

Myra threw the glass in the sink and held on to the end of the counter, as she gained her composure. The yells from the customers wanting their orders brought her back to her senses.

Anthony waited in his office, not knowing what to say once she did come. He sat in his chair, facing the back wall. He didn't know if he liked her working for him. This complicated the relationship he hoped for, as she had walked into his secret world. Here he could be him without apologizing. He took whomever he wanted into his office and there was no one to judge him. Tashia was family and he didn't want this to be her opinion of him. He heard the knock and wished he had left it alone. This was her secret, too. Now it was too late to back away from his decision.

"Come in," he beckoned.

He heard her enter the room and invited her to sit. He remained staring at the wall and realized he had his back to her for a while. He turned in his seat and saw the recognition and horror on her face and regret overcame him, yet again.

"Hello, Shia!" he said, trying not to sound like the deejay. "This is a side of you I did not expect." He was feeling her out. "I like to meet all of my employees so here we are."

She said nothing. He wondered what she was thinking. Was it shame or embarrassment? Her poker face had him puzzled. She intrigued him even more.

Tashia looked at him with a smirk on her face. He waited for her to say something, but she didn't.

"Was there a question in there somewhere?" She crossed her legs.

Oh my, this girl is amazing.

He looked her over then leaned back in his chair. He smiled back at her. "Your secret is safe with me."

"I didn't ask you to keep any *secrets* for me," she said, emphasizing secrets. "There are areas of my life I choose not to share, but they are a part of my life, so I won't lie about them either."

"Ditto."

"So does Preston know you own this?" she asked, waving her hand around the room.

"What I do is none of my brother's business. I'm his keeper not the other way around." Anthony studied her, again, for a reaction, but she gave none. She watched him as though studying his next move. "I don't know if me being your boss is a good idea."

"Then don't be my boss," she offered.

Anthony chuckled and leaned back in his chair, not taking his eyes from her. "I think I like SSSHHIAAA," he said, now imitating the deejay. He saw a slight smile on her lips as she cocked her head to the side. "Make sure one of the guys walks you to your car and I will see you tomorrow."

Tashia stood and tightened the belt of her trench. "I'll be okay," she replied. "Besides, everyone is busy."

"Then I guess I will have to walk you," he said, standing to his feet. "You gonna need someone to make sure you get there with that sack of money," he teased.

"If you must, I'll even let you carry my sack," she teased, handing him her purse. Anthony dutifully took her purse and realized he had been had. She wanted him to walk her to her car.

When they left his office, Myra was standing near his office door. He instantly became annoyed. "Will you be right back?" she asked, rubbing his chest and eyeing Tashia sideways.

"Who is at the bar if you are back here?"

"One of the barmaids is covering. We slowed down," she answered, stepping in close and personal.

Anthony pushed past her even more annoyed that she believed she meant something to him. He didn't like the way she looked at Tashia either.

Tashia knew girls like Myra and they did not intimidate her. She stopped in front of the insecure girl. "Is this something you need to take care of, Anthony?"

"No." He continued walking.

Left standing in the hall, watching them leave out the back door, a deflated Myra yelled, "Who is this bitch?"

"Looks like your new competition," one of the dancers answered.

"No. That would be her replacement," another mused.

Myra entered Anthony's office and waited for his return. She wanted answers. What was she to him? Who was she and where did she come from?

She was sure her face was flushed. He couldn't just toss her aside without an explanation. He needed to make a decision. She was sure she wasn't willing to satisfy his dark appetites as she did.

When Anthony entered his office, Myra was sitting in his chair. He said something to one of the girls and turned his attention to her. Leaving the door open, he approached his desk. "You need to be at the bar or go home," he instructed. "But know that if you go home, do not come back," he said coldly. "Now get the hell out of my office."

Angered by his dismissal, Myra asked, "Who is she, Anthony?"

"*She* is not your concern." His accent was heavy now. He stood at the door, waiting for her to leave.

"You're not going to fuck me and then dismiss me," she told him, not moving from the chair. "You owe me an explanation!" she yelled.

"Girl! I owe you a paycheck every Friday and that's all I owe you and everything else has been paid in full," he said through clinched teeth. "Now, get your ass out of my chair and get out of my office." Two bouncers walked into the office to put her out.

"Oh, so now you are throwing me out?" She was seething with anger. Her chest rose and fell as her breathing picked up.

"Your choice. Either take your ass back to work or leave on your own. Or, we can go with option three and I can throw you out. Choose!"

Myra sat for a moment. She needed this job. If she left, it would be on her terms. "All over this new chick?" Anthony didn't answer. Myra walked past the bouncers and went back to work. The smirks on her way were almost unbearable. She knew she earned them. How many times had she snubbed them?

Snow appeared in his door. "You're too late. Fire her after this weekend," he instructed.

"Who will replace her?" Snow asked frustrated.

"Don't worry. We will find someone. I will go shopping."

"So you know Tashia?"

Anthony didn't answer him as he ignored the question when Myra asked. "I will look for three girls. We were short anyway."

"If you stop sleeping with the help we can stop replacing them," Snow murmured, as he stormed past Anthony.

He received a text message and looked at his phone. It was Tashia letting him know she was safely in her apartment. Anthony closed the door behind him and made his way back to the floor.

Tashia stepped out of the shower, toweled, and moisturized with lotion before heading to bed. She was tired and still had to go to work at the hospital in the morning. She got another nurse to cover her until nine, so she could get a few more hours of sleep.

She pulled her sheet up to her shoulder and thought about the events of the evening. Anthony intrigued her. She loved his swagger and he didn't take anything from anyone. She especially liked the way he tried to protect her. It had been a while since she felt protected. Although she didn't feel like she needed protection, it was nice to know someone had her back.

She already put her money in a strong box. She collected over five hundred dollars. Not bad for the first night back. Once she had a following, the money would get better. She needed money for a down payment on a house. She wanted her kids to be able to play outside and not worry about stray bullets or someone taking advantage of them. She wasn't so naïve to believe those things didn't happen elsewhere, but where they lived, it was expected.

Her phone beeped.

Anthony: Good night SSSHHHIIAAA!

Tashia: Goodnight Boss

Shut Up and Drive

W ork at the hospital was difficult. Tashia worked in the Intensive Care unit. The day dragged; she was still tired from the night before. She was looking forward to being off the following day.

She spoke to the boys who were excited about going to the motocross track with Preston, and Solana was enjoying her little cousin Callia and her Aunt Cuyler. She felt she was doing the right thing. Soon they would be in a better place.

After leaving the hospital, she went straight to the club. She needed to get some time in on the pole before they opened.

There were very few people there. Anthony had not arrived, but Myra was there to watch her every move. Tashia nodded to her and continued to the back to put her things down.

After changing into her shorts and top, she headed to the deejay with her music. He wasn't in the room, so Snow took her to him and introduced them. "Terrance, this is Tashia. She was going to practice and needed you to spin for her."

Terrance appeared to be too young to be in the club as well. Tashia thought about Mouse and smiled at the thought of setting them up.

Terrance was as slender as Mouse. He was taller than Anthony, which made him around six feet four inches. He was a dark chocolate brown and had a little peanut head. His smile made her instantly like him.

"No problem," he answered.

Tashia joined him in his booth and told him what she needed then headed for the stage. She could feel Myra's eyes on her the entire time, but chose not to acknowledge her. She dealt with girls like her all her life and the best thing to do with them was to ignore them.

Once onstage, she got a running start and swung stiff-armed around the pole. She had not warmed up or stretched, so she didn't want to do too much. Terrance queued up her music and she began dancing. She wanted to try something using a rap song. She strutted slow, then fast with the music. Dropping into a squatting position, she stayed there, bouncing, then twerking. Once close enough, she went into a headstand and allowed her legs to slowly lower onto the pole until she could grip it with her thighs. She raised her torso until her thighs totally supported her. Seductively, she climbed the pole to the top and bent back until she was upside down. On beat, she dropped until her face was almost to the floor and she came to an abrupt stop. She pulled up and twisted down into a split on the floor. Swinging the front leg behind her, she pushed up from the floor and stood.

She could see Myra still watching her. She ran, swung with her arms stiff and legs spread and straight out with the pole between, but not touching it. She held the position, dropped about a foot, and stopped, repeating the move twice before planting her feet on the floor again. Once again, she ran, but this time throwing her legs in the air, gripping the pole upside down. She looked up and saw Anthony sitting in a chair in front of her. She smiled.

She waved to Terrance to queue up the next song. Smiling, she danced for him, throwing everything she had. She kept eye contact, as she did during her show once she determined where her biggest tips would come from. The song slowed toward the end for her finale. He locked his eyes on her, as if in a trance. One of the workers whispered something to him. He answered, never looking away from her, causing her to blush. When the finale came, she spun down the pole and stopped almost at the bottom with her head bent back, looking at him.

Anthony stood and clapped. Tashia dismounted and took her bows and came down to join him.

"That was magnificent!" he said sincerely.

"Thank you. It's a little harder than it should be, but I'm out of practice."

"Only you know how hard it was. You performed it effortlessly."

"Thanks. I need to go eat before I perform. I haven't had a chance to do that."

Anthony felt she was baiting him, again. He bit. "Go get dressed and I'll take you to get something," he offered.

"Okay," she said, and was off to her dressing area to get ready.

When Tashia entered the dressing room, Myra was there waiting for her. Tashia glanced at her and continued on to her things. She pulled her leather shorts from her bag and threw her fishnet style sweater over her workout bra. Myra sat in silence. Tashia waited, but she said nothing to her. Tashia was putting on her boots when Myra found her voice.

"So you think he's yours now?" Myra was looking her over.

Tashia smiled, as she tied her boots. Stretching her strong legs, she admired how the boots made her legs look, making Myra wait for her answer just as she waited for the question.

Once dressed, she stood and checked herself in the mirror. She wasn't wearing any makeup, but she liked what she saw. Her long, jet-black curls framed her face, giving her an angelic look.

"The problem with women like you is you believe you can tame a man like him. He's no more mine than he is yours." Tashia left, giving her something to ponder.

Anthony was leaning on the wall outside the room. She knew he heard and blushed. "I'll drive," he said, and led her out the building.

Anthony took her to a Reggae supper club. The atmosphere was quaint and the music inviting. Most were at the bar, laughing and drinking, while others sat in the booths, eating. Anthony found a table and asked her what she wanted to eat.

"You choose for me."

She watched him go to the bar to order. She didn't know why she found him to be sexy. He was tall with broad shoulders. His legs were long and he was on the slender side. She figured his entire family specialized in butts because he had a nice one like his brother, Preston. Unlike his refined brother, Anthony was wild and abrupt. She would not have given him a single thought if he were like Preston.

He returned to the table with a number and placed it in the center. He was watching her, again. The average person would become uneasy, but it didn't bother her.

"How long ago did you buy the club?"

"About a year now. I'm trying to make some changes to upscale it a little . You want to dance?" He stood up.

"They said you were not a talker." She watched him, as she evaded his invitation. The last thing she wanted to do was get any closer to him. He turned her on.

After not receiving an answer, she took his hand and went to the floor. She seductively danced around him, smiling and occasionally tossing her hair to the reggae beat. His dancing skills surprised her. She watched the smirk that danced on his lips, which were slightly curled at the corners. His eyes penetrated her soul, causing her to blush.

She saw the waitress bring the food to the table. Grabbing Anthony's hand, she led him back to the booth.

Tashia didn't realize how hungry she was. She quickly blessed the food and began eating. "You better jump in if you want some. I'm not as polite as my sister," she warned.

Anthony leaned back in his booth seat and let her eat." Did you eat today?"

"No!"

"Unless you want to get sick flipping upside down you better slow down."

"Why aren't you eating?"

"I eat one meal a day. I'm too busy the rest."

"You know that's not healthy?"

"Why haven't you asked me about Myra?"

"She's irrelevant and none of my business, but apparently you want me to know about you and her." Tashia put her fork down. He was right, if she kept eating at this rate she would get sick.

Anthony smiled. He really liked her. "Let me get you back before your fans get there."

"Just when I thought you were opening up to me," she joked.

Anthony took her back to the club to prepare for her set. This time he walked her through the front door to ensure the patrons knew she was returning to the stage. The regulars turned and watched as she walked by. Her thigh high boots, leather shorts, and fish net sweater turned heads alone. She always came dressed seductively, so the payers could get a peak. When she left, she wore defensive clothes so no one knew whom she was. As she walked, she realized she also received stares from Myra. Eventually, there would be a showdown, because of Myra's insecurity, but it wouldn't be her first.

Tashia was thinking about her routine and debated changing it. She brought costumes for both. She was about to get dressed when Myra entered the room. She sat in the chair next to Tashia, so Tashia stood to get dress.

"You know that he doesn't stay with one person long?"

"Is that what happened to you?" Tashia side eyed her.

"I'm just warning you."

"Thanks for warning, but you must have me twisted with you," Tashia started. "First, I've never had a man leave me. Second, you are under the impression I want him. To be honest, by the way you are looking at me, I think you want me!" Tashia smiled at her. "You wouldn't be the first woman."

Tashia walked her now totally nude body over to the rack and pulled her chaps off their hanger. She turned and saw Myra was still watching her. Slowly, she pulled the chaps up until her bare behind dropped into the two cutout holes. Although they were long, the inside of her thighs were cutout so she could still grip the pole when she needed to stop.

Tashia reached for her vest, which fit only through the chest in order for her breasts not to drop out when flipping and spinning off. Myra continued to watch.

Snow poked his head in the doorway. "Fifteen minutes," he told Tashia, looking at Myra. "Aren't you supposed to be at the bar?"

"I'm on my break," Myra informed him.

"Well the last time I looked this was not the break room."

Reluctantly Myra walked out of the room.

"Sorry. I'm strictly dickly. If I change my mind I'll let you know," Tashia said over her shoulder and continued to prepare.

"Is everything okay?" Snow asked.

"I'm good. She's not ready for me, Snow. Tell Terrance to play the second song, please," she yelled, as he closed the door.

Snow made his way to the deejay box to give Terrance Tashia's music instructions when he encountered Anthony. "You need to check your girl. She was just in the dressing room with Shia, harassing her."

Myra's persistence angered Anthony. "I will handle her after her shift," he assured Snow. Anthony was making his way to Tashia when she walked up on him in the hall. Reaching out, he wrapped his arm around her waist and pulled her to the side.

"What did she want with you?" he asked angrily.

"She wanted to tell me all the dirty things you two have been doing." She smiled and watched him squirm.

Anger flashed across his face and Anthony turned to deal with her right away. Tashia quickly grabbed his arm to pull him back, but had to jump in front of him instead.

"Woo, cowboy, I was just kidding. I can handle her!" She got in close to him. "Now go sit front and center. I have a treat for you. It will probably piss her off more, but that's my specialty." Tashia walked toward the stage to prepare for her introduction.

Terrance saw her standing in the wings and began. "She decided to return for a second night. She said what she got she promise it's a killer. Please, welcome back to the stage...SSSHHIAA!"

Tashia sauntered onto the stage, swinging on each poll when the beat stopped. She spotted Anthony making his way to a chair. Tonight she wouldn't stay in the back. She went straight to where he sat and mounted the pole, climbing for her death drop.

Her entire performance she danced at Anthony. She stayed high on the pole and slowly dropped, stopped, posed, then dropped more until she was totally in a split on the floor. She looked seriously at Anthony, not avoiding his eyes.

She came from the stage, which was not her norm, and danced around him, capturing his full attention. Sitting in his lap, she gave him a lap dance.

She turned and straddled his thighs, bouncing faster and faster as though riding him. Leaning all the way back until her head almost hit the floor, she arched her back as though she was in the heat of passion. Coming back up, she panted, running her hands down the side of her face, mouth open and eyes closed. She could feel him growing between her thighs.

She kissed him lightly and as quickly as she came off the stage she climbed back to prepare for her finale. The patrons went wild, slapping Anthony on the back, congratulating him. Once finished, she sauntered off the stage as though walking off into the sunset, looking back once over her shoulder at him. He was watching her every move. Not once had Tashia looked in Myra's direction, but she knew Myra's eyes never once left her.

When off stage and back in the dressing room, she leaned against the wall behind the changing screen, trying to regain her composure. Quickly, she changed into her jeans, knit shirt, and boots. She was trying to affect Anthony and found she was more affected. The fire within her rose. It had been years since she was that close to a man and he had awakened the sleeping desire within her.

"Girl! You in a hurry?"

Tashia didn't know the girl. Her bright Kool-Aid hair made her smile.

"I have to be at work in the morning."

"Do you think you can help me sometimes to do better?" The young girl they called Mouse was shyly looking down as she waited for Tashia's answer.

Tashia slowed down and looked at the young girl. She was skinny, but Tashia saw potential in her look. Tashia wondered how old she was and what was her story. Everyone there had one. No one chose to work in a gentleman's club.

"Sorry, I don't have the time, but I will watch you the next time you dance and give you some suggestions," she promised. She grabbed her bag and glanced at the girl before leaving.

Tashia walked into the night air, breathing in its coolness. The club was hot and she welcomed the chill. The door swung open, startling her. It was Snow.

"You know the rules. You don't go to your car without an escort."

"I had to get out of there, Snow. It was too hot," she said, still walking to her car.

Snow smiled. He saw she was running. "You are playing with fire, girl. You know he's looking for you?" It was more a statement than a question.

"I know." She took in another deep breath and let it out slowly. It was what she needed to put out the fire that was slowly kindling inside her.

Snow skipped down the steps and approached her. "Com'on. Let me walk you to your car." He said, putting his arm around her shoulder.

Tashia leaned on her old buddy, Snow, as they walked to her car. He always looked out for her when she was there before. The previous owner made her a proposition that she declined. He even tried to force himself on her once, but Snow took care of him, although she needed no help. That's when she decided to leave.

Her friend tucked her in her car and buckled her seat belt. "He's a good person, Tashia, but he will hurt you. Leave him alone. He's intrigued with you now, but he quickly loses interest." She looked at him. "Even in you, Princess."

Snow closed her car door. Tashia started the engine and hesitated for a moment. She saw the light from the back door of the club illuminate the parking lot in her rearview mirror. Anthony was coming her way, frantically. Trying not to be obvious, Tashia pulled out of her parking space slowly and rolled out of the parking lot, watching as Anthony became smaller in her rearview mirror.

She did not trust herself to go home. He would come for her and she was too weak to avoid him. The heat between them was real and she was not ready to become involved with anyone, especially intriguing and sexy Anthony. Besides, what did she really know about him?

He was nothing like his brother who was refined and conservative. This man was wild and untamed. He reminded her of Jesus the way he commanded people and played no games. This was why he was respected in the streets and Anthony was respected and feared in his club.

All lights were off at the Washington's except the one coming from the back of the house. She knew Preston and Cuyler would be there, probably asleep. She debated whether to use her key and go in. Even if he found her there, he would never knock on the door this time of night.

No sooner than she turned off her car, her phone rang. Anthony had been texting her since she left the club, but she didn't pick up her phone to read the messages. The effect he had on her was greater than she expected or needed in her life.

"Hello," she answered, trying to sound irritated.

"Tashia. Where are you?" he asked calmly.

"I'm safe," she answered, not wanting to reveal her location.

"I was worried. You never texted to say you made it home." His voice was strained.

"Where are you, Anthony?"

He didn't answer her, but she already knew the answer. "Let's talk," he finally answered. "Meet me."

"Not tonight."

"Where are you?" She heard the command in his voice. He tried to hide it, but it was there.

She didn't answer. "I'd like to hear your story one day, Anthony." Tashia disconnected the call, not wanting to hear his voice any longer. He enticed her, taking her to a place she had not been in a while. She had made bad decisions in the past and she didn't want to make another. Her children would pay if her decisions were bad.

Tashia closed her eyes and leaned her head back on the headrest. He had her mind spinning. She recognized who Anthony was—that boy who couldn't be tamed. As a child, he was disobedient and uncontrollable. He was that man who would eventually break her heart because he was insatiable. He would never be pleased with one woman. If his brother was not married to her sister she would go for that ride as long as she could, but after he was done with her he would still be in her life, appearing at family events.

Even with her eyes closed, Tashia was aware of her surroundings. She felt the shade that suddenly covered her window, blocking the light from lamppost. Opening her eyes, she turned her head to see Anthony standing outside her window.

Myra watched Tashia dance. She was definitely good. Compared to the other girls there was a lot more structure to her routine. She always had a theme, making sure her routines were different and more exciting than the dance before.

Myra felt the resentment rise in her. They were nothing alike. Tashia was everything she was not. She was confident and cocky. It was evident in her dance, the way she flipped her hair and looked directly in the men's eyes, pulling them into her fantasy, and then left at the end of the night, without giving any of them a second thought.

She could see it as she watched her spin each man in the room into her web, trapping each in the fantasy. She knew what Tashia said was true. No woman could hold Anthony down. She thought she would break him by allowing him to do what he wanted with her, but he didn't touch her anymore. His attention was elsewhere, and she discarded.

Getting a man was never an issue for her. Didn't she fight them off all night at the bar? Her five-foot-five-inch frame showcased a slender one hundred twenty-six pounds. Tashia was maybe two or three inches taller and thicker by far. Myra liked her redbone status. Her hair was died golden and she wore it bone straight. Although she had two children, she was proud of her flat stomach. She didn't know Tashia's heritage. She appeared to look Latino. Her skin was an Aztec bronze and her hair was curly, but defined and not bushy. She was very curvy and the men followed her when she walked through the room. She definitely made a great contender.

She watched Tashia ride Anthony and hurt resonated through her body. She turned away and served the men at the bar. She would apologize later and let it go. Maybe she could get a bartending job at another club.

Myra heard the patrons talk about Tashia's performance. They sounded like groupies. It was definitely time for her to leave. She watched as Anthony went back to his office afterward. Tashia would be with him soon.

Myra continued to take care of her guests and took her mind off the situation. She was distracted thirty minutes later when she saw Anthony rush through the room with his leather jacket on. She wondered what was happening.

Anthony went back to his office after Tashia's dance. He expected her to come there once she changed so he could walk her to her car, but she never came. He walked to the dressing room to see if she maybe had another encounter with Myra, but a few of the other girls were all that occupied the humble room. He didn't ask the question, but they knew who he was looking for.

Melissa spoke up and answered the unasked question. "She left about five minutes ago. She said she worked in the morning."

Anthony looked at the young girl, noticing her for the first time, and nodded to her. He knew her information was inaccurate because she didn't work in the morning. He walked to the back to locate Snow who he was sure was close by and pulled out his phone to see if he missed a text message, but there were none.

Snow was nowhere to be found. Anthony headed to the back door. There was a slight briskness in the air when he opened it, but he didn't feel it. Snow was standing outside of Tashia's car, talking to her. His pace picked up when he descended the steps, but she pulled off before he reached the bottom. Disappointment set in, knowing she didn't come to see him.

"I gotcha, boss." Snow walked back to the door.

Anthony felt better, but wondered why she didn't say good-bye. "I'll be back. If I don't make it back before closing, wrap things up for me," he instructed.

"Go. I got this." Snow smiled, as Anthony walked away. He had never seen him act like this and he enjoyed it. Tashia was going to be a hard conquest. He had his work cut out for him. She quit before because the previous owner tried to get in her pants and wouldn't take no for an answer, so one night without warning she didn't returned.

Once in his car, Anthony texted her, but received no answer. When he arrived at her apartment, there was no answer at the door. Now he was worried. Then he thought he was assuming too much. Surely, a woman like Tashia had a man. But, if that were true where was he during her recent ordeal? Then it hit him; she may have gone to Preston's because the kids were there.

Tashia wasn't shocked to see Anthony standing outside her window. She rolled it down. "What are you doing here?" She didn't look at him, afraid to betray her feelings and show her annoyance.

"I wanted to make sure you were okay."

"I told you that on the phone, so why did you really come?"

"Come with me. Let's talk." He was ready to lay everything bare for her and he wasn't willing to do that for anyone. She captivated him. She had for over a year now.

"Why?"

"Because you have questions." He could see she was at a crossroad and was not going any further unless she had answers.

"Where?"

"We can go back where we had dinner. It's a club right now and they are open until four." He waited for her answer.

Tashia saw the light go out in the back room of the house. "Okay. I'll follow you." She didn't want to leave her car in the driveway and have someone wonder where she was.

Anthony read her mind. "We can park your car around the corner and you can ride with me. I don't want you to disappear again." Without waiting for her answer, he walked back to his car.

Tashia's heart was racing, as she followed him and parked her car where he suggested. He waited, holding her door open. She climbed in and quickly buckled up. She was bothered by his presence.

They rode a few blocks in silence, before Anthony broke the ice. "Why did you leave without saying goodbye?"

Tashia didn't answer. She stared out of the window at the scenery. "Is that a requirement of my job?" Cutting her eyes, she watched him.

Anthony began to wonder if Myra had said something to her. "No, but I told you to make sure you don't walk to your car alone."

"And I didn't. Snow walked me."

There was an apparent difference in her demeanor from when they went to dinner. He didn't question her anymore. He could feel her become more closed with each question he asked.

The parking lot at Reggae was almost full. He pulled up to the back door in a spot appearing to be private. He walked to her side of the car, opened the door, and took her hand to help her out. Placing his hand in the small of her back, he guided her through the parking lot to the front door. Although she tried not to show she was flustered by his touch, he felt her body quiver.

Finding a seat wasn't difficult because the floor was packed. They found a seat in the back corner booth and sat together. He watched her turn her attention to the crowd.

"What would you like to drink?" he asked, bending into her so she could hear him over the music.

He was too close. His breath was on her neck and his lips beckoned to be kissed. Her breath picked up and she held her breath to control her breathing. "A Pain Killer." She smiled at the name of the drink. It was just what she needed right now.

He found his regular waitress and told her what he wanted. She quickly returned with his order, as she made the drinks personally. Tipping her well, he returned to Tashia, handing her the drink. He slid in close so she could hear him, but she wouldn't look at him. She continued to watch the dance floor.

He watched her sip her drink. Cautiously, he ran his hand down the side of her face, turning it to him. When he looked in her eyes, she was watching him with that same poker face she always showed him. He couldn't take it anymore and moved in to kiss her, but she quickly turned her head.

He watched her chest rise and fall, and turned her head to face him again. "I need to breathe, Tashia, and I can't breathe." He moved in again, but this time she didn't turn her head. He kissed her lightly first and she lightly kissed him back. Pulling back, he looked at her. "Damn your eyes," he said and kissed her, again, but this time yielding to the passion he had for her. She responded to him, her breath picking up.

Tashia could feel him watching her during their ride to Reggae. She couldn't breathe. He kept asking her questions when all she wanted to do was be with him, to know him, to possess him. His touch on her back pulled her closer into his world: It was like fire reaching to the depths of her soul.

Once inside, they were able to find a seat off to the side in the back away from the flow of traffic. She couldn't concentrate. He asked her what she wanted to drink. She tried to joke. When he left the table to get their drinks, Tashia slowly let out her breath. His cologne filled her senses and his accent made her weak. She knew she had made a mistake by coming with him and didn't know how much longer she could resist him.

She watched him return from across the room in his all black. His fitted shirt showed off the length of his torso and the ripples of his abs. His arms were sizable from working out. His sex appeal was pulling her in deeper. She looked away when he got closer, afraid he would see it on her face, but he turned her face back to him and was about to kiss her. She wanted to run and knew it was the best thing to do. She looked away, but he turned her face to him again. She could fight him no longer, as her head spun out of control. She kissed him back, giving him permission to linger there.

Pulling away, Tashia took his hand and pulled him to the dance floor. She couldn't sit any longer. She could do him right there in the booth. She danced to the grooves, trying not to get too close, but it didn't matter, because his mere glance rekindled her fire, sending her higher.

He was smooth with his moves. He squatted almost in a limbo stance and grabbed Tashia around the waist, rocking side to side, shifting his weight from one leg to the other, taking her on a ride with him. The heat continued to rise between them. He stood still, holding her around her waist, shifting behind her now. Pulling her close, he swiveled in circles, pressing against her to allow her to feel him.

Tashia tried to wiggle out of his hold, to change position, to run, but he pulled her in tighter.

"What's wrong? You can dish it out, but can't take it," he whispered in her ear, kissing the back of her lobe, reminding her of the dance she gave him earlier. She became dizzy with passion.

Tashia tore away and headed for the ladies room, but Anthony pursued her. She reached to open the bathroom door only to have it pulled from her hand. Anthony gathered her by the waist and pushed her against the wall, pinning her with his body.

"You see, Tashia, I don't think you came to talk. I know the female's anatomy very well and it tells me you want more." He spun her around and kissed her long and hard. She died and he revived her. Her chest rose and fell. He moved to her neck and she pulled him, unable to fight him any longer. Gripping his baldhead, she pressed it between her breasts.

"Anthony." She couldn't let herself go. His world was a dangerous game, even she knew that. She promised herself to be smarter in her decisions with men and she understood the hold a man like Anthony had on a woman. She witnessed Myra unraveling before her eyes. Didn't she just tell her a woman could not tame a man like

Anthony? "Anthony," she cried, but his fire had been lit and she knew it would not be put out by words. He was no longer in control. Her pleas fell on death ears.

She pushed him away from her. They stood, watching each other, breathing deep, carnal breaths. Anthony bit his bottom lip and walked away, getting lost in the crowd. He didn't like he had lost control with her.

Tashia stood in the hall with her head on the wall and eyes closed. He was right. She didn't come to listen to his story. She came to fan the flame he ignited within her.

She walked into the bathroom. The mirror reflected her lack of control. Her hair was unruly. Her messy bun was now a mess. She pulled the band, which barely held it, and allowed her hair to fall. Her face was damp. Grabbing a paper towel, she wiped it and her neck.

She looked at the lonely girl in the mirror and knew before returning to him she had to make a decision. Anthony was not a man to toy with. He brought out Shia in her. To be with Anthony meant moving on. She took a deep breath and let out the cleansing breath. "Let's go get 'em."

Anthony returned to his seat. The waitress from earlier came over. "Did you need anything else, Mr. Laurent?"

"A cold shower," he answered. "Have we added that to the menu?"

The girl smiled and answered, "No, sir."

"Then I'm good," he answered, nodding to her in dismissal.

Shia pushed past the waitress and pulled Anthony from his seat by the hand. She pulled him through the crowded floor and out the door. She had let her hair down and it now blew in the wind. She was silent.

He unlocked the door and reached across her to buckle her in. The fire in her stare told him indecisive Tashia was gone and Shia was in control.

The drive was silent and he wondered what she was thinking. "I'm sorry I lost control with you, Tashia. It won't happen again," he said, breaking the silence.

"Shut up and drive faster."

Anthony watched her for a moment. "Where are we going?"

Tashia thought for a moment. "Your place," she answered, not hesitating.

"Yes, ma'am." Anthony cranked the Hell Cat into over drive.

Happy Endings

The house was dark, but Tashia could see it was sizable. There were four doors on the long garage and the second door came to life when they pulled into the driveway. Anthony backed the car skillfully into the garage and the door came down.

Tashia waited impatiently for him to come to her door. She had already removed her seatbelt by the time he got there. He helped her from the car as he had twice earlier. Her eyes no longer looked away to hide what she wanted. She knew why she came and it was not to talk. She was sure his story was interesting, but storytelling was not on her mind.

"Tashia, are you sure you want to do this? Because if it's exclusive you want I'm not that man."

She heard what he said, but her desire had not changed. She pushed him against the Black pickup truck parked beside them and picked up where they left off in the hallway at the club, catching him totally off guard. She leaped into his arms, straddling him like the poles she dominated at the club. Again, they were lost in their passion.

Anthony carried her to the door and entered his security code. He maneuvered to the screaming alarm to silence it.

Tashia never lost sight of her objective, never once taking her eyes from him. She pulled his shirt above his head, dropping it to the floor. She was still gripping his sides with her powerful legs. His chest now bare showed he took care of his body. She ran her fingers across his chest, leaned in, and sucked gently on his bare nipple.

Leaning back, she allowed Anthony to pull her sweater over her head, dropping it to the floor as well. Her bra was next. Tashia arched her back and leaned backward as though he was a pole. She watched him. Running his hands across her abdomen, she allowed him to feel she was as fit.

Anthony grabbed a throw blanket from the back of his sofa and continued to walk. "Damn. Get there already!" She was impatient and afraid she would change her mind if he didn't get there soon.

A low animal laugh came bellowing from his chest and his perfect smile shined through the darkness of the room, contrasting his beautiful black skin. He draped the chaise lounge with the blanket and laid her on it. He unzipped her boots and removed them, only leaving her jeans. He looked at her, taking in her nude body.

"You've seen it before, in the light."

"Not like this," he said, removing his pants.

Tashia took in the view. He was gorgeous. She could see why Myra didn't want to let him go and it came to her that she had no protection. She didn't want anything that chicken head may have. She knew her status. She had not been with any other man since Jesus and he was five years deceased.

"I'll be back," Anthony said, disappearing into another room.

Tashia closed her eyes and wondered how she got here. Although she had known Anthony since Callia's birth, she never pictured herself here, in his house, ready to know him. "Oh my, God."

"It sounds like Tashia has returned," he mused from the doorway. "I wondered where she went."

Tashia sat up from her laying position. Nothing had changed about her desire for him, but her mind caught up with her irresponsible behavior. Pregnancy and disease never crossed her mind. She just knew she wanted this man and didn't weigh the cost of having him.

Anthony came to her still full. Lying next to her, he pulled her back down with him. She looked in his eyes and saw no disappointment. He had an all-knowing smirk on his face. "We can have that conversation now, if you'd like," he offered.

She didn't want conversation, but she knew she couldn't finish what she came for, not yet. "Yes. I would like that conversation now, please," she conceded.

Anthony moved his head between her breasts and lightly sucked, as his hand continued between her thighs. Lightly he bit the end of her nipple and she softly cried out.

"But let me take that edge off first," he offered and ran his tongue down between her thighs.

"Oh my, God," she cried out, but there was neither protest nor indecisiveness.

Love Pains

Gemma was quiet and to herself. She was good at helping Caden to get organize. Pastor asked if she could help with the gala. He thought it would be good for both of them. Caden didn't know what her story was and really didn't know her at all, but he found her to be organized, efficient, motivated and a lifesaver.

Gemma was five-four and weighed one hundred five pounds. Caden found her a little skinny for his taste. They worked well together and she began to pick up on his direction instinctively. She made him miss India who was great at anticipating his needs and desires.

Caden found her to be very private. The times he offered to drive her home, she declined, choosing to take the bus, so when they met, Caden tried to pick locations close to where he believed she lived and always ending their planning before dark to ensure her safe passage home.

They were to meet tonight, but she did not show. Caden attempted to call her, but received no answer. He hoped she was fine, but her absence pulled at his spirit. Caden said a silent prayer that she would call and at least let him know she was fine and then returned to work. He deliberately stayed at their meeting spot in case she was running late, but after two hours, he gave up on her coming. Reaching a stopping point, he packed his things. He wanted to stop and see Callia on his way home.

His phone rang. It was Gemma.

"Hey! Is everything okay? I missed you for the meeting."

"Everything is fine. I am sorry I didn't call you earlier, but I got tied up." She spoke so low Caden almost couldn't hear her.

Caden was not convinced. The tone of her voice didn't sound right. "Don't worry about missing the meeting. I appreciate all that you do to help get this organized, but are you sure you are okay?"

"I'm fine. I have to go," she blurted and quickly disconnected.

Standing in the middle of the café, Caden was in shock at how abruptly she disconnected the call. There was something wrong, but he couldn't help her if she wouldn't let him.

Forfeiting his visit with Callia, Caden went straight home and video messaged her. After his shower, he decided to turn in. He knelt at the window chair, but he couldn't see the moon tonight.

The house was abnormally quiet without Callia there. She was spending time with her cousins, which allowed him to pray in peace.

He prayed for his new family, including his brother, Jacque. They had met a few times and were rebuilding their relationship. He made a promise to India to forgive him and he did, but he did not trust him. Not yet. He prayed for Gemma.

Gemma lay in bed with her eyes opened. She needed to go to the bathroom, but Jason had his arm wrapped around her and she couldn't move. He was sound asleep and she didn't want to wake him.

She felt bad for upsetting him earlier. He said he was tired when he came home. She should have listened, but as usual, she aggravated him, talking about all she had to get done. She didn't want to upset him further by waking him. He had not too long fallen asleep.

When he finally released her and rolled over, she slowly eased from the bed, taking care not shake it much. She gasped at the pain in her rib and looked back at Jason before moving further. He was still asleep.

The bathroom floor was chilly. Slowly, she sat on the commode and released what she had been holding for hours. She felt much better. After a few minutes, she held her side and got up slowly, careful not to bump it. Deciding not to flush, she washed her hands and returned to bed before he woke.

Lying was painful, so she decided to sit up instead. Jason turned and grabbed her. She gasped. He looked up. "You okay?"

"I'm okay," she lied. She rubbed his head that was now in her lap. She didn't want to burden him with her issues. He had to get up early to go to work. She was sure it would pass.

She and Jason had been together for five years. She was in her last year of college and almost flunked out, spending so much time with him. When she graduated, Jason found a job in Washington,

D.C., so she came back to the area with him. He had changed position twice since there and was now in charge of a team of people.

Jason didn't want her to work although she wanted to. He said he wanted her home when he got there and for her to take care of things. They talked about marrying, but Jason wanted to wait until he could get them a house. She offered to work to get there faster, but he wouldn't hear of it. Because he took such great care of her, she felt loved.

Becoming pregnant the year before unraveled Jason, because he thought it would ruin all the plans he had for them. Gemma was disappointed he wasn't as excited as she, but she lost the baby, resolving the issue.

She spent her spare time volunteering so when pastor said Caden may need help she was happy to have something to keep her occupied. She felt badly she couldn't meet with him this evening, but with circumstances as they were, it couldn't be helped. She would make sure she sent him an update in the morning after she washed clothes.

Palace Laurent

Tashia lay in Anthony's arms, looking up at him as he talked. He had long since taken the edge off and it was everything she expected from him.

"First, I want you to know I'm not your conventional guy. I don't have a woman because my lifestyle doesn't yield me the time to invest in a relationship. I have the club and the boys. They are my girlfriends." Anthony stopped to see if she was still awake. He saw she was listening intently. "This is why I was upset with Myra. I made it perfectly clear to her from the beginning that I belong to no one."

"What made you buy the club?" She wanted to change the focus from Myra. She really didn't care what was going on between them.

"Am I boring you, Tashia?"

"Oh, I'm sorry. I thought you were done talking about her."

He smiled at her sarcasm. "*Shiaaa*,"he said, exaggerating her name. "Do I sense jealousy over Myra?"

Tashia laughed. "Not at all, but I'd rather hear about you."

"What do you want to hear about me?"

"How long have you been here? I know why Preston came, but why did you come?"

"Which question do you want me to answer?" he teased. Anthony was not big on sharing details of his personal life, but he was compelled to tell her everything about himself. He wanted, *needed*, someone to share his dreams with. He had accomplished much and he didn't have anyone.

Tashia was like her sister in many ways, yet so different. She was his type of beauty. She was edgy and made it clear she didn't need his protection. She had a quick wit about her and he didn't see her involved in mindless games. He leaned slowly, waiting for her to protest, but she didn't. Their lips met and he kissed her softly. Leaning her back onto the chaise, he kissed her more intimately. He pulled her body closer to his, now spooning, and kissed the back of her neck, shoulders, down to her fingers and back up her arm to her neck. He could feel her release her breath as he moved his hand between her thighs. Reaching under the pillow, he pulled out a condom and shook it in the air jokingly. "A man should always be prepared," he joked, opening the pack. "I don't know your status," he said.

Tashia laughed at his humor, but became more relaxed under his hold. "It's you who have been with questionable people."

"Shia, that wasn't nice."

"I know, right!"

Anthony flipped her over to her stomach and kissed her long neck to the base of her back while playing between her thighs. His dark side rose up, but he didn't know what she would think about that side of him, so he kept him in the box.

He raised Tashia to her knees and covered his manhood with the condom, guiding his way between her thighs where he had been playing, until the two became one. He sat her in his lap while on his knees and held her closely with his arm wrapped around her waist. Still kissing her neck and nibbling her ears, he began to move forward then back. He moaned and withdrew quickly, laying her on her back. She excited him, making him feel like an inexperienced teenaged boy. He traveled down her stomach, visiting her caverns, again, to give him time to regroup, but she protested, gripping him under his arms with her strong thighs.

"Give me what I want, damn it," she told him. She loosened her grip from around his ribs and slid down. Pushing him to his back, she mounted him and rode him like a bull.

Anthony knew he was not going to last in this position and flipped her back over. Again, he withdrew, pacing himself. "It's not going anywhere, Tashia, slow down or it will," he warned. "Now let me work."

Tashia relaxed and let Anthony work, and work he did. He kissed her in places she had never been kissed, reaching spots with his tongue that had never been explored. She could tell he was searching for her spots and he found them. She could feel the ripples slowly rising in her. "Cum with me, Anthony," she begged.

Anthony got her meaning and reentered her one final time. He draped her legs over his shoulders, pitching deep to a spot he found earlier and spun back and forth. He could see her hold her breath as she gripped the sides of the chaise and pitch her head back before moaning a low moan that gained momentum as she peaked. A scream came from the pit of her belly, letting him know she was gone.

"Anthony!" she yelled, allowing herself to enjoy the moment. When she opened her eyes, he was smiling at her. She laughed a deep hearty laughed, as she watched the amusement etch across his face.

"I believe you screamed my name, S-h-h-i-i-i-a."

"Yes, but it will be mine that will remain on your mind," she challenged back.

"No doubt." He watched her, smiling at her happiness, but remorse set in. "Tashia. We need to talk. I need you to understand me because I never want to hurt you."

"Sh-h-h." She pressed her finger against his lips, silencing him. "Let me enjoy this moment. It sounds like you about to mess it up. Besides, you're an old man and you need your sleep before round two."

Anthony heeded her wishes and decided to save the conversation for a not so intimate time. Tashia was resting on his chest and almost asleep. "But I put *you* to sleep," he whispered.

As she slept, Anthony watched her. She looked so serene. He had never seen her like this. She was always running around and never still. She had to learn to be still.

Anthony wondered how the kid's father was killed. Was she there? Was she able to move on? He wondered by telling her he was not attachable if he scared her off, but everything they just did answered that question. Truth told, he was not worried about her, it was his feelings he was guarding. She was already in his thoughts. He already valued her feelings and worried about her and her kids. There was a connection between them. He couldn't afford to become vested in her. There were too many secrets to guard.

Anthony had been watching her over the past two years at every family event, but he never thought they would hook up. They both had too much to lose if things did not work out and he never had time to be vested with any woman. Tashia captured his heart long before Zander's event; he just would not allow himself to venture there.

81

Anthony slowly got up from the chaise and covered her with another throw. He wasn't much on sleep, so he decided to go to his office and look over the accounts and complete some orders. But, before going, he cleaned up their play area and checked his messages. He had three texts from Myra.

Myra: I hope everything is okay.

Myra: You left here so fast and didn't return.

Myra: Not stalking just checking on you. I do care about you, but I understand.

Anthony placed a call to Snow. He answered immediately. "Is everything fine?"

"Stop worrying, Anthony. I promise I've done this before," Snow assured him. "I took care of that problem. She's gone."

"Call her back and tell her you misunderstood what I was saying."

"You call her. She almost took my head off!"

Anthony chuckled, imagining hot-tempered Myra going after Snow. "Okay, Snow, I'll take care of it. Go ahead and finish closing and have a great Sunday."

Anthony sighed and dialed Myra's number. What was happening was his fault. He wanted to make sure she could still take care of her children.

"Snow fired me!" she yelled when she answered the phone. "Did you tell him to fire me!" She was sobbing into the phone.

"Calm down, Myra..."

"Don't tell me to calm down because calm down won't get my rent paid. What am I going to do? I'm sorry I made trouble for you. I just love you, Anthony. I know you told me not to, but it just happened. Please give me my job back. I need it," she sobbed into the phone.

Anthony knew a drunk when he heard one. "Myra, how much did you have to drink? Where are you?"

"I don't know how much. I took a bottle of Goose. I'm sorry," she began apologizing again. "You can take it out of my check."

"Where are you," he asked, again, impatiently.

"In front of my mother's house."

"Myra, get some rest. A friend of mine is hiring you for his restaurant. It will be better for you there. Plus, I will still need you to train your replacement at my place, so you will be able to make some extra money if you would like," he assured her.

She was quiet now, but he could hear her whimpering. "Thank you, Anthony. Thank you," was all he could make out.

"But, if you continue to be disrespectful I'm going to have my friend let you go. I never lied to you. You knew who I was before we started this." Again, that guilt played at him. Tashia. "I will call you later today to give you the details." He hung up.

Anthony decided to let his accounting wait, instead he went to his room to run some bath water. He set the temperature for his water heater, which kept the water recycling and warm. His housekeeper had already replenished the towels in the rack and there was nothing left for him to do except get his guest.

When he returned to where he left Tashia, she was standing at the back patio door. When he kissed her shoulder, she leaned back and rested on his strong chest. "Come go with me," he whispered to her and led her by the hand up the spiral steps to his bedroom.

Tashia marveled at how elegant his home was; this did not look like the Anthony she knew. But, did she really know him? The master suite looked more like a palace suite rather than a master suite. His bed sat on a marble platform floor and there were two steps up to the bed, surrounded by marble flooring.

Anthony led her to the bath he prepared. The tub mimicked his bed with steps leading to the entrance and sat in the middle of the bathroom. The light was dim on the three-tier chandelier that hung above the tub. Against one wall was a bench covered in tiger print.

"Your home is beautiful, Anthony," she said, taking in the room.

"Thank you." He took the opportunity to take in the sight as well. "I don't get to see it that often."

Anthony helped her into the tub and held her hand until she was seated. He gently followed, trying not to disturb the water. Sitting opposite her, he took her in.

Tashia was only one of two women he had ever allowed in his home. The women he spent time with didn't know anything about him. "Is the water comfortable?"

"It's good," she answered, tying her hair atop her head. Leaning back, she put her head on the pillow behind her head.

Anthony watched her intently. "You look like you belong here," he said, smiling at her.

Her eyes were closed. "While that may be true I don't think that would happen with me or any other woman." Her eyes opened, examining him. When he didn't comment, she closed them again. "Hmm," she said, acknowledging she was right. When he didn't say anything for a while, she reopened her eyes and saw him still watching her.

"What time did you need to pick up the kids?"

"I am meeting them at dinnertime."

Anthony reached for the new puffball he found in the linen closet and added soap. He moved to her side of the tub and pulled her by the legs, sending her unexpectedly under the water. She immediately resurfaced. Her hair was wet and had come loose.

"Damn you, Anthony. Don't you know to never get a Black woman's hair wet?" He dipped her, again, and they laughed and played in the water like kids splashing one another.

Anthony snatched her into his chest and kissed her, taking her under the water with him where they kissed until her lungs could hold no longer. He moved to the side and lifted her out of the water, laying her on the cold step. She arched her back from the unexpected chill of the marble, but was quickly pressed down by the weight of his body on top of her. He reached to the edge of the tub behind her and grabbed the package he left when preparing the water.

He entered her quicker than Tashia expected. He rode her, gripping her behind, pulling her in, and allowing him to go deeper. Occasionally, he pressed deep and held it, letting her to feel his fullness. She cried out in pain.

"Are you okay?" he whispered in her ear, but she didn't answer. Anthony pulled back and looked in her face. "I told you I'm a wild boy, so if I hurt you please tell me."

"Damn, don't you ever shut up?" she teased. "I'm not that girl. If I don't like it, I'll let you know. So, shut up and ride." Anthony smiled and did what she commanded.

He continued to test her limits, trying different positions first. He found her to be very flexible as he raised and lowered her legs. For his last litmus test, he placed her legs on his shoulders and rode. Unexpectedly to her, he slid his thumb in her rear. Still riding, her breathing quickened and she grunted with each thrust.

"Anthony!" she yelled and he moved his thumb back and forth, sending her higher. She gripped his sides with her legs, squeezing with each wave that rippled through her body. Her curls bounced each time he pounded. Now he turned his thumb like a cork and covered her breast with his mouth, sucking gently. Her legs tightened one last time, squeezing him as she climaxed. Anthony continued to ride beyond her point and allowed himself to enjoy her. She was holding him around his neck, nibbling his ear as she twisted his nipple between her thumb and forefinger. Now it was him who cried out as he filled to capacity and exploded.

Leaning on the ledge of the tub, he gently put her down. Climbing back into the tub, he pulled her with him under the water, again, and back up. He reached for the scrub ball and began washing her gently. Then, he washed himself and helped her from the tub, giving her the towel he had already put out. She took it and first dried her hair before drying the rest of her.

"Do you have a comb or I'm gonna be in trouble?" She pointed to her hair.

Anthony pointed to his head, giving her a blank stare.

"Point made," she said, smiling at his baldhead. "I think I have one in my gym bag," she said.

"I'll get it for you. You can lie on the bed and I'll be right back."

Anthony was back within minutes with her purse. "This was all I found. I guess your gym bag is in your car."

She forgot she switched cars. She looked at the image in the mirror in the recessed ceiling. Her hair looked like a wild mane. "This is your fault."

Anthony dove in bed, laughing at her hair. He ran his fingers through the now tangled mane of curls. He didn't care what her hair looked like. He enjoyed her company and for the first time, he realized he was lonely.

Hugging her, he whispered, "I'm very vulnerable right now, so don't hurt me."

She giggled at his comment and looked at the clock on the wall. It was out of place for the rest of the decor. It was loud and digital. She did see it was five in the morning. "I have to meet my kids in twelve hours, so go to sleep."

The two slept in one another's arms.

Sheep

Church was good. Preston sat with Solana in his lap and a jealous Callia glared every so often from Caden's. He and the boys had a great weekend. Preston tried to convince Cuyler to let him purchase them their own bikes. She advised him to speak with Tashia first.

The message was about everything they had belonged to God and they were to share with the less fortunate. Preston had been thinking about offering one of his rentals to Tashia to rent for her and her kids. He received his confirmation from the sermon that this is what he was supposed to do. He would talk to Cuyler about his decision later.

Pastor was dismissing them, so they stood, but Solana wouldn't let him put her down. Cuyler smiled and looked away before Callia saw her. She was still glaring at Solana. Cuyler thought that maybe they should have a boy. Callia didn't like sharing her papa with another female other than Cuyler.

"Hey, I have to talk to pastor before I leave." Caden leaned to hand Callia to Cuyler, but she reached for Preston.

"Papa. Je t'aime *(Daddy, I love you)*," she whined.

"Papa vous aime trop. Daddy loves you, too," he said, taking her from Caden.

Zander saw the peril and took Solana from Preston. "You my girl," he said, smothering her with kisses. "Let's go outside." Winking at Preston, he took his little sister outside followed by his brother.

Preston sat with Callia. "Pourquoi pleures-tu? Why are you crying?" He asked a now tearful Callia.

"Mon papa *(My daddy)*," she said through tears.

Preston held her close, rubbing her back to soothe her. "Oui, votre papa. Yes, your papa." He knew she didn't understand. She never had to share him before. "Je t'aime tellement. I love you so much." He wiped her tears. "Pouvons nous aller chercher Solana? Can we go get Solana?" He asked.

"No!"

Preston laughed at her honesty. "Okay. What about later?"

"Bien (Good)," she conceded, but she would not let him go.

They walked outside and joined Cuyler and the boys. Callia tightened her grip around his neck when she saw Solana, who attempted to run to them, but Zander caught her. He stooped to her level and spoke to her. She nodded a couple times and held his hand, looking over her shoulder.

"Solana looks sad," he told Callia. "She doesn't have a papa." Callia turned and looked at Preston. "Elle n'a pas de papa (She doesn't have a Papa)."

Callia watched Preston and thought for a minute. She pushed to get down and ran to Solana. Taking her hand, she pulled her to Preston. She pushed Solana to Preston. "Votre papa trop," she told Solana.

"What did she say, uncle?"

"She said she would share." Preston smiled at his little girl proudly.

"Thank you, Callia." The two girls walked together holding hands.

Caden informed the pastor he would be a part of the youth department, but felt inadequate because he was learning everything himself. "Some of these kids have been here since birth. They could probably teach me."

"I'm sure they could, but I need them to see your success. They need to see you can be good looking and love God. They can be smart, athletic, and successful and love God."

Caden thought about what he said. "I can do that." He got up to leave, but Pastor Jenkins stopped him.

"Have you talked to Gemma?"

"I spoke to her yesterday. We were supposed to meet, but she couldn't make it."

"Okay. She wasn't here for any committee meetings, so I was wondering."

"You don't think anything is wrong?"

"No. Sheep sometimes disappear. All we can do is pray for them."

Caden processed his comment and went out the door. He was led to pray for her, again, and hoped everything was fine.

Diva Dorreen

Gemma's Secrets

Gemma was awakened by her throbbing headache. The frozen bag of peas had thawed long ago. She was home alone now. Jason went out and said he would be back at dinnertime. Closing her eyes, she tried to go back to sleep, but the pain brought on tears.

She didn't understand why he had become so angry. He called her nasty and trifling for not flushing the toilet the night before, but when she tried to explain why she had not, he slapped her twice.

Although shocked by the outburst, she was not shocked he had slapped her. This was not the first time, but usually she had a warning if he were not in the mood. Gemma's parents had never hit her. She experienced time outs and restrictions, but never spankings.

Her father was from England and her mother from New York City. Her dad met her mother while in college and they fell in love and married. When they moved to Washington, DC from upstate New York, Gemma was six years old. Her dad took a job at the United Nations as a linguist and her mother worked for the state department as an analyst.

Gemma and her brother, Emmanuel, went to the French Emersion School and were both fluent in French. From there, she attended the National Cathedral School and then college at High Point in North Carolina where she majored in international studies.

She was always a good girl and an honor student, but was bad at picking men. She often picked those who wanted to control her. Her first boyfriend, Parren, and she did everything together. After she stopped seeing him, he would show up wherever she went. She thought it was cute and he did this because he loved her, but soon found he wanted to know everywhere she went and with whom. He also threatened whomever she was with. He never hit her, but she had to put a restraining order on him. Soon after her brother had a 'private' talk with him, he moved on to another girl.

Gemma met Jason at a poetry reading. He was one of the poets. He saw her in the crowd and recited poetry to her his entire performance. Afterward, he introduced himself. They didn't hit it off immediately, but he soon grew on her.

Jason and Gemma dated for months. He complimented her about everything. He wanted to do everything with her and questioned when she had plans outside of him. When she met up with him, again, he always seemed agitated. He would apologize and say he had no one other than her and he missed her or he was lonely while she was gone. He said he loved her and she believed him.

After seeing him for a year, he suggested they move in together, especially since he was going to marry her anyway. She thought it was the natural progression of their relationship and she did love him deeply. However, after a couple months, she met Jason's mean side. He often said her parents didn't love her. He told her if they loved her, they would not have allowed her to move with him. He said his daughter wouldn't move with any man unless she was married to him. Her parents wanted to get rid of her, he told her. No one loved her except him. Once they had fallen on hard times when Jason was between jobs. When her father refused to help her unless she left him, she believed Jason.

The first time Jason hit her was because she talked back to him. They got in an argument about what she was wearing. When she told him if she wanted her daddy, she would go home. Her lips were busted for two weeks and she told everyone she was kicked in the mouth during kickboxing class and she had never taken kickboxing. When Jason hit her a second time, she realized the first time his fist met her lips was not an accident. He had a problem and now she did, too.

She never knew when it was coming. It was as though he waited to catch her off guard to hurt her. She had nowhere to go because her relationship with her parents was estranged. She also quit her job, per his request, and was no longer able to support herself. She had lost count of the number of times she had been hit, strangled, or threatened, but this time Jason had really hurt her and it was the first time she feared for her life.

She remembered she needed to send Caden an update of her research. The throbbing was so great she decided it could wait until she was at least able to sit up. Closing her eyes, she went back to sleep.

The Swap

Anthony sat in his office with the new girl. She was the same waitress who served him and Tashia the previous weekend. He did a swap and offered her the opportunity to work at the gentlemen's club and she said yes. Myra would go there in her place.

Myra knocked and poked her head in the office. She was there to get instructions and train the new girl. She liked the opportunity to make the extra money by working at both locations until the girl was trained.

"Come in, Myra," Anthony said, waving her in. "This is Rhonda and you will be training her for the club."

Myra entered the office and sized up Rhonda. The girl was skinny and lanky. Anthony liked a woman and she was a girl. Her hair was in a ponytail and she wore no makeup. Besides, she was dark and Tashia was the darkest woman she had ever seen Anthony with, so she was not going to be a threat to Tashia and she couldn't hold a candle to her either. Why Anthony wanted this girl in the club she didn't understand. The men weren't going to look at her and her tips would be minimal.

"Hello, Rhonda," she said, extending her hand.

Rhonda accepted her hand and returned her attention to Anthony. Myra could see she was caught in his web, like every other woman who worked for him. The only person she ever saw not caught up was Tashia. She looked at him like a challenge, but not one she wanted to keep. Anthony appeared to be a game to her.

Myra didn't always have the attention of the men. When she was in high school, her popularity heightened after she slept with Sony, the captain of the basketball team. She became his girl. She changed the style of her clothes and she dressed a little more provocative. Her jeans and tops became tighter, showing off her ample bosom and behind, which she used to draw attention. She learned what the boys liked and played with them.

Anthony was different. He controlled his world and took orders from no one. He also had a dark side and liked sexual pleasures that she was sure Tashia would not accommodate. He would be back and she would be waiting.

Smiling, she pretended to listen to his instructions to the new girl, but she watched how his shirt played on his muscles, and the whiteness of his teeth. What did she need to listen for- she already knew what to do.

So caught up in Anthony, Myra didn't hear him dismiss them. She took the cue from the new girl and stood to her feet. The new girl looked at Myra for direction. "You know where the bar is, right?"

The new girl's smile suddenly disappeared at Myra's rudeness. "Yes. Anthony showed me around."

Myra smiled at her response, knowing Anthony had not shown her around like he showed her eight months ago. "Okay. I will meet you there. I need to speak with Anthony for a minute."

The girl looked at Myra in amazement, but quickly turned her attention back to Anthony to hide her disdain. She extended her hand. "Thank you, *Mr. Laurent*, for the opportunity."

Myra turned her attention back to Anthony once the skinny girl was clear of the room and smiled. "Thank you for giving me my job back and I apologize for being disrespectful."

Anthony smiled at her as he covered his mouth. He watched her as if he wanted to say something, but did not. After the awkward silence between them, Myra excused herself.

"Myra. Understand that I believe in second chances, but there will be no third. Also, be nice to Rhonda." He was still smiling at her, which made her blush. She quickly left his office and headed for the bar.

The night went well with training Rhonda. She caught on quickly and Myra was sure she would have things in order by Friday when the traffic picked up. She saw Anthony across the room talking to one of the dancers. She was smiling and giggling as he conversed with her. Myra observed the girl laugh and run backstage. The heat rose to her face as she watched him head toward the bar, no doubt to check on Rhonda's progress. Myra pretended to wash dirty glasses.

"I washed those already, Myra," Rhonda reminded her.

Myra looked at her and smiled. "Oh, I didn't know." Myra deliberately bent to put the glasses away, with her behind tooted in the air. She heard Anthony talking to Rhonda and stood.

"So how is she doing, Myra?"

"Great! She will be a pro by Friday's rush."

"Wonderful." He smiled at Myra as he watched her trying to be nonchalant. "Do you think you need to review anything with her tomorrow?"

"Why don't I come back on Wednesday so I can see what she retained from today and see if she has questions?"

"Good idea."

"Okay. Well, is it okay for me to leave now? My mother has the kids and I have to go to Reggae tomorrow?"

"Sure. Thanks for your help and we will see you on Wednesday." Anthony leaned back on the bar, smiling.

She knew he could see right through her attempts to pretend she was no longer interested in him, but she didn't care. He would come to her and she would be ready.

Not My Mother

Zander finished reading his homework and reviewing for his test. He felt ready. He leaned back on his pillow and looked up at the ceiling, remembering the weekend and the fun he had, wishing every weekend could be like that, but he knew his mother couldn't afford anything like it.

The soft rap on the door brought him back to reality.

"Zander, can I speak with you for a moment?" his mother asked, sticking her head through his door. Zane was already asleep, as well as Solana.

Zander joined his mother in the living room and sat on the oversized pillow couch. "What's up, Mom?"

Tashia was beaming. She met with Preston earlier and he took her to a house near work and offered it as a rental for her and the kids. The house, though small, was much larger than their apartment and was somewhere her kids would be able to play outside, without her fearing they would come to harm. She couldn't wait to share the information with Zander.

"Uncle Preston showed me a house this evening that we could rent. It's a really awesome house that I know you guys would love, but it would require you to change schools."

Zander tried to hide his disappointment, but he was never good at pretending with his mother. "That sounds great, Mom. When do we move?"

Tashia saw his apprehension. "What's wrong? I know you grew up here, Zander, but I thought it would be a great experience for you guys." She moved in closer to her son and pulled his chin up. "You can still go to the center after school, I wouldn't stop you guys from going there, and the school is much better for you so you wouldn't have to go so early in the morning."

"Mom, I'm sure everything will work out." Zander hugged his mother to hide the expression on his face. "I'm just so used to being here, is all." He didn't want to ruin her excitement and knew she worked hard to get them out of the neighborhood. Lately was the happiest he had seen her in a while.

His mother pulled away and looked at him. She knew her son and he was covering up something. "What's wrong, Zander?" Her voice held concern.

Zander leaned back on the couch. He didn't know whether he should tell her or not about his morning activities and why it was important for him to be on time. He knew she wouldn't like it, but it was something he felt good about doing. "It's just starting over will be hard, especially now that I'm older," he lied.

"You will make new friends, I'm sure, Zander. You have always been outgoing and I know they will love you!" She was smiling a huge smile and he couldn't take that away from her. He would figure things out on his own.

The next morning, Zander dragged as he walked onto school property. He dreaded sharing his news. Cutting through the school, he went out the back to the field bleachers. Dwayne was waiting for him as he had done for the past three weeks. Zander climbed the steps, heavy with the information he had to share.

"We are gonna run out of time if you don't hurry, Zander." The boy, not much older than he, with the scar from being cut by a broken glass bottle when he was ten, rushed Zander. Scar had a book in his hand and papers that still reflected the folds from being in his pocket in the other. "Can you look over my assignment to make sure I did it right and tell me what to do tonight?"

Zander took the boy's papers and began reviewing the assignment with him. He told him what he missed and why. Zander was shocked when Scar came to him and asked him to teach him to read. He said if he was going to have his own crew one day he had to know how to run it and be able to handle his business so he wouldn't have to trust others to do it for him. He had witnessed too much stealing on the inside of the organization and wanted to be smarter than that. Zander thought he was smart for figuring this out and hoped one day he figured out the rest and leave the gang life.

They reviewed the next assignment as well before Zander explained to him what he was told the night before. "Dwayne. We are moving and I will be going to another school."

"Where are you moving?"

"I don't know. Somewhere near the hospital where my mother works."

"How you get dough like that?"

"I don't know."

"I heard your mother was dancing at a club. I didn't want to say nothing because that's her business, but maybe that's how she's doing it."

Zander looked at Scar, astounded by his words. "My mother don't work at no club. She works at the hospital!" Zander said, with his fist balled up.

"Zander, don't get mad at me. I'm telling you what I heard. Besides, she has to be doing something in order for you to move into that area," Scar said, defending his words. "You and I are cool. I appreciate you keeping my secret and helping me out." Scar raised his hands, palms open to ensure Zander knew he wasn't challenging him. "We'll figure out something. I'll come to you. I gotta go," Scar said, and ran down the bleachers.

Zander sat on the bleacher, defeated by Scar's words, but he was right. Where would they get money like that? The first bell rang and he knew he should be making his way back to the building, but he couldn't. The second bell rang, but he remained where Scar had left him: On the third row of the bleachers.

A New Home

Tashia met Anthony at his truck in the hospital garage. This was a new experience for them, because he had never come to her job before. The first thing she noticed was that dirt filled the back of his black pickup truck. As he opened the door, Anthony handed her a brown paper bag of something that smelled heavenly.

"Hey beautiful. How long is lunch?"

"Forty-five minutes. Now forty minutes." Tashia showed him her phone with the big digital clock counting down the time.

"Okay then let's go."

They drove for about ten minutes while she ate. Anthony pulled up to an abandoned building, with barred windows and broken out glass. Debris was scattered in the parking lot.

Smiling, he opened her door and helped her down.

"Wow! This is beautiful," she joked.

Anthony grabbed her and pulled her into his chest. "It will be once it's fixed up. This is going to be the new boy's center so we can do more things for them," he proudly announced. "Don't say anything to anyone. No one knows that I want the building. If we tell anyone, the price may go up. I think I will be able to purchase it in about six months to a year."

Tashia watched him as his big smile beamed across his face. She saw the love he had for the boys and how much he wanted to help them. A sense of pride filled her, knowing he shared this information with her first. "It's going to be beautiful, Anthony. The boys could really use this."

Tashia pushed from his hold and went up to the window to look in. Anthony quickly pulled her back. "You will see the inside soon enough, but right now there are occupants that will have to be vacated, so don't get too close."

He directed her back to the truck and opened the door. The ride back was silent as she thought of how harshly he handled Myra, but how gentle he was with her and the boys. He was very complicated, just as she was. This was probably why they got along so well. The past month had been great with him. He made no demands to see her and she put none on him. Often, she wondered if he were seeing other women, but made herself stop before she went mad. They had set no boundaries for one another and she was fine with that for now.

Anthony was talking to her, but she was lost in her own thoughts. It wasn't until he called her name that she realized he had asked her a question. "What?"

"I'm rambling," he said, apologetically.

"No, I was just imagining everything and how great it will be. I hope Zander is learning to give back to others as people have sown into him."

"Zander is going to be great! He's a good and smart kid. He helps the other kids at the center now." She didn't know that, but she could picture him helping.

They pulled back into the garage and Anthony offered his hand to help her out of the truck. As she walked away, he grabbed her hand and pulled her back.

"You are going to make me late, Anthony!"

"You are off tomorrow, right?"

"Yes."

"So spend the day with me."

The twinkle in his eyes was new to her. She was used to tough Anthony and had never seen mellow Anthony. "I'll let you know tonight."

"I'm not letting you go until you say yes."

"I need to work on the yard tomorrow, Anthony."

"The boys and I will take care of that on Saturday while you are at work."

He seemed to have an answer for everything. How could she say no to him? "You're gonna make me late!"

"Then say yes and I'll let you go," he promised. Leaning into her, he lightly kissed her. "*Please*," he whispered in her ear.

Tashia laughed and pulled away. "Thanks for lunch Anthony and I will see you tomorrow morning."

Anthony smiled, as she disappeared into the brick building. He liked the way she made him feel when he was with her. He felt safe.

Tashia quickly ran up the stairs that led to her area. She put her purse away and checked the board to see what needed to be done. Nosey Tonya, the floor secretary, turned the corner and smiled. Tashia smiled and turned back to avoid unnecessary conversation with the busy body.

"Your young man is handsome."

Tashia didn't want to explain that he was not hers, so she didn't feed into the conversation. "Thank you."

Tonya did, however, make Tashia wonder where she was going with this relationship. She genuinely liked Anthony and looked forward to their daily interactions, whether she saw him or it were only by phone. Her children loved him although they knew nothing about their relationship. He was Zander's mentor and confidant. She felt she was setting herself up for hurt or worse, becoming Myra. If she asked for more, she could lose him. Maybe she would start dating others.

Tashia looked out into her beautiful yard. Anthony had already taken care of it before picking her up for lunch. When she arrived home, she was totally surprised. She couldn't believe where life had led her from one call. Her children were safe and she was in a home she could have never afforded on her own. The kids had adjusted and everyone seemed happy, but there was something different about Zander. He seemed to have questions for her that he wouldn't have asked, and he finally requested to speak to her when the kids went to sleep. She smiled at his referring to them as the kids.

Solana went to Auntie Khadada's after school and she and her cousin had become inseparable. They were like she and Cuyler as children, except Callia was the one in charge. Solana definitely had her Aunt Cuyler's gentle, but fighting spirit. Sometimes she thought they had the wrong children. Her family's lives were coming together.

The only part of her life that was confusing was Anthony. She had convinced herself she would give the young doctor, Cliff, the opportunity to take her out, especially since her address had changed, she was no longer embarrassed about her zip code, but she backed out, not wanting to waste his time. Just the other day he brought her lunch when he found out she had not eaten. She thought it was thoughtful of him. He was the man she should have been looking at, but found herself attracted to danger and heartbreak.

Closing the curtains, she retreated to Solana's room to tuck her in. Her little girl loved her new room. Anthony helped Zander to paint it lavender, her favorite color. Tashia was able to buy her a new green and purple comforter. She found furniture at a yard sale and painted it green to match her room. She was looking for a short bookcase to complete the room.

"Hey, Sunshine," she said, snuggling with Solana. "You brush your teeth?"

"Zander made me." Solana put her book on her nightstand. "Mommy, does Uncle Anthony have a girlfriend?"

Tashia smiled at her question. "I don't know. Why?"

"He doesn't have a family and I don't want him to be alone at night."

Tashia snuggled her nose in her neck. "I don't think uncle is alone, honey. He has us."

"Can he stay sometimes?"

"Of course. Now get under your covers and go to sleep." Tashia tucked her in and kissed her goodnight.

Zane was already sleeping when she reached his room. He had been tired a lot lately, so she made a doctor's appointment for him. Tashia ran her hand down his face. He had a slight temperature and she saw a new bruise on his arm.

"He tried to wait up for you, but I see he didn't make it." Zander approached his brother's bed. "Is he okay?"

"He goes to the doctors Monday. I'm sure he probably just has a bug or low blood." Tashia pushed the braids from his face. He started growing them after he saw Caden's hair as a little boy. Now his hair was halfway down his back and held by a hair tie. She covered him with a blanket and turned off the lamp on his nightstand.

She and Zander left Zane's room. Zander stood still, watching his mother walk to his room. She looked tired. Following her to his room, he closed the door behind him. He watched her sit in the chair by his window. This was a new addition to his room. It was the only other thing he wanted. Caden was teaching him how to pray and talked about the chair in his room.

"What's wrong?" he asked.

"I'm tired." She watched him and saw he was tired, too. "Come sit with me and tell me what's on your mind," she said, patting his chair. Zander felt ashamed to bring up the subject now. He was doing it because he was angry with her for lying about what she was doing on the weekends. Now he saw Tashia, the woman, tired, who would do what was necessary to take care of her children. "It's not important anymore. You look tired. Go to bed."

"No. You have been pondering something for weeks now and I want you to talk to me or someone, Zander." She stood and hugged her big boy. "I'll always be here for you."

"I know, Mom, but it really isn't important anymore. I just worked everything out in my head and everything is good."

It had been a while since she held him like this. He held her because she needed it and had no one else to hug her. He held her because she was his mother and he promised to take care of her.

Mr. Wood

Cuyler sat in her office, reviewing a new file from her old firm. She read the files and decided not to take this case. It was above her expertise and she was sure Preston would not agree. She had already made the call. They informed her they would send a messenger to pick up the file.

She leaned back and looked family at the portrait that sat on her desk. It wasn't that long ago when she had none of them. Now, she was pregnant with another angel. Her stomach fluttered as though hearing her thoughts. She pressed her hand on the growing mound.

"You ready to go?" Preston stood in the doorway, watching her.

"Ready." She stood. They had an appointment for her sonogram and were about twenty weeks, so the doctor wanted to validate her due date. She could see he was anxious.

During her sonogram, Cuyler realized she was in the same room from her first pregnancy. The same brown spot was on the ceiling. She held the water quietly this time. She knew the routine and knew it would not be long. Preston was sitting in a chair at her side, looking intently, trying to understand what he was seeing.

"Do we want to know the sex?" he asked.

"No. Let it be a surprise." Cuyler answered.

They both watched as the technician scanned her belly. Cuyler thought she knew what it was, but didn't share with Preston. She watched his kid-like reactions to the process and smiled.

The vibration of her phone distracted her. She looked to her purse.

"Whoever it is can wait," Preston said, ignoring the vibration.

"Okay, you may relieve yourself. Get dressed and the doctor will be in to answer any questions."

Cuyler jumped from the table, almost losing her cover-up, and hurried to the restroom. Preston laughed at her urgency. She returned, relieved, and checked her caller ID. It was her old employer. She made a face, wondering if she'd forgotten something.

"Everything okay?" Preston asked.

"It was the firm. I will call them back after we're done here."

The doctor entered, reviewing her sonogram with them. He honored their wishes by not telling them the sex and informed them they were twenty-two weeks pregnant.

Back in the home office, Cuyler called the firm. It appeared the client was insisting she was his lawyer.

"Sam, I don't want it. Besides, Preston is not going to let me take another case like that. He wasn't pleased when I took the last one. Also, I've no expertise in this area. I would be doing the client a disservice." She paced as she spoke.

"Well, we gave him your office number. He will be calling you to convince you," Sam advised.

"Then I will kindly tell him I cannot help him," she told Sam. "I don't take sex-related cases, Sam, and this is incest involving his child. No!"

Cuyler didn't like the last case she took, but she believed the defendant was being trapped or she would not have taken it. The result was positive, but she never felt comfortable.

Later, Cuyler explained the offer from the firm to Preston. He said exactly what she knew he would say.

"No."

"I already told them no. They said he would be calling me anyway because he liked my work on the last case."

"I'm glad he liked your work, but the answer is still *no*, Cuyler! Why did you tell them you had to discuss this with me? You already knew what my answer would be." He was irritated now.

"You are right. I shouldn't have put you in the middle." Snuggling under his arm, she placed his hand on her growing stomach. The baby was kicking and stretching.

"The baby said no, too," he joked. "I don't want you taking cases like that, okay? And, thank you for telling me about it. I want you to be safe."

He pulled her as close as he could. Callia was asleep in his lap. She attempted to wait up for Caden, but with the Gala only months away, he had his hands full.

"Have you talked to Caden?"

"He said he would be working late, again, but he would still try and come by to see her, but I will text him to let him know she is sleep."

"I'm going to take her up for bed."

Preston stood to take Callia upstairs and the doorbell chimed. "It's probably Caden." The two walked to the door to let Caden in, but it was not him. Instead, a man dressed in a suit greeted them.

"How can we help you?" Preston handed Callia to Cuyler.

"I hate to disturb you, but my name is Steven Wood and I needed to speak with Cuyler Washington about representation," the stranger said, extending his perfectly manicured hand. His slightly receding hairline exposed his big forehead, and his overly small waist exaggerated his oversized thighs.

"Well, the best place to speak to her concerning representation would be at her office," Preston informed him. He would not take the man's hand. "She doesn't take calls in our home. Who referred you?" He was agitated and took a defensive stance.

"I got her information from her old firm. I believe they have been speaking with her concerning representing me, and she told them she didn't feel equipped to handle the case, but I don't trust anyone else to handle my defense. I heard she was fair and very good."

"Well, Mr. Wood, as I said, she doesn't bring her work into our home, and she cannot take your case because, as you can see, she is pregnant and is not taking on anything big or extensive. You are more than welcome to call her tomorrow at the office, but you would be wasting your time unless you are calling for a referral." Preston watched the man. He didn't like him and definitely did not trust him. Coming up behind the man, he saw Caden approaching.

Caden checked the man out and then looked at Preston. Preston's look was stern and guarded. Caden immediately took a defensive stance. "Is everything okay?" He walked past the man slowly and took a stance next to Preston.

"Everything is fine. This is Mr. Wood. He was just leaving. He came to talk to Cuyler about taking his case, but I informed him she has already made a decision and would not be able to take on his case." Preston's attention never left the man. "Goodnight Mr. Wood. I wish you luck in finding someone."

"Thank you, Mr. Washington. I am sorry I disturbed your evening," the stranger said, and walked to his car. Preston watched him climb into the Lincoln Sedan and pull out of the driveway.

"What's going on?" Caden asked, concerned about the polite exchange.

"The firm called Cuyler today to see if she would take his case and she told them no because the case was sex-related. We have an agreement that she will not become involved with these cases. The firm called her back and said this guy is adamant about having her represent him and gave him her office's direct number, but this bastard shows up to my house!" Visibly, Preston was angered.

"Hey, Caden," Cuyler said from the steps. "She's in her bed, but you can go and see her. She went back to sleep, so I'm not sure how much interaction you will get from her."

Caden heard her, but turned his attention back to Preston who was shaken. "I'll be back."

Preston stood with his hands on his waist. He looked at Cuyler, who looked frightened. He took a few short breaths and tried to calm down. "Come here," he said, extending his hand. He held her in his arms and rubbed her back. "Why don't you go take a bath to relax and we can talk about this later. Okay?"

"Okay," she conceded and disappeared up the steps.

Preston checked all the entrances and windows downstairs and returned to the sunroom. The visitor bothered him. He leaned his head back on the couch and closed his eyes. He didn't have an answer for this one. He didn't know what to do to protect her.

"She needs to have a restraining order placed on this guy," Caden said, entering the room. "I know it won't help his case, but that was bold!"

Preston opened his eyes, not realizing Caden was in the room with him. "If needed, I will personally handle this. It's my job to keep her safe!" He looked at Caden. He would go to the firm on Monday.

If Caden had learned anything about Preston over the past two years, it was not to press him when he was agitated and the other was not to overstep his boundaries when it came to Cuyler. "I will come by and pick Callia up around noon tomorrow. I need to make time for her." Caden stood to leave.

Preston saw Caden out the door and headed to his bedroom. Cuyler was in the tub, leaning back on her bath pillow. Quickly, he undressed and met her in the water. Her silence let him know she was still shaken by the incident. Leaning her forward, he sat behind her and became her pillow. He could feel her tension subsiding. Revisiting why he did not want her to handle these cases was no longer necessary. Now she understood why.

"Is Caden still picking her up tomorrow?" she asked.

He knew from the question she did not want to talk about what had just transpired, but it was necessary. "You can't avoid it, Cuyler. We have to talk about this." He rubbed her arms and kissed her neck.

"He came to our door! What if you were not here?"

"Exactly! What if I were not here? Would you know what to do? I need to know you would."

She turned her body to face him and lay on his chest. "I like to think I would know what to do."

"I need to *know* you know what to do, Cuyler, so we will work on a plan that will work for any dangerous situation. Okay?"

"Okay."

"It will be okay. I just need you to be more aware of your surroundings right now."

He stroked her hair while thinking about their situation more. He couldn't be with her always, so he needed to have his private investigator find out more about this man. He would have to broach the subject with her in the morning about filing a restraining order as well, so there would be some type of file on him. It was his job to keep his family safe.

Honesty

After her set, Tashia headed for the dressing room. Her new little mousy friend was there. She had been giving the young girl pointers after her sets and giving her various strengthening exercises to do. She could see improvement in her dancing, although dancing was not the young girl's calling.

"That was great, Tashia!" the young girl told her.

"Thank you. I see you have been doing some of your new moves as well. Good job." Tashia tried to encourage her as much as she could, without making her feel like this was a permanent lifestyle. "How is school coming?"

"I have a paper due Monday, but I'm on top of things."

The door opened and Anthony entered. The girls looked to see if he was signaling them to leave, but he did not. They returned to what they were doing.

Anthony sat and watched Tashia take off her cat woman costume. The only thing she had left on was her thong and dominatrix bra. She stepped into her jeans, slowly pulling them over her ample behind, aware he would be looking, and finished dressing. After packing her bag, she put on her leather jacket and headed to the door where Anthony waited for her.

"Goodnight, Mouse," she said over her shoulder. "Ladies."

"Goodnight, Tashia," they sang back.

Anthony escorted her to her car. "You are very quiet this evening. What is going on?" Anthony asked, taking her hand.

"I'm just tired. I've been working a lot lately."

She stepped into Anthony's arms. He was the closest thing she had to a confident.

"Why don't you take tomorrow off and spend time with the kids," Anthony suggested. "I will come over and spend some time with them as well."

"That would be nice. Thank you. I will take you up on your offer, boss."

Her presence calmed him. Her eyes were sincere and honest. He couldn't think of anyone with that power over him. Damn her eyes on him. She had so much control over him and she was unaware.

"Call me to let me know you made it home." Opening her door, he helped her in the car. After closing her door, he rapped on the top twice and returned to the building.

Her ride home was peaceful. She decided to call Cuyler to see if she wanted to go and visit Brenda with her. It had been a while since Cuyler had seen their mother and it bothered Brenda.

"Hey, Mommy! How are you feeling?"

"Hey, Shia! I'm a little tired, but nothing I can't handle."

"I was thinking about either taking the kids past Mom's tomorrow or inviting her over. I wanted you with me either way." There was silence. The silence was so long she tested to make sure Cuyler was still there. "Hello?"

"Shia, I don't know. The last time we were together we got into it."

"Cuyler, you can't expect her to change her ways after all these years. She may be sober, but she is still Brenda Davidson." Again, Tashia heard silence from the opposite end of the phone. "Come on, Cuyler, she is still our mother."

"She's your mother. You were my mother."

"Fine then. I will cook tomorrow at my house and you may come and Brenda may be there as well."

"I don't know if I could tolerate her through dinner. She will say something to piss me off before the night is over. And if she calls me a snob one more time I swear I will jump on her!"

Tashia thought about their last encounter and the exchange between her mother and sister. Brenda revealed she told India that Caden would never be hers, and he would always want her daughter no matter what she did. Cuyler told their mother not to bring that ghetto mess to her house and that Caden did love India. Brenda called her snobby and uppity, and it was all downhill from there.

"For the kids, Cuyler?"

"My children won't miss a thing if she was not a part of their lives, and if she treats them badly I will handle her, Shia!"

Tashia was quiet. She wondered if Cuyler felt the same about her. They were different. She never lived the life Tashia had lived. She sighed and tried to shake the thought from her mind. "Think about it, Cuyler, and call me in the morning so I can prepare. I am still going to invite her to the house just in case you change your mind. I love you."

"I love you, too, Shia."

When she pulled into the driveway, the house was dark except the front door light. Once inside, she made her rounds to check on her children.

Zander was asleep with his plugs in his ear, listening to music from his iPod. His birthday was coming in a couple of weeks and he would be spending it with his uncles. They called it 'man business'. She dared not remove the plugs or turn off the music because she knew he would definitely awaken. Backing out of his bedroom, she closed the door behind her.

Solana was half on and half off her bed. Tashia tucked her back into her bed and kissed her. After leaving her bedroom, she walked into Zane's bedroom. Slowly, she walked to his bed. He was awake.

"Hi, Momma," he said in a weak voice. Tashia ran her hands through his braids and brushed one from his face.

"What are you doing up, monkey?"

"I just got something to drink and went to the bathroom," he answered, sounding weak.

Lying with him, she rubbed his back until he was asleep. A tiny bead of preparation covered his forehead. Carefully, she stood so she wouldn't wake him.

She thought about her conversation with Cuyler and began to compare their lives. She wondered why Cuyler never checked on her and the kids after Jesus' death. She knew she had spoiled and sheltered her as a child, but she never thought her sweet Cuyler would have become so privileged. She reminded Tashia of the rich white people who looked down at her as a child, except she wasn't rude. She was still sweet Cuyler through her jaded views. Where did she fit in Cuyler's perfect world?

Her phone buzzed in her pocket. She was sure it was Anthony. She had not called nor texted him to let him know she was home. She looked at her phone.

Open the back door.

When she reached the door, he stood starring at her. No, he was starring through her. Quickly, she opened the door and pushed him back. She could no longer hold her emotions. She dropped to her knees and cried.

"Tashia," he whispered in her ear, now on the ground with her, holding her. "I'm sorry. I should not have let you leave. Shhhh," he whispered.

He held her until she pushed from him and stood. He stood with her. "What happened?" She didn't answer. Instead, she buried her head in his chest and held onto him. "What happened," he asked again.

"Nothing. I'm just tired." She looked to him, wondering what he thought of his tough girl now. She needed him to be her safe place. She needed him. "Why are you here?"

"I should have left with you. I should not have let you leave when I saw you were upset." He looked at her. "I'm here for you. What's going on?"

"I had a disagreement with Cuyler and realized I have nothing in common with her," she said through tears flowing down her cheeks.

Anthony looked through her and felt her hurt. There were those eye, again, piercing his heart. She was one of the strongest women he had ever met, but when it came to her family, she was transparent.

He held her in his arms and she melted into him. He felt needed. He felt wanted. She made him feel all the things he knew would make him hurt if she ever betrayed him and he allowed his transparency to show for once. "I'm staying," he announced.

Anthony walked her back inside the house and locked the door behind them, placing the stick back in its protective spot. He guided her to her bedroom and laid her down.

"The kids," she started.

"I'm not leaving you, again, when I want to be with you. We will have to talk to the kids in the morning, if needed, but I will be with you tonight."

"What are we doing, Anthony?" She waited patiently for an answer.

He thought about it. "Entering the unknown. We will have to figure it out as we go. I just know I need you with me."

"Before I cross that line with you or anyone, I need to know we are exclusive. I've been hurt before and I won't invest in a relationship that has no potential to become more." Watching his expression explained everything. She saw the small twitch of his jaw and the light sheen of perspiration. He was scared of her, but she would not let him off so easily. "Where are we going with this?"

"I will give you all I can. That's the only promise I can make. I have never been here before." His vulnerability was showing. She watched him search her face for acceptance.

"If you hurt me I'll kill you." She searched his face, again, and saw the smile that warmed her heart more times than he knew. "Oh, and I need to know your status because I don't like condoms and you have been with some questionable people. I have my paperwork."

Anthony smiled, knowing she was referring to Myra. "I think you are jealous of Myra." The two laughed at his comment.

They lay on her bed and he held her while she slept. He could not sleep.

Zander was first to awake. He could hear his mother cooking in the kitchen. He made his way through the quiet house, but was shocked to see Anthony there instead. He stood watching and wondering when he arrived. "Hey, Anthony."

Anthony turned and smiled at him. "Good morning, Zander. I was wondering when someone would come to help me. Grab a plate so I can put these waffles on it."

Zander reached in the cabinet, slowly getting a plate as asked. He put it on the table and reached for a bowl to begin mixing eggs. "How long have you been here?" he asked.

"Since earlier this morning," Anthony answered.

"Does my mom know you are here?"

"Yes. She let me in. She is asleep now." Anthony poured the batter into the iron and turned to look at a now quiet Zander. He knew he had more questions, but he was trying to be polite. "You have questions, Zander, so ask, but always know they may not be the answers you want, so be careful."

Zander watched Anthony and thought about what he said. He wasn't afraid. "Why are you here?"

Anthony turned to flip the iron. "Your mother was upset so I came to check on her."

"She called you?"

Things had just gotten complicated. "No."

"Then how did you know she was upset?" Zander wanted him to answer the questions that had been pulling at him for weeks, but could not ask his mother. "Were you with her?"

"Yes."

"After work?"

"Yes."

"Instead of me asking you one question at a time why don't you tell me where the two of you were last night, or this morning?"

Anthony smiled at Zander, but he didn't smile back. He knew where his mother was and he wanted Anthony to confirm.

"Where do you believe your mother was, Zander?"

"You gonna lie to me, too?"

Anthony saw his balled fists. He was angry. "Do you believe that is what she has been doing? Lying to you?" Anthony watched as Zander labored through his thoughts and waited for an answer.

"She said she was at work. The streets say differently."

"What do the streets say, Zander."

"I think you know."

Anthony saw the tears that now shined in the young boy's eyes. He was challenging him, daring him to lie. He was hurt. "It is all relative, Zander. If your mom said she was at work then that is where she was."

"She's a stripper. Did you know that?" His anger overflowed and the tears now fell.

"Your mother will never be a stripper, Zander. She is a dancer, yes, but she is no stripper. She has much too much class for that."

"So, you were there watching her?" he asked, his voice beginning to elevate through the cracks, indicating his transition from boyhood.

"First, lower your voice. We can talk and I will answer your questions, but if you want me to treat you like a man you will act like one." Anthony's voice was stern. He handed the crying boy a napkin. "Fix your face."

Anthony waited for him to gather himself and gestured for him to sit. "Zander, do you believe your mother loves you?" Zander nodded. "Your mother would do what she needs to take care of you guys, but she, too, has boundaries."

"Then why did she lie to me?"

"What did she say? That she went to work?" Anthony waited for an answer, but Zander was silent. "There was no lie in her statement. You are a child."

Zander looked at Anthony through hurt eyes, revealing the childhood he lost five years ago. "I haven't been a child since my father died," Zander told Anthony, now standing to his feet.

Anthony studied Zander and saw his own life. He had not been a boy since he was six years old and he stepped off the boat in Antigua. He, too, watched his father die, which introduced him to manhood early. He could not remember being a boy anymore. He would not treat Zander as though he was a child either.

"Zander, I'm sure your mother finds no pride in some of the things she has done. In a world of imperfection, parents want to always be seen as perfect in their child's eyes. She doesn't want to display her imperfections to you. Can you understand that?"

The boy nodded and contemplated Anthony's words.

"Most times what someone else thinks about us is more important than how we view ourselves. Never be that person. Always know who you are, or someone else will define you."

"Are you seeing my mother?"

Anthony thought he was prepared for their talk, but Zander was hitting with the hard questions. "I think we are getting to know one another, but I don't want my and your mother's relationship to interfere with our relationship, so let's not confuse the two. Promise me that."

"Do you love my mother?"

Anthony never thought about what the boy was asking him. He cared deeply for Tashia, but he had not experienced love. He only loved his family. He looked at Zander and sat with him. He wanted to answer the question as truthfully as possible. "I don't know, Zander. I can tell you she is very special to me and I will be here for her."

"She deserves someone who loves her," the young boy told him.

Anthony rubbed his head. "She does and I'm not saying I don't. What I am saying is I am not equipped to answer that question and be honest with you and myself." Anthony tapped the table and stood to continue cooking. He threw away the now burnt waffles.

"Good morning," Solana said, entering the kitchen. She climbed into her brother's lap and he kissed her forehead. "Uncle Anthony why are you cooking? Momma at work?" she asked.

"No, Sunshine. Momma is asleep," he answered, happy she came to save him from Zander's many questions.

"No, Momma isn't," Tashia said, entering the kitchen. "What's going on in here?"

"Uncle Anthony is making breakfast!" Solana yelled.

"Not so loud, Solana," Zander told her, covering her mouth.

Tashia kissed her children and smiled at Anthony. She was still wearing the clothes she wore to bed. "I'm going to see what Zane is doing." He nodded to her and watched as she went to his bedroom and disappeared behind his door.

Tashia tipped to his bed and lay with him. He was still asleep and she didn't want to wake him. Lying next to her son, she moved in close. Soon she was asleep with him.

Anthony peeped in Zane's room and saw they were both asleep, so he quietly retreated and returned to Zander and Solana. Solana was telling a silly story and Zander pretended to be entertained. Zander looked up and saw he returned alone.

"Go and take your shower, Solana, and pick out something nice to wear," Zander instructed.

"Where are we going?" she asked.

"I don't know yet," he answered.

"Then how will I know what to wear?"

"You can wear whatever you want today." Solana was happy with that and ran to her room to prepare for her bath.

Zander studied Anthony and saw that he protected his mother's secrets. He liked Anthony. He reminded him of his dad. He was strong and take-charge. He offered a sense of security. If he was seeing his mother that was fine with him.

"Are we okay with this morning's conversation?" Anthony asked. Zander nodded. "Do not embarrass your mother by asking her where she is working on the weekends."

"I won't," Zander promised, looking down. He was not proud he talked about his mother, but he appreciated Anthony's honesty. "Thanks for being honest with me."

Mama Drama

Tashia was happy Cuyler conceded and decided to come for dinner. Brenda arrived early and was playing with the kids when she, Preston, and Callia arrived. Although small, the house accommodated everyone nicely.

Anthony went to Reggae earlier and brought back jerked chicken, curried chicken roti, monkey bread, and oxtails. Tashia made red beans and rice, a salad and veggie empanadas. She let Zander make the tea and lemonade, which proved to be lethally sweet.

Cuyler kissed Tashia and was shocked that Anthony was there. She went to the living room, kissed her mother, and took a seat on the couch. Callia had long ago disappeared with her cousin into her bedroom.

Tashia fidgeted in the kitchen, feeling the tension between her sister and mother. She also wondered if everything looked okay. Did her couch look too old? Were there enough decorations? Should she get more décor for her home?

Running back and forth, she put the food on the small dining room table. She didn't realize she was tense until Anthony stopped her in the kitchen by grabbing her around her waist.

"Slow down. Tell me what you need me to do."

"Tell me why I decided to do this?"

Anthony ran his fingers through the roots of her hair and took the last few things to the dining room. Preston was standing near the table, smiling. Anthony ignored him, cutting his eyes, and returning to the kitchen to see what else Tashia needed him to do.

"That's everything. We can eat now."

Gathering everyone to the living room, Tashia asked Preston to bless the food.

"Thank you, Lord, for the food we are about to receive. Thank you for another opportunity for our families to come together and break bread. We thank you for the gracious hostess who invited us here today into her beautiful home and continue to bless her and her family as they transition in their lives. Amen."

Everyone fixed their plates and Tashia and Cuyler fixed plates for the girls.

"How did Anthony end up here today?" Cuyler asked Tashia.

"You know he spends a lot of time with the boys so I invited him."

"Oh. Okay."

Tashia side eyed her little sister, reading all the meaning in her words. "Why do you say 'Oh. Okay'?" she asked, mocking her.

"I didn't mean anything by it. If it were more than that I would be shocked because he doesn't seem like your type."

Tashia stopped fixing Solana's plate. "Tell me what my type is, Cuyler," she said, with a little more edge than she wanted.

Shocked by her sister's defensive stance, Cuyler looked at her. "He's rude, for one, and a bully."

"Then you don't know him."

"Why are you defending him? I remember not too long ago you threatened him for threatening me!"

Tashia remembered that time. It was when Anthony found out there was history between Cuyler and Caden. He told Cuyler he would be watching her and she had better not hurt his brother. "And I realized he hadn't said anything I would not have told Preston if I thought he was out of line with you. You know what? The two of you are grown, so fight your own battles!"

Tashia left the room when she saw her mother headed their way. She seated Solana on the patio and Callia soon followed with Cuyler and her plate. Callia was glaring at Tashia and Tashia smiled, realizing Callia was defending her mother. She was definitely like her auntie; always ready to fight and protect. Callia didn't smile back. "You don't want any part of me, little girl," she teased and tickled Callia, who gave in to her laughter.

"I just want you to be happy, Tashia," Cuyler said in a low whisper. "I wasn't trying to—"

"Forget about it, Cuyler. Let's just eat." Tashia was irritated and didn't want to defend her relationship with Anthony nor justify it to Cuyler.

Diva Dorreen

Her sister had this perfect life with the exception of the two-year meltdown of her relationship with Caden, who in the end tried to win her back. Tashia's entire life of relationships was out of necessity. She was tired of being in survival mode. She was ready to love and be loved.

Brenda was sitting on the living room couch when Cuyler and Tashia joined her. The men were outside with the kids. Brenda watched them as they sat and Tashia was sure she heard their conversation in the dining room. She didn't want any comments from her mother afraid that Cuyler would bolt from the room.

"How is the baby, Cuyler?" Brenda asked, turning her attention to her youngest child.

"Everything is fine. We went to the doctors the other day and I am twenty-two weeks." Cuyler beamed talking about the birth of her new child.

Tashia wanted that. She wanted to be able to be happy about something. She wanted an uncomplicated life, but could Anthony give her that? Everything about him was complicated. Even his smile was complicated and meant several different things.

"Callia has really grown. I haven't seen her in a while and she speaks three languages!" Brenda smiled with pride. "She has so much more than you girls had. I'm sorry I wasn't there for you more."

Tashia listened to her mother go on about Callia's accomplishments and realized there would be no compliments given to her children. With each word her mother spoke, she felt the weight of her inadequacies. Her children were as amazing, too. Solana was the sweetest child she knew. She had a heart that Tashia knew would be her greatest downfall one day. Zane could carry on a conversation with any adult and talk politics to sports. Zander was so perceptive and quick the sky was the limit for him, but she was sure all her mother saw were three ghetto children.

She was distracted and didn't hear her mother ask her a question.

"Tashia, I haven't seen much of you lately either."

"Mom, I told you that I've been working more, but I do come to see you when I can." It had been a long time since she felt like she was competing with Cuyler. Even when she was with Jesus, she felt Cuyler was her competition. Jesus was always worried about where she was

120

when she went out and would send one of his muses to watch her from afar. He spoke of her beauty often and spoke of Tashia's as though it were an afterthought.

"Where else are you working? I heard you took on a second job."

Her mother looked at Tashia with those knowing motherly eyes, accusing her. She knew she was being baited, but her anger was on the surface now. "Why don't you talk more about Callia with Cuyler? It's not like you get to see her that often." Tashia challenged her mother like she did when she was a drunk and addict.

"Watch yourself, little girl," her mother dared.

"Oh! Now I'm a little girl! I don't ever remember being that!" Tashia spat angrily.

"Tashia! Where is the steak sauce?" Anthony called from the kitchen. "Can you help me look for it?"

Tashia was glaring at her mother, not answering nor moving to Anthony's request. She wanted to say more, but with the day already ruined, she didn't want to destroy it. She was sitting on a powder keg and she didn't know why. She was overly agitated about things she would have normally shrugged off.

"Tashia!" Anthony was standing in the kitchen doorway now, watching her, calling her with his eyes. He didn't move until she stood.

Tashia walked into the kitchen and Anthony was leaning on the fridge. She could hear her mother talking to Cuyler, again.

"It's great to see your mother and Cuyler getting along."

"Yeah. Great!" she replied with a slight edge in her voice. She opened the fridge, found the half bottle of steak sauce, and put it in his hand, but he was still watching her. She began to walk away, but he pulled her back.

"What's going on with you?" He rubbed the side of her face and she began to calm down.

"Nothing. Everything. I don't know!"

Anthony watched the stubborn Tashia he first met stare back, challenging him to come for her, too. He smiled at her, amused. "Put your guns away. I'm not coming for you."

She dropped her defense and laughed. She leaned her head on his chest and let go of the tension that had risen up within her. She no longer felt like company and didn't want to go back out to the circus her mother was trying to manipulate.

"Are you staying tonight?"

"I can do that if you want me to. But, you can't stay in here forever."

Tashia turned and made her way back to the living room. Her mother was still telling Cuyler how proud she was of her accomplishments, including her marriage to Preston. Tashia decided to sit quietly and listen to her mother's rantings instead of joining the charade.

The group ate and enjoyed the evening together. Tashia moved to the patio with the kids and enjoyed their multiple conversations when she could no longer listen to Brenda. She laughed and savored the ease between Preston and Anthony and wished things were as simple with Cuyler, but she had built up a wall a long time ago between them.

She watched Anthony. He was relaxed with her children and them with him. Zander seemed to be the boy he was supposed to be at almost thirteen instead of the man he was forced to be at seven. Although she still didn't know where she wanted to take the relationship, it seemed more and more it was guiding itself without waiting for her approval.

She sat quietly, absorbing the exchange between the two. Zane looked at Anthony like a boy would look at a father she was sure he had long forgotten. Solana was in love. She cooed freely over Anthony in a way Tashia would not let herself. She was seeing so much through her children's eyes, yet she held a piece of herself back.

Before Cuyler left, Tashia apologized for her earlier outburst and hugged her goodnight. She wanted what Preston and Anthony had, but she no longer wanted to feel like she was Cuyler's keeper.

Tashia tucked Solana and Zane in after their showers. Zane was still clammy, but he seemed a little better. Zander was helping Anthony finish the kitchen.

"Are you staying tonight, Anthony?" Zander asked. "She seems better when you're around." The young boy waited for an answer.

"I may stay a while. Your mother is okay."

"I didn't say she wasn't. I said she's better with you."

Anthony sometimes felt inadequate when talking to Zander. He was much more intelligent than his years. "Then maybe I will." He hugged Zander goodnight and watched him leave.

When he met Tashia in the great room, she was sitting on the couch, listening to music. He sat with her, putting his arm around her neck. "That boy amazes me," he informed her.

Tashia hummed in reply, letting him know she understood what he was saying. "I know. He's an old soul," she said, relaxing in his arms.

The day was long, but he enjoyed having a family. He had never been away from his businesses, but he felt she needed him more. "You've never talked about his father before."

Tashia looked up at him. "You never asked, but is that what other women do, bare all to you?"

He knew she was teasing him. "Sometimes they mistake me for a priest and cry, confessing all at the altar of Anthony and then they bare all," he teased back.

Tashia laughed. "I can see that happening."

Anthony looked at her, no longer smiling. "What happened today, Tashia?"

A sigh came in place of the reply he expected. He saw her apprehension and changed the subject. "If you won't tell me about tonight tell me about Jesus."

She could love this man with her whole heart, but she saw the dark side of him as well, but what she saw in the shadows would not allow her to trust him completely with her heart.

Hurt lurked just beyond his smile. The ease of his conversations were somewhat rehearsed as though he learned over the years what to say and not. He was once an old soul, she was sure, but now he was bits and pieces of a past that haunted his spirit. Even with her, she could see he could run at any minute, yet there was an unknown that kept him in place.

He caught her off guard asking her about Jesus. She had never talked about him to anyone, but when she looked at Anthony, she saw he truly wanted to know and was not questioning her just to make conversation. Worse, he saw through her soul, seeing her, under all her walls of deception she had carried since the day in the corridor under the steps when she was fourteen, alone and wounded.

A crack had begun in the first brick laid to protect her over the years. Fear filled her as she questioned whether she was worthy of love. She knew her anger with Cuyler earlier was because of her choices before him, causing her to question if he were just another bad choice in her life.

She watched him, weighing her options while she still had them, yet she could feel the crack become wider the longer she delayed. She had carried her family for so long she didn't know how to let her duties go. Today was all about her need to be normal and her crazy life was everything but normal. Normal would never be a part of her future if she continued with Anthony, but he understood her crazy and accepted her.

The tears were hot on her cheeks. She didn't know when they started, but she needed to shed them.

"I see you," he was saying to her and no one had seen her not even Jesus. "It's okay not to be okay," he said, but in her world to show your vulnerability was death. It was what had gotten Jesus killed. They were his vulnerability and his desire to protect his family got him killed. That night he could have escaped, but he needed to make sure they were okay.

Her soul screamed *no*, but this man disarmed her. She wanted to trust him with her secrets. She needed to talk about her past and he made her feel safe to do that. "What do you want to know?" she asked.

"I want to know the you that is hidden away. I want the true Tashia not this watered down tough girl version. I see *you* and that is the woman I want to know."

Tashia looked at him and challenged, "Will I get the same from you? I have a lot more to lose than you, Anthony. I am trusting you with the hearts of my children, so will you show me the true you as well?" She could see the battle that waged within him. She knew he had more secrets than she could ever have.

Anthony released her and sat forward, clasping his hands. He looked back at her and after a few moments of contemplating what she asked of him, he answered, "I can do that, but I can't promise you will still want to be with me after."

His fear was real. Tashia could see it in his face. She stood, took his hand, and led him to her bedroom, closing the door behind them.

Anthony stood in Tashia's bedroom feeling completely vulnerable. The dark part of him wanted to run. He wanted to escape the promise he made, leaving his dignity and vulnerability intact. He felt like that little boy hiding on the top shelf of the closet where his father put him when the men came to kill him. Anthony knew he could do nothing to help, but nonetheless he wanted to save his dad from the men.

He remained in that closet ever since that day, afraid to come out. He was still on the top shelf as he stood before Tashia ready to lay bare what he guarded all his life.

She saw his apprehension and came to him, kissing him lightly first. His breathing quickened as she pulled back his layers with each piece of clothing she removed. Finally, he stood nude in the middle of her room, but in truth, he had been naked since the first day he met her. He knew she would be the one to whom he told his secrets.

Slowly, she undressed, allowing him to take her in. He came to her, pushing her back on the bed. It creaked slightly under his additional two hundred pounds. Tashia reached into the top nightstand drawer and withdrew the small packet of protection she had recently purchased. Once in place she guided him inside her.

Slowly, they rode together as they both relaxed in one another's arms. Anthony reached between her thighs and stroked her to help her get to his level. She responded immediately to his touch, letting him know he was beginning to know her.

They took turns taking lead. They gave themselves totally with no fear or apprehension. His moans guiding her and her cries directed him. He pleased her with his tongue, showing her the skills he acquired from his many years of practice and her wild innocence pushed him to please her more. She in turn showed her appreciation by gifting him in like manner until they became one, again, and met in that mutual place where they could ride the wave together as they experienced the deathless death.

Tashia lay in his arms, feeling free of the bondage that had entrapped her for years, but to be truly free she knew she had to tell her story, so she no longer feared the past.

Anthony must have seen the turmoil rising in her. "You can let go with me," he repeated, as he had told her earlier. He could see her eyes flood with emotion. "You don't have to keep your tough girl act with me. I see you." She was still watching him as though weighing his words. "It's okay not to be okay, Shia," he repeated.

Tashia took a deep breath and began the story she promised.

Me Too

"I met Jesus when I was only twelve. He was fourteen. He was a drug runner and always on the corner near my building. He would tease and joke every time I passed him, always making me smile, but he would never approach me." Tashia smiled, remembering his shyness, but her mood quickly changed when she remembered why they did begin to speak.

"This went on for two years and I was crushing hard, but I was too afraid to say anything other than answer his questions or respond back to him."

Tashia stopped before continuing. She would share with Anthony what she chose to never share with her mother or sister. Remembering made her emotional and she didn't want to relive the experience, but knew she could trust Anthony with the information.

She continued. "One day, when I went home, Momma needed me to go to the corner store. Cuyler wanted to come with me, but I didn't want her to because I wanted to say something to Jesus this time.

"On my way back from the store, he was correcting one of the guys on the corner so I didn't stop. He was more intense than usual. You see, he had been elevated and ran some of the corners. When I walked in the building, there was a man who I didn't know. He was dressed in overalls and old beat up leather shoes. His skin was light and eyes light blue, but there was something scary about him. He spoke to me, but I said nothing because I didn't know him.

"He knocked the bags from my hands and grabbed me by my ponytail, dragging me to the basement. I fought with everything I had because I knew nothing good was going to happen in the basement." She stopped. Cringing, she vibrated, as though cold, as she remembered the stench of his breath and dirt on his clothes. Anthony pulled the sheet around them.

She wanted to be freed from the shame and shadows that chased and whispered to her over the years, telling her she was dirty and nasty, making her feel not worthy of a healthy or normal relationship. The memories held her captive, telling her it was her fault and if she had acknowledged the dirty man it would not have happened. The tears fell and the bars of her prison pushed in on her. Embarrassment and shame pressed down on her and she began regretting she had ever started.

Anthony rubbed her arm and drew her in close. "Shhhh! He's not here, Shia. It's just us," he reminded her. "Breathe." He continued rubbing her arm and instructed until her breathing became normal.

"He took me to the back of the basement under some steps. A young boy playing saw and ran out of the basement. I hoped he would help, but he was *so* little. He couldn't help.

"I knew what was next. Things like this happened in our neighborhood every day.

"The man reeked. I can still smell the alcohol from his breath panting on me. His hands were like sandpaper on my skin as he gripped me, moving them over my body as if smoothing out its imperfections.

"I squirmed, trying to get out of his hold, so he smacked me and choked me until I lay still. I lay there, anticipating, crying, knowing no one was coming and this was happening. He ripped my panties off and discarded them as if annoyed I had any on. I tightened my thighs to keep him out, but he tightened his grip on my neck, causing me to choke. He said he could kill me and make things easier.

"I thought about my sweet Cuyler and wondered had I brought her with me if the same would have happened or would he have taken us both, using our love for each other to have his way with us both. I knew she could not have endured."

Anthony was so quiet, Tashia looked up to see if he was still listening. His face was very intent, searching hers, waiting for her to go on. She laid her head on his outstretched arm, feeling the strength that made her feel safe.

"I remembered the stories the girls shared of their first time. 'Relax and it won't hurt', they would say. I couldn't relax. He stunk and I wanted him off of me, but I knew if I let him have me, he would finish faster and he would be done. He was rough and in an obvious hurry. He pushed hard and my flesh was on fire. He looked at me surprised I was still a virgin and smiled saying 'Oh, I picked a good one this time'. But, it hurt so bad I started fighting him again, so he hit me over and over until I was still.

"The man flipped me over and had his way with me again, but this time from the back, tearing me there, too. The pain was so great I wished for darkness to come, but it didn't. I couldn't move under his weight so I cried.

"My chest felt like it would burst or I would smother to death from his weight pressing down on me. I tried to holler, but couldn't.

"I heard noises behind us and the man suddenly stopped and was gone. I rolled over to run, but couldn't because what I saw paralyzed me. Jesus had the man from behind, slitting his throat. He tossed him to the floor like a rag. I watched the man jerking on the floor like a slaughtered chicken.

"I ran to the man and kicked him over and over. Jesus let me vent before grabbing me and carrying me out of the basement, kicking and fighting to go back and finish.

"Jesus looked me over and knew he was too late, but he never looked at me in pity. Instead, he hugged me and apologized for not getting there sooner. He had gone to another corner to check on their progress. That little boy ran to find him to help me." Tashia paused. "He called me Shia for the first time." She was crying again. "He told me no one would ever touch me, again, and they didn't.

"I was a mess. My face was bruised, my clothes were torn, and somewhere in the struggle I had lost a shoe, so I wouldn't let him take me home. I didn't want Cuyler to see me like that." Tashia laughed, thinking that on that day she had lost more than a shoe, she had lost what she could never give to that special person. She looked in Anthony's face and saw no pity. She saw hurt and anger. "I always protected Cuyler. She was my baby. I never wanted anything like that to happen to her.

"Jesus barked orders and his crew scurried. The boys picked up the contents of the bag, taking them to our apartment. They told Cuyler I asked them to bring them, but the bag broke.

"Jesus took me to his home in his car. His mother rushed to me when she saw my state and gave orders to Jesus. She was the sweetest woman I ever met. She taught me how to love my children and loved me, never judging. I am saddened that my children will not grow up knowing her or that side of his family.

"His mother bathed and soothed me in a way my mother had never done. She held me when I cried and prayed for me. Jesus brought some of his sister's clothes and she dressed me before Jesus took me back to my apartment. After that point, we were inseparable."

"When I came home, I stayed to myself. Jesus took me to his mother's daily and she checked me and used some of her home remedies to make sure I healed. I couldn't go to the hospital because a man was dead and they were afraid it would come back to Jesus. I didn't know how to feel about a man dying because of me, but I felt safer, because he was dead. Jesus gained a rep in the neighborhood and was feared even more.

"Zander is so much like his dad; he scares me sometimes. I think this is why I was afraid for him. I know my son's capabilities." She looked at Anthony and saw the storm that was just there had calmed. "He made me feel safe. I was Jesus' girl. Cuyler and I had food, clothes, and protection. Not even the girls who taunted us because we wore the same clothes teased us anymore.

"I felt I owed him the world, but he never made me feel like I owed him anything. He gave freely from his heart.

"We had Zander when I was eighteen. He was such a proud father and spent as much time as he could with him. Zander knew how to manage people before he was five. He could make a decision on how to handle a situation by the time he was six. Jesus made sure his son could think for himself.

"He told Zander he was going to be the first generation in his family to go to college and he was going to be a bigtime business man. He explained to him the drug trade was a business and not a game of power to be toyed with. He told him he didn't want him to be trapped in the same situation. Zander saw more than any seven-year-old should have been exposed to, but his dad wanted him not to be fooled by the game.

"Then there was a rumor there was someone who wanted to take Jesus' post." Tashia laughed a cynical laugh. "He only had to ask and

Jesus may have given it to him. He wanted out, but there were too many people depending on him.

"The day before they came, he begged me to leave. He knew they were getting closer and he had a traitor in his camp, but I wouldn't go. I felt safer with him in danger than I did leaving and being without him.

"When they came they were swift and quiet. Jesus' right hand man came in the room and yelled to get strapped. Jesus yelled to me to get his children and go into the safe room. He handed me a glock and pushed me down the hall. I heard gunfire and chaos behind me. I had Solana in my arms, she was just a baby. I went into the boys' room and my Zander already had his brother ready to go and the door open to the safe room. We barely made it inside the little room before someone came into the boys' room, shooting.

"In safety and behind the safe room door I turned on the cameras and told Zander to turn around. I saw Jesus." She stopped.

Anthony stroked her. "I get the picture, Shia. You don't have to tell me anymore," Anthony said, consoling her.

"I saw them gun him down like a dog in the street. When they realized they couldn't get to us and they heard the police cars, they left. When I turned, I saw the horror on Zander's face. He had seen it, too!

"I thought he was dead, but he hung on for us. Everything he did was for us. I told Zander to lock the door behind me and I went to him.

"He lay on the floor in his blood. There was so much blood. I thought surely he was dead, but when I held him, he heard me cry and opened his eyes.

"He told me he loved me since he was twelve and to take care of his children and keep them out of the game. He told me not to cry for him. He knew his life would be short, but he was happy we were in it. He asked me to leave there and not to look back." Tashia fell silent. "When he left me that day I never cried for him, again, until now. He became my strength from his grave."

Anthony could see why she was attracted to him. He wasn't that different from Jesus. He, too, loved his family and had done things to protect them, not caring about himself. They always came before him and he always felt expendable. He viewed Tashia and her children as his family, although he never spoke those words to her.

He saw her vulnerability long before she showed him. He knew she had been through something, because she was too guarded. Her eyes showed him more than she wanted to reveal to him: They spoke to his heart. Now her tears tore at his soul, breaking down his inner turmoil. He thought if he held her closer and absorb her hurt his own demons would go away.

Tashia looked up at him strangely. He was trembling. Tashia cried in Anthony's arms, realizing she had been living in shadows. She left Tashia in that room the night Jesus died. She became a hardened soldier now exposed to so much warfare she was desensitized to the battle around her. Her job was to protect the civilians, her children; being in Anthony's arms allowed her to become a civilian, if only for a while.

She was about to tell him about Zane's heritage when she realized he was still trembling. She looked up to see he wasn't okay at all. At first, she thought it was her story, but she realized he was in his own hurt, trying to hold back for her.

She kissed him and waited for him to speak, but he didn't. He reminded her of Jesus, holding everyone else's world together, with no one to take care of him. The more she kissed him the more broken he became. He tried to push away and get up, but she pulled him back and held him tighter. "I'm sorry no one was there for you, Anthony. I'm here now. I'm not going anywhere."

She felt his body relax in her arms and she hurt for the man who seemed like a fortress, realizing that everyone had issues, never dealing with them. She was so wrapped in her losses and world she never stopped to think that maybe he was dealing with things of his own. She understood why he was so compassionate, even for Myra, by not wanting to see her and her children in the street because of her actions at the club. He had been doing this all his life.

She saw her son for the first time through Anthony's hurt. She didn't like him when she first met him years ago, because she didn't like the way he looked at her sister with contempt in his eyes. She saw how he watched her every move when she was around Caden, but now she understood that he was protecting his brother.

She saw life for the first time and realized everyone was bruised from their past. The past sometimes made it difficult to follow your heart. Hadn't she tried to run away from him when she realized she had more feeling for him than she wanted? She had been running from relationships since Jesus. She didn't want to be close to anyone other than for the obvious comforts.

"I'm sorry," he said repeatedly.

"It's okay. You don't have to be sorry," she said, but he continued to say it, and she realized he wasn't talking to her at all. He was dealing with the demons chasing him, his demons. He wasn't the bad boy she thought he was. She realized what he showed was an illusion and his secret was safe with her. Now, the inner most secret part of him lay bare and he chose to expose himself to her.

He was apologizing, but now to her. He rolled her on her back and gently made love to her, apologizing. The fears once screaming inside her for loving him were now silenced by the honest love he showed her. He had been showing her for a while, but now she got it. He was afraid, too.

He looked her in her face and apologized again. "I'm sorry."

"It's okay not to be okay," she repeated his words back to him.

"Tashia," he started, but then stopped. She saw the shine in his eyes and knew he was still vulnerable.

She silenced him with a kiss and rolled him on his back. There she lay in his arms and they slept exhausted by the events of the day. Theirs was a different kind of love. Neither was safe any longer.

Monkey Business

Tashia woke to an empty house. There was a note on the
pillow next to her from Anthony.

*Took Zander and Solana to school. Zane's still sleeping.
I need to take care of some business this morning so text me if you
need anything. I will see you soon.*
P.S. - Thanks for last night.

Tashia smiled, thinking about him. She was in love. She
stretched and realized she heard a faint sound coming from the great
room. She made her way to the door and peeped to see a napping
Zane on the couch. She threw on her sweats and T-shirt and went to
check on her child.

There was a glass on the table with a thick drink of some kind.
"Anthony made it for me. He said if I drink it all before he got back
he would get me pizza."

"I thought you were sleep, monkey."

"Is Anthony your boyfriend now?"

"I dare you to ask him," she challenged.

She sat and put his head in her lap. He seemed like he had more
energy.

"Are you still achy?"

"Some."

"I can give you something for that."

"No thank you."

Zane was the darkest of her children. His dad was dark skinned,
tall and muscular, which was the total opposite of Jesus who was only
five feet nine, one hundred sixty pounds and fit. She always knew that
one day he would be much bigger than his brother. He was a
handsome little boy, but he was not as sure of himself as Zander,
although he was raised in the same household. He looked up to his
brother for guidance, direction, and love. He desperately wanted to be
like him. Over the years, Zander had become his father as she had
been Cuyler's mother.

Tashia tickled him. He laughed, but she could sense he didn't feel like playing so she stopped. "Why don't you take a nap?"

"I'm not sleepy."

"Okay, then watch television and I am going to clean my room." She went to the fridge to get a bottle of water. When she returned to the living room, Zane was asleep. She smiled, covered him, and returned to her room to strip her bed and wash her linen.

The day was quiet. Just when she was finished cleaning the room and making the bed, Anthony appeared in the bedroom doorway.

"Hey."

"Hey yourself. Where you been?"

"Taking care of business. How is Zane? I see he drank his drink," Anthony said, still standing in the doorway.

"He's been sleep off and on. What was in that glass?"

"Spinach, broccoli, apples, pineapple, protein, and some other stuff. I was trying to get him to build his strength."

Tashia stopped and looked at him. He looked different. He seemed less edgy. She went to him and attempted to kiss him, but he put his finger to her lip.

"Go back to the other side of the room before I take you," he moaned in her ear and ran the back of his hand down the side of her face. "I have some calls to make and a few more things to do before I go to the center. I came by to see if you needed anything."

Tashia attempted to kiss him again. He allowed her the small indulgence, breathing her in slowly. He knew her scent. "I've got to get this work done, Shia," he moaned, still kissing her. "Stop," he said, again, teasing and laughing. He kicked the door closed behind him, backing her to the freshly made bed.

"Stop," she teased back, "I just cleaned this," but he ignored her, stripping her of her sweats. "You planning on keeping your clothes on?" she asked, in all her nudity.

Anthony stopped and stared at her. "I am going to keep mine on because I do have to go. I just wanted to check on you guys and to see you." He laughed at the expression on her face and helped her up, lifting her, allowing her legs to wrap around his waist. "Now I can go back to work and I will see you later." He put her back on the bed, lying with her. "I will bring the kids home before I go to the club tonight. Stay here with little man and you get some rest, too." Anthony rose from the bed, looking back at her from the door and then he was gone.

"You're not the boss of me, Anthony," she mumbled, still naked and dejected on her bed where he left her.⬛

Myra's Promotion

A nthony's day was full. He was working on staffing his locations and preparing the band for the upcoming gala. Caden asked them to participate, again. He accepted with the same enthusiasm he had before.

Myra, though calm, still had sexual undertones with him. She came to his office, pretending to be unfazed by his presence. She now knew he owned both the gentlemen's club and Reggae, which was more information than he wanted her to have.

"I hear Tashia is no longer dancing. I knew she wouldn't last. Everyone isn't as faithful as they pretend," she said, gloating. "Does that mean I can come back to the club now that she is gone?"

Anthony smiled at her jealousy. "I thought maybe you wanted to stay here and be more than just a bartender." Anthony watched her perk up, turning her attention to him.

"What did you want me to do here?"

"I thought I would move you up to management and put you in charge of my inventory and training."

"Is that more money?" she asked, smiling.

"Yes," he answered an eager Myra.

"How much more?"

She was still the untamed girl he met his first day at the club. "We can discuss your salary, but first I have to know if you're interested."

"Yes!" she said, excitedly.

Anthony discussed salary and hours with Myra. She signed some confidentiality papers and he stressed their importance. A grateful Myra came to his side of the desk. Anthony folded his hands, knowing what would come next.

When she saw he would not hug her, she pouted. "I miss you, Anthony." She started rubbing his neck. When he didn't protest, she bent to kiss him.

Anthony raised his hand in protest. "You are a part of management now, Myra. Don't make me regret this decision. I told you before there was never any us. It was sex and that was it. When are you going to stop thinking with your pussy and use the brain in your head? You are a very smart girl and have the potential to go far."

Myra took in what he was saying, but it did not change her feelings for him. "Why can't it be more than just sex? I always wanted you to be more than that."

"Because that's the way you started things, and *you* started it." Anthony waited for reality to set in, but her look told him she was not going to give up. "Can you handle that, Myra?"

Myra looked long and hard at him. "I guess I don't have a choice," she finally answered and left his office. Anthony knew she wasn't done, but for now, he would accept their truce.

As he did his inspection, he watched her deliberately swing her hips as she crossed the restaurant. He saw her at work and knew she could have the pick of whomever she wanted, but his heart was not available.

He looked at his watch and realized he had to get to the center. He asked his cook to bag some food and to let him know when it was ready. He spotted Myra from across the room, watching his every move. She was training a new waiter, showing him how to key in his order. Anthony turned his back to Myra and called Tashia.

"Hello."

"Hey. I'm bringing diner so relax and enjoy Zane."

"I think there is still food from yesterday."

"Well I guess you won't have to cook for a couple of days."

"We're watching television and talking, so take your time."

Roscoe came to Anthony with the bag of food. "Here, Mr. Laurent," he said, handing him the bag.

"Thanks, Roscoe. I will check in tomorrow. Call me if you need anything tonight."

Anthony headed for his car, but Myra stopped him. "You gonna eat all of that alone?"

He continued to his car. "Stay in your lane, Myra," he replied, waving over his head and getting inside the car.

Anthony started his engine and backed out without hesitation. He could see Myra standing in the parking lot with her hands on her hips. He shifted the sports car into overdrive and sped away.

When he entered the house, he had Solana, the meal and a small pizza for Zane. He found Tashia and Zane together on the couch watching television. Tashia looked up and smiled.

"I promised a certain young man a pizza if he finished his drink." Anthony saw an empty glass and a smiling Zane. He handed the frail boy the entire box of pizza and picked up the glass from the table. "Thank you for putting in the effort."

Zane opened the box of pizza and immediately dove in.

"Zane! You are not going to eat all of that are you?" Tashia asked.

"Yes," he answered and they all laughed.

"I may not see you tonight, but I will drop Zander off." Anthony winked at Tashia, kissed Solana, and headed back out the door, realizing he had just made his life more complicated, but he didn't care because for the first time in a long time he was happy. He had a family.▢

Janet's Return

The club was quiet when Anthony arrived. Dancers were scurrying, trying to get in place. When Anthony entered his office, Snow was waiting.

Anthony walked by the albino, hung his jacket on the wall hook, and sat hard behind his desk. Scanning his desk, he saw there was a drink already poured. He looked at Snow and knew whatever he had to tell him was going to be heavy so he lifted the glass and threw his head back, drinking it all in one gulp. He returned the now empty glass to the desk and Snow refilled his glass. Anthony looked at him long before lifting the glass, again, and repeated his previous task. When he returned the glass to his desk, he placed it upside down. "Spill it."

"Janet's back," Snow said, calmly.

Anthony fell silent. He leaned his head back in the tall chair. Janet was before Myra, and Janet was wild. She was loud and brash. What he enjoyed most was her freakiness. "That's not a problem," he said, trying more to convince himself.

Snow tilted his head to the side. "I just freshly painted my nails and I don't want no shit out of you bitches. You know she is wild and out of control. I think you need to stay your ass back here tonight. You are in a good place with Tashia and I have never seen you this happy or calm. Let's keep you there." Snow threw his head back and crossed his legs, irritated by the entire situation.

"That's fine, because I *am* in a good place and don't want any drama either. If she ask I'm working and don't have time." Anthony unlocked his desk drawer and pulled out his ledger to begin working.

"Good," Snow replied and stood to leave. "If you need something call my cell," he added and left the office.

After Snow left, Anthony did think about Janet for the first time in months. He thought she moved on and found a man. He wondered if she still did the tricks they used to do. He used to tell her that Halloween had nothing on her, she was trick and treat all in one.

He reached for his phone and called Tashia. She answered just when he was about to hang up. "Hey, what are you doing," he asked.

"Taking a nap before you come through."

"Who said I was coming through and why do you need to rest before I get there?" he asked, smiling.

"I don't want to fall asleep on you." He could hear her smile through the phone. Just hearing her smile made him want to leave now and he thought it might be a good idea with Janet in the club.

"Maybe I'll come now and come back here in the morning."

"That would be great."

"Then I'm on my way," he said, packing everything back in his desk. Anthony grabbed his jacket off the hook on the wall and made his way to the back door. He heard the commotion behind him, but didn't turn, allowing his bouncers to handle it. He had been driving his sports car recently. He usually didn't drive it, but Tashia asked him why he had it if he wasn't going to drive it.

When he arrived, the house was dark. He texted her to open the door so he wouldn't wake the kids. He saw the door open and Tashia stepped outside in a short robe. Her hair was straight and hung past the middle of her back. He had never seen her hair straight before. He found it to be sexy.

He climbed his long legs from the car and met her on the porch. They entered the small home and sat in the great room. When she sat with him, he ran his hands through her hair almost instinctively. Grabbing her hair, he pulled her in closer and softly kissed her. "You're beautiful," he whispered in her ear, grabbing under her thighs to pull her even closer.

"Stop." She interlocked her fingers with his. "How was your day?"

"Long. No very long," he answered, still smiling. "How is my boy? Did he finish his pizza?"

"He wants to go back to school tomorrow."

"If you want we can pick up where we left off."

Tashia smiled and leaned on his chest. "I like this, but I go back to work tomorrow."

Anthony thought about his visitor and guessed it best to share that part of his past with her. He knew that eventually she would run into her at the club.

"I do want to talk to you about something," he started. "I had a visitor today."

"Who? Myra?"

"*No*," he answered, shaking his head. "About a year ago I was with a girl named Janet. She's wild and unruly, rude, brash, and the list can go on. Well she showed up at the club today." He didn't see any change in her poker face, but he felt a slight tension change in her body. "No worries. I just wanted to tell you because I didn't speak to her so I'm sure she'll be back."

"Why did you tell me this?"

"I used to be involved with her," he said, looking her in her eyes. There was no change.

"Okay."

He ran his hand down the side of her face. "I was no angel when you met me and I come with a past. I just don't want my past to interfere with us. I figured if I let you know what's going on, no one can catch you off guard."

"Okay, thanks for telling me, but is that the real reason you left early?" she asked, looking into his eyes now for the truth.

"Partially," he started. "When Snow told me she was there I thought about you and how happy I've been over these past days and I didn't feel like the drama. I like the place I'm in and the feeling I get when with you, so here I am."

Tashia smiled. "You are a sweet talker."

"You still tired?" he asked, smiling.

"I just got a second wind."

Anthony ran his hand under her rob, feeling her teddy. "If you were going to bed early what's all this?" He pulled her in close and kissed her to let her know he missed her. "Can Zander keep an eye out and we make a run?" he asked.

"For how long?"

"A couple hours."

"I'll get dressed and let him know." She left him on the couch with his thoughts.

Anthony led Tashia into Reggae and sat at their table in the back, although the people on the wait list protested.

"Who do you know that we never have to wait?" she asked.

"The owner." He smiled.

Myra was across the room, so he nodded to her. He saw her jaws twitch as she realized she was wrong in her assumptions earlier. He whispered in the hostess's ear and a woman appeared and took their order. "Did you want something to eat?"

"No. I want a Jolly Rancher," she told the waitress.

Anthony told the waitress what he wanted and she disappeared. Anthony leaned over her with his arm around her shoulder. He whispered in her ear. "Don't look, but here comes your favorite friend." He purposely kissed Tashia long and very intimately. Myra stopped her approach and walked back across the room. He deliberately lingered at Tashia's neck with hopes Myra would get the message and leave him alone.

"Be nice," Tashia said, pushing him. But, he just kissed her again, this time moving to her breast. Tashia laughed at his silliness.

Their drinks came and Anthony moved in closer so they would not have to yell to one another. "How are you today?" he asked.

Tashia thought about his question. "I feel better when I'm with you."

"Good," he whispered and ran his hand down her arm, sending chills through her body.

She watched him and saw he was in a playful mood. He was relaxed. She saw something else in his eyes. She saw surrender. He bit his lower lip, which always turned her on. Trying to cover her desire, she turned her head and looked across the room, but he just turned it back to face him again. Smiling, she looked away again.

"You want me, don't you?" he asked, smiling.

Tashia looked back at him, enjoying this fun side, and moved in closer. Leaning into him, she pretended to kiss him and when he leaned into her, she diverted to his neck, slowly moving to his chest, biting lightly on his nipple through his shirt.

"Oh, shit," he whispered. "You're playing dirty now because I can't do that."

Diva Dorreen

He bit his lower lip, again. "Te quiero, bebe *(I love you, bebe)*," she said in Spanish. "Pense en ti todo el dia. *(I thought of you all day)*" She kissed his neck, again. "I want you and I've been thinking about you..."

"I know what it means. I speak very fluent Española," he whispered, catching her lips with his teeth. His tongue darted past her lips as he forgot where he was.

Tashia could feel his heart beating heavily in his chest. His kisses were intoxicating and soon her breathing picked up to meet his. "Can we go back to your place? I want you right now." She pulled away, searching his face for an answer.

Anthony appeared to be contemplating something. Without warning, he pulled her from the booth, almost dragging her with his arm around her waist. He waved to the waitress and pointed to the table, letting her know they were done with it.

Tashia's feet barely skimmed the floor as he took her down the back hall to a door next to the kitchen. He pulled out a key and unlocked the door. Tashia looked at him puzzled. *How did he get keys?* Before she could think much longer, she was in the room and he was locking the door behind them.

"Anthony who's—"

"Shut up, Shia, and let me drive," he said, remembering her words their first night together. "I want you now and have thought about nothing but making love to you all day." He pulled her shirt over her head and she did the rest while he undressed himself. Once they were both naked, he stopped to take her in with only the moonlight through the blinds. Her straightened hair hung covering her breast down to her naval. Her Aztec bronze skin glowed even through the natural night light. "My God, you are beautiful." Running his hand between her breasts, moving down to her ready and wet creases, he played gently between her folds. "Damn, you're wet."

"Callarse y unidad," she said, leaping into his arms and wrapping her legs around him. "Shut up and drive."

Anthony watched Tashia as she danced for him while putting her clothes back on. She was smiling at him, making exotic moves. He walked to her and held her as she continued to dance. He sambaed with her for a few stances, whispering in her ear, "We have to get out of this room before the manager comes back here with *his* key."

"Who's office is this?" she asked, as she continued to dance all around him.

Anthony knew she already knew the answer to that. "You already know."

They both dressed and headed out of the office.

"Wait! How do I look?" she asked, smiling.

He smiled and opened the door, thrusting them back in the hustle and bustle of the restaurant. "Let me get you home, because this is a school night for Zander and you have to go to work tomorrow."

Anthony held Tashia under his arm as they walked through the crowded restaurant. He heard his name called through the room and looked up to see Janet standing at their table. She made her way to them, ignoring Tashia.

"I came past the club and you left without acknowledging I was there," she said, with her hands on her ample hips and head shaking.

"Hello, Janet," was all he said. He could feel Tashia shift and pulled her closer. Janet noticed and looked Tashia up and down.

Tashia didn't break eye contact. She had a different level of confidence than Myra and Janet reminded her of the bold girls in her hood. Tashia looked up to Anthony and asked, "You ready?"

"Yes," he answered. "I hope all is well with you, Janet, but you need not stop by again. Take care of yourself."

Anthony continued to guide Tashia through the crowd and out the door. He was quiet during the walk, not knowing what to say. He had never been in this position. He actually cared what this woman thought.

"Breathe, Anthony, I'm good," she said, pinning him to the car to change the mood. She kissed him to rekindle what they shared just moments ago.

He lifted her, placing her on the hood of his car. "Let's go home," he whispered, kissing her neck.

Janet watched from the back door of the restaurant. She was upset that she had been dismissed. She would come back to see him, again, and he *would* talk to her.

145

Happy Anniversary

Preston held Cuyler, rubbing her growing belly. He felt the tiny foot kick. The anticipation of the baby's arrival was exciting. He couldn't sleep, so he watched her as she slept. She glowed and seemed much calmer than her previous pregnancy. She was much happier and less emotional.

He was still worried about the visitor and stopped past her office often. He no longer saw any fear in her concerning the incident and she seemed to have put it behind her. He made sure to remind her always to have her guard up and watch her surroundings. She now had a permit to carry her gun, and she did.

"Go to sleep, Preston."

"I'm sorry. I didn't mean to wake you."

"You didn't wake me. The baby did," she explained. "Why are you up?"

"Looking at you."

She rolled over and looked to see him. "Why are you up, Preston?"

"I was thinking about having a family dinner for our anniversary."

"You were up for that?" Cuyler looked him in the eyes. "Liar," she said, laughing and snuggling under him. "You worry too much."

"As long as you don't have to, I'm good with that. I was thinking we could go to my dad's for a little. School is almost out and we could take Tashia's kids and Callia."

"I like that idea."

"I already talked to my dad and he would love to have us all."

"I miss him so much." Her forehead wrinkled as she thought on her words. "It's funny, I think about him every day and I don't think of my own mother at all." She was wide-awake now.

"Hmm," Preston responded more out of sympathy for their relationship. He still thought about his mother, even though she was deceased.

"Blaine will be in town next week. He said they are coming for some special concert or something. He wants to spend a couple of days with us and he is bringing a guest."

Cuyler perked up at the thought of Blaine bringing someone. He was such a playboy. She giggled, imagining him fawning over someone. "Blaine has a girl?"

"I know, right?" He teased her using a line he heard her use with Meagan and Candace.

"This is going to be interesting to see," she said, chuckling.

Cuyler ran her hand down Preston's smooth chest. "Now that you have me fully awake, do you think you can put me back to sleep?" she whispered in his ear.

His laughter started from the depth of his belly. She always amazed him. Lately she was insatiable. "You're so nasty," he whispered, grabbing her behind, pulling her in closer and the festivities began. He knew what she wanted and he would make sure to take care of her.

When Cuyler awoke, she looked at the clock and saw it was eight-thirty. "Oh my, God," she said, flopping back down on the pillows. She had a ten o'clock appointment and needed to start her day. The house was silent, which told her Preston and Callia were gone. She vaguely remembered Callia lying next to her, stroking her hair calling her. She smiled thinking of her angel.

"Time to make the donuts," she said, and got out of bed to start her day. She got on her knees to pray for her family.

147

Group

Marissa sat in group, listening to members discuss their trespasses and how sorry they were for them. She was quiet, not willing to participate, but mostly she was quiet because her medication subdued her senses.

"Marissa. Would you like to say something?" Dr. Davis asked for the fifteenth time since being at the facility.

"No." She was so tired of him trying to get her to participate. She just wanted to do her time and get out. They had her on a series of medication that helped her to separate reality from her vivid imagination. The voices she heard had dissipated as well. There was nothing there telling her things about people and she was left to discern them on her own.

When the meeting was over, Dr. Davis asked her to stay. She was sure he was going to talk to her about participating, again, but he surprised her when he did not.

"Are you getting anything from group, Marissa?"

She wanted to tell him she didn't belong there, and these people needed help. She wanted to tell him there was nothing wrong with her, but then she would have to explain why she shot her fiancé Preston.

She had been there for over two years and had learned the game. "Oh, yes! The sessions are helping a lot. I just don't want to have them look at me like I am crazy." She smiled at her humor.

"You have to participate if you plan to ever get out of here. I have nothing to put in my reports if you don't."

Marissa thought about what he was saying. She needed to leave there before Preston forgot about her. When he went away to school, the distance made him forget about her. He started seeing another woman and she had to visit her to let her know he was hers. She didn't realize at first, but after several visits, she soon understood.

"I understand, Dr. Davis. I will try, but I don't like to talk to everyone about my issues, because they will look at me differently."

"Group is for everyone, but mostly it's there to help you to work out some things before you meet with me. I will meet with you later and we can talk more."

Marissa went to the game room. She would watch the guys play chess and maybe a card game or two would be going on.

Things Fall Apart

Fridays were always hectic for Anthony. It was one of the busiest days at the club and the restaurant. Sometimes he had to go back and forth between the two. He tried to be at the club on Fridays because it was one of Tashia's only nights to work and the crowd was a little rowdier.

He sat in his office reviewing two weeks of neglected book entries. Everything seemed to be in order, but he could see the income on alcohol had declined while the supply price increased. This usually indicated he had a thief. He would have to spend a little more time in the building. Since he and Tashia were together, he was mainly there when she was there. He had to get his business back in order.

There was a knock at the door. Snow poked his head in. "Feel like company?"

Anthony motioned for him to come in. Carrying a drink in his hand, Snow made his way across the room, placing the drink in from of Anthony. Anthony looked at the drink then to Snow. The last time he brought him a drink Janet was there. He leaned back in his chair and sighed.

"Do I need to drink first or can I wait?" Snow looked at him in silence. Anthony picked up the drink and swallowed in one gulp. "Ahhhh!"

"Janet is back."

"So? I told her not to come back, but as long as she is a paying customer and not causing any trouble I cannot do anything about her coming," Anthony said, irritated by the new situation. His father always said he couldn't outrun his past.

Snow pulled a flask out of his coat pocket and poured Anthony another drink. "Take your time with that one," he suggested.

"I don't have time for this bull, Snow. Take me to the plot of this story!"

Snow sighed. "She met Tashia in the parking lot and had words with her," Snow began the tale, but before he could continue Anthony was out of his seat and headed for the door.

"Stop! She asked me to tell you she would speak with you later. She needed to get her head together before her set!"

Anthony stood with the door half-open, still ready to spurt down the hall to the dancer's lounge. He was debating on whether to honor her request or go anyway. "Damn it! Damn it! Damn it!" he yelled, slamming the door. Just when he was at his happiest. He wondered what Janet said to Tashia to have her shook, because she could not be easily shaken. She knew how to deal with women like Janet. "Did she say anything else?"

"She told me to tell you to talk to her because if she gets in her face, again, she would handle her."

Anthony came back to his desk and sat down hard, causing the chair to roll backward. The last thing he wanted to do was to speak with Janet. He didn't want to go back to that ratchet life.

Janet had gotten the closest to him of all the woman of his past. She was a gold digger. She used him until she met one of the local ballers and left. He didn't miss her, but to know she lied and schemed irritated him. He felt as though she had taken him off his game. He was totally oblivious to what was happening and hadn't figured her out to be the using bitch she was.

He knew he was a dog, but he never presented himself as anything other than. He never led anyone on to believe their relationship was going to be a love story. Janet spun a web of trickery. "Go ahead and find her and show her back to my office."

Snow left the office to do Anthony's bidding. He wanted this over as well. He couldn't have his number one upset and the quicker Anthony could resolve the situation the better.

Tashia sat on the floor, stretching and pretending to meditate. She knew nothing about meditation, but she felt it would keep others from asking her questions, but she could feel their eyes on her. When she entered the club with a wild woman in tow, she handled the situation the best she could without flaking on her. The information she shared had Tashia's head swimming although she knew it had nothing to do with her. She could not hold him accountable for things that happened before them, but nonetheless she couldn't shake it.

She stood and looked in her wardrobe. Anthony had gotten her one so she could leave her costumes at the club and not take them home after every show. She felt nasty tonight, so she pulled out the most seductive costume she had. The costume exposed her cheeks in a way the chaps couldn't. In the chaps, her front and thighs were covered. This costume left nothing to the imagination. The top was simply a bustier.

After donning her costume, she looked at her body in the mirror and began to have second thoughts about her decision. She looked damn good and knew this would be trouble. She wanted to go and let Anthony know she was calm and okay, knowing he would worry.

She didn't hear Snow come in. "Where the hell are you wearing that?" he asked with concern. "Tashia! I know you are upset, but they will tear the freaking club up!"

"I don't have time to change now!" she said, looking at the time. "Tell Anthony I will dance with him tonight and that will keep the club calm." She winked and danced around Snow, knowing it did nothing for him.

"If I wasn't gay I would do you right now in that outfit," he told her.

Tashia laughed now, feeling lighter and kissed Snow on the mouth. "You still feel gay?"

Snow pushed her away, laughing. "Damn, girl, that ass is still looking good."

One of the barmaids burst in the room. "Snow, we need the key to get some liquor out of the special inventory. We have a VIP in the house."

"Here I come." He stood and left with the barmaid.

"Don't forget to tell Anthony!" Tashia yelled, but Snow was gone. She would have to tell Anthony herself.

Anthony sat irritated across the desk from Janet. She had been coy about her message since she walked into the office and he wanted her to get to the point.

Before Tashia, he would have marveled at her still tight body. Her small waist flared to an ample bottom that seemed a little larger than normal, but she wore it well. She had died her hair blond, which accented her green eyes. She was lighter than Tashia and slightly shorter. He saw she had a breast job and her new breasts were spilling over her top. She was still the beautiful woman he remembered.

Before he could finish taking inventory, someone knocked on his door. It was security. They had a VIP in the house and wanted to know if he wanted them to close off a section.

"We go over this for a reason. If I am not here everyone should know what to do," he answered, irritated. He covered his mouth with his hand and thought for a minute. "Put them in section one and rope it off. Assign two team members and an exclusive barmaid. Tell them to get a card number and run a tab."

When security left, Janet was still digging, trying to get information out of him. "Your girl is on fleek," she started. "She has a mouth on her, too, but I didn't peg you as a dancer type. I saw you with someone much classier." She uncrossed her legs and crossed them again.

She still played games. He could see through her now. He knew her game. "Look, Sharon Stone, unless you have something to say to me, I need to get to work...."

"You have a daughter, Anthony," she said. Now standing, she faced him, waiting for a reaction, but he didn't react.

Anthony's mind caught up to the meaning of what she was saying. He stood and walked to the file cabinets that flanked the back wall, pulling at his mouth. "What are you talking about? We haven't been together—"

"Since last year. I know. I didn't tell you sooner because my friend said he would raise her as his, but I needed to give you the opportunity by letting you know the truth." She sat on the end of the desk.

Anthony wondered what her game was this time. Child support? He didn't trust her. "What kind of game are you playing, Janet?"

"It's not a game! She's yours!"

Janet stood again, looking at him, waiting. He put on his best poker face and sat at his desk, again. "Why are you really here, Janet?"

"I told you, to let you know you had a child," she answered calmly.

Snow entered. He seemed surprised that Anthony was still in the office. "Oh, I'm sorry, I thought you would be on the floor in light of what's happening. I just need the key to the special inventory room. I forgot you changed the locks and I didn't change mine out."

Anthony saw he was trying to give him a way out, if he needed. He reached in his pocket and tossed the key to him, shooing him, letting him know he was fine. Snow retreated from the room and nodded to Anthony, pointing to his watch to remind him Tashia was about to go on. Anthony threw his head back in acknowledgment.

"I know I played games with you in the past, but this is a child's life. I'm not going to play with my child.

"I know I did you dirty, but it was just sex. Remember?" she added, reminding him of their conversations.

"We used protection, so how did this happen?"

"No protection is one hundred, Anthony." He could feel her looking for some sign from him, but he still gave none.

"Then there is nothing left but to take a paternity test and we can talk, again, once the results come back."

An angered Janet came around the desk. Anthony stood, remembering her being very aggressive. He didn't want to be caught off guard. She reached for him, grabbing him in the chest.

"This is not one of your business deals, Anthony! You are still a cold son of a bitch! All cool and collected. This is our child you are talking about like she is a transaction. You may have treated me like business, but if that's how you are going to treat her then screw you, Anthony," she yelled at him, now crying. "Do you know how hard it was for me to come here? I could have let my friend raise her and you would have never known."

The smooth collected Janet had unraveled. He watched her, but had no compassion. "You came here, Janet, because I am your back up plan in case he finds out the baby is not his." He smiled at her, now understanding her true intent for coming to tell him. "Maybe we should both be tested at the same time," he said, calmly.

The door to his office swung open again. "Damn it! Does anyone ever fucking knock?" he yelled, instantly regretting his words. It was Tashia. "Tashia, I will talk to you later, close my door!"

Janet still had her hands in his chest and he held her wrist. He could see Tashia go from zero to one hundred. She left his office with not so much as a word. Now he was angry again. "Call me when you have a date and time set," he said, pulling her hands from his shirt.

"She is yours and I will bury you with this one," she said, angrily.

"Call me, don't come by, when you have a date and time set up. I'm not angry, but there is nothing to discuss until I have proof." He returned to his seat. "Good night, Janet."

A disgruntled Janet stormed out of the office. Security peeped into the office and Anthony gave him the cut sign, which indicated he wanted her out of his club.

Sitting in his chair, he tried to gather his thoughts. He could not wrap his mind around what she was telling him. *A baby?* If he had to deal with her for eighteen years, he didn't know what he would do. He closed his eyes, but knew he needed to go to the floor for Tashia's set.

Gathering himself, he left his office and made his way down the hall and went to the front. He saw that the VIP section had been set up correctly. The VIP was one of the Island's most popular actors right now. He made his way to the front and saw Tashia for the first time. He stopped in his steps. He caught the look on Snow's face as he looked away from Anthony.

Tashia twisted and contorted up and down the pole as he had become accustomed, but she was almost naked. She was hot nonetheless but he didn't like the type of attention she was getting.

She dismounted off the stage, which she only did when he was seated in front of her for her protection, but she was angry and he could tell by the edginess in her dance. She went to their guest of honor and became his private dancer.

Tashia finished, stretching and put on her prizefighter robe. She didn't know if Snow had said anything to Anthony, so she made her way to his office. When she opened the door, she was not prepared to see Janet almost in Anthony's arms. She knew he didn't know it was her when he cursed, but he knew who she was when he dismissed her.

She left his office angry, but more importantly she didn't have time to change her costume. She stormed down the hall and was about to walk through the room to mount from the floor, but Snow grabbed her.

"I can't let you do this, Shia! They will tear this place up." She tried to pull from his grip, but his strong arms held her. "Calm down before someone sees you like this. Breathe! Breathe! Don't let her get the best of you. She doesn't mean anything to him," he whispered in her ear. "You are going to have to dance in what you have on, but promise me you will not go on the floor."

His words calmed her. Her breathing slowed. "I'm good, Snow. Let me go," she said, releasing her breath slowly. Tashia walked to the top of the stairs and after a moment, she raised her fingers, indicating which song she wanted Terrance to play.

"Now back after a short hiatus, she will leave you breathless. I know I loose my breath every time she dances. Back by popular demand is SSSSSHHHHHIIIIIIIAAA!" Terrance announced.

Tashia sauntered on the floor, slow and deliberate, with the music she chose. She needed to be a little edgier tonight. She needed to dance hard to cut her tension.

She mounted the first pole swinging slowly with graceful ballerina type moves. Then she moved to the second pole, swinging faster.

She was oblivious to the patrons in the room as she escaped into her own world. She hid in that place where only she existed, remaining there as long as she could.

She dropped the prize fighter robe, revealing her seductive prize fighter costume. Her movements brought back memories of when she was a young girl, dancing to forget her hardships. Her graceful moves stretched her limbs to their limit, taking the patrons to her world – Shia's world. By the time she reached the first pole, the crowd was wildly pressing against the stage to get closer to her.

She climbed to the top of the pole. She could feel the patrons waiting for her death drop, but she did them one better. She spun and worked her way back up the pole and spun like an acrobat, again, down the pole. On her third trip up the pole, she gave them what they wanted—the death drop. At the completion of the drop, her back arched and she was looking their VIP guest in the eye. She also saw

Anthony making his way to the front of the section, but he was too late.

Tashia quickly gripped the pole and dismounted, making her way to their guest. When she reached him, she saw Anthony stop his advancement. She danced around their guest, dragging her hand up his shoulder then around his neck. She came back around and straddled him just for an instant, hopping back up, turning in the other direction she sat on his lap and then stood and twerked for an instant.

The crowd began to push in at the ropes and security held them back, but she could see she had to return to the stage before someone got hurt. Hands were reaching in, trying to get a feel, but they were not able to get close.

Tashia sat on his lap and spun one last time, preparing to make her way back to the stage and it happened. The guest reached down and grabbed her crouch full frontal.

"How much?" he whispered, sliding his finger inside of her.

Tashia turned and smacked him across his face, but he just laughed and became more physical, pulling her into his chest. "My God, you're beautiful," he said, his mouth on her neck now.

"No touching," she heard security yell at him, but he was unable to get to her for pushing the crowd back.

Tashia kneed the guest in his groin and hit him in the nose upward, sending him reeling back in pain. She was about to kick him when she felt herself being lifted off her feet.

Anthony shielded her as he rushed her through the crowd to the back corridor, carrying her in his arms. He kept moving until they were in his office and behind closed doors. An angry Tashia fought to get out of his grip, but failed.

"What the hell were you thinking, Tashia!" he yelled, not putting her down. "I have rules in place for a reason. You could have been hurt!"

She balled up in his arms, somewhat shaken by the incident, not saying anything. What *was* she thinking? What did she believe she would accomplish by her actions? She was out of control. This man had her twisted, caught up in his game.

She didn't respond to his words, half understanding what he was saying, and then she realized he was speaking in his native tongue. "What!" she yelled.

"Did he touch you? What happened? Are you okay?" he was bombarding her with the questions all at once and her head was spinning. Now calm she didn't want him to put her down. She felt safe.

Anthony was whispering in her ear now softly, trying to calm down. "Did he touch you, Tashia?" She heard the edge in his voice.

She didn't answer, knowing how he would react. He was a protector and he could lose everything he worked for because of her stupidity. "I," she started. "I'm okay, Anthony. I'm okay," she said, calmly.

"Don't lie to me, Tashia," he said, his chest still rising and falling from the adrenaline pumping through him. She could feel the tension in the muscles of his arms. "You smacked him, so don't you lie to me. You were ready to kick him."

He was frightening her now with his heightened rage. She knew he knew the truth and needed her conformation to go back to the club floor to finish what she had begun. She held him tightly, tears streaming down her face because of what she had started, because she could not be an adult concerning their earlier altercation.

"Stay here with me, Anthony. Don't lose everything you've worked for because I was being a stupid, angry girl," she pleaded. "Please, let it go. Please," she begged and kissed him lightly. "I'm sorry."

He sat with her in his lap, holding her until Snow entered.

Anthony held her, hoping this would be enough to subdue his anger, but he was not sure it would be. He saw the surprise on her face when she turned and slapped their VIP. If he had not reached her she would have kicked, clawed, and scratched his eyes out.

Snow entered the office. "We got everyone calmed down. Our guest was escorted out. Security told him it was for his safety," Snow updated Anthony. "Tashia, here is your bag so you can remain here until you are ready to be escorted out."

"Thank you, Snow," she replied. "I'm sorry."

"You know how to close out a night, I'll give you that, but are you okay? He grabbed you pretty hard!"

"I'm okay, Snow," she said, cutting him off. He winked and returned to the club.

She trembled in Anthony's arms and he realized she was cold. He picked up the throw on the couch and placed it around her shoulders. "Better?" he asked.

"No," she answered. "I feel foolish."

"You should feel naked." He chuckled.

She chuckled as well, realizing how much she was not wearing. She snuggled closer to him.

"Why don't you get what you need out of your bag so you can get warm," he suggested. "I am going back to the floor to make sure everything has calmed down."

Once out of his office, Anthony immediately looked for Snow. He wanted to know what happened. He couldn't let it go. He had let her down, being caught up in his past.

Snow was directing some of the girls when he approached.

"Is our girl okay?"

"She'll be okay. Just a little heated."

"I'm glad you got her when you did. She was about to let him have it, but he deserved it."

"Do you believe he meant to grab her?"

Snow looked at Anthony. "I guess he accidentally went in her panties, too!" he said in disbelief, but quickly realized Anthony wasn't sure what happened. He was baiting him. "Hey, man, he's gone. Good riddance. Let it go. She handled herself."

"I know, but I should have been there." Anthony headed back to the office to clean up his mess.

Tashia was fully dressed in her jeans when he entered the office. She wouldn't look at him. She was still angry. He approached her, but she picked up her bag and pushed past him.

"I'm sorry about what happened in your place. I'll get Snow to walk me out."

Anthony pushed the door closed, causing her to stop. "Let's talk," he whispered in her ear. "Explain what part of what I did made you so angry you thought it was a good idea to go out half naked. Tell me that, Tashia," he said, as calmly as he could, now angry about how she was handled.

"Anthony, I don't want to talk about this now. I want to go home," she said, tensely.

"You are going to get to go home, but we will talk first."

Tashia spun around, dropping her bag on the floor. She walked to the coach and flopped down. "So talk."

Anthony walked to her and stooped to her sitting level. "Why did you do this?"

Tashia didn't answer him. She sat staring. When she did not answer, he stood and sat next to her on the coach. He pulled her closer and sighed. "What did I do, Tashia?"

"If you don't know you will do it again."

"You're right. If I don't know, I will do it again. So tell me."

Tashia was tight-lipped initially. "I wasn't supposed to dance for him I was supposed to be dancing for you. When I came into your office and you were with Janet she was all up in your chest and you treated me like you did Myra the day she walked in on us."

Anthony nodded his head. Pulling her with him, he leaned back on the coach. He could feel her body relax in his arms. "I apologize for that, but I can say her hands on my chest were not a friendly gesture. She was grabbing me up. The reason I was short with you is because I didn't know it was you initially. When I saw it was you I didn't want you here at that moment," he tried to explain. "I apologize for my tone. I was not trying to make you feel little or make her feel she was important. When you walked in we were in a heated argument."

"I was stupid and angry," she said. "I am sorry."

Anthony looked away to ask the hard questions. "What happened, Tashia?" he turned to search her face. "And don't tell me nothing."

Tashia attempted to pull away, but couldn't. "Leave it alone, Anthony. Everything that happened I brought on myself." She looked at him now searching him. "What we do here is one step away from being a whore. That's why men come here. They come for the fantasy. That's why I do what I do when I leave. Some girls get caught up and believe these men calling their names are some kind of celebrity status. The bottom line is they want to have sex with you.

"I know who I am and I know my worth. I don't need a man having sex with me or wanting to have sex with me to validate my womanhood. Some do.

"That's why I don't blame him for what happened tonight. I crossed that line. This environment and places like this give men like him the false impression that we are nothing." He could hear the hurt in her words. "I removed all those barriers that limited him when I went on that floor," she said, her voice cracking, but she quickly recomposed herself. "Leave it alone, Anthony."

He marinated on her words, but they didn't put any closure on what he was feeling. "No."

Tashia attempted to get up again, but could not. "Let me go home, Anthony!"

"If I had not gotten to you, you would have really hurt him. You were angry and I want to know what happened, Tashia? What did he do to take you to that place?" He held her face, forcing her to look at him. "Just say it. I promise I won't do anything to retaliate."

He watched the tears stream down her face as she shed what he wanted to shed so many times and had no one to shed them with. He understood her anger. He had been that angry before. He was always angry as a child, but the patience of a father calmed an angry little boy many years ago. He learned, as she had, to keep them below the surface, hidden away from the rest of the world.

"He took me back to that basement where I said I would never go again, but I escorted him there. I invited him and teased him, daring him. I created that fantasy, but I gave him the false allusion that the fantasy was real, so he touched me in my most inner private parts." She grabbed between her legs. "I didn't want him to touch me, but I led him there," she cried. "So leave it alone, Anthony, because it was my fault." She pulled away from him and picked up her discarded bag. "I'm damn good at what I do and that is why I dance in those boundaries, because for some of them the fantasy is real."

Anthony saw the raw uncut Tashia. The pain she hid between her cracks was showing. He grabbed her around her waist to keep her from leaving again. To keep her from opening it, he put his hand on the door and pressed her against it, keeping her from escaping her feelings. He whispered in her ear, "Stop pretending with me, Shia. You're not okay. Be real with me," he told her. "You can trust me with your most intimate secrets. I'm here for you."

"Is that what you're doing with *me*? Sharing your most intimate parts?" she asked. "You broke down on me and you shoved your feelings right back in their hiding place." She turned to face him and saw the torment on his face. "I show you mine and you keep yours?"

He knew she was waiting for his answer. He wasn't afraid of her knowing his secrets; he was afraid of her leaving him once she knew his dark, seedy life. "I don't know if you can handle my secrets, Tashia. I barely have a hold of them."

"What I just heard was trust me, Tashia, but I can't trust you." She stared at him, waiting, but he couldn't deny nor confirm her beliefs. "That's what I thought." She turned back to the door. "I will get Snow to walk me to my car." She looked over her shoulder. "My friend told me once 'it's okay not to be okay'."

Tashia opened the door, but before she left, she turned and hugged him like she had the night of his breakdown. "I love you with all my heart. I would never hurt you. You have to trust someone, Anthony. Call me when you are ready to trust me with your deepest private secrets. But, we can't go any further until you can trust me fully with *your* secrets." Tashia kissed him intimately. "Goodbye."

Tashia left Anthony standing in his office alone as he was the night she first walked into his club.

Tashia found Snow running around in the back. She walked to him. "Snow, can you get me out of here?" she asked about to breakdown.

Snow looked back to Anthony's office and saw the door was closed. "Sure, Princess, but where is Anthony?"

"Snow, I can't hold this together much longer. Please!"

"Sure. Sure."

Snow dropped the prop on the floor and put his arm around her shoulder. He escorted her through the crowded hallway to the back door. All eyes were on her, but Snow pulled her closer. She heard a few people whispering.

"Is she okay?"

"Where is the Boss?"

"She's so pretty."

Once at her car, she broke down. He held her until she pulled herself together. "Tomorrow is my last night, so can you pack my things when you get in, Snow?"

"Your last night!"

"If tonight taught me anything it was just because I'm good at it doesn't mean I have to do it." She laughed, but became serious. "Take care of him, Snow. He is so dear to me and he needs someone. He just doesn't know it." Tashia hugged and kissed him before getting into her car.

When Snow entered the office, Anthony was somber. He watched Snow as he sat in the chair on the other side of the desk. "This was a hell of a night."

"She's on her way home. She was pretty upset."

"I know," Anthony said, letting him into his secret circle. "Damn it!" he yelled, throwing his cup at the wall. The plastic cup bounced off the wall and fell to the floor, spilling its contents. "I didn't see tonight coming. I should have been there!"

"She's a good one, boss, and she's good for you. I've been working for you for over a year and I've never seen you this calm and happy." Snow paused. "Tonight, not included, of course."

Anthony looked at the peculiar man, taking in his words. He knew they were true. He needed a break. Maybe he would go away for a while. Maybe he needed to visit with his father.

Twenty minutes past with Snow babbling and him listening. His phone went off. It was Tashia texting she was home okay. "She's home okay."

"Fix this, Anthony. Don't let her slip through your fingers."

"Stay in your lane, Snow."

"When that girl balled at her car it wasn't about the guest. She was crying for you. She wanted to make sure *you* were taken care of. She asked me to take care of you."

Anthony tapped his fingers on the desk in silence.

Shall We Dance

The next two weeks were hard for Tashia. She had gotten accustomed to being with Anthony daily and she desperately missed his companionship. She missed him holding her, their conversations and the smell of his cologne. She missed his smart mouth, jokes, and him playing with the kids. In the short time they were together, they understood each other.

Zander picked up on her mood change. One day he asked why Anthony didn't come in when he dropped them off. Tashia told him Anthony was working on some things, but she knew he didn't believe that. Every day he dropped the kids off he texted her to see if they needed anything, but she always said no. She knew if they started any conversation she would let him back in and he would continue to hide. She needed him to trust her for their relationship to grow.

Today would be the first time she saw him in almost two weeks. She didn't know if she was going to Cuyler and Preston's party to celebrate their union or to see him. She wanted to see that he was okay.

She finished her makeup and put on her clothes. She didn't hear Zander come to the door.

"He's not going to be able to look at anyone else tonight, Mom, you look beautiful." Zander watched his mother check out herself in the mirror. "I hope you two fix things. He looks miserable and I can tell he wants to come in when he sees your car. I don't know what happened, but you need to fix it. This isn't working for either of you." When Tashia turned to speak, Zander was gone. He was too smart for his age.

Tashia sat in her car starring at the house. Preston had decorated the tree in the yard and the lights flickered. The kids helped decorate the tree the last weekend they visited. It reminded her of Christmas.

She looked down at her dress and wondered if it was too tight. She flat ironed her hair and wore it in a ponytail. She could still hear Zander's words echo in here head. What was she supposed to do when she saw him? What if he didn't come? Fear overtook her and she started her car. Just when she thought she had the nerve to go in, she decided to leave. The rap on her window startled her. It was Anthony.

He opened her door. "You leaving?" he asked.

She felt like a schoolgirl who the jock noticed. "No," she lied. "I was warming up before I went in."

Anthony smiled his wide grin, disarming her. "Stick with the truth, Tashia. You are not a good liar." He extended his hand and helped her out of her car. Reaching inside the car, he turned off the engine and the two walked to the door.

When Preston opened the door, he smiled at them standing there together. "Come in. We were waiting for you to get started. Tashia, you know your sister is pregnant and could eat all day."

Cuyler came around the corner. "Come on in. What took so long?" She hugged her sister and Anthony. "Now we can eat," she said, clapping her hands. The four laughed at her enthusiasm.

Anthony escorted Tashia to the dining area where the remaining guests were waiting. Preston blessed the food and everyone ate.

Preston seated Anthony and Tashia together, explaining they were the odd ones out. Everyone else there was coupled. Anthony assured him it was fine.

Tashia didn't eat much. She was much too nervous. She could feel Anthony watching her. She peeped at him and smiled nervously. In the middle of discussion with the guests, he put his hand on her leg, more out of habit, causing her to tremble.

A man who introduced himself as one of Cuyler's associates from her old law firm challenged Anthony on the subject of youth today and urban development.

"I hear you have a youth center for the underprivileged. I believe the youth of today is in the state they are because of their lack of guidance and supervision," the gentleman said.

Tashia saw Cuyler duck her head for fear of where the conversation would go. She felt Anthony tense at his words.

"Which youth are we referring to, the urban? Or, are you talking in general?" Anthony asked.

"Why yes, the urban youth," the gentleman answered.

"What is your name?" Anthony asked, now putting down his fork.

Tashia heard Meagan from the opposite side of her mumble, "Oh, shit," under her breath.

"My name is Malcolm, Malcolm Ross," he announced, as though he was James Bond.

"Well, Malcolm, can I call you Malcolm or would you prefer Mr. Ross?" Anthony asked, sounding very English as she had heard him do before.

"Malcolm would be fine."

"And you may call me Anthony. This urban generation, let's call them, have been forced to be adults way before their time, because they have been raised by parents who don't have a purpose or direction themselves. Do you have a purpose, Malcolm?" Anthony asked, leaning in.

"You don't have to answer that question it was rhetorical," he started. "Well a man who doesn't see his purpose in life floats aimlessly in life with no direction. He lives his life just surviving for his next check, the next meal, the next relationship, the next orgasm, whatever, but always waiting for the next thing he believes will make him happy.

"He doesn't care about anything, because this world has proved it doesn't care about him. His first lesson taught when he went to school and the teachers were as rude as those in his home. He is shown disrespect by those who are teaching him to be a leader in his community, disrespected by the police, who have been hired to protect him, and who use their authority as if they are above the very law they are hired to uphold, then he goes home to be disrespectfully called stupid, dumb, and told no one loves him by those who have never experienced love.

He is told he is disrespectful. He doesn't care if he lives because death has to be better than the hell he experiences on a daily basis. He is given no direction because a man with no purpose cannot direct.

"Then there are his offspring who, just by existing, daily remind him of his failures and the failure he is. Their directions become everything they see on the tele. They can't get direction from school, because the majority of those who teach them have taken jobs in their school, because no one else wanted to teach there. They are the leftovers who don't care if Jaquan, Davon, or Quanisha learn anything. They put in their time until they can find a teaching job in a *more desirable* area," Anthony said, with conviction. He was about to let Malcolm have it, but Tashia squeezed his thigh, disarming him by her touch.

"I think what Anthony is trying to say is, that's a broad subject and it could be discussed from so many angles, but I don't think we will resolve these issues in one night," Tashia offered, smiling, to bring the atmosphere back to normal. "If we could we would all be on some special task force, right?" she finished, laughing.

Malcolm laughed at her joke. "Anthony your wife is very smart."

"Oh, Anthony is not my husband. I am Cuyler's sister, Tashia. I was one of those urban children as was Cuyler, but we turned out just fine," she retorted now annoyed and tired of the gentleman.

This time, Anthony touched Tashia's leg to calm her. She couldn't breathe.

"Excuse me." She rose from the table. Some of the men at the table stood and watched as she walked from the dining area. She was sure Anthony watched as she departed. Again, she wondered if her dress was too tight.

"I didn't mean to offend her." Malcolm sounded concerned.

"Je ne sais pas s'il connait le sens du mot. *(I'm not sure if he knows the meaning of the word)*," Anthony said in French for Preston's ears only.

"That's not fair, Anthony, the rest of us were unable to understand what you just said," Malcolm scolded.

"I didn't want to offend anyone," Anthony said, standing to his feet. "I will go and make sure the young lady is okay."

"It was my fault. I can do that," Malcolm volunteered.

"You've done and said enough for one evening, Malcolm." Anthony went to look for Tashia.

Once in the small hallway, Tashia made her way to the powder room just in the foyer, but it was occupied. She took the stairs to the upper level and made her way to the hall bathroom. Once inside the door, she breathed for the first time since she had seen Anthony.

Tashia caught a glimpse of herself in the mirror and was amazed at how stunning she looked. Her dress was snug, but she did wear it well. Her makeup, though light, was flawless. She was glad she decided to wear her hair in a ponytail. The look was more effective than if she had worn it down.

She heard the faint knock on the door. "I'll be out in a minute," she announced and turned the water on and washed her hands before leaving the bathroom. When she opened the door, Anthony stood in the hall, leaning on the wall.

Anthony watched as Tashia excused herself from the table. He could feel his stomach drop as she walked across the room. He also saw the eyes of the other men in the room follow her. Tired of Malcolm and his ignorance, he stood and excused himself.

When he entered the foyer, another guest was leaving the bathroom. Looking around he didn't see her. Taking the stairs two at a time, he made his way upstairs and saw the light from the hall bathroom. He knocked lightly and heard her voice, making his stomach drop again. Leaning against the wall, he waited.

When the door opened, he could tell she was caught off guard to see him there. "Tashia," he said, not sure what her reaction would be. "I didn't get to tell you earlier that you look exquisite tonight."

"Just tonight?" she teased.

Anthony laughed lightly from his depths. She could always make him smile. He could see her breathing pick up.

"Well, I will see you downstairs," she announced and proceeded down the hall, leaving him there alone to deal with his feelings.

The night wore on and the guests moved to dancing in the basement. Candace and Meagan flanked Tashia. They asked about the kids and spoke briefly of their lives.

"I'm glad you came," Candace was saying, but she was not into the conversation as she watched available women in the room pursuing Anthony. She could feel his eyes burning through her soul as he stole glimpses of her.

Candace and Meagan moved on and she was grateful to be alone. She was about to walk over to Anthony when she was stopped by Malcolm. "Hello, my name is Malcolm. I used to work with your sister."

Tashia turned to see the good looking, but rude, Malcolm smiling at her. His tuxedo jacket showed off his broad shoulders and his piercing blue eyes were evident even in the dim lighting. "Pleased to meet you," she said, nodding.

"I can see beauty runs in your family. You are as beautiful as your sister," he said, as if giving her a compliment. What he didn't understand was Tashia never liked being compared to Cuyler. All her life she heard how beautiful Cuyler was.

Anthony caught her eye and she watched him walk to the deejay as she tried to carry on a conversation with Malcolm. Tashia never paid attention before, but realized for the first time that Terrance was spinning. Then she heard it, the first song they danced to, "We are Not Alone" by Demi Grace.

Anthony made his way across the room to her before the song had completed its first verse and Malcolm could start another conversation. He took her by the hand. "Excuse us, Malcolm, I would like to dance with the wife," he joked, pulling her to the dance floor.

Anthony was a great dancer. Whenever they danced to this song, he tangoed and half-sambaed with her. He moved his feet, spinning her and pulling her back, and then held her close, moving her with him and before she could get comfortable, he tangoed or spun her.

His cologne and closeness was too much for her to bear. She wanted him right then and there. It reminded her of their first night together. He leaned into her and whispered, "He pensado en nada mas que en ti desde esa noche en mi oficina, SShiiaaa, *(I've thought of nothing but you since that night in my office, Shia),*" he said in Spanish, half hissing her name, setting her on fire.

His words danced in her head. She had thought of nothing, but him since the night, too.

"I miss you," he whispered breathy in her ear. "Tashia, I have been breathless, because you are the air I breathe," he said, continuing to speak to her in Spanish. "You do that to me."

Her head was spinning. The drumline beat, sending her back to a motherland she had never experienced. Her chest rose and fell as her breath became more intense. They danced as though making love, oblivious of the presence of the audience that watched.

The song should have been over, but she realized Terrance was remixing it, making it seem endless. Anthony was working her, spinning then pulling her back. He held her, grinding in circles, holding her close, dancing behind her, taking her almost to the floor in a sitting position as he held her up with his strong thighs so she could feel his condition. "I want you, Tashia," he said, still speaking to her in Spanish."

She couldn't breathe. She couldn't speak. She saw him nod at Terrance as he rocked her from side to side. She heard the song chant, causing her to feel drugged as though in a trance.

Anthony was looking down, watching her as the last verses played out. "You can have all of me as long as I don't have to live another day without you, but be careful what you ask for, Tashia. My story isn't pretty." He lightly kissed her as the song ended and the small group erupted in cheers. For the first time they realized they had an audience and were not alone as the song indicated.

Anthony took Tashia by the hand and led her off the floor. He held her protectively around her small waist as he guided her through the room. He walked past Malcolm and patted him on his shoulder, whispering, "You were talking too much."

Preston was standing at the bar, grinning at him. Anthony approached and leaned into him and whispered something. Preston whispered back and Anthony guided Tashia up the steps and through the kitchen to the back yard. When they reached the guesthouse, the key was where Preston told him it would be. He unlocked the door, returned the key to its resting place, and entered with Tashia. He pushed the door closed behind them and immediately began to undress her.

"I couldn't watch you another second and not touch you. I missed you so much, Tashia. Please, don't ever leave me again. Tashia, you—"

"Some things change and some remain the same. Damn, man, shut up and drive," she said, breathing heavily. "I'm not leaving ever again," she whispered in his ear.

Cuyler came to a smiling Preston at the bar. She watched her sister light up the floor with Anthony and there was more going on than dancing. It was dirty, sexy, and breathtaking.

Preston saw her coming and turned away to laugh. He saw the fire Tashia had lit in Anthony a long time ago. For a while, he thought he would miss out because he was moving too slow, but the joke was on him.

"Is someone going to fill me in?" Cuyler asked, punching him in the arm.

"On what? I don't know anything," he said, recoiling and covering up.

Cuyler eyed him in disbelief. He was smiling too much to know nothing. "Then why are you grinning?" she asked, beginning to laugh herself.

"I could see it in his eyes and body language long ago and I kept saying to myself if he plans on catching her he had better pick up his pace. I was the one who needed to pick up the pace."

"Do you think they've been seeing each other?"

"I don't see why not. He brings her boys home every day. He did her yard and keeps it up. They have been together enough to learn one another. And tonight was definitely not the first time they have danced together." Preston pulled her closer to whisper. "I think your friend, Julie, had an orgasm."

Cuyler laughed and hit him. "She was jocking him. She will give him her number before she leaves tonight." The two laughed again. "Where did they go?"

"Let's just say they have left the building!" he teased. "We know how to throw a party, Mrs. Washington."

"Yes we do, Mr. Washington."

Tashia lay in Anthony's arms, once again, feeling secure and safe. She missed him so much over the past couple of weeks. She rolled onto his chest, leaning up to see his face. He was smiling.

"I had to come get you. Malcolm was breathing in all my air," he told her laughing. "You never looked as beautiful as you do right now." He grabbed both sides of her face, rolling her over to her back and kissed her.

"I didn't know you could dance like that. I thought I was going to have an orgasm right there on the floor," she said, whimsically.

"Now tell me the truth, were you leaving when I opened your car door?"

"Yes. I wasn't ready to see you."

"I do that to you?" he asked, smiling.

A blushing Tashia answered, "You do that to me."

Anthony lay for a minute then said, "I need to tell you a few things." He sighed.

"Not tonight. Please, not tonight," she begged. "We have time. I'm not going anywhere."

He sighed. "Tashia, why couldn't I have met you before?"

"Because you wouldn't be you. Everything we experience is what makes us who we are."

He thought about what she said then asked, "Do you want to drive?" They laughed.

The light shining through the window blinds awakened Tashia. She jumped and looked for her phone, realizing it was still in the house. "Mierda! *(shit)*" she mouthed, trying not to awaken Anthony.

Sliding from under the covers, she got out of the bed they finally found in the night and dressed. She found paper and pen and wrote a quick thank you note. She placed it on the door and left with her shoes in her hand.

Tipping past the pool, she hoped the kitchen door was still unlocked, and it was. The chimes of the alarm sang, letting the occupants know someone had entered. "Mierda," she mouthed again, forgetting about the chimes.

She closed the door and heard an all too familiar voice. "Taking that walk of shame?" She turned to see Cuyler sitting in the corner of the kitchen in her chaise lounge.

"Busted," she answered.

Cuyler slid from the chaise, struggling a little with her growing belly, to stand and made her way to her sister. She hugged her arm, smiling, and led her to the conservatory. She closed the double doors behind her and went to the couch.

"So, how long have you been seeing Anthony?" she asked, beaming, waiting for an answer.

"I don't know." She grinned. "Ummm, I guess since we moved into the house. There was no formal announcement. He was always there and it just progressed."

"Oh my, God, that dance last night got men laid and it was foreplay for the women. I didn't know you could dance like that!"

Tashia scratched her head and let her hair down. "Oh, I can dance," she replied.

"I think Malcolm is even more in love with you than before he came. He was like 'Oh, Cuyler, your sister is so beautiful. I have to take her out. Can you hook me up'?" Cuyler giggled, reminding Tashia of when she was a little girl. "He was oblivious to the fact that you just left to dance with the guy he had a verbal war with!"

Tashia laughed at the encounter. "I had to put my hand on Anthony's leg to keep him from jumping across the table," Tashia said, recollecting the evening.

"You really like him?" Cuyler asked, remembering her encounter in the hospital when Preston was shot almost three years ago.

"Yes. He's really a good guy, Cuyler." She was beaming. Somehow, she felt like she was in Cuyler's courtroom and, at some point, the hammer would drop.

"But, what do you really know about him?"

And, there it was, the doubt.

Tashia felt the wave, again. She had been feeling it more often lately. She felt this shift between her and Cuyler that she couldn't explain or understand. At that moment, she felt she had to defend Anthony, and he was not a man who needed defending,

"Well," she started, "He's a lot like his brother. He's very generous and kind. He has a big heart and is very protective of his family." Tashia stopped to think about the secrets he promised to share with her. So, did she really know him? "When you think about it, Cuyler, who really knows anybody? People show you the person they want you to see, but eventually the true man shows up."

Tashia felt Cuyler didn't trust her judgment in men. Yes, she didn't make a great choice when it came to Zane's dad, but she learned from the experience. Her sister's questioning was starting to irritate her. "He feels me, Cuyler. He gets me. He understands me. The last two weeks were the longest days of my life. I love him and I'm not going to apologize for that.

"Look at my life! It has not been perfect, so who am I to judge him? All I know is he doesn't make me feel ashamed about the choices I've made in my life. When I'm not happy and everything in my life is falling apart, he tells me it's okay not to be okay."

Cuyler saw her sister as she became emotional over a man that scared her. She was afraid Tashia had made another bad choice, but this time the kids would be the ones to suffer.

"He's had my back in more ways than I can explain Cuy. He's protective and he loves my kids."

"What about the kids, Tashia?" Cuyler asked.

Tashia looked at Cuyler for a moment and stood to leave. "Enough of this interrogation! Puedes ser tan egoista *(You can be so selfish)*," she said, abruptly ending the conversation. "You can be so selfish, and speaking of kids, I need to go home to mine."

"Tashia, I didn't mean—"

"Cuyler, you never *mean* to, you just say. For once, I have the storybook life with a man I am not going to give up," she said much louder than she meant.

"Hey, hey what's going on in here? Why all the yelling?" Preston asked, as he entered the room. Anthony entered through the kitchen door as Tashia had.

"Nothing," Cuyler said, and turned away as not to show the shine in her eyes, but Preston had already read the emotion on her face.

Preston looked at Tashia for an explanation. "Hormones," she said, picking up her shoes from the floor to leave. She didn't need him to start questioning her too.

Anthony followed Tashia.

Tashia was upset that Cuyler was giving her the third degree about her relationship with Anthony. She knew Cuyler didn't like him, but her loving him was none of her business. She was crying by the time Anthony caught up with her.

"Tashia! Tashia! What happened?" he asked her, concerned.

"Nothing!" she lied.

"You're upset so it can't be nothing so stop and talk to me!" Anthony was getting angry.

"Anthony, I don't want to talk about it now. Can we just go home to the kids?" she asked, now calmer.

Anthony smiled, causing her to smile through her tears. "Why are you smiling?" she asked.

"You said home," he answered, still smiling. He kissed her. "Yes, let's go home. I will let them know we are leaving."

Tashia watched as he jogged back to the sunroom He could always make her smile, and what could be wrong with that? There was nothing Cuyler could tell her about Anthony to make her leave him.

Anthony came back in a few minutes. They left.

Preston sat with Cuyler. She was quiet. She laid her head on his chest, but her mind was somewhere else. "What happened?" he asked, stroking her arm.

Cuyler turned, looking up to him, smiling. "I don't know. I guess she thought I didn't want to see her happy. I just know with the kids she needs to make sure she's not getting into anything too fast," Cuyler answered. "Then she got defensive."

"Hmm."

"What does that mean?"

"Now look who's defensive. I guess it runs in the family." Preston held her closer so he could wrap his arms around her belly. "Are you sure you weren't projecting your feelings about Anthony onto her."

Cuyler thought about his words. He always seemed to make her nervous. "Maybe. I think I hurt her feelings, so I will call her later to apologize. I wasn't trying to judge her or put Anthony down."

"What did you say?"

"I asked her how well she knew him."

"Hmmm. Definitely projecting. Leave them be and let them find their way."

"But, Preston!"

Preston had never seen his brother as happy as he did the night before. She made him happy and he understood that. Anthony was always assertive and it took the right woman to handle him, but this was different. Tashia mellowed him and he saw a calmer, tamer man. "Leave them be, Cuyler. He loves her. I can see it in his every fiber. Give them a chance."

Cuyler looked long and hard at Preston. He knew she didn't want to see her sister hurt. "He won't hurt her." He was calm, as he stroked her face. "Trust me."

175

Journey To Trust

Zander was asleep on the couch when they arrived to the house. Tashia first went to check on Zane who was asleep. She touched his face and he was warm, but not hot as before. He pushed her hand away. "I'm fine," he moaned, irritated. She smiled, knowing that he was.

Solana was not in her room when she checked. Tashia came out to the living room and she was not there either. She saw the dim light in her room and when she entered, she found her curled up next to Anthony who was half-asleep already.

Tashia lay on the other side of Solana and held her close. She looked at Anthony and stroked his face. He closed his eyes and was soon asleep.

When Tashia awoke, Solana was rubbing her face. "Good morning, Mommy," she said, still stroking her face.

"Good morning, Sunshine." She looked over to see Anthony still asleep. She had never known him to sleep so long and decided to let him rest.

"I put water in the bath for you, Mommy," Solana told her.

"You did!" Tashia followed Solana to the bathroom to find a tub filled with hot water.

"It's too hot now," she said, realizing her mistake. "Don't get in yet."

"Mommy would love a bath. I'll fix it." Tashia turned off the water, opened the stopper to allow some water to escape, and replaced it with cold. "This was a great idea, Solana. I really need a bath."

Solana smiled at her. "You looked sad and I wanted to make you happy, again."

Tashia was touched she had noticed. She looked at the little girl who looked more and more like her aunt every day. She was going to be much more beautiful than her mother. All the jealousy she felt toward Cuyler came rushing back and she felt ashamed.

"Okay, Solana, I'm going to get in now, so why don't you make some cereal and Mommy will make you your favorite dinner later. Okay?" She kissed a beaming Solana. "Thank you."

"You're welcome. Love you, Mommy," she said and ran from the room before Tashia could reply.

Tashia undressed and pinned her hair up. Once in the bath, she slid down and enjoyed the heat. She thought about what Cuyler was saying and realized she was upset because she was right. She didn't know anything about Anthony. She only knew she felt safe with him.

She relaxed, trying to clear her mind of the morning's events. The kids were going to Antigua and maybe she would take Anthony up on his offer and go. That would be great!

Anthony tipped into the bathroom and locked the door. "Anthony, the kids are awake."

"I won't be long. I only came to wash your back." He reached for her bath sponge. "I need to go and get some work done and we can talk tonight."

"It's Saturday. You can't play hooky and spend the day with me catching up?" She pouted.

"I'll tell you what, I will do what I have to do and come right back and we can spend the evening together," he said after he finished washing her back and left.

The restaurant was empty when Anthony entered. He had to look at his books, again, to see where he was losing money. He did a quick walkthrough after turning the alarm off to make sure no repairs were needed. Everything seemed fine so he went back to the alarm to turn it back on so he would know if someone entered while he was in his office.

Once in his office, the memories of him and Tashia making love invaded his thoughts. She put a smile on his face. *Focus, Anthony, focus.*

The file cabinet was locked, as it should be. The keys were on his key ring. After unlocking the cabinet, he pulled out his recent orders' receipts and sat at his desk to look through them. He turned on his computer to match them with the invoices emailed to him. Everything seemed to be in order.

He leaned back in his chair. Whoever was stealing from him knew his system, which narrowed his offenders down to three, maybe four people. He thought about everyone's situations and their longevity with him. He prided himself in being a good judge of character. Everything pointed back to one person, but that didn't make sense.

Anthony pulled out his ledger and looked at the sales to compare the orders. What he was looking for, he didn't know. He combed through the files, frustrated. It appeared the losses were at the club and not the restaurant, but then he saw it: the pattern.

He made copies of everything he needed and returned the files to the cabinet and locked it. Sitting back in his chair, he sighed. If what he found was true, he had a lot of work to do in a short time.

He could smell dinner when he entered the house. The boys were on the couch playing Xbox. Anthony watched a drained Zane trying to keep up with his brother. He looked a little livelier than he had been over the past couple of days.

"Did you guys already eat?" he asked.

"No. We were waiting on you," Zander answered, never once looking up.

Anthony walked to the kitchen and found Solana with flour in her hair standing at the sink washing a few dishes and a tired Tashia in the corner chair. The table was already set. "Do you want me to tell the boys to come?" he asked after lightly kissing her hello.

"Yes."

Anthony lifted Solana from her chair, grinning as she screamed for help. He gathered the boys and they all met back at the table.

The chatter was loud as each child took turns vying for his attention. Watching Tashia across the table, he saw her smile as she enjoy their conversations. He wondered if she would wear that same smile after knowing his secrets.

Staling, Anthony played the game with Tashia while the kids cleaned the kitchen under protest. When they finished, Tashia gave instructions to each and she and Anthony retreated to her room. He was nervous. His palms were sweaty from the fear that gripped him. He watched her turn on the television, although neither were avid watchers. He had already gone home and showered and was now dressed in his workout clothes. Her eyes washed over his body and he could feel the warmth rush to his face.

"I've missed you," she told him, barely audible, but the words rang loud in his ears.

With one finger, he summoned her and she came. He held her in his arms for what seemed like a glimmer, but minutes rolled by. He sighed and let her go. Their journey was in its infantry and he knew they would have to work through some things before moving forward.

Pushing her back, he lay with her. He began his story and their journey of truth.

I Loved My Father

"I sat next to my father on the steps of our small one-bedroom home. My mother had long since left the house. She would wander back later, as she usually did. I often wondered where she went, but that was not a child's business to know.

"May, our neighbor, brought the fish my dad had taken to her earlier to prepare. May was the old woman of the neighborhood. Everyone took care of her by bringing food and other necessities. She watched the neighborhood kids and received money or other things for payment. My dad taught me that's what a village did. They took care of each other.

"May didn't like my mother much. Whenever my mother was around, May side eyed her and responded to my mother's hellos under her breath. I heard the other women talking about my mother, calling her names.

"She was beautiful and my father worshiped her. If she was not faithful, he didn't seem to care.

"Jasper Laurent was his name and he was not a small man. He was a giant to me. My dad's arms were like big tree trunks and his chest massive. His ebony skin was so dark that some called him blue. The women smiled and waved to him when he walked by. He could have had his pick, but he chose Pillar Brevard."

Tashia knew where Anthony inherited most of his attributes, including his dark, ebony, smooth skin and broad, mischievous smile.

He remembered everyone telling him one day he would be fine like his father.

The times he spent with his dad were fun times. He taught him how to fish and hunt. He also took him on hikes and taught him how to take care of himself in the wilderness. Anthony always felt he was in training for something, but he didn't know what.

"My dad and I got up early one morning and went fishing. When we returned to the house, my mother was still gone, so my father took the fish next door to May to prepare. This was the fish May brought back.

"My father laughed at how I was blowing the fish while in my mouth. He told me I was going to choke and to stop. I was trying to eat mine because I knew he would give me his once I finished—and he did end up sharing his fish with me that day. He just laughed and broke off a piece." Anthony smiled as though reliving the moment and then became silent again. "That was the last time we spent together."

"My dad handed me the remainder of his fish and stood looking far off down the road. He was watching the two trucks coming fast in the distance. He told me, 'Boy, go in the house and hide on the top shelf of the closet like I taught you'. He didn't look at me. His eyes were on those trucks speeding toward us. He said, 'Don't you come down until I tell you and don't you make a sound!' My dad looked down on me for the first time and yelled, 'Move, boy!' when I didn't respond.

"I scrambled to my feet and did as he instructed. It wasn't the first time he had to hide me there. He hid me in that spot whenever men came to talk to him. Most times, I fell asleep in the cramped area when I was scared.

"I heard the sound of tires skidding into the yard. I lay in the spot, quietly listening. I heard four different voices outside. Their tones became more tensed as they asked my dad questions."

"*Who you been talking to?*" one man yelled.

"*I'm not crazy, Caesar. I don't talk to no one!*" his father responded.

Anthony heard the scuffle move from the porch to inside the cramped house. His father struggled to push the men out, but they overpowered him. Anthony watched the men beat his father. He wanted to come out of his hiding place and help, but fear gripped his limbs and he couldn't move.

"*You've been talking to someone. Where is that brat of yours? Maybe if we had him you would remember who you been talking to.*" He was taunting Jasper.

Jasper picked up the small man and threw him across the room. One man pulled out a knife and stabbed him in the side.

"Kill him!" the little man ordered to the other two men.

"They took turns trying to stab my father, but he fought like a caged animal until the last wound rendered him helpless on the floor. One man kicked him twice and he gasped as his last breath seeped from his lungs. When I could no longer hear his labored breathing, I knew he was dead.

"I cried on the top shelf of that closet and watched my father's dead corpse lying on the floor. Blood encircled his body and streamed across the room like a tiny river. It seemed like hours before anyone came to the house, but May came.

"She gasped when she saw him on the floor. The old woman frantically looked around for me and I think she was expecting to find my dead body, too. She called for me twice before I answered. May made her way to me and instructed me to come down. I was too scared to move. She assured me the men were gone. I was five at the time.

"May carried me from our small home, turning my face away from my father. I stayed with her for a day before my mother came to get me and so began my life in hell."

Tashia wiped away the tear that ran down the side of his face. He trembled as he had before.

"I have never been so helpless in my life. I wanted to come down, but I couldn't move."

"If you had come down you would have been dead alongside your father, Anthony. You were a boy; almost a baby."

Shame resonated on his face. His silence magnified in the room. Minutes ticked away.

"Anthony? Do you need more time? I don't have to hear everything today."

He turned and glared at her. The chill of his glare frightened her. "I will only tell this story once and I *will* tell it today!" He was visibly shaking now and for the first time, Tashia feared what was to come. He proceeded.

Hiding

"We hid from home to home, but not in our neighborhood. Everyone there was afraid to help for fear the same would happen to them. When I asked why we had to hide, my mother said people were looking for us, the same who had killed my father.

"My mother found a room to rent. We never had money in the house, so I didn't know where she was getting the money to take care of us, but I didn't understand money.

"Pillar began bringing strange men back to our room. She would tell me to go and play and not to come back unless she called. I dared not disobey, because my mother could be harsh with her punishment.

"One day I came back too early and found a man on top my mother, pounding into her brutally and pulling her long hair. She yelled to me to leave, but I stood there staring. I thought he was hurting her and we had been found. I couldn't let her die, too. I debated what to do, but I was not leaving her with him. I was only five.

"The man turned, staring at me with a vulgar smile and he continued to ride my mother. 'I think he likes to watch', the man said. My mother looked petrified and yelled at me to run, but, I would not.

"I picked up the chair and tried to hit him with it, but it was almost too heavy for me to lift. The man let my mother go and she tried desperately to avert his attention back to her, but he was distracted.

"With one hand, the man snatched me up and I fought him with all I had. Pillar scrambled to get to her feet, because she knew the strange appetites of her customer.

"My heart pounded in my chest as he dragged me to the bed. The naked man pushed Pillar across the room when she came to rescue me from his grip. Before she could recover, the man snatched my pants down around my ankles and pinned me on the bed. Pillar jumped onto the man's back, punching and yelling, but he was too big for her. Again, he pushed her across the room.

"The pain was excruciating as he pushed inside me, riding as he had my mother. I screamed, but no one came except a desperate mother who was frantic to rescue her child.

"I could feel the ripping with each thrust. I remember him celebrating, yelling, 'Oh this is a nicer ass! I will pay you double for him'."

Anthony clinched his fist and the tears flowed down his cheeks freely now. Tashia was mortified, listening to his experience. She was fourteen when she experienced the same, but he was a mere five years old. She wondered how he was sane today after living through the ordeal. Now, she understood his aggressiveness and protectiveness of his family.

"Shhh!" It was her turn to console him as he had her previously. She wondered how people could be so cruel to children and understood his desire to help the helpless. "It's over. I'm here with you. I won't let anyone ever hurt you again!"

"That is why I was so upset the night you danced. You were on my watch and I let you down. I wasn't there to protect you!" His voice was loud. "If I ever see him, again, I will hurt him, Tashia. It's there in my dark side and I can't shake the thoughts of what I would do to him."

"I'm okay, Anthony!"

Anthony lay staring at the ceiling silent. The big, strong man who was there for her and her family so many times before appeared tiny and vulnerable. She was beginning to realize they were all flawed. The experiences of their past formed them and led them to each other. Their experiences were not that different. They were born beautiful creatures to be shaped and molded by events and choices. Well, she chose him, in all his imperfections, his strength manifested from tragedy of his past and his desire not to see his family suffer through senseless acts by the hands of others. That was the man his past had created and she loved him with all her heart.

Tashia watched him attempt to speak, but he couldn't. She silenced him with her kisses, letting him know she was there for him. She stroked his face evoking the pain he held back from her, in his efforts, again, to protect his loved ones from the pain he had experienced. His body shook as he made his last efforts to contain the emotions awakened in him.

"I didn't know what violated was until later, but it did not adequately describe my feelings," he whispered. "I didn't know why he did that to me. I was a good boy who obeyed his parents and honored his elders. Why was I being punished?" He wiped the tears from the side of his face. "My father was good and kind to me and my mother... I didn't understand why my dad was taken from me.

"I walked in a daze for weeks after that day. I remembered my mother and I moving from one place to another, again, hiding until one day we boarded a boat and left a place that held nothing but bad memories for me.

"I don't sleep well. When I close my eyes I am haunted by the sight of my father lying in his blood on the floor of our home or I see the evil in the face of the man who took me."

Up until then, she had been shaken by his story, but was present for him. She could no longer hold back the tears she held inside and they came without warning. She had Jesus to help her get by her tragedies, but Anthony was still on that island he escaped as a child.

"I'm sorry no one was there for you." She sobbed, holding him tightly. "I'm here now and I won't let anything happen to you."

Anthony smiled at her words. "Oh, you won't?" He tried to joke to lighten the mood. He buried his head in her neck exhausted and Tashia held him there.

"Shhh." She stroked his strong arms and ran her hands over his massive shoulders, soothing him. "Thank you for trusting me."

Anthony lay in Tashia's arms, relieved he was able to tell somebody of his childhood horror. He had never repeated his story to anyone before. He didn't want to return to that place, not even in his mind, but the bondage was gone and he felt a release.

In the past, he felt dirty, soiled tainted, but she didn't make him feel that way. Before, sex was an act of control for him and he was the controller. With Tashia, he reached a level of oneness and an intimacy he could not feel with anyone else.

Sleep was better when he was with her. It was like his demons were afraid of her. She was already his protector and didn't know it. She was his angel.

He needed to clear the air about Janet. They were in a good place and he didn't need any other incidents.

"Hey!"

"Yes?"

"Remember when you came into my office and Janet and I were arguing?"

"Yes."

"She came to tell me she had a child and she was mine."

She was silent for a moment, causing him to look up. She was looking down at him with the same poker face he had grown accustomed to.

"Have you seen her yet?"

"No. We just did the paternity test last week so I am waiting for the results. I don't want to become a part of her life unless I know for sure she is mine." Anthony watched her expressions. She was in deep thought. "If she is mine I will be a part of her life, Tashia. Will that be a deal breaker for us?"

Tashia kissed him. "What deal are we making?" She smiled at him, letting him know everything would be okay.

Anthony was full of emotion. His fear had crippled him and would have caused him to lose her. He knew now it wasn't fear it was shame that had crippled him. He was afraid she would see him, instead of the act, as vulgar. They had both suffered tragedy and survived.

"What deal would you like to make, Tashia?"

Tashia smiled. "I missed you and I don't want to be apart from you ever again. Can you handle that?"

Anthony sat up and looked at her being silly. "What are you asking?" He made his eyes big and covered his mouth. "Oh my! Are you asking me to marry you?" Anthony hopped from the bed and ran into the living room. "Zander! Zander! I believe your mother just asked me to marry her!"

Tashia ran out the room behind him, laughing. Anthony ran back to her, lifted her in the air, and screamed, "Yes! Yes! I will!" He swung her around, holding her tight. "Yes, Tashia! I will spend the rest of my life with you!" Anthony looked at her seriously. "Yes, Tashia. I want to spend the rest of my life with you." He watched her expression and knew her answer.◻

The Proposal

Preston watched Cuyler as she slept. She was more fatigued the bigger she became. She was still the beautiful woman he married. Her skin glowed and her hair shined from the vitamins she took daily. He thought about getting a housekeeper, but he knew she would protest. He wanted her to quit working, but he knew she wouldn't do that either.

Shaking her gently, he woke her up. "Hey, dinner is on the table and everyone is waiting for you to wake from your nap. Are you coming downstairs or do you need to sleep more," he asked.

Cuyler watched him, trying to gather her senses. She looked to the nightstand for the time and quickly sat up. "Why did you let me sleep so long?" she asked, holding her spinning head.

"You okay?"

"Yes. I just sat up too fast. Preston, I've been asleep for four hours. You should have awakened me," she scolded.

"We all had it under control so all you have to do is come and join us." He extended his hand to help her up. "Go wash your face. You have a little something running down the side," he teased.

She swung at him playfully and made her way to the bathroom to fix her face. When she returned, the two went downstairs to join the others.

Everything was prepared and everyone seated in the dining room when they entered. Cuyler was still sleepy, but she loved these times with her family.

The christening was great. Callia spoke in French the entire time, even when the pastor asked her questions, she responded in French. The congregation thought that was funny, but little Callia was irritated by their laughter. She thought they were laughing at her. Preston explained to her they were not laughing at her. She told Preston she still did not like it.

Sitting in Caden's lap, she leaned back into his arms, an indication she should have taken a nap with Cuyler. She was oblivious to the conversations around her and began blinking more often. "Callia, are you ready to take a nap?" Cuyler asked.

"No!" she answered, shaking her head and hiding her face in Caden's arm as he stroked her. Everyone laughed.

Cuyler sat in the chair next to Preston. When she looked down their long dining room table she saw Anthony holding Tashia's hand. She smiled at Tashia. She saw Jacque, Meagan, Candace, Gemma, Aunt Khadada, and Brenda as they should be, but for the first time she realized Caden was alone.

"Let's join hands and bless the food," Caden said. Everyone did as instructed. "Lord God, we thank you for this day. We thank you for each of our family members here today and those who couldn't be here. Thank you for the food and the fellowship we are about to share and bless the hands of the cook who prepared it, in Jesus' name we pray. Amen"

Cuyler watched him hold Callia and realized he wasn't alone at all. He stroked the now sleeping child with the same love she once knew. Caden was having a love affair with his child. She was his priority. She had a newfound respect for him.

"Do you want to lay her in her bed?" she asked him.

"So she can wake up and be angry with me? No," he answered.

Aunt Khadada began passing the food around. Cuyler watched Anthony prepare Solana's plate and hand it to her. Solana beamed at Anthony the way she did Preston. She was at peace with him. Cuyler thought that maybe she should be, too. Her sister and her family loved him.

Cuyler turned her attention to the boys and immediately noticed that Zane was playing in his food. "You're not hungry, Zane?"

Zane looked up, not realizing anyone was watching. "A little."

"I have never had anyone complain about my food before," Aunt Khadada said playfully.

"Your food is good," Zane reassured her and looked to his mother and Anthony for a bailout.

Anthony rose from the table and gestured for Zane to come with him. "It's not a big deal, Anthony," Cuyler said with a slight attitude, wishing she had never said anything. She looked to Tashia in question, but her sister never looked her way.

Anthony and Zane disappeared into the kitchen. Cuyler could feel her anger rising as her sister sat and did nothing. Preston placed his hand on her lap to settle her, but she couldn't shake her anger. She felt her sister was making a bad decision, again. Why hadn't she gone to the kitchen with him? He was her child. *He better not touch him.*

All attention turned to the kitchen at the sound of the blender. Preston rose and went to the kitchen to assist. He gave Cuyler a warning look before he left the room. Cuyler looked down the table and Tashia was now playing in her food. Cuyler could see her mood had changed and wondered what was going on.

"Excuse me," Tashia said, and went into the kitchen to join the others and check on Zane.

"Zane's been sick," Solana announced to everyone at the table.

"Oh really? What's wrong with him?" she asked her niece.

"I don't know."

"That's enough, Solana," Zander said in a warning tone.

"I'll be back," Cuyler said, standing slowly to adjust her large belly.

"No you won't," her mother said. "You are going to sit right there and entertain us while the men take care of that."

Cuyler complied with her mother's wishes, and sat back in her seat. She was no longer hungry and stirred her food around her plate. When the door opened, the entourage returned to the table and Zane carried a smoothie, with him smiling. Preston returned to his seat and resumed eating. Cuyler assumed everything was fine and returned to eating as well.

"You ready for that baby?" her mother asked.

"I am ready to have my personal space back, and I know Preston can't wait."

"Are you going to be able to fly to Antigua so close to your date?" Tashia asked.

"I have been cleared to fly," she answered.

Anthony turned to Brenda and asked, "How soon can you get your passport?"

"Why? I'm not going anywhere," Brenda answered.

"Well you are going to miss the event of the year then," he told her, as he got down on one knee next to Tashia and pulled a box out of his pocket.

Cuyler watched as her sister covered her mouth, smiling at Anthony. Cuyler looked at Preston who was smiling and felt betrayed that she was not told anything.

"Tashia, I have known you for a while and knew the first time you got smart with me and rolled your eyes that you were the woman for me. You have calmed my inner beast and accepted me as I am, with all my faults and imperfections. You accept the bad boy I can sometimes be and have welcomed me into your family, trusting me to be a part of even your children's lives. You trust me with your secrets and dreams and you have not condemned me for mine. The two weeks we spent apart were the longest days of my life. I couldn't eat, sleep, or function because you were not there to make my reality sane. I never want to be without you, again, and wish to spend the rest of my life with you and become a part of your family, if you will have me. I know you asked me first," he joked, "but I thought I would do it the right way and ask you in front of our family as witnesses."

Cuyler watched her sister's tears stream down her face as he spoke to her so gently and kind. Cuyler could see from her end of the table that the ring was nice and the rock big. Tashia hugged Anthony around his neck and kissed him, saying yes through her tears. Yet another side of Anthony was revealed. Tashia had changed him into a gentle giant. He was always rough and abrupt when she saw him. She also saw peace on her sister's face she had never seen: even with Jesus. They were happy. Cuyler wondered if her sister was pregnant.

She was so deep into her own thoughts; Preston had to nudge her when everyone went to congratulate the couple. He helped Cuyler to her feet and they both made their way. Cuyler wiped the tears from her sister's face, kissed her cheeks, and hugged her. Tashia wiped away the tears from her face as well. "You look so happy and if you are happy so am I," she told her sister. "I'm sorry about our last talk. I only want the best for you. You deserve it and if he puts that smile on your face and makes you beam like this then he's the best for you," Cuyler whispered in her sister's ear. "I love you so much, Shia. You have always been there for me."

"Okay, Cuyler, move and let someone else get in there," Caden said from behind. He had taken Callia to her room and laid her down.

"Sorry," she said, wiping her tears away and moving out the way.

"He beat me to it, Shia. I guess I moved too slow," Caden joked, as he hugged her. Caden went to Anthony and shook his hand. "Congrats man."

Cuyler watched Zander beam at his mother and Anthony. Anthony was holding Solana in his arms and his other arm was around Zane's shoulders, holding him close. They were already a family.

Anthony looked at her mother and said, "So you see why we need you to get that passport? We are getting married in Antigua," he announced. "Preston has started a tradition now."

"Where are we all going to stay?" Tashia asked.

"I got that covered," Anthony answered. "I figured if I get everything set before we leave we can stay for the summer and get married before we come back to give everyone a chance to prepare."

Cuyler became sad, realizing she would probably miss the wedding. She didn't know if she could fly back to the states that late in her pregnancy. Preston read her mind. "We will talk later, mon amour. Anthony and I already have this thought out," he whispered in her ear.

She looked at her little planner and wondered what he had in store for her. He always surprised her.

"Is everyone done eating? We can take this to the conservatory."

Preston hired a few people from Reggae to help with dinner so he gave them instructions on what to do with the food and instructed them to bring dessert into the other room. The kids went to the family room and the grownups went to the conservatory.

While walking to the other room, she saw Tashia checking Zane's forehead. He was still drinking the mixture Anthony had fixed for him and shaking his head, no, while pushing Tashia's hand away. She kissed him and he disappeared into the room with the other kids.

All of their guests were scattered throughout the room. Meagan and Candace were admiring her ring. Her mother sat next to Anthony and he held her hand. The sight of them holding hands warmed her. Jacque was standing with Caden, Gemma and Cuyler's secretary talking. Preston helped Cuyler get comfortable on the chaise lounge and joined her.

"They look happy, C," he said. "I never thought he would find anyone to tame his wild spirit, but she has definitely done that. Look at how he keeps checking on her. He's in love and this side of Anthony I have never seen."

Cuyler hoped for the best for them, but she couldn't help but wonder how much Tashia knew about him. She had seen his dark side before and wondered how much Anthony had shown her. She was happy for them, but was not completely convinced.

Nellie

The following week was hectic. Anthony made sure everyone's passports were finalized. He had to expedite Tashia's and the kids'. Brenda would come later so there was no rush for her. There was also the matter of the missing alcohol in the inventory, so he called a meeting with Snow to review everything.

Snow entered the club office and sat on the other side of the desk from Anthony with two cups and a bottle. He smiled, still happy with the news he shared with him. He was careful not to share the information with anyone else; he knew it would affect some more than others.

"So, someone finally tied you down and I knew it would be Tashia the first time I saw you look at her." Snow poured a little bourbon in each cup. "Salute!" he said and the two toasted to the happy occasion.

After celebrating, Anthony opened the file on his desk. "We have a problem," he began. "One of the servers is stealing from me." Anthony slid the file to Snow. "You look at this and tell me what you see."

Anthony leaned back in the chair and watched Snow scan through the file. He closed the file and leaned back in his chair. "What do you want me to do about it?"

Anthony pulled at his lips. "I don't have any options. I'm not in business to lose money. I have a family to take care of now, so I'm going to have to cut ties."

"I know that, but how. We can't accuse with no evidence."

Anthony circled his thumbs as he thought how to handle the situation. "Let it play out as usual, but this time set the trap," Anthony suggested. "Let me come up with the how and I will let you know as soon as I figure out something."

Anthony didn't have long to get things settled. The trip was coming up in a couple of weeks and he had a lot of closure to make it happen. He and Snow decided to run things as usual, but they would have to watch a little closer.

The club was full. He asked Tashia to come and be with him for the evening. He needed her to distract while he and Snow watched. When she walked in, he knew he would be the one distracted.

He watched as she walked toward him smiling. She wore white fitted stretch pants and a white halter-top, exposing her midriff. Her shapely legs showed through the fitted pants, forming every curve. Three-inch heels exposed her freshly manicured toes, and her hair was wild as it swung back and forth.

The warmth rose in him as she approached. She entered his arms with no reservation of who was watching. She didn't care. He was hers. Holding her tightly, he kissed her, not caring who saw and hoping that ever one had. "I'm not going to get anything done and the dancers won't make any money tonight as long as you are looking like this," he moaned in Spanish in her ear. "S-s-s-h-h-i-a-a," he teased. "You want to go back in my office?"

"I want to go to your place when we leave from here. The kids are at Preston and Cuyler's for the evening," she whispered back in Spanish. "So let's get this started," she added, removing his hands from her behind.

Tashia made her way to Anthony's office. She put her purse in his bottom drawer and closed it. She was about to leave when she saw a picture of the most beautiful child. She was about three months old and had the prettiest almond shaped green eyes: Anthony's eyes. Her smile was wide and contagious. On the back of the picture: Fatimah, three months. When she returned the picture to the desk, she saw a piece of paper from the lab. *Fatimah is his.* Tashia put everything back and went to the door. There was nothing she could do about the results.

The hall was busy as she remembered. Everyone greeted her as though she was an icon. She headed to the dancers lounge to say hello before she had to go to the bar and pretend she could mix drinks. Snow intercepted her.

"I know that fine ass anywhere," she heard him say from behind and her feet left the floor.

Tashia turned her head and saw the albino smile a big welcoming smile. "Hey, beautiful," he said. "I missed you."

After putting her down, Tashia hugged Snow. He had always been her protector in this place. He watched out for her and got her out of many situations. He was like the big brother she never had.

"You keep holding me like this and I'm going to have to go back into the closet," he said, laughing. Tashia pushed Snow away from her and continued down the hall to the dancer's room.

When she entered the room, all heads turned. Mouse ran to her, giving her a huge hug. Others shouted *hey* and a few asked if she was back. Tashia responded to everyone's questions and saw relief from some. She looked around the room and saw the changes she suggested had been made including the cubicle like dressing areas. Everyone had their own spaces and there was a circular bench in the middle of the floor for additional seating.

"It's nice, isn't it?" Mouse asked.

"Very."

"Not as nice as that rock on your finger," someone said across the room.

Tashia, forgetting about the ring, looked down at her finger. She forgot to remove it from her hand, but it was too late now. She tried to smile it off, but more questions came.

"All I know is if Myra finds out heads are gonna roll," someone said and they all laughed.

Mouse smiled and said, "I'm happy for you."

"I've got to go and earn my coin. Make sure you make yours, ladies!" Tashia said, waving her hand over her head as she left the room.

Anthony was already at the bar. He was hanging glasses and having words with one of the girls who appeared to look new. He barked a few orders and she went scurrying to the back.

"What was that all about?" Tashia asked.

"Nothing. She's just young. Caught her messing with one of the guards and I had to tell her we don't do that here. If she finds she wants to get involved with one of my guys then one of them will have to leave. I can't chance the disruption."

"So, what do you want me to do?"

"I need you to keep an eye on any of the girls who disappear for a long period of time or who are giving out free drinks. Our issue is more with the latter because of the quantity missing, but it could be both things."

"Okay. I can do that." Tashia waved to Terrance as he walked to the bar.

"Hey, Tony," he said to Anthony. It had become a joke whenever Anthony was missing for long periods of time. He hugged Tashia, rocking her and trying to salsa with her as Anthony had the night at Preston's.

Anthony cut in and showed him how it was done. "The name is Anthony, and don't touch my woman, again," he told Terrance, jokingly. The three laughed.

"It's time to unlock the doors, Anthony!" Snow yelled from the back.

"Butch already unlocked the doors," Terrance announced to Anthony. "Tell Snow he can cool it. You're here tonight."

"Then go and turn off that mix and you start mixing," Anthony said, reminding him he was out of position.

"Yes, sir. See you later, Tashia," he replied and headed back to his station with the drink Tashia made for him in tow.

"That's where my liquor is going," Anthony said, shaking his head. "Call me if you need me and Bruce is your guard for the night."

"I don't need a guard," she announced.

"You are still a celeb here, Tashia," he said looking back at her. "And your outfit isn't exactly helping either." Anthony looked her up and down, warming her.

"Go to work, *Tony.*"

Tashia was left alone to deal with the heat he had ignited within her. She took a deep breath and looked around to see the bar was beginning to fill. She had not seen it from this side. Usually, by the time she came out the bar was packed. A young lady from Reggae entered the bar area.

"Oh, hello," she said, surprised to see Tashia. "I didn't know you were back. This means our tips will pick up tonight."

"I'm not back to dance. Anthony asked me to help out at the bar tonight. I just hope I am more a help than a hindrance!"

A man walked to the bar, smiling. "Can I get an Atom Bomb?"

"I got it Shi—"

"Tashia," she corrected the girl. Shia was her stage name and she didn't want any attention brought to her while at the bar. "Your drink is coming. Is there anything else?" she asked, realizing it was a stupid question. He looked her up and down. "Okay that's a no." Tashia took the man's money and handed him his drink. He continued to stare until finally recognition set in.

"You're Shia!" he said as though she was a star.

"Shhh," she said. "Not anymore."

"You will always be Shia," the man answered and the realization of the truth of his words rang strong in her ears.

"I guess you're right," she conceded.

The man left without his change, smiling and looking back every couple of feet. Tashia thought about the obstacle and wondered if they were making a mistake having her there to help.

"I will put the change in our tip jar and we will split it at the end of the night."

"That's fine."

As they worked through the night, Tashia realized there were more guests at the bar than the stage. She could tell she was not a welcomed distraction and she had to change things and fast.

More girls arrived for their shift at the bar and were happy about the crowd, but Tashia was not. Nothing abnormal was happening and time was passing.

Things were overwhelming. Men were yelling to Tashia to dance for them and she pretended to act like she didn't know what they were talking about. She smiled and took their money. They emptied the tip jar three times and the night was nowhere near being done. When she attempted to leave the bar to get whatever they had depleted, Bruce met her at the swinging door, and he was a welcoming sight.

"Where do you need to go, Ms. Tashia?" he asked, making her feel old.

"I need a break, Bruce. I think I need to go to the office for a minute."

The two walked toward the back hall. Bruce pushed back those who attempted to approach her and she was grateful Anthony had assigned him to her. She didn't like the attention. Bruce stood in position while she escaped the madness and went into the office. Tashia stopped abruptly. She was caught off guard to see Anthony in the office and he was not alone.

"Oh! I didn't know you would be here," she said apologetically.

Janet cut her eyes at Tashia and smiled. Anthony was leaning back in his chair and she was standing at the corner of his desk. She liked taunting Tashia, but Tashia knew her. Janet was much like her.

"Come and sit with me," he offered Tashia. "I know you are tired." Anthony gestured for her to join him.

Tashia saw the sails leave Janet's posture. This was where they differed. Tashia strutted across the room deliberately and sat in Anthony's lap, leaning into his welcoming arms. This time it was she who smiled.

"I saw you slinging drinks behind the bar," Janet said. "It's hard work being a barmaid."

"I'm just helping. I'm an RN by trade," Tashia replied.

"Oh, is that what you call your dancing?"

"Ouch. Touché," Tashia said, cooing. She smiled at Janet as her eyes dropped to Anthony massaging her back. Tashia could sense her uneasiness and laid back into Anthony's hard chest. She whispered in Spanish. "You need me to leave so you can handle this?"

"Si. Vamos a hablar mas tarde," he answered, indicating he would talk to her later about the conversation. "Tenemos algunas cosas que discutir (*We have some things to discuss*)."

"Bueno," she answered, standing to her tired feet.

"Being dismissed, again?" Janet asked, trying to kindle a fire in Tashia.

With that comment, Anthony stood with her and escorted her to the door. He bent, kissing her passionately, to soothe any doubt she may have had. He didn't want a repeat of the last time the three of them were together. "Te deseo pero eso tendra que esperar hasta mas tarde (*I want you, but that will have to wait until later*)."

Once again, Tashia was in the mix of the madness. One of the girls approached her. "The VIP wants to know if you are dancing tonight and if not can he meet you."

Tashia looked at Bruce. "Who is this?"

"A rapper named Nelly Brown," Bruce answered.

Tashia knew who he was referring to and thought it couldn't hurt the club to go meet him and then return to her post at the bar. "Okay, Bruce let's go."

She led Bruce to the VIP section through the crowd, which seemed to have doubled since she went to the office, but she realized she really had not paid attention when going there. As they got closer to the area, security got deeper and she felt better.

She saw a good-looking man sitting in his chair surrounded by his entourage. He was young and appeared to be full of himself. His group catered to his whims, feeding his ego as he threw money at the stage. They laughed as he balled up the bills and tried to bounce them off the dancer's behinds. Tashia felt herself become instantly irritated and wished she had not agreed to the meeting. Her fear was it would not turn out well for the club.

The waitress who had approached her ran to Nelly Brown eager to announce her triumph. He looked over to Tashia and smiled. He quickly tipped the girl for her triumph. Leaning over he whispered to his partner and she moved one seat over, leaving the only available seat beside him. Bruce whispered to one of the guards who quickly disappeared to the back hall to the offices.

"Hello," he said, looking her from head to toe slowly. His guest watched, looking wounded. Some of his entourage snickered.

Tashia politely smiled and lowered her eyes and looked back up, meeting his. She could see he was not used to a challenge. His jaw twitched. "Was that seat for me?" she asked, pointing. She looked to Bruce for approval. He nodded.

Nelly looked to Bruce as well. "Is this your man? He had to give you approval?"

"Oh, no Mr. Nelly," she cooed. "That was not for approval. That was letting him know that I would be good. You see, I don't usually get this close to the guests. When I do, bad things happen. I let him know I would be good." Tashia saw his cockiness and confidence come down a notch. She stuck out her hand. "I am Shia," she said to his guest. She then turned to Nelly. "I am pleased to meet you as well. I hope everyone has given you first class hospitality."

Nelly looked her from head to toe again, but this time it was not with lust but with respect. "Yes, they have, thank you. We were hoping to see you perform tonight. We were disappointed when we heard you would not be."

He was better spoken than she expected. She listened to him praise the growth of the club and how it was much nicer than the first time he had come years ago.

"New management can bring about positive change," she said, looking past him to the bar. She watched as the young girl conversed with the guard. She whispered to one of the others and slid out from behind the bar heading towards the kitchen. She came back as though she had forgotten something, reached under the bar to retrieve it, and ran off again. She looked back toward the offices and saw Anthony standing against the wall, watching her. She looked toward the kitchen and he quickly followed her gaze and headed in that direction.

"Am I boring you?" Nelly asked.

Tashia smiled and bowed her head as though embarrassed. "I'm sorry, you caught me. Always thinking about work, but now you have my undivided attention."

The crowd around them had gotten dense. She looked to Bruce. He lifted his hand mid-way, looked at a couple of the guards, and signaled to them. They quickly sprung to action, moving the crowd back.

"What do I have to do to meet Shia?" and "What, we ain't VIP?" were just a few of the comments she heard from the thickening crowd and knew she couldn't stay there long.

"Why are you in town?" she asked, not really caring.

"Just passing through to our next gig in New York."

Bruce bent down and whispered in her ear. She nodded and turned back to Nelly. "It was great meeting you, but I was informed that for safety purposes I have to move. I want to keep you as safe as possible." She added and stood.

Nelly and his guests stood and each shook her hand. "I appreciate you." He looked her up and down slowly again. "Damn, you fine. Maybe the next time I'm in town I can look you up?"

Tashia smiled and said, "Next time you are in town, call the club and I'll make sure I'm here," she promised and walked away before he could ask her anything else. She could feel his eyes on her behind as she walked.

Bruce crowded in, draping his arm around her shoulder to shield her from the crowd. She could feel the crowd pushing in around them. They were rowdy and bold. Bruce pushed a few men back who were a little bolder. Tashia tried to turn toward the bar, but Bruce redirected her back to the office. The guards at the end of the hall prevented anyone from following to the back. He opened the office door, allowed her to enter, and took up his post outside.

Tashia made her way to the inviting couch and stretched out, looking up to the ceiling. Her phone vibrated. She unclipped it and looked to see it was Anthony.

"Where are you?" he yelled into the phone. "It's crazy out here."

"In the office," she answered as she stretched.

"I saw you bunned up with Nelly. Is there something you want to tell me?" She could hear him smiling as he talked. "We got them. I will tell you all about it when I come to the back. Take a nap. You're going to need one."

Tashia closed her eyes, knowing she was safe with Bruce outside the door. It was one in the morning.

Anthony placed the stolen liquor back in the storage area. He was still smiling from talking to Tashia. Snow watched as he hoisted the boxes on top of one another.

"They better be glad you're in love because the old Anthony would have been explosive. I still can't believe you let them go."

"They tried it, Snow. They lose their last paychecks. I got my liquor and can't prove what they've already taken. We're done. I don't have time for the courts and paper. Besides, I have other plans tonight." He winked at Snow.

"Yeah I saw Nelly pushing hard."

"I'm not worried about him, Snow. I'm not worried about any other man as long as I'm taking care of my end."

"What did she say about the Janet thing?"

There was a time he would have told Snow to stay in his lane but the two had kindled a friendship of sorts. "I haven't told her the test results yet. I just got them myself today, but we will talk about it tomorrow." Anthony laughed to himself, remembering how she handled Janet earlier. "Shia really put Janet in her place earlier. It was magical to watch."

"You better be careful because Janet wants you back. You recognize that, right?"

"I thought as much, but she don't want me, she wants a check."

"What do you want me to do about replacing those two?"

"They shouldn't be hard to replace. I will look into it tomorrow, but right now, my friend, I have to go and check the bar and you need to check on the girls."

"You mean you need to check on Shia," Snow said and laughed.

Anthony laughed as he walked back to the floor. The crowd had not been this thick since Tashia danced. He supposed that some of the guests called their friends to let them know they had seen her there. The bar was packed as well and he had an extra person working to cover the loss he knew he would suffer.

As he walked through the crowd, he heard various patrons asking when Tashia was going to dance. The crowd was beginning to get restless and impatient..

Anthony approached one of the security staff, told him to tell the door they were at capacity, and made his way to his office. Bruce stood outside his door so he knew Tashia would be inside. He entered the office and found her asleep on the couch. He lay with her and rubbed her back until she began to stir.

"Is it time to go?" she asked, stretching.

"Not yet, but I do have a favor to ask," he began. "Apparently, many are here tonight because they thought you were going to dance. They are getting a little rowdy and I—"

"You were wondering if I would dance tonight?" she said blowing hard. "Anthony, I don't even have a costume to wear!" she yelled.

"Wear what you have on. Hey, you don't have to do it. Just come on stage and say hello." Tashia looked hard at him. "I know. That wouldn't work." He shrugged and paced the floor. When he turned, Tashia was stripped to her shimmering gold undergarments. Anthony stood, watching her in amazement. "Was that for me?" he asked as he approached.

"Yes, but if you want me to share it with the rest of the world I will," she said, teasing him as she stretched to warm up. Swinging her leg to the wall, she reached in a split position and repeated the move on the opposite side.

Anthony walked to her and picked her up. "I'm not sharing you with anyone anymore," he murmured and laid her down on the couch. "I can handle the crowd," he said, kissing her repeatedly.

"This is not exactly where I wanted to spend the evening, but it's a start." He laid there for a moment, caressing her, rolling his head between her breasts before there was a knock on the door.

"Anthony, I need your help," Snow yelled from the door. "We may need to close the doors before things get out of hand."

"Mmmm," he hummed in her ear. He gripped her behind and squeezed. Sliding down her stomach, he stopped at her shimmering underwear and took a deep breath. "I've got to go back to work."

Slowly, he got up from the couch and covered her. Watching her, he backed to the door. "Don't leave this room. I *will* be back," he said and disappeared on the other side.

Tashia lay on the couch, still feeling the imprint of his touch. The heat he aroused in her wouldn't allow her to go back to sleep.

She got up from the couch and redressed. Bruce was still outside the door. "Come on, Bruce. It looks like I have to go back to work." Bruce followed her to the dancer's lounge.

Mouse was sitting in her booth with her books opened. Tashia smiled at the young girl's diligence. She entered her space and sat on her trunk. "Mouse, do you still have the things I gave you?" she asked.

The young girl looked bewildered. "Oh, you mean your old costumes?"

"Yes."

The young girl's face brightened. "Are you going to dance tonight?"

"It looks that way."

"I have most of it in my chest. The rest I haven't brought back from washing."

The two opened the chest. Tashia immediately found her chaps, which she felt would work perfectly with what she had in mind. Mouse helped her pull everything together before running to Snow with her instructions.

Once dressed, she entered the madness of the hall with Bruce in tow. She met Snow at the base of the steps and peeped round the corner to see Anthony where she instructed Snow to have him. She was ready to get her night started and calm the madness of the crowd. She listened to Terrance as he cued her music and introduce her. "Tonight, we have a special guest. She heard your pleas and cries and decided to return to the stage one last time to give a proper goodbye. Everyone welcome to the stage, Sh-h-hi-i-i--a-a!"

Tashia hopped onto the stage, whip in hand, swinging and snapping it in the air. She strutted to the first pole, dropping the whip to the floor and running to swing up the poll and the style she was known for. Once inverted she dropped, catching herself with her thighs and picking up the whip while upside down. She curled up using her strong abs and dismounted from the poll. She danced to the second poll, riding off the adrenaline of the crowd and mounted it, but this time dropping slowly and curling up at the same time, watching Anthony as she came up. Once her feet were close enough she stood and danced to the first poll in front of their guest of honor. There she danced and swirled around the poll. She danced in representation of her last dance. Money was flying, hitting her as she rose and dropped on the pole. Combining all her dances, she gave them a grand send off.

It was now time for her finale. She looked at Anthony, letting him know this dance was for him; a dance of lust and love, embodying everything she felt for him, igniting the fire he had started in her. She locked eyes with him, calling, beckoning, and pleading. She was at the end of the stage now and he was there, right where she wanted him.

She lowered herself into his strong arms, wrapping the whip around his neck, and he became her pole. She danced around him, occasionally cutting her eyes, and smiling at Nellie who was now at the end of his seat as though anticipating he was next. She wrapped her legs around his waist and lifted his shirt over his head, showing off his defined abs. The crowd cheered. She bent backward and back up as though riding him. She repeated the move until she pretended to climax and she pulled his head between her breasts, panted, holding his head there.

She felt the thud of his chest and he, too, panted. His muscles glistened under the lights from the perspiration that had formed. She looked in his eyes and saw he wanted her as badly as she wanted him.

Gently, she unfurled the whip from his neck and he placed her back onto the stage. Pulling back, she playfully hit him once with the whip, barely touching him, but opening a small spot where the whip touched him. Tashia was instantly sorry for accidentally striking him, but she saw a look of pleasure on his face as he gave her that wolfish smile, heating her. She licked his wound and sucked lightly on his nipple before the dance began, again. She played on the pole, swirling, dropping and spinning.

Turning her back to her audience, she gave a little twerk, and strutted to the second pole. There she twerked again, sending the crowd into a frenzy when she looked over her shoulder and waved goodbye, blowing a kiss to them, murdering men and women as she slowly glided off the stage, disappearing into the back. Finally her time grinding Monday to Friday and working Friday to Sunday was over officially.

Bruce waited for her where he dropped her off. Mouse hugged her, giddy with excitement. "Go and get the money on the stage. Use it for school," she whispered in the girl's ear. Mouse hugged her and ran to the stage to collect the greens that covered the entire floor.

Tashia walked back to the office with Bruce. She could still hear the crowd. She entered the office with Anthony right behind her, closing the door behind him. He slid her top over her shoulders and pulled her chaps down, lifting her into his arms, pushing, then falling on top of her as he laid her on the couch.

"Damn, Tashia," he whispered in her ear. She could feel his heart pounding against her chest as he entered her hard and strong. Tashia arched her back as she lifted to meet his thrust. She gripped his butt, pulling him in closer until she could take no more. The heat of his tongue all over her body sent waves like waterfalls, landing and rippling, flooding her mind and raising her, again, and, again, to meet each thrust.

Abruptly he stopped, snatching her, lifting her freshly waxed and wet purse in the air where he dove in and sucked as though drawing her juices with every taste.

"Uh, na, na, na," she babbled, barely audible but clear to his ears. She felt the curl of his lips as he smiled, hearing her audible pleasure.

His fingers entered both cavities, sending her pleasure to a new level. Again, her back arched, receiving all he had to give. She felt the small ripples within her trying to build and she held her breath as though she needed to save it in case later came now.

"Todavia no. Not yet, Tashia," he whispered.

She tried to hold back, but his lovemaking and her love for him wouldn't let her. "No, No, no. No puedo sostenerlo mi amor!" she pleaded. "I can't hold it! Por favor."

He stopped and ran his tongue from her caverns, to her navel and between her breasts where he stopped and nipped at the end of her nipple. She tried to push him off. She wanted to be in control. She liked being in control, but he laughed, grabbing her hands and pulling them above her head, locking them in his grip.

"Shia," he whispered in his ear. "Quiero toda de ti *(I want all of you)*."

"You have all of me," she answered back not understanding his meaning. "I'm yours."

"No I don't." He didn't know whether to continue or not. They had shared so much recently, but he didn't want to frighten her. "There are things I would like to do with you that are on the fringe."

She tried to understand what he was saying. "Oh, so you want to tie me up and whip me," she teased, staring into the depths of his eyes.

He smiled that irresistible smile and answered, "Yes."

Tashia's face changed as she gave thought to what he was saying. She could see he was serious and her heart raced. She smiled with excitement. "Can we finish what we started here first?" She asked, smiling from the high she felt.

The knock on the door jolted them back to reality. Tashia dropped her head back. She wanted to finish. She no longer wanted to wait for the ride back to his house.

While donning his clothes, he walked to the door and cracked it slightly. It was Snow. He knew he would not have come had it been something he could handle. "What's wrong?"

"Tashia has a request from Nelly. He wanted to say goodbye," he said, smiling at Anthony.

"Tell that mother—"

"Anthony!" Tashia yelled, as she slid into his shirt hanging from the rack. "Tell Nelly I will be out once I have changed, Snow," she said, peeping under Anthony's arm and she pushed the door closed.

"You don't have to meet and greet! You didn't do it when you worked here and you don't have to do it now!" Anthony was angry she agreed to meet with him.

Tashia jumped into his arms. "Are you jealous, Mr. Laurent?" she asked, kissing all over him and smiling.

"I don't want a repeat of the last time, and if you go back on the floor it will be crazy, Tashia. I don't want you back out there!" he said louder than he wanted.

"Well, well why don't I get dressed and then you can invite him back to the office. You can be here and Bruce will be outside the door, but it would be good in changing the image of the club. Right?" Tashia searched his face for an answer.

Anthony carried her around the office, as he thought. She did have a good idea. He looked into her face and her searching eyes dissolved his anger. "It's a good idea, so I will do it. I will send for your clothes."

Mouse came to the office with Tashia's clothes and her money. She laid Tashia's clothes on the couch and looked around the office in awe. "I brought your money, too," she told Tashia, still looking around the room.

"I said you can have it and I meant it. But, I only want you to use it for school." Tashia thought. "Why are you still here? Go home and do your homework."

"I dance, again, in thirty minutes."

"I danced for you so go home and keep the money."

"But it's too much and I wouldn't feel right keeping it all."

Tashia wondered how much the girl made dancing. "How much is it, Mouse?" she asked.

"It was over five thousand dollars!" Mouse answered, bouncing and smiling, proud of Tashia.

Tashia looked at her in amazement. She hugged Mouse. "That was for you because I said it was. I don't care how much it is. I want you to fulfill your dreams, Mouse. That money is yours. Okay?" She let the young girl go. "I started dancing to feed my kids and put myself through school, too."

"Did you finish!" the young girl asked amazed.

"Yes I did. I am a Registered Nurse and have a four-year degree in management as well, so go and get it done. If you need more, this," she said, waving around the room, "will still be here."

Anthony watched Tashia reach into her purse and give the young girl her card. "Here is my number if you ever need encouragement or just someone to talk to. Okay?"

"Thank you," Mouse said, with tears in her eyes.

"Don't cry or you will make me cry," Tashia told her. "Why don't you go and get Nelly and escort him back here to the office."

"Leave your money here, Mouse, and I will have someone walk you to your car later," Anthony offered from his desk.

"Okay here," the young girl said, handing him all the money she had.

"Tell Snow I said to remove you from the line up," he added, as she was leaving the office.

"Yes, sir."

Anthony turned to Tashia. "You will interview for her position. I have enough to do before we leave."

"She needs to go. She lied on her application. That girl is not twenty-one."

Tashia was fully dressed again. Anthony watched her from his desk, impatient for this meeting. He was ready to go, and as long as he did not take Tashia through the club, things would begin to quiet down.

He watched the curves of her body and knew why men went crazy and the women were jealous, but it was more than that. Her personality was approachable. She had a heart for others, which was evident by what she had done for Mouse. Her tough exterior gave her a level of confidence that said 'not today'.

She turned and looked at him and he wanted to finish what he started. He was biting his lip. Her gaze matched the heat of his.

"Come here and sit with me," he said, barely audible and she came to him, straddling him in his chair. He buried his head in her breasts, taking in her scent, which now was a mixture of sweat and musk oil. Cupping her breasts, he nibbled through her shirt, sending her, again, to the place where they had left off. She grasped his face and pulled his lips to hers, savoring every drop of moisture.

The soft knock on the door almost went unheard. "Go fix yourself for our guest," Anthony whispered in her ear. "I'm not in the mood for a lot of bull tonight, Tashia," he warned as she headed into his private bathroom.

Mouse knocked again. "Come in," Anthony beaconed.

Mouse entered with Nellie and his entourage. Once everyone was in the office, Mouse attempted to leave. "Jazmine stay," Anthony said, shocking the young girl that he even knew her name. "Tashia will be out in a minute," he announced to the others. "Would you like a drink?"

The group gave their order and Mouse was on her way to get drinks. Anthony smiled when Tashia entered the room. She had redone her hair wetting it a little to make it lay and she had her heels back on.

"Mouse just left to get drinks. I ordered for you," he said, as he motioned for her to sit in his lap.

She cut her eyes at him, walking to their guests, embracing each before making her way to Anthony, not wanting to ruin her happy ending for the night. Once seated between his muscular thighs, he placed his hand on her butt as if marking his territory.

"I want to say I am honored you came through our place tonight," Anthony said. "Tashia's dancing was a surprise even to me."

"You were awesome," the young lady with Nelly offered. "I told Nelly that I had to have you in my next video!" She was much more energetic than before. Nelly calmed her.

"Thank you for dancing. I know when we talked earlier you said you were retired," Nelly said, not looking at Anthony.

"I did it as a kind of farewell and as a favor for management," she explained.

"Well I am glad you came out of retirement while we were here." Nelly boldly looked at her and Anthony shifted his weight under her.

Mouse returned to the office with help from Snow just in time to redirect. "Here are our drinks," Tashia said as she tried to rise to help Mouse serve, but Anthony had a grip that told her he wanted her to remain where she was. She crossed her legs to play off the movement on his lap.

"Rest. You've been on your feet all night," Anthony said, smiling.

Nelly took his drink and sipped it while Anthony took his and downed it in one gulp. He was ready to end the meeting.

He was not good at niceties and didn't like the disrespect Nelly was showing him. He wanted to throw him out of his office. Tashia looked at him, reminding him she was with him, and her heart was his, once again, able to soothe the beast that threatened to rise.

"What is your name again?" she asked his guest.

"Aiden," she answered.

"Aiden, give my assistant your information with the details and my manager and I will discuss it and get back to you," Tashia offered, ignoring Nelly's boldness and gesturing toward Mouse.

Mouse looked bewildered, but quickly picked up and got a pad and pen off Anthony's desk and handed it to Aiden.

"We will have to invite you back, again, when we have something special or maybe out at the house," Anthony suggested. He stood to his feet with Tashia. "I don't want to appear to be rude, but we have to be off. We have to be somewhere else and are very overdue." Anthony made his way around the desk and shook everyone's hand and Tashia did the same as he led her to the door. "Snow. See our guests out and Jazmine call me tomorrow and I will get you taken care of, okay?"

"Yes, sir," she answered as Anthony led Tashia from the office.

Once the door closed, he turned to Tashia. "I told you I had no patience for bull tonight. He's an arrogant bastard."

Bruce smiled as he walked them down the hall and out the back door. Once she was settled in her car, Anthony closed the door behind her. "I will see you at the house."

Anthony followed Tashia to his house. She was proud of the way he handled Nelly, because she saw the entire situation going differently. Her phone rang.

Tashia hit her Bluetooth button. "Hello!"

"Hi, Tashia. This is Jazmine. Nelly wanted to talk to you, but I didn't want to give him your number. I told him it wasn't mine to give."

"You did well, Mouse. Go ahead and put him on," she instructed.

There was a quiet exchange in the background. "Hello," Nelly said, smiling through the receiver.

"Hello, Nelly," she answered. "What can I help you with?"

"I want to take you out," he said.

Tashia fell silent.

"Hello?"

"I'm here, Nelly. Why do you want to take me out?"

"You intrigue me," he answered.

"Why because I danced?"

"No, you intrigued me long before I saw you dance. When you sat to talk with us I was expecting you to be different, but you were dope."

"I'm flattered, Nelly, but I'm not available for anything so intimate."

"I'm not asking to sleep with you, Tashia, just to meet with you."

She could hear him waiting for her answer, but she already knew what that answer was. "I am sure we will see each other again, but I am unable to accommodate your request, as flattering as it is. I do have something coming soon and I will make sure to send you an invite?

Tashia could hear him sigh in the phone. "Okay. I had to try," he said. "Until I see you again, Tashia."

Tashia disconnected the line. Her phone rang again.

"I'm sorry, Tashia, but he kept bugging me and I didn't know what to do," Jazmine said.

"You did fine. Now go home. It's late. Make sure someone walks you to your car, okay?"

"They always do," she said and then was silent. "And, thank you, Tashia. No one has done anything like this for me."

"One day you will be able to pay it forward to someone else. Okay? Goodnight."

Anthony opened the gate from his car and Tashia followed him in. He drove around her, parked his car in the garage, and came out to meet her. He escorted her into the house and they picked up where they left off earlier.

Their exploration left a trail of clothes behind them that led to the master bedroom. She watched his body shine in the moonlight peering in from the window. Each ripple glistened. He tried to reach for her, but she retreated, encircling him and taking in every muscle and ripple. She wondered when he had time to work out.

Anthony was a take-charge man, but this time she wanted to be in charge. She stood behind him, running her hands down the sides of his hard thighs as she moved to the music streaming from his ceiling speakers. Once again, he became her pole and she climbed him, holding on with just her legs around his waist. He throbbed between her thighs, beating steadily against her butt like a stick to a drum— bump, bump, bump.

She climbed higher, his head resting between her breasts. He nibbled as he had earlier, but she slapped him. Looking down she saw the smile dance across his lips and he tried to nibble again, but this time she slapped him twice and slid down, stopping when their eyes met. She bit his lower lip, sucking hard. Her hand reached between her thighs and guided him inside her already saturated purse that waited to cash in on what she had been deprived of all evening.

Like synchronized skaters, the two moved with precision. She glided up and down his body, clamping her purse closed to ensure its contents didn't spill. His gasp let her know when to stop and hold him tightly as she waited for his stick to stop beating with such high velocity and the dance began again.

She covered his nipple and slightly sucked sending his head back. The ride began, again, with her circling around and around, twisting, gripping, and turning.

He walked to the bed where he laid her on her back at the very top. Reaching, he pulled up a strap that hung on the back of the bed and placed it around her wrist. He saw no fear in her face so he repeated the same with the other. The only things free now were her legs, which she gripped even tighter around his waist.

He smiled, again, and retreated from within, lifting her buttocks until her purse was in his face and he sampled its contents, finding her to be as sweet as she had been his first sample. Her legs, once locked, were now spread wide as he sent her back to the mountain peak where he had taken her earlier.

She panted, breathing harder and harder as the altitude changed with each lick, poke, or nibble. "A-a-a-a, Anthony, Anthony, Anthony," she called to him with no release in sight.

She felt his fingers enter her, sliding back and forth, heightening her pleasure. She arched her back again, begging to him, awaiting relief, feeling she would burst.

He slid up her body, entering her hard, causing her back to arch further. Thrusting deep, finding that spot where he fit so perfectly, as if he always knew it was there, causing the waves that had been waiting all evening to escape.

The sound, low at first, gushed as they rode the waves of an overdue happy ending together, crashing like water against rocks meeting the waterfalls, hard and violent. Her back arched with each wave as he pushed deeper to hold his spot in that secret corner. The ripples were never-ending and came one after another without a break. "A no, no, no," she babbled as the final wave came and subsided. She went limp, unable to catch her breath.

Anthony laid his head on her stomach, now committing the experience to memory, erasing the negative that occupied his thoughts for too long. He reached over her head, untied the straps around her wrists, and pulled the sheet over them. She turned and faced him, drawing in closer.

"You okay?" he asked, not knowing her feelings concerning the straps.

She let out a low hum. "I think you've started something, Mr. Laurent."

"I have more."

She's Mine

The sun shone through the window, waking Anthony. He grabbed the remote and closed the blinds, grateful the previous owner had invested in it. He could hear his housekeeper moving around downstairs and looked at the clock on the wall to see it was eleven o'clock. He never slept this late. *What are you doing to me, Tashia?*

Looking down he saw she had moved under his arm and was still sleep. Slowly, he slid from under her and the covers, trying to be quiet and headed to the shower.

He welcomed the heat of the water pounding his body as he thought about his events for the day. They only had another week before leaving for Antigua and he had to hire three people before then. He also needed to set up something for Fatimah. He didn't know how he felt about that situation yet.

Nails running lightly down his back interrupted his thoughts. Tashia slipped in front of him, sharing the shower. She ran her hands across his nipples, bringing a smile to his lips. Cupping her chin, he tilted her head to him and covered her lips with his. "We have a few things to talk about and interviews to set up."

She moaned, indicating her protest. The two took turns washing one another and Anthony received his first lesson in washing her hair. He left the shower and indicated he needed to do some things in his office before they left.

Once Tashia finished blow-drying her hair, she met Anthony in his office. She was wearing his football shirt from his closet. She went to the couch by his bay window and sat in it, tucking her legs.

Anthony leaned back in his chair before standing and coming to meet her. He sat on the couch and handed her a picture. Tashia recognized it as the baby from the office. Looking up, she met his eyes. "Is she yours?" She already knew the answer.

"Yes."

"Are you going to see her before we leave?"

Anthony pulled his lips. "I don't know." He looked at her, searching for answers.

"We don't have to go for the entire summer, Anthony. We will figure it out."

Anthony knew it wouldn't be that simple. Fatimah's mother was nothing like Myra. She would fight for him no matter how often he told her no. Maybe it would be better to let Fatimah go, or maybe he should fight for custody.

He leaned back on the couch and sighed. "It's not going to be that simple with her mother."

"What happened with the two of you? I get distinctive vibes that she wants you back and she may leverage the baby to get what she wants, Anthony."

"I dated her when I first came to the area. She couldn't adjust to my lifestyle and she left me to date a baller. Told me that was what she wanted anyway. She said she never wanted me and bounced."

Tashia saw something in his face that told a different story. "She hurt you, didn't she?"

"She didn't get me like you do, so she didn't understand my ways. I admit I was cold and often short, but I was under the pressure of trying to build two businesses and start the mentorship. She felt I didn't give her enough attention so she started dating this high profile guy. Everyone warned me and told me she was a gold digger, but I didn't see it. So, when she announced she was done with us I was completely blindsided.

"I guess when she left she was pregnant and didn't know it, but I'm sure he wasn't fully convinced it was his and here we are."

"Do you still have feelings for her? And be honest with yourself."

Anthony pulled her close. "No. I used to care about her, but she has no place in my heart. I guess that was evident because I buried myself into my businesses so she could not be the one. I would give this up," he said, raising his hands to the sky, "entirely for you, Tashia. I can't breathe without you. When she was gone my air was just fine." He grabbed her hand.

"Then, why were you hurt when she left?"

"I was already having a hard time believing women. She told me she loved me and wanted to spend her life with me and I believed her.

Then she left to be with someone who had more money. When she came by yesterday it was to bring the test results and ask if I was going to be a part of *her* life."

"What did you tell her?"

"I told her no. Her feelings were hurt. I have you and the kids. I told her the dynamics of my life have changed and that doesn't mean they are going to change back because now she wants me to be a part of hers."

"So why don't you invite her over and we both can talk to her so she knows we are together and she can drop this hope of getting you back? The only thing that needs to be discussed is visitation."

Anthony kissed her. "That's why you are my girl," he said. "Now let's change the subject and you tell me what Nelly wanted when he called you last night."

Tashia watched his face and he was serious. "How did you know Nelly called me?"

"Jazmine called about the video information and she apologized." Anthony watched her waiting for an answer.

"He wanted to spend some time with me and I told him that I was not an available woman."

"I told you I didn't like the way that disrespectful bastard was looking at you. Then he openly stared you down when in the office."

"You need to create a lounge atmosphere in the back to host guests. You have the room," she suggested.

"Don't change the subject, Tashia. I don't like him and I don't trust him. Okay?"

"He could help elevate the status of the club, so keep it business. I can handle him, Anthony. "

"I'm sure, but I don't want to have to *handle* him."

She could feel his tension. He was so sexy when he got dark. He licked his bottom lip, and she leaned in to kiss him, but he turned his head, agitated she disagreed with him. She sat in his lap and tried again, but he laughed and turned his head again.

The two played and rolled on the floor until she was seated on his chest. "I smell you, Tashia, and I need to get some work done before we pick up the kids. Now get off of me before we get started again."

"Would that be so bad?" she teased, nibbling his earlobe. "I want you, again. You saying you don't want me?"

Throwing her to the floor, he got to his feet and ran from the room, leaving her lying alone.

Out of the Mouths of Babes

Cuyler sat with Preston in the chaise lounge, watching a movie with the kids. She smiled every time she watched Solana and Callia. Callia had started her Spanish lessons and Solana spoke to her in Spanish when they were together. Now Callia had her head in Solana's lap, napping. They reminded her of her childhood with Tashia.

She didn't know what was going on between the two of them. Tashia seemed hostile at times toward her. She was only trying to protect her from being hurt by Anthony. Preston didn't believe she needed protection, but to Cuyler he was scary.

She thought about their trip to Antigua and hoped they could mend their differences. They had just reunited and she didn't want to lose ground.

"How are we all going to fit in Dad's house?"

Preston wondered how long she had been thinking about that. "Anthony has his own home on the island so I am sure he will stay there."

"Oh! Where does he live there?"

Preston didn't answer immediately. "Why all the questions, C? Are you still worried?" Preston was becoming annoyed and Cuyler could hear it in his voice.

"She's my sister, Preston!"

"She's a grown ass woman, Cuyler! Did you not see how happy they are together? Now leave them alone!" he said louder than he wanted.

Zander turned to look at them. He heard their conversation and wondered why his aunt hated Anthony. He turned back to watch the movie.

"Leave them alone. You sound like he did with you and me. Do you remember how it made you feel? The difference is Anthony doesn't give a damn what you or anyone else thinks. Enough!"

Cuyler's feelings were hurt. She didn't understand why he defended him so hard. She was quietly sulking.

Preston pulled her close and whispered in her ear. "I don't want you worrying about anything except this baby. I don't want you worried and wound up like you were with Callia. What is gonna be will be whether you want it or not." He rubbed her arm with his thumb.

Cuyler rested in his arms and thought he was right, but she wanted so much more for her sister. She deserved it. She had so much hardship in her life and she wanted peace for her sister.

Cuyler slid out of Preston's arms and made her way to the bathroom. Then, she went into the kitchen to get something to drink. She turned from the fridge and Zander stood in the doorway, watching her.

"Why don't you like Anthony, Auntie?"

"Who said I didn't like him?"

"You don't have to say it."

Shame swept over her. "I don't dislike Anthony." She didn't trust the person she believed he was.

"They are good for one another. She is happier than she was when my dad was alive and I didn't believe that was possible. They were apart once and they were miserable. He loves her. I see it when she walks in and his face lights up. I saw it before she saw it. He's protective of her and us..."

"He has a family now, Auntie. He was all alone before. We're his family," Solana said from the doorway, crying. "I don't want him to be alone again."

Zander picked up his sister and consoled her. "Shhh. Anthony's not going anywhere," he assured her. "Now go wash your face so you don't upset Callia."

"She's sleep," she said, wiping her tears.

"Anthony isn't going anywhere. He's not leaving us. Okay?"

Solana nodded her reassurance, slid from her brother's arms and ran to the bathroom.

Cuyler felt small and sorry she had upset her nephew and niece. "I'm sorry you heard my conversation. I just want the best for your mom."

"She's in good hands." Zander turned when Solana came back down the hall. "Go and watch the movie, Sunshine."

Cuyler was shocked at Zander's maturity. He spoke to her not as a child but an adult. The silence made her uneasy as he watched her, waiting for her to say something. His eyes were accusing and showed disappointment.

"I trust your judgment, Zander. I will trust him and do better." Maneuvering her growing belly, she hugged the young boy.

The Shadows

Tashia parked her car in the garage and hopped into Anthony's with him. They needed to go to the club to meet with a few people from the restaurant who had shown interest in working there.

She wore white shorts and a blouse almost equally long in white. Her four-inch heels exaggerated her thick, muscular legs. Anthony watched her as she fidgeted with her seat belt. Her hair was blown straight and she wore it up in a ponytail.

When they arrived to the club, the applicants were there already, as well as Myra. Nothing had changed between them. Myra scanned her as she walked by.

"Hello, Myra," Tashia said. "How are the kids?"

"Fine and yours?" Myra asked, taken off guard.

"They're good. Are the applicants ready?"

Myra looked at Anthony in question, confused by Tashia's involvement. "You two can handle this. I need to meet with Snow," he said, answering her unspoken question and continued walking to the back.

Myra turned and looked at Tashia. "So I guess I'm following your lead?"

"No. I'm here to help you. Anthony totally trusts you and feels you've been doing a great job."

Myra looked shocked. "He talks about me?"

"He talks about work and especially his key people. You are one of his key people. So, what are we doing?" Tashia went to the bar and had a seat.

Myra's calm told Tashia she had won her over for the time being. She watched Myra walk to the bar and gather her papers. "We are going to talk to the two girls who want to come over and see who the best fit is. And that's about it."

Tashia realized Myra didn't have a plan, but allowed her to continue. "Well, let's get started." Slapping her thighs, Tashia jumped from the barstool.

"I heard you danced last night," Myra said. "Do you miss it?"

Tashia thought about the question before answering. "I miss the art of it. I don't miss feeling or being viewed as less than a person."

Tashia saw Myra's eyes move slowly to her ring and back to her eyes. "I see you were able to do what no one was able to do. Congratulations. We can take them one at a time to one of the tables, I guess."

A now deflated Myra approached a pretty Latino girl and ushered her past Tashia to a table near the stage. Tashia followed the two and the three sat.

The girl looked Tashia over. "I like your outfit, but I like everything you wear to the restaurant."

"Thank you."

"My name is Catalena Martinez," the girl said.

"Mi nombre es Tasha y ella es, Myra. Tu tienes que ganarte la atencion de ella, porque ella toma la decisión final," Tasha said, warning Catalena that she needed to suck up to Myra and not her.

Catalena smiled. "Gracias."

Tashia could see Myra was getting annoyed. "I welcomed Catalena to our meeting and told her good luck. Let's get started," she lied.

After Myra completely reviewed the girl's application, Tashia looked her in the eyes and asked her the hard questions. "Why do you want to work at the club? The guests are rude and disrespectful. There are often fights and a lot of ass grabbing. Are you that girl, Catalena?"

"I have four brothers, the restaurant has its share of rude and disrespectful people, and no one touches my ass unless I put it there," she answered, smiling.

Tashia liked her. She was edgy, but she was no barmaid. "I don't have any additional questions, do you Myra?"

The two interviewed the last girl. She was Caucasian with long skinny legs. Her reasoning for coming to the bar was to make more money.

After the interviews were over, Myra turned to Tashia and said, "I think Catalena would be a better fit here."

Tashia agreed, but she knew Myra's motives were not pure. She thought Catalena would be a distraction for Anthony and she was too pretty for her to compete with at the restaurant, but Tashia had other plans for Catalena. "I want them both," she said, surprising Myra.

"But then I will be short *two* girls at the restaurant!"

"You will be short one girl. Call Mouse. She needs something with better hours for school. You can teach her how to serve, and she is just pretty enough." Tashia knew she would not understand the meaning of her last words. Mouse was a pretty girl, but was no real competition for Myra.

"I thought Anthony said he only needed one waitress?"

"We need a dancer as well. I will train her when we get back." Tashia looked back at Catalena. She was a prize if she could dance with the same attitude she gave.

"When you get back?"

Tashia stood and patted Myra on her back lightly. "That's why you get paid the big bucks."

A puzzled Myra watched as Tashia headed back to the office.

The kids were in the kitchen eating when Tashia and Anthony arrived. Solana ran to Anthony and jumped in his arms. He swung her around as he always did and carried her back to her chair.

"Finish eating, Sunshine."

He went to greet Preston and Cuyler and noticed Cuyler was not as standoffish as she usually was with him, but he also noticed that Tashia stood back not approaching Cuyler at all. Instead, she waited for Cuyler to come to her.

"Hi, Shia. You look beautiful as usual," Preston said, hugging her.

Cuyler came quickly to her sister and hugged her, not sensing Tashia's mood. Anthony placed Solana in his lap and watched. Never noticing before, he realized Tashia always stayed back when Cuyler was around. She appeared to be shy and quiet.

"Did you guys already eat?" Preston asked.

"No. We had to take care of a lot today," Anthony answered.

"Well, have a seat, Tashia, and I will make you a plate."

224

"I don't want a lot. I do have to wear a bathing suit next week," she joked, as she sat in the chair next to Zane who was nursing a shake Preston had made for him.

"If you and your sister came from the same genes I'm sure you're not worried about that," Preston joked.

Anthony saw it again. There was a shift in Tashia's demeanor.

"Tashia has always been the one with the body," Cuyler threw in, as she sat in the chaise in the corner.

Preston gave Tashia her plate, but she played in it, pushing her food around. She looked across to him and he winked at her. She gave him an uncomfortable smile. Anthony announced, "You know what, I forgot we were supposed to meet my manager on the way home and I don't want to hold him, so, I will take mine to go unless I'm being rude."

"It has never stopped you before," Preston replied, pulling a to-go box from the pantry. He prepared the box for his brother and got another for Tashia.

"Thank you," she said, handing him her plate.

Tashia rubbed Zane's head and kissed it. She played with various strands of curls and put them back in place.

"Okay! Does everyone have their things at the door?" Anthony asked, standing with Solana still in his arms.

"My things are at the door!" Solana answered, pushing from his arms. She disappeared around the corner with Callia following like a shadow.

Zane stood with his drink bottle in hand and Zander removed their plates from the table, loading them into the dishwasher. The boys hugged them both, said their thanks, and headed for the door as well.

"The car is unlocked if you want to get them loaded up. I'm coming," he told Tashia and lightly kissed her. He watched her hug Cuyler and Preston before disappearing down the hallway.

Preston looked at him, puzzled.

"Can I speak with you for a minute?" Anthony asked, gesturing to Preston's office.

"Sure."

"Excuse us," Anthony told Cuyler, to make it clear she was not invited.

The two men went to the office and Preston closed the door. "Have a seat," Preston told him.

"No, this won't take long. I wanted to let you know that I found out yesterday that I have a child. Tashia knew it was a possibility and she's fine with it, but I'm not sure what I'm going to do."

"What do you mean 'What you are going to do'?"

"If I didn't have Tashia and the kids it would be a no brainer, but I do and don't want to complicate things. She's my child and so of course I want to be a part of her life, but her mother's a handful and I don't want to chance that with Tashia."

Preston laughed. "Tashia is a handful and I think she can handle her own. You may have a rough road, but you have the right woman to travel it with," he reassured.

Anthony pulled his lip. He had been thinking the same, but it took his sensible brother to reassure him. "You're right. I am worrying too much about this thing."

"So, girl or boy? How old? Name?" Preston flooded him with questions.

Anthony laughed about the situation. "Girl. Her name is Fatimah. She is four months old." For the first time since her paternity was confirmed he wanted to meet Fatimah.

Preston patted him on the back and walked him to the office door. Anthony stopped abruptly, wondering if he should breach the subject of Cuyler and Tashia, but thought better of it.

"What?" Preston asked.

Anthony shook his head and walked out of the office. He hugged Preston, "Thanks, man."

"I feel honored that my big brother trusted my opinion enough to ask me."

When they turned the corner, he was surprised to see that Tashia was still standing at the door. Cuyler was talking to her, but he knew that stubborn look, and Tashia was not complying.

"You ready to go?" Anthony asked, as he approached.

"Yes," she answered relieved. "Bye, Cuyler," she said, turning to hug her sister.

Cuyler hugged her sister, but Anthony saw the disappointment on her face. He opened the door and ushered Tashia out. "If this summer is going to work you two need to talk," he whispered in her ear.

"I'm not going to Antigua. Just the kids!"

"I'm not leaving you here alone. You are coming," he said. "What is going on?" he asked, but she said nothing. "Come on. We won't do this here."

Tashia lay looking at Anthony as he talked. She didn't want to talk about her and Cuyler. She almost wished the years between them had never been disturbed, but then she would not have met Anthony.

"Where are you, Shia? What has you so shutdown?"

"Let's talk about you instead," she suggested, changing the subject. "Did you set up the meeting with Janet?"

"Yes. We meet with her tomorrow evening. She is going to bring the baby and I told her you were coming. She fought me at first, but I told her this was the only way this was going to work, so she said she would come, but would make no promises."

"Good. I'm excited for you."

"We're not done. What is going on between you and your sister?"

"Nothing."

"Oh yes there is. Whenever she is around, it looks like your light goes out. You take a back seat as though you are hiding."

She turned on her back and looked up at the ceiling. She didn't know what was wrong. She only knew that Cuyler annoyed her lately. She felt somewhat jealous, but that wasn't really it. She was secure in her skin. "I don't know what it is. She hasn't done anything to me, but her very presence irritates me."

"She can be irritating," he teased.

Tashia hit him. "You can't talk about my sister, but I can. She is a brat and always has been. She could never do anything wrong, even as a child." She turned and looked at Anthony. "I love my sister, Anthony, with all my heart and soul. I'm just....I don't know," she said, jumping up from the bed. She twirled around to face him. "It's like when I am with her she's good and I'm bad; she's perfect and I'm flawed; she's important and I'm not. She's....beautiful and I am pretty! Can you understand that?"

He knew all too well what she was feeling. He was not his father's natural child, so he always felt he had to be that much more perfect than his siblings. He was always trying to please his father so he would love him the same, although his father never treated him differently. "Yes. I was not my father's natural child and I always felt like the servant or the keeper, but separate from the family. Funny thing is it never came from him; it was the role I stepped into by choice. No one made me; I wore it because it was comfortable." He stood from the bed and came to her. "It's all in *your* head. Cuyler sees you as her big sister and those are some big shoes to fill. I know because I rub them every day," he said, laughing. Tashia laughed and pushed him. He had a way of making her issues seem silly.

Janet's Melt Down

J anet sat at the bar, waiting for Anthony and Tashia. Although early, she felt annoyed they were not there. Nervous, not knowing what to expect from this new Anthony, she played with the ice in her now empty glass.

Looking down she checked to see how her outfit looked. She wore his favorite color, orange, hoping he would notice her. She heard he was getting married, but he had not said 'I do' yet.

Snow approached the bar and informed her Anthony said they would be there in five minutes, and brought her another drink.

They! The word stuck in her head, agitating her more as she waited. She would play the game, but she felt Tashia had no place in this meeting. Once Anthony became attached to Fatimah, she would have a few demands of her own or she would change the game.

The venom from her bitterness was like a shadow over her. She should have never left him but she thought he would come after her. He never did. Days, weeks, months past and there was not as much as a phone call. His new girl, Tashia, had some game with her, but she didn't understand what he wanted with a woman who had three suitcases behind her.

The host and hostess entered the bar. Tashia was dressed stylish in her boyfriend jeans, white pumps and half lace asymmetrical blouse. Her hair was in massive curls and pulled to her face making her look totally Latino.

Anthony extended his hand to shake hers and she looked at it, hurt he would treat her like a business appointment. "Hey! Sorry we're late. There was an accident so we had to take a detour. Let's go back to my office."

"I am going to grab water. Does anyone else want one?" Tashia asked.

"You can bring me one."

"I have a drink already," Janet indicated by lifting her glass.

Anthony directed Janet back to his office, noticing her reserve. He smiled, knowing she was salty about Tashia's presence.

Snow had turned on the air conditioning before they came as Anthony had instructed so the office was cool and comfortable. "You can have a seat, Janet. I thought you would have brought Fatimah with you."

She loved the way he accented her name differently, making it sound even more beautiful than Janet thought when she chose it. "She's in the car asleep with my sister. I wanted to see how the meeting went before we took things to the next level."

Looking above the rim of his shades, he studied her, wondering if she was still playing games or acting on her motherly instincts. His thoughts were interrupted when Tashia walked into the office.

"Sorry. I had to go to the storage to get it. I hope you didn't wait for me."

Janet observed her movements as Tashia crossed the office to Anthony. She wondered why she was there. They were not married *yet.* She wondered how she would treat her daughter. Would she love her like her own, or discard her as interference? She sat in the chair in front of his desk. "Let's get started."

To Janet's surprise, Tashia sat in the seat next to her.

Janet looked at her blankly. "Why is she here? You are not married yet."

That was the Janet he knew. Perhaps Snow was correct in believing she still wanted him, but he didn't care.

"Tashia *will* be my wife. She will be a big help to me, but mostly she is here so you will be comfortable when Fatimah is with me to know that everyone will have her best interest in mind."

"Who said she will be with you alone?"

"What are you saying?"

"I'm not ready for that."

"That's understandable. But, when will you be ready?" Tashia could see the disappointment on his face and saw that Janet saw it, too. She watched the young woman settle in her seat as she recognized that she held the reigns. Her heart felt for him as she realized the journey he was about travel.

She watched Anthony regain his composure, but was sure Janet had already recognized the minor change in his demeanor. Picking up the envelope on the desk, which held the debit card he ordered for Fatimah's care earlier that week, he flipped it several times, deep in thought, before opening his desk drawer and dropping it inside.

"How do you want to do this, Janet? What do you want?"

"I *expect* you to be a father to your child and take care of her."

"And what are your *expectation*?" he asked, over emphasizing the word. Tashia could see he was angered now.

"I expect you to take care of her financially, of course."

"So, it's just the money you want from me. How much?"

"What are you offering?"

"What do you want!" he asked, slowly standing to his feet.

Tashia stood and moved to his side, rubbing his back. He was trembling.

"That's right! Get your boy!" Janet told Tashia.

Tashia turned to Janet. She could see she wanted to hurt him and she was going to use Fatimah to do it. The hurt showed clearly on her face and her being there only added to it. "Sit down, Anthony," she said softly. His muscles relaxed under her touch and he returned to his seat.

"Oh you sit and fetch now. I always knew you had a little dog in you. Woof, woof," she barked, imitating a small dog.

Tashia quickly sat in his lap to keep him from rising again. "Everyone calm down. We are here for Fatimah and what's best for her."

"We? I don't know what *you* are here for, because *you* don't have anything to do with this!" Now it was Janet who stood.

"I'm here for the reasons Anthony said. I have three children, Janet, and before I would ever let them go with anyone I have to know they will be safe. They trust me to keep them safe.

"Anthony wants to be a part of Fatimah's life. Family is everything to him. He makes sure my children are safe and I don't see him doing any less for your child. He will keep her safe and make sure she wants for nothing.

"It's important that he is a part of her life so she will feel complete. No one can do that except the two of you."

"You damn right, so why are you here!"

Tashia could see her presence complicated the situation. Janet was breathing heavily and openly daring her. Anthony thighs tensed. "Let me say this and then I am going to leave. My kids' father died six years ago and they have not been the same since. He was an important part of their lives. They miss him in ways they will never understand.

"Anthony has filled that void in their lives. He is great with them and they love and trust him. *I* trust him with their lives. He wants to be a part of Fatimah's life. That's important to him, but if you two cannot make this work, she will be the one who loses out.

"I see something in your attitude that says you are making this about you and it isn't."

"You don't know me. You come here and dance and turn him on and now all of a sudden he thinks he's in love and wants to be this great man! Well let me tell you, Anthony will throw you out like trash when he is bored with you and he will as soon as someone else comes along who can do better tricks!"

"But this isn't abought me and Anthony or you and Anthony. This is about Fatimah and her father."

"So, I am supposed to wait for him to throw her away like he does everyone else!" She glared at Tashia, as though waiting for an answer.

"I didn't throw you away, Janet. You left me for what you thought was a better meal ticket! So is that what I will be, another cash transaction?" Anthony asked. "Don't deflect on me!"

"You told me not to expect anything from you. Remember? You could not give me what I wanted is what you told me. Why was I going to waste my time?"

"So, why are you angry with me? Because I was honest? I don't know any other way to be."

"You two need to talk, so I am going." Tashia stood to leave. "Don't forget you two are here for Fatimah, so say what you need to say to one another, but don't forget your objective."

Tashia went to the bar to get another bottle of water. Seated at the bar was a dark complexion woman holding a baby she knew had to be Fatimah.

"Hi. Can I help you?" she asked, as she approached.

When she came closer, she could see it was not a woman, but rather a young girl who appeared to be about sixteen. Tashia saw she was shy and protective of the baby as she pulled her closer when Tashia approached.

"No. The white-haired man gave me something to drink."

Tashia came around to see her closer and the girl adjusted to keep Tashia in view. She walked into the bar area instead, feeling the bar would make her feel more at ease knowing there was something between them.

Fatimah smiled when she saw Tashia and kicked both legs. "I see you," she cooed at the baby. Fatimah bounced up and down. "What's your name?"

"Her name is Fatimah, but I call her fatty because she's so juicy," the girl said, smiling for the first time.

"I was talking about you. What's your name?"

The girl immediately shrank in disposition again. "Jeanie," she answered. Slowly, the girl scanned the room wondering if anyone was watching.

"How old are you?"

She clammed up and did not answer. Tashia thought her demeanor was strange, so she decided to stop asking her questions. "My name is Tashia and I am going in the back to find a snack. Would you like something?"

"No thank you."

Tashia went to the back and found Snow cleaning the storage room. He looked up and stopped cleaning. "Hey. You're done?"

"No. I left the two of them together to fight it out. That girl wasn't going to hear anything he had to offer as long as I was there." Tashia reached for another bottle of water.

"You're gonna need something stronger than water when they are done."

"And you need a man to stay out of here." Tashia looked at him confused. "Why are you always here?"

"Because I don't have a man." He smiled and started cleaning again.

"Did you see little Fatimah? Isn't she a cutie?"

"Yes and did you see her strange bodyguard?"

Peeking out the door, Tashia made sure the girl was in the same spot where she left her and she was. "Did you speak with her?"

"A little."

"Strange."

After a while, the sound of voices caught both their attention. There was no screaming or shouting. Tashia decided not to shake the delicate balance and stayed in the storage room with Snow. Here phone rang. It was Anthony trying to find her.

"Where are you?"

"In the storage room with Snow."

"Well come, we have to get going."

Tashia jumped from the box and waved goodbye to Snow. "On my way."

Anthony was holding his daughter, smiling, when she entered the bar area. He was talking to Fatimah in baby talk and she was kicking and laughing at him. Janet stood nearby watching their interaction taking in everything Anthony did. Jeanie sat where Tashia left her at the bar, watching little Fatimah with Anthony.

"She's beautiful, Janet," Tashia said, as she approached.

A pink-eyed Janet turned to Tashia. She said nothing and looked back to Anthony. Jeanie looked at Tashia, but quickly to Janet. She was visibly afraid.

"I will be in and out of town for the next few months but money will be deposited on the first of every month into the account. I will pick her up the first weekend of next month."

"Send me the papers and I will sign them and send them back to your lawyer."

Janet took Fatimah and started for the door once Tashia was close. Tashia could see there was still going to be a problem while she was in the picture. Nothing was resolved.

Denial

C aden sat with Gemma reviewing and finalizing more arrangements for the gala. She seemed to be moving a little slower than usual, but it was not the first time he had seen her in pain. Over the months, he had been praying for her, but didn't know if his prayers were being heard. More than once, he could see she wore makeup to cover the bruises on her face. He long ago stopped asking her what was going on, believing she would tell him when she was ready.

He could see she was thinner than she had ever been since he first met her and he always met her at a restaurant to make sure she ate. Never finishing her food, he couldn't get her to take the rest home for later either.

They were beginning to wrap things up and he saw her wince from the pain. He wanted to ask her, again, but was stopped by Jacque who walked up on them.

"Hey, man! What are you doing here?" Jacque was carrying his gym bag over his shoulder. He was alone.

Caden stood and embraced his brother. They had come a long way since their reunion in his home before India's death. Caden had forgiven him and started a new bond, which was much different from their childhood.

Jacque reached down to hug Gemma; she winced and slightly cried out. "You all right?" Jacque asked, afraid he had squeezed too tightly.

"I'm okay," Gemma lied.

"No you're not," Caden said, concerned. "You have been favoring that side all night and you can barely breathe. You need to go to the hospital, Gemma."

She protested and stood to her feet ready to go. "I will be all right, but I have to go." She gathered her things, still wincing through the pain. "I will email you my update tomorrow and you can let me know what else you need me to finish." She walked away, leaving the two men dumbfounded.

Jacque turned to his brother for answers. Caden shrugged and sat back in his seat. "I think she's being beaten by someone, but she won't let anyone help her."

Jacque sat where Gemma once sat and looked at the food on her plate. "That girl needs to eat. She barely ate anything."

"She never does and won't take it with her."

Jacque pushed the food out of his way and called the waitress over to order. He ordered his salad and turned his attention back to Caden.

New Allies

Marissa waited for her turn to speak during group. She was doing what Dr. Davis told her to do in order for her to leave the institution. During her last session, he praised her for her improvement and told her he was recommending she be moved to a less secure facility.

Standing, she began, "I was born on the island of Antigua, and I fell in love with a boy. We were best friends most of our lives and I knew we would spend the rest of our lives together.

"After we graduated from prep school he worked at his father's import/export shipping company and two years later came to America to go to college. I was so proud of him, but didn't want him to leave. Many times when our men come here, they do not come back and do not marry girls from home. They want an American woman. He was no different.

"I waited and waited for him to come back to me, but he never did. When I questioned his family they would say he was doing well, but he never asked about me, or said he missed me. Then one day I found out he had a girlfriend. I had lost him.

"I didn't eat or drink for weeks. I stayed in my bed. They said I had a nervous breakdown, but to me I died. I should have, because I didn't want to live. I tried to take my life twice, but each time someone found me. I thought he would come if he understood how much I loved him."

"You could have had any man you wanted. Look at you," one of the patients said. "Why him?"

Marissa watched the man, annoyed he interrupted her. She knew no one would understand her love for Preston. There would never be any other man for her. "Preston is kind and patient," she began. "He is smart and hard working. He has a beautiful voice and can play any sport."

"You sound like you still want him!" the patient said, still interrupting.

Marissa watched the man again, but this time she listened to what he was saying. She *did* sound like she still wanted Preston. If she wanted to leave this place she could not let on that she still loved him. "Wayne, I do still care for and love Preston and probably always will, but Dr. Davis helped me to put these feelings into prospective. He helped me to understand people come and go in our lives and sometimes relationships are not forever, but we can sometimes still feel. I learned to understand that this is fine, but we have to pick up and move on or get lost in life." She was now looking at Wayne, warning him to keep his mouth shut.

Rolling her eyes, Marissa put on a smile and continued with her story. "I do want a man with the same qualities one day, but Preston has moved on and it's time for me to do the same." Marissa flashed a big smile as everyone applauded, except Wayne. She saw he was not buying her act. If she could persuade him, she knew she would be able to persuade Dr. Davis to release her.

After the meeting, she approached the scrawny man. He looked at her, astonished she had any conversation for him. "Hello, Wayne."

"Hi, Marissa."

"May I talk to you for a minute?"

"Sure."

"I wanted to know why you feel I still have a thing for Preston?" She smiled her best smile and tried to be as tame as she could. Blinking her catlike green eyes, she tried to win him over, but saw he was still apprehensive.

"Your eyes get all mushy and you look dreamy when you talk about him. You smile too much when you say his name." He looked at her, debating whether to say more. "You are still in love with him and as long as you don't know how to hide it you will remain here. You need to think of someone you like, but just not in the same way when you talk about him and that will help to convince Dr. Davis, otherwise you will be here for a while." The man looked at her blankly and walked away.

She ran behind him, circling him to make him stop walking. "Why are you here, Wayne?"

"Why?"

"Because you seem like you have a good head on your shoulder."

"I do." He pushed past her.

Again, she ran around him and stopped him. "Then why are you here with me?"

He looked her in the green eyes he knew she used to get what she wanted from most. He had to admit, they were hypnotizing, but he didn't want to start all over again. "Because I *am* crazy." He walked by her and disappeared down the hall.

The next morning, Marissa approached the peculiar little man, again. He was bored. She mystified him. He agreed to help her.

A Time to Pray

Caden's prayer list was getting long, but he didn't mind. He started praying for Gemma long before he knew she was in trouble. He was compelled to do so.

Sitting in his chair, he looked at the moon. It was big and aluminous. He no longer cried for India, but he still missed her and there was not a day that went by when he did not think of her.

Although busy, he began to feel lonely, knowing Callia was about to leave him for months. He would miss her so much. She would be two this fall and he could not believe how much time had passed. She spoke three languages and she would be going to school part of the day, beginning in the fall.

Smiling, Caden thought about how bossy and take-charge she was. Her mother referred to it as being 'fire'. When she became wound up, they said she was 'catching fire'. He was so blessed to have had her no matter how she came. He thanked God that Cuyler did not abort her, which she had every right to do since at the time he was missing in her life, but she chose life and he felt blessed by that choice.

Opening his prayer log, he glanced at his list and began praying.

Another Move

Anthony helped Zander with the last box from the truck. They spent the last week painting rooms and getting everything set up so when they returned they would not have to do so much. Anthony decided they would move in his home temporarily, but wanted to find a different house or have another built. His house was not created for children. For the time being, he painted the kids' rooms the colors they chose. The only one who had seen them was Zander because of his involvement in the project.

Solana's room was painted lavender, highlighted in green and pink. Tashia purchased accents to create a room for a princess. She had a bouquet of faux flowers on one nightstand while the other had a lacy green lamp. Her cover was furry and pink, lavender and green. There was a table in the corner for her and Callia to play and shelves with books and dolls alternately arranged.

Zane's colors were blue and grays. Zane was into cars, but they thought he was too big to get a car bed so they did a futon bed combination in case he had company. His shelves had cars, puzzles, and books. He also had a table in the corner of his room so he could assemble his models.

Zander's room was the guest room in the house. He had his own bathroom and a modestly decorated room. His colors were black, gray, and gold. He also had a sliding glass door that led out onto a private deck. Anthony had conversations with him about his limitations and the temptations his room offered. His final suggestion for him was not to think about it.

"How did your interviews go yesterday?" His mother had taken him to two prep school interviews.

"Why do I have to go to a prep school?"

"We figured it would give you better opportunities for when you go to college."

"They are stuffy. They aren't my kind of people."

"Zander, I don't see you with anyone, so tell me, who are your kind of people?"

Zander didn't answer. He didn't hang with anyone when he was younger because he was always with his dad, and after his death he watched his brother and sister. He couldn't answer the questions.

"I graduated from prep school," Anthony said, smiling. "So what are you trying to say about me?" Anthony smile, again, and patted the boy on the back. "It will be a good experience for you to know that the haves are more messed up than the have nots."

"What do you do for a living, because this house is fat?"

"I own some businesses," he answered.

"What kind?"

"I have a restaurant and club."

"Can I get a job there?"

"We can work out something."

The two climbed back into the truck. "Let's get this back so we can go to Preston and Cuyler's to eat."

"Why doesn't Aunt Cuyler like you?"

"You sure are full of questions for a boy who normally says nothing." They both laughed. "Your aunt doesn't like me because I was mean to her when I first met her. I believed she was going to hurt my brother and I supposed I was protecting him."

"Auntie is cool people."

"Yes, she turned out to be okay."

"I think she believes she is doing the same."

"I know."

Zander was quiet for a moment. "Thank you for making my mother so happy. I haven't seen her happy since before my dad died."

"Your mom is good people and she deserves to be taken care of and protected."

Anthony pulled into the truck rental parking lot and jumped from the truck. When he returned he signaled for Zander to get out. Once Anthony signed the paperwork, the two headed for his car.

"Okay, let's go on holiday!"

Home

A nthony watched the island rise to meet the plane. He didn't know what to feel about returning to his home. All he knew was he missed his dad.

Mr. Washington sat at the head of the dinner table, happy his family was there. He watched Anthony and Preston fight over who would sit at the head of the opposite end, smiling at the rivalry that had ensued for years. Eventually, Anthony won, as he usually did, and Preston sat next to him, laughing.

Cuyler beamed and he liked the calm and happiness surrounding this pregnancy. Callia was a well-adjusted little girl and he was shocked she remembered him. She sat next to him, chattering away in Spanish, with her cousin, Solana. Tashia sat to Anthony's right and the boys filled in the middle with Zander between Cuyler and Solana.

The men put the food together while the women unpacked their things. The next day they had planned to have a party at the house and the other family members and friends would be there. Blaine was flying in later with a guest and Annetta would come to the house later. Anthony asked her to go and open his house and she had been staying there until they came.

"Why Annetta still at the house, Pop?" Anthony asked. "I thought she would be here today."

"The pool man is coming and she wanted to make sure he did what he was supposed to do."

"Well, we will head over as soon as we finish up here. I didn't want her to have to do all that."

Cuyler looked at Preston, confused. "I thought we would all stay here."

"Anthony has a couple of homes here. Annetta stays in one and he stays in the other when he is here. We can ride over, too, and help them get settled." He turned and looked at his father. "As long as Dad doesn't need us to do anything here."

"Oh no. I may ride with you. It's been a while since I've been there."

Anthony walked around his property, evaluating the work done in the yard. The landscaping was beautiful and the tropical plants were blossoming.

Tashia walked close to him, marveling at it all. It was beautiful!

He went to the back. The pool man was still working on the pool. It was closed because he had not been there in a while. He would come more often now so they could all enjoy why he worked so hard. He never had anyone he wanted to share it with before.

"Mr. Laurent, I will be done in a moment. You still cannot use it until tomorrow, because I just shocked it." The pool man was vacuuming the debris that had settled on the top and bottom.

Tashia walked around the yard and saw a garden off to the side. The yard was shaded by a series of trees and there were pathways leading to different parts of the yard. Beyond the trees was a beach. She could see there was a sign, but couldn't make out what it said. She walked closer and saw it read private. So, he had a private beach. Smiling, she thought of the fun they could have out there.

"Hey. This is really nice!" Cuyler waddled over to her with her shoes in her hand.

"Yeah. He likes nice things," Tashia said playfully.

"I never asked Preston, but what does Anthony do?"

Tashia could feel the shadows beginning to rise in her, again, and remembered what Anthony told her. "He owns a restaurant and a club, and who knows whatever else." She smiled at her sister and turned back to the water.

"Tashia. Let's not argue. I want us to enjoy ourselves together and have a good time. Okay?"

Cuyler stood looking like Solana with her sad face. How could she remain angry with her? She didn't even understand why she was angry with her now.

Smiling, she walked to her very pregnant sister and hugged her. Tashia was happy for the first time in a long time and she did not want to disrupt that feeling over stupidity.

"Are you planning on coming inside?" Anthony stood at the end of the shrubs, watching the two, smiling. When they reached him, he lifted Tashia and carried her. "I would pick you up Cuyler, but my brother is a great fighter and I don't want any bloodshed," he teased, carrying Tashia the rest of the way to the house.

Preston saw the dilemma and came quickly to lift his wife as well, pretending she was too heavy. The four laughed at the brotherly competition and proceeded inside.

Anthony put Tashia down and let her take in the view of the quant house. They were standing in the great room, which was small with three sofas that formed a U and a coffee table in the middle. A bay window overlooked the front garden and a beautiful French door with stained windowpanes framed the eastern wall nicely. Tastefully decorated, the cottage held various forms of art pieces. Flanking the walls, all around the room, were bookcases and cabinets that stopped just below the windows. Off from small kitchen area, in the back of the great room, was the sliding glass door to the pool. A bar hung over the kitchen counter, towards the great room, with five barstools that matched the sofas. The counters were some type of stone and the appliances were stainless steel.

Tashia had not realized she stood in one spot, spinning around until Anthony stopped her and asked if she wanted to see the rest of the house.

"This is amazing. Did you decorate it?"

"Of course, he did. I've been telling him for years that there was a little woman inside of him," Preston teased.

Tashia made her way to the hallway that ran around the back of the kitchen. There were three bedrooms and two bathrooms. The first bedroom had two twin beds and she thought it to be perfect for the boys. The second room was more like an office with a day bed. The master suite had its own bathroom area and there was a second at the end of the hall.

"We already bought everything inside. I told Zander he could have the office to give him his space from the other two. Solana and Zane will take the front room, if that's okay with you."

"That's fine."

"The kids are outside exploring. They have the girls, and I instructed them not to go near the pool."

Tashia could hear the girls screaming as they ran around outside and she smiled knowing her children were happy and safe.

It's Just Dinner

G emma finished cooking dinner just before Jason arrived from work. He was quieter than normal when he entered the tiny apartment, so she knew he had a bad day.

"Hey. How was your day?"

"Bad," he answered, throwing the mail on the table. "What's for dinner?"

"Pork chops, couscous and spinach," she answered. "Are you ready to eat right now?"

"No. I'm gonna change my clothes first."

She watched him disappear into their bedroom before letting out a long breath she did not realize she was holding. Her heart was pounding, expecting a different Jason to show up. Usually when he had a bad day at work, she caught the brunt of it. She wanted to talk to him about her returning to work again, but she would not be able to do it now. Although she volunteered to help Caden, he still gave her money every now and then. She deposited it into an account Jason didn't know about, because he would be angry.

When he returned he was wearing his shorts and tank. He sat at the table and waited for her to bring his food. "What did you do today?"

"Nothing much."

She came and sat with him once she had her plate, wondering if she should bring up the job, but decided against it. "What happened at work?"

He continued to eat. "These are a little dry."

Gemma tensed. She waited for him to say something to understand where the conversation was going. From previous experience, she knew no matter what she said it would not ease his tension. She would allow him to vent and criticize her cooking for the evening and they would move on, but she didn't dare add any additional stress.

She had to find the opportunity to text Caden and let him know she would not be able to meet him tonight. He would worry if she didn't.

"I can't eat this. What else do you have?" He waited for her to answer. She knew whatever she said would not please him, but she tried.

"Maybe it's just that one. Do you want me to get you another?"

"Why would I want another when this one is dry?" Jason pushed the plate away from him. "Find me something else."

She heard the tension in his voice, so she stood to get something else out of the fridge. She walked the long way to the fridge so he would have no reason to touch her.

"What are you doing? I don't want any leftovers. Fix me something else." He stood and went to their bedroom.

Gemma looked to see what she had that could be fixed quickly. She saw the rice from the other day and vegetables. She took out a frozen chicken breast and put in in a pan on low heat so it wouldn't cook on the outside before the inside was thawed. Once melted down, she cut the breast in stripes and mixed the vegetables in. Adding water to the rice she had heated, making sure it wasn't hard or burned. Quickly she fixed his plate and placed it on the table where he sat.

She was nervous. Days like this never ended well. Now, cold she threw her meal in the trash and her plate in the sink and went to tell him his food was ready. He was asleep. Leaning against the door, she cried. The dilemma was now whether to wake him or let him sleep.

Gemma wiped her eyes and entered the room. Tipping to the bed, she rubbed his back and called his name lightly. He moaned. "Your food is ready."

He looked at her through sleepy eyes and sat up. Slowly, he stood and walked to the table. "What's this?" he asked groggy.

"Chicken, vegetables and rice." She was now shaking.

He tasted the food. "That's better."

Gemma went to the kitchen and began cleaning. She then went to the bathroom to make Jason's bath. The night was young, he was still edgy, and she was afraid.

It's a Start

Blaine sat on his father's patio with his brothers eating breakfast. The calm his brother Anthony displayed was welcoming. Before, he was always edgy and in charge. Now he was relaxed and carefree.

"So, why didn't you introduce me to the sister when you married Cuyler, bro," he asked Preston. "Those sisters must have some powerful mojo," he added, circling his hips. "I didn't think you would ever calm down enough for anyone, Anthony. What did she do to you?"

Anthony smiled. "Well, we are fresh out of sisters so I guess you will never know." He patted his brother on the leg. "So who is this girl you brought with you?"

"Oh I met her on the road and brought her along."

"You were supposed to come to our anniversary dinner. Is this the same girl?" Preston asked.

"Yes that's her."

"Then are we planning a double wedding?" Anthony teased.

Blaine sat up in his chair. "No! No!"

The brothers laughed. Tashia came outside with a platter of food for them. "You guys need to eat if you are going to drink Kool-Aid all day." She placed the platter down and four plates.

"Are you joining us?" Blaine asked, smiling.

Tashia smiled. "No, but your dad is coming to join you."

Anthony leaned back in the chair and watched his brother flirt with Tashia, smiling at the interaction. Tashia flirted back, causing Blaine to sit forward and take the challenge.

"Okay, little man," Anthony interjected after a few exchanges. He pulled Tashia and sat her in his lap. "Your girl is in the house asleep. This one belongs to me." He whispered in her ear and she laughed, stood, and disappeared into the house.

"Man. I don't know if I can get used to this mellow you. You used to be bossy and mean and cold! Now you're a big old teddy," Blaine teased.

"We can have a match out there on the sand and you will see there is nothing soft about me!"

"There will be no match today, boys," Mr. Washington said, approaching the bunch.

"Hey, Dad!" Blaine stood and hugged his father. They each took turns hugging Mr. Washington, returning to their seats.

"Who is that white woman in my living room on the couch?"

Preston and Anthony looked at one another and smiled. Leaning back, they waited for Blaine's response.

Blaine fidgeted in his seat. Tilting his head, he looked to Preston and Anthony for support.

"What are you looking at them for? I asked you the question."

"She's just a friend, Dad."

"You never brought just a friend home before." Mr. Washington side eyed him through slanted eyes. "So, is she just a friend or more?"

Blaine squirmed in his seat and picked up his plate. "For now, Dad, she's just a friend."

Preston and Anthony laughed aloud at Blaine's uneasiness and picked up their plates to eat. Blaine glared at them.

"Well, the next time you bring a half-naked woman in my home make sure you cover her backside. An old man doesn't need to see what he can't have."

Their laughter was explosive at their father's comment.

"Yes, sir."

"There they go!" Cuyler said, smiling. "I never get tired of hearing them laugh at one another."

Cuyler turned to look at Tashia when she did not respond, but saw her looking through the window, smiling at them as well. She wished they could laugh, again, like they used to and realized they had not shared that kind of laughter in almost a decade. "Since the kids are with Annetta why don't we go and sit on the beach and spend some time together?"

Tashia turned, contemplating what she offered. "Okay."

Cuyler grabbed a thermos from the pantry and rinsed it. She filled it with ice and water.

Tashia was getting a few pieces of fruit and left to get her beach bag, which contained her sunscreen and other beach items. She returned to the kitchen, added the fruit to the bag, and picked up the thermos. "Let's go!"

The beach was breezy but sunny. Cuyler knew they would not be able to spend much time there, because the sun would soon push them back to the house. There were already chairs in a semi-circle and umbrella's buried in the sand.

Tashia helped Cuyler into the chair and knew she would have to do the same when they left. She was due in a few months and Tashia was surprised when she was cleared to fly. Placing the thermos between them, Tashia realized she had not brought any cups. "I need to go back and get cups!"

"For what? We can drink from the same."

Tashia sat next to her, looked out at the water coming in and going out, and thought it was a metaphor of her life. The good was finally coming in, the bad was being washed away. Taking a deep breath, she let it go slowly to cleanse her mind.

"This is so nice, isn't it? I remembered the first time I was here. It rejuvenated me." Cuyler closed her eyes and allowed the sun to wash over her.

"I guess we should put some sunscreen on." Tashia reached into her beach bag and pulled out a bottle of sunscreen. She thought for a moment and pulled the fitted sundress over her head deciding to wear only her panties. Cuyler, who had always mimicked her sister, did the same, reminding Tashia of when they were children and how Cuyler always wanted to do what she did.

Tashia put sunscreen on Cuyler first then herself. Leaning back in the chair, she felt free. The slight breeze brushed past her and she breathed it in. Although her eyes where closed she could feel her sister's eyes on her. "What, Cuyler?"

"You used to do that when we were kids and I always wondered how you knew."

"I can feel you. I could always feel you. I knew when you were in trouble, when you were scared. I even knew the day you lost your virginity."

"When!"

"You were wearing my white dress and K-Swiss. You spent all day putting your hair up, then taking it down. You stared at yourself forever naked in the mirror after taking your shower. You took my favorite lotion and perfume from my dresser and bathed in it." Eyes still closed, Tashia laughed as if reliving the memory. "I thought I would gag.

"When Caden picked you up he was super nervous as well, so I knew the two of you were up to something!" She laughed again. "You were past a reasonable hour and you had not called to say you would be late. I sat in a chair in the living room and waited for you like you were my child coming home from the prom. I never felt you were in danger. I never got that feeling and Caden was such the gentleman, but you know those are the crazies, girl!" She laughed, again, to herself.

Tashia opened her eyes and looked at her sister. "When you did come home that night the two of you were so sweet and I could see the innocence was gone. He looked at you like he didn't want to let you go, almost like he needed you to come with him and you looked at him the same." Tashia's tears fell, reminiscing about a special moment she shared with her sister in time. "In that look he said everything, and yet he said nothing. In that moment, I knew my baby was a woman and that soon you would be gone."

Cuyler tears came as well. "I didn't know you were there!" Cuyler whispered through her tears.

"Hmm." Tashia knew there were many times her sister did not know she was there, but she had always been there. She also remembered the day her sister broke her heart. The day she left. "In two months you were gone."

"I thought you would be glad to get rid of me."

"You were not thinking of me when you left. You were in love."

Cuyler didn't respond. She was a honey badger in the courtroom, but she was no contender for her sister. She liked the place they were in and in that moment she learned so much about a sister she was beginning to realize she knew nothing about.

The two lay in the sun in silence. Tashia made Cuyler drink every now and, again, taking her turn as well. The sun was getting hotter and the kids would be back soon.

"Hey!" Tashia heard Anthony say from the tree line. "Where are your clothes?" he exclaimed.

"Who needs clothes? We're on holiday," Tashia said, imitating his words. "It's too nice for clothes." Her eyes closed, she did not see Preston with him. Anthony lifted her from the chair, locking her in his arms and walked toward the water. "No, Anthony! Remember our conversation about a black girl's hair?" she pleaded.

Anthony just smiled and continued to walk toward the water as Preston helped Cuyler from her seat and into her sundress.

Tashia was kicking now and pleading for him to put her down, but Anthony, knowing her legs were strong, locked them with his strong arms and plunged into the warm, salt water, taking her under with him.

Tashia held on as he swam with her under the water. When she opened her eyes, she was amazed at what she saw. The colors of the fish that scattered away from them as they invaded their territory were brilliant. The pretty coral against the almost white sand was something she had only seen in the magazines. She saw the ocean crashing on the surface above them and immediately understood its' power.

Anthony resurfaced with her and they both breathed. "You ready?"

"Yes."

He took her back under the water, pulling her and pointing to different things. He showed her how suddenly the shoreline dropped off, and hermit crabs crawling on the bottom. She saw more coral and got closer to it this time and then up they went.

"Anthony, it's beautiful. I can't wait for the kids to see this."

He was staring at her. She knew the look and searched the beach. It was empty. This time he went under water without her and she could feel the slight pull, and then she was nude.

The Family Party

Annetta stepped onto the patio and immediately saw her brother, Blaine. She hugged and kissed him all over his face like she did when he was a baby. Suddenly, she slapped him in the back of his head.

"Who dat white woman you brought here with no damn manners? She backside in the sky for all to see in your father's house and there are children running around here! Your father still got blood pumpin' through his veins. You want he to have a heart attack?" She waited for Blain's explanation, but instead she got a smile. "Take that stupid smile from your face and take care of dat!"

Blaine kissed his sister and entered the house to take care of his guest.

Annetta watched the children splash around in the pool. Zander was holding Callia on his shoulders, because she did not like the splashing. They were wonderfully behaved children. She wondered when she would meet Fatimah.

She joined her father at the table and kissed him. "Good morning, Dada."

"Good morning, Beauty." Beauty was a name given her by her father years ago when their mother made her feel ugly because of her complexion.

She was the darkest of the clan and her dad said she got her color from his mother. He constantly told her she was beautiful until she believed it. He nicknamed her Black Beauty and over the years had shortened it to Beauty. When she went to prep school the battle began again, but it was different. The girls teased her and the boys adored her. Then there was the rumor one girl started who said she put out because there was no other explanation for the boys' attraction to her. Annetta wanted to leave the school, but her dad told her she would stay and endure, explaining there would always be someone who would challenge her in life.

Her dad wanted her to meet someone and to get married, but Annetta loved her father's company and could never find anyone like him. Now he had a house full of children, so she hoped that would end the conversation for a moment.

"Did they give you a hard time?"

"I raised sneakier and meaner than they. That Solana is a heart thief. She will have the right Dada for the job. They will be afraid to come to the door. And, Zander is a heartthrob. The little girls are already asking."

Mr. Washington watched the children change and could see Anthony had changed them as much as they had changed him. He was happy for his son. Tashia seemed like a good woman. He had only interacted with her a couple of times and she seemed much like his son, always on watch. Maybe they would allow one another to breathe.

In the distance, he saw Cuyler and Preston making their way and Blaine was coming from the house with his guest.

She yawned and stretch. Annetta rolled her eyes. Blaine smiled at his sister's annoyance and waited for Preston and Cuyler to make his introduction. "Everyone I would like for you to meet Jessica. Jessica, this is my father, Kei Washington, my brother, Preston and his very pregnant wife, Cuyler. This is my lovely and bossy sister, Annetta, and swiftly approaching is Cuyler and Preston's daughter, Callia."

"Hello, everyone! It's so nice meeting you." Jessica sat in the chair that was pulled out for her. "This is a beautiful place you have here, Mr. Washington."

"Where are Anthony and Tashia?" Blaine asked.

"Under water," Preston answered, winking.

"Okay."

Annetta returned from the kitchen with another plate. "Would you like something to eat?" She put the plate and fork down in front of the girl and handed her what the boys had not eaten on the plater.

Cuyler looked at Annetta, shocked she offered the girl cold food. She could see the disdain for her on Annetta's face.

Jessica looked at Annetta and smiled. "Thank you. I will have some fruit. I don't eat much in the morning." Jessica picked through the fruit, getting all she wanted and smiled nervously at Blaine who was now seated next to her.

"Here come the slackers," Preston said, as he watched the couple come through the trees and up the yard.

Anthony smiled as he approached. Tashia was laughing at something he said and punched him in the arm.

"That was quick," Blaine shot at his brother once he was in earshot. Standing he walked to the edge of the concrete patio.

"You worry about you," Anthony volleyed back.

"Is that what I should expect when I get as old as you?"

Anthony laughed at his younger brother. Lifting him in the air, he locked Blaine's arms, making him absorb the wetness of his clothes. He let him drop then pushed him before he could retaliate.

Blaine, once again, did the introductions to Jessica and then informed them that they needed to set up the equipment for the night. The three brothers sprang into action and began setting up the yard. Zander and Zane were called from the pool to help.

Tashia bathed Callia and Solana and the women met in Preston's bedroom to prepare the little ones. As they did the girl's hair, they spoke about the night's events.

"Have you ever seen Blaine perform, Jessica?" Cuyler asked.

"No. He's always behind the scenes when I see him."

"Well, you're in for a treat. The boys are a big thing here," Cuyler told her, excited to hear them perform again.

"Where are you from?" Tashia asked.

"My mom is from the Philippians and my dad from Puerto Rico. I've lived in both, but now we live in Miami."

"Bienvenido a la famillia," Tashia told her, welcoming her to the family.

"Gracias."

Annetta entered the room, letting everyone know that the caterer was setting up and the guest would start arriving soon. The men went to Anthony's to get ready and would be back shortly.

"When are you getting ready, Annetta?" Cuyler asked.

"I will in a minute."

Annetta left and the women went back to their conversation. Callia's hair was done and Cuyler tied a scarf around it and laid her down on the pillows because she had fallen asleep. Jessica had already taken her shower so Cuyler went next.

"When is she due?" Jessica asked Tashia.

Tashia stopped to think and realized she didn't know the exact date. "Soon," she said, laughing.

Jessica watched as Tashia talked and coordinated outfits the best they could considering all of Tashia's clothes were not there. When Cuyler put on her sundress, the two tied a sash below her belly to make her a little sexier.

Solana ran back and forth, as they got dressed. Tashia warned her that if she did not take a nap she was going to fall asleep before Callia, who was still napping, but she would not lie down.

The women heard the boys warming up on their instruments and knew it was time to leave the tiny room. Quietly, they left and closed the door behind them, leaving Callia asleep.

When the three came from the house, the yard was already filling. People were eating and children were playing. Tashia noticed the cover that now covered the pool, with locks in place to hold it taut.

The food was beyond what Tashia expected and she wondered if their wedding reception would be this lavish. Zane stood behind a set of bongos, lightly tapping them as Anthony directed him. Zander was on the steel drums, rubbing with what appeared to be a brush with long hair. She was shocked because she did not know they could play anything yet.

The three made their way across the yard and Tashia saw Anthony smile as he watched her approach. She patiently waited on the side as he continued to warm up. Jessica stood along the side of her while Cuyler greeted the many relatives who already knew her. She watched as they kissed and hugged her and she could feel her going to that dark place again. She fidgeted with her hands and smiled at those who ventured her way to greet her. She felt awkward standing alone and wished Cuyler had thought to take her and Jessica with her and introduce them.

When the band broke, she felt better because Anthony joined her. Solana was roaming the yard with her new grandpa, who introduced her to the family.

"You okay?" Anthony whispered in her ear.

"Yes. I just feel a little awkward because I don't know anyone."

Grabbing her hands, he lifted them and examined her outfit. "Even nicer than the anniversary party and I didn't believe you could top that dress." He winked at her and led her to the people he wanted her to meet. Glancing over her shoulder, she checked on Jessica to make sure she was not left alone, but saw Blaine was taking her on her rounds.

The boys were eating and having a good time. She smiled, as she saw a young girl who kept looking at Zander, knowing they were about to venture into a new era. Solana found her way into Anthony's arms and made the rounds with them, charming everyone as they went along.

"Solana, go and see if your cousin is still asleep," Tashia said, and off she went. In minutes, she returned, pulling along a crying Callia.

"She couldn't get out of the room!" Solana was yelling to her mother. Tashia made her way to Callia, lifted and consoled her. Soon Preston and Cuyler were close by. A still upset Callia put her hands out to Preston who took her.

"Estas bien niña, Papa te tiene. Its okay, baby girl. Papa has you," Preston whispered to her, rubbing her back until she calmed.

"Let me take her to wash her face and get her dressed," Tashia offered, but she would not leave Preston.

"We will take her," Cuyler told Tashia and pulled Preston to follow her.

Left standing with Anthony, Tashia was about to suggest that they get something to eat but she was distracted by a woman who watched Preston and Cuyler go back to the house. She was tall and shapely with long hair. She wore a tight fitting dress, showing of her perfect silhouette and flat shoes as not to exaggerate her height.

"Anthony, who is that over there?" she asked, but when she turned the woman was gone. "She was right there, but I don't see her now."

"She'll show up, again, I'm sure."

Cuyler and Preston returned and the guys played to an excited and loyal crowd. Jessica watched, tickled that Blaine could play and sing.

Tashia was equally surprised when Zander stepped to the mic and sang a popular song. Again, she saw the young, shy girl standing on the side of the stage, bouncing to the music. Another young girl, a little bolder, stood directly in front of him and danced. Tashia was amused at the events unfolding. Preston walked to Zander, still playing his bass, and whispered in the boy's ear.

Zander took his instruction and jumped from the stage, going to the girl. He took her hand and began singing to her. The young girl jumped up and down, covering her mouth. Zander let the young girl's hand go and walked to the young, quiet girl who stood on the side of the stage and did the same. As he neared the end of the song, he hopped back on the stage.

Smiling, Anthony was looking at a beaming Tashia as she covered her mouth, amazed at the talent she didn't know her son had. She was moved to tears, hearing the reception he received when he finished the song and returned to the steel drums.

"He's very good and very marketable," Jessica told Tashia. "If he ever wants to do something with it, let me know."

Tashia was still very surprised and couldn't comprehend what had just happened. After two more songs, the band took a break. Tashia couldn't get to Zander because so many girls surrounded him.

"Let him have his play." Anthony put his arms around her shoulder. "He can speak to you later. Leave him be. It's a great confidence booster."

Tashia turned to face him. "Why didn't you tell me!"

"He wanted to surprise you. He's been working hard on that piece. That's why he always falls asleep with his earplugs in."

Others came up to Preston, Blaine, and Anthony, telling them the music was amazing and asking who Zander was. The rumor was he was Anthony's son. Zander didn't deny the rumor and Anthony walked around with his chest out.

The group cranked back up and the local favorite, Preston, stepped to the mic. He played the base and nursed the mic as if he were making love to it as he sang.

Jessica smiled at Cuyler. "That man is singing to you." Cuyler blushed.

Tashia saw the woman, again. She was smiling at Preston as he sang. "Weirdo."

They danced, ate, and sang all day, enjoying the hospitality and meeting new family. As the children fell asleep, they were put to bed until only Zander remained awake.

Zander entertained his new friends by telling stories of his home. The girls giggled at his accent and begged him to sing again. He only had the one song prepared, but knew countless songs so he sang for them.

Blaine, Anthony, and Preston shared chairs with their women and the brothers joked amongst each other. The day was long and exciting.

Someone watched from the edge of the trees.

A Cry For Help

The ringing in her ears was a low murmur. She needed help, but cried because she had no one. Jason had shut everyone out of her life. Her parents cut her off the last time she borrowed money from them. Her father told her to come home and he would take care of her, but he would not take care of her and a grown man.

It was becoming difficult to stay alert and she could hear her phone ringing. It was right next to her, but she was dazed. She tried to reach for it, but nothing happened. She felt as though she were in a half-dream state. She pushed harder to answer and her hand finally moved forward. She slid her finger up the glass screen. A name appeared, but she couldn't read it because her vision was blurred.

"Hello," was all she said repeatedly.

"Gemma! Gemma!" Caden called out.

Gemma could hear Caden's voice. "Can you help me? Please!" she cried into the phone, but she couldn't make out what he was saying.

"Gemma," he said calmly. "Where are you?" He got no response from her. "Gemma! What's wrong?" She was still unresponsive.

Gemma could hear Caden, but was unable to answer. Her sight became spotty and the darkness started from the corners of her vision moving in slowly, consuming her, sending her spiraling into a dark abyss.

Caden re-entered the church. The line was still open to Gemma's phone, but she was not answering. She sounded drugged and groggy. She was in trouble.

Pastor was still in his office. "Gemma's in trouble!" He announced when he entered. "I have her on the phone, but she is not answering. Do you have her home address?"

"No. She has never given us an address!" Pastor picked up the phone and dialed 911. "Hello, this is Pastor Jenkins. I have a member that may be in trouble. She has passed 0ut on a member's cell phone and she needs help. We don't have an address for her." Pastor Jenkin's followed the instructions of the operator while Caden remained on the line until help reached Gemma.

The sterile smell of the hospital room met Gemma when she awakened. The light in her room was dim and the pain in her head had diminished. She was afraid to open her eyes for fear the pain would return, but she had to see her surroundings.

Slowly, she opened her eyes and viewed her room. It was small and quant. Hers was the only bed in the room. She looked at the clock on the wall. It was eight-thirty. Under the clock, Caden slept in a nearby chair. She supposed he was the one who called.

Quickly, she looked for Jason. He wouldn't like Caden being there with her knowing their secrets, but he wasn't there. He loved her, so she expected him to be there. Maybe he went to get something to eat out of one of those vending machines, or some coffee, she thought to herself. Maybe he was okay with Caden being there.

Her throat was tight and dry. She pushed the nurse's button. The intercom came on quickly and a male voice screamed through the speaker. Gemma closed her eyes to the sound. She could feel the dull thud in her head, but it was somewhat numb. Squeezing her eyes, she tried to shut out the sound. She didn't answer back.

When the sound died, she reopened her eyes to see Caden standing at her bed. He wiped away the tear streaming down her check. "What do you need?" he asked softly.

She watched him for a moment before answering, afraid to disturb the calm that had returned. "Water," she answered in a quiet whisper. The pain in her jaw resonated through her head and for the first time she felt the wire in her mouth.

Caden gently rubbed her head. He had a look of pity on his face and she knew her secret was out. "Where is Jason?" she asked through clenched teeth.

"In jail," Caden said.

For the first time, she felt free to cry about her circumstance in front of someone. No longer did she have to cry in secret.

Caden continued to rub her head. "You have a broken jaw, rib, and concussion. You are on some heavy meds right now to cut the edge of your pain..."

In the mist of his explanation, the male nurse from the intercom exploded into the room. He pulled on a pair of gloves from the dispenser and approached her bed. He checked her monitors then turned to her. "Do you need any more pain meds?"

"No," she answered, shaking her head, which was a mistake. She instantly became dizzy and the dull pain returned. She closed her eyes to subdue the nausea she now felt.

"You don't want to move your head too abruptly. You have a concussion." The nurse recognized the look on her face, sat her head up slowly and retrieved the dish from her nightstand, placing it below her mouth. Gemma heaved a couple of times expelling the minimal contents of her stomach. The nurse went to the sink and wet a rag. He returned and placed it gently to her mouth, wiping away the residue.

No one heard the tall white man enter the room. He stood back with a look of horror on his face and tears filled his eyes. Caden heard him first and abruptly turned. Instantly, he knew he was the man he spoke to on the phone. He was Gemma's dad.

Mr. Warner watched his baby girl in horror. Caden thought he saw a glimpse of shame on his face. Slowly, he approached her bed. When Gemma saw him, the flood gates opened. Her dad rubbed her arm, unsure if he should touch her at all.

"I'm sorry, Daddy," she said through the flow of tears.

Gemma's dad wailed in anguish and Caden understood his pain, but he quickly hugged him and removed him from the room. Once outside the room he cried out, "How did I not know? How did I not see?"

"She hid it well, sir." Caden waited until the anguished man calmed.

Extending his hand, he introduced himself. "I'm Earl Warner, Gemma's dad. I guess you're the young man who called me earlier?"

"Yes, sir."

"Thank you."

"I would want the same courtesy if something happened to my daughter," Caden started. "I pulled you out of the room because she has a concussion and loud noises hurt her head right now. Go back in and spend time with her. Tell Gemma I will come by and check on her tomorrow."

Aria began her shift early. She looked at the board to get familiar with the patients in her unit. The battered patient, Gemma, had already been assigned to her. She looked at her chart and saw she had been prescribed some heavy painkillers.

Gemma was asleep when she entered her room. Aria updated her board so she would know her name and today's date. Many times the patients lose time so it helped them to keep their days in order.

Aria looked at her vitals and marked them on her chart. She then looked at the woman who lay in the bed. Her face was bruised and now purplish. Her left eye was swollen and black. Aria had memories of her ordeal with the man who promised to save her from her destiny.

When she met him, he was the most wonderful man in the world. He lavished her with gifts and affection. He took her to a house with a picket fence. Then within weeks, the beatings and sexual abuse began. He liked beating her. Not because she didn't do what she was told, but because he liked it. He was a sadist.

Gemma wasn't a beautiful girl; she was rather plain, but pretty. She was a little on the skinny side, which may have been from stress of the abuse. Aria smiled and rubbed her hand. She was going to need help. She was sure she was not done with him.

Abruptly, she was distracted by a sound at the door. It was Caden. He came daily to check on her. "Hey, Caden."

"How is she doing?"

"Her vitals look fine, but that isn't the part she will have to deal with. She will have to fight her emotions. These wounds will heal. We were made that way, you know; to rejuvenate. It's the mind that sometimes never rejuvenates." She rubbed Gemma's hand again.

Aria's mind was in the past, dealing with her experience. She was not the same girl who was rescued from her captive years ago. Shaking her feelings, she placed Gemma's hand back on her covers. "I need to check on my other patients."

Caden reached out and grabbed Aria's hand as she passed by. "How are you?"

She smiled and nodded. "I'm good, Caden." She found him difficult to read. She didn't know if he was genuinely nice or he was hitting on her half the time. The first day she met him she told him her story. He made her feel at peace. There was something special about him.

When released, it would be Aria's job to convince Gemma to attend meetings and rescue herself from the danger she lived in.

Gemma left the women's shelter to meet Caden. She had been working very hard on the gala and had many updates to give him. She recently had the wire removed from her jaw and could now eat, and whenever they met, Caden seemed to bombard her with food. Today they were meeting at a steakhouse.

Caden always told her where he wanted to eat and let her choose. She knew what he was asking. He wanted to make sure he was not taking her to a place associated with Jason. Her dad begged her to come home. She told him she would soon, but she had to finish this chapter in her life. She needed to know why she chose Jason and what she missed in their dating process that she didn't see.

Caden was not allowed to know the location of the house, so she met him on the bus line. He was parked where he always waited, but she still felt apprehensive when she got off the bus. Although Jason was behind bars, she couldn't shake the fear.

Caden saw her coming and opened the car door. "Hello, Miss Gemma. You are looking refreshed this evening, "he said. "I hope you are famished because I am."

Gemma sat quietly as she rode to the restaurant. There was a question on her mind and she trusted his judgment. "Caden, do you think I should go back home?"

"I think you should have peace of mind and be happy wherever you choose to be."

Gemma thought about his words. She loved it here. This had become her home and she didn't want to live with her parents. She didn't want to run from Jason, but she was always scared even though he was behind bars. "Do you know of a good place where I can take a self-defense class?"

"I'll ask my brother, Jacque. That's his thing, not mine."

"I didn't know you had a brother. You don't talk about him."

"We were estranged for some years, but we are working on rebuilding our relationship."

"Oh."

When they arrived at the restaurant, Caden escorted Gemma to her seat. After looking over the menu, they ordered and began discussing the plans for the gala. There was a question pressing on Caden that he felt comfortable asking. "Was Jason your first?" The look she gave Caden made him realize he had to cleanup his question. "That didn't come out right." Caden laughed, embarrassed.

"I know what you meant. The answer is I don't know." Gemma thought about her answer before she continued. "I guess my dad is abusive in some ways. He was harsh with his words to my mum. He probably made her feel that as a Black woman she should be grateful to be with a white man. He probably made her feel like as a Black woman she was the lowest of woman. That's what I felt for her."

Gemma looked in Caden's face, watching his reaction. He could feel her looking for confirmation. "Maybe you need to go home to face your new feelings and see how your mother felt or feels. Maybe she needs someone to tell her this isn't right."

Gemma was saved from answering when the food arrived. "Let's eat." She realized she was now famished as well. She was embarrassed, exposing her family's imperfections.

Caden saw the shame on her face. He reached across to her now shaking hand and steadied it. "Don't be ashamed. No one I know, including myself, has a perfect family. It's the issues in our life that mold us into the people we become. We need to embrace our past and learn from it so we can help someone else. If we don't share our stories, we can't free ourselves and grow. Our testimonies help others. Never be ashamed of what happened; share it with someone who needs to hear your story. Let's bless the food."

Facing Fear

Gemma thought for days about what Caden shared with her. She was too shy to get in front of people so she didn't know how she would share. Caden said it would come when she needed to speak.

Aria shared her story while Gemma was in the hospital. She, too, had been battered, but she went from one bad relationship to another until her last boyfriend almost killed her. She told Gemma that if she stayed she would have been dead. She told her to go to the meeting first and become involved, if she still thought she deserved the treatment she was getting then stay. After hearing so many stories similar to hers, she knew it was time and the last incident was her near miss.

She waited for Jacque to pick her up from the bus stop. She told him what she would be wearing so he could find her, but she picked him out immediately. He resembled his brother with slight differences, but she could see the body build and couldn't deny the good looks.

"Gemma?"

"Yes," she answered, extending her hand to him.

"Hello. My name is Jacque." Jacque looked at her clothing and saw she was dressed as he instructed. "Good. You wore what I asked. We are going to run to our workout place. It's not far and will get your muscles warmed up. We will run at your pace, if you're ready."

Gemma liked running so the run didn't bother her. She ran when she was a teen so she wouldn't get fat. She often heard her dad refer to her mother as 'fat ass' and she didn't want him calling her that. He would use her as an example to her mother, telling her she should take lessons from Gemma. Gemma remembered feeling good when he said it because his compliments were far and few, but she would see how hurt her mother looked and her joy was short lived.

Jacque gently guided her when he wanted her to turn. When they arrived at the gym, it was pretty empty. There were a few working on bags and a couple of guys sparing in the ring.

"Hey Jacque," one of the guys yelled to him as he approached. "Hello young lady. I hear you come to learn from this kickass." He turned to Jacque and reminded him of the gym rules.

Turning his attention back to Gemma, he guided her to the corner of the room. "We will start on some basic defense moves and once you have those down, you can graduate to fighting. Okay?"

Gemma nodded and began her new journey.

Gemma's mother was on her mind constantly. She spoke with her many times since the incident, but needed to feel the warmth of her touch. After working with Jacque for three weeks, he saw her focus dropping and encouraged her to go home for a visit.

There were so many emotions stirred from the group meetings and memories awakened that needed answers. Gemma looked around the room she once called hers. Opening the jewelry box, she remembered when her dad gave it to her for her seventh birthday. The ballerina circled the parameter of the box. When she was little, Gemma wondered how she didn't get dizzy. Thinking of the question made her laugh at herself.

Her track trophies lined the top shelf of her bookcase and her medals where mounted in the frame on the wall. She touched them and realized her mother kept them dusted.

She heard her mother moving around the house. She was sure she was eager to see her, but Gemma was not there for pleasantries: she was there to help her mother and she knew from experience if her mother didn't want help she would not hear Gemma, but she had to try. After weeks of therapy, she didn't consider herself an expert, but she had the beginnings of a conversation.

Gemma looked at her body in the mirror. She could see the definition beginning to develop from her training with Jacque. Jason liked her hair long so she cut it off to prove to herself she was done with him. Her workouts with Jacque were therapeutic as well. She could push herself hard on those days she found difficult to get through. She dressed in her workout gear and prepared for her morning run.

Her mother was sitting in the front room reading her book. "Good morning, Mum." Gemma went to her mother, kissing her on her cheek.

"Hello, sweetheart. I was wondering when you were going to make it out of your room. What time did you get in?"

Gemma could feel her mother looking her over as if examining for scars. "I'm okay, Mum," she reassured her, taking her hands. They were shaking slightly. "Mum, I'm okay," she said again. "I'm going for a run and we can catch up when I get back, okay?" Gemma didn't wait for an answer. She headed for the door and walked out into the morning air.

It was slightly cool, but Gemma felt it made her run easier. She started her slow jog and thought about her transformation over the past weeks. Her training with Jacque made her feel empowered. Despite her feeling, she could defend herself if attacked, although fear danced in the shadows of her mind.

She wondered if her mother was fearful of her father or tolerant. She didn't know how she was going to broach the conversation with her. The journey was personal. Would she be receptive? She needed to talk with her while her dad was away from the house, so she hurried back to take her shower.

Gemma entered the small laundry room where her mother was folding and washing clothes. "What can I do to help?"

"Nothing. Just have a seat and keep me company." Her mother pulled out a chair and gestured for her to sit. She took a double take at Gemma and said, "You need to eat, Gemma. You are entirely too small."

Gemma pulled up her shirt and lifted her shorts to show her mother how cut she had become. "I've been working out. When I get back I will increase my protein intake and I will bulk up a little," she explained to her mother.

Gemma's mother's eyes widened in amazement. "You look great!" her mother exclaimed, but as quickly as she complimented Gemma, she became critical. "I know you've been through some things, but you're not starting to like girls, are you?"

Gemma laughed at her mother. She was so naïve. "No!" She had not laughed like that in a while. As quickly as she laughed, she became serious. Now was the perfect time to start her conversation.

She walked to her mother and took her hands. "I don't want to feel defenseless ever again. When Jason and I were together I was always afraid." She let her mother's hands go and returned to her chair. "I was afraid he would leave me, beat me, not like me, reject me, you name it and I was afraid of it, but all the things I was afraid of had nothing to do with me. I only cared about making him happy."

Her mother looked at her with pity and it angered Gemma that she didn't see herself in the situation. She examined the small scar on the side of her face and Gemma smiled at her. "That's not from Jason, Mom. That is from my sparring partner."

"Your what?"

"My fight partner. I have a kickboxing class. When Jason hurt me, he made sure I covered my scars. He didn't want anyone to know."

"I could kill him for putting his hands on you like that," her mother said.

"He has his own demons to deal with and I have mine. I can only take care of me for now." Gemma looked for a reaction from her mother, but she gave none.

Her mother hung her head. "What demons are those?" she asked as she absently folded her clothes.

"I've found that the road to my destruction started a long time ago. We are who we are through a series of things in our lives. The outcome is based on our choices when they happened. Or something like that," Gemma answered, waving off her thoughts, now afraid to go back or forward, but she had to go on. "Mom, do you think Dad was mean to us?"

"What are you talking about, Gemma? Your father is who he is. He is a good provider and father." She paused. "You are not suggesting that Jason's beating you was your father's fault, are you!" She had her mother's full attention now. "Your father loves you, Gemma, and he never laid a hand on you! Your father cried like a baby after he came from seeing you in the hospital."

"And why didn't you come to see me, Mum?" Gemma waited for an answer. "Did he tell you it was your fault I was there? I am sure he didn't take any blame, but I'm sure he told you it was yours."

"You will not talk about your father, Gemma!" Her mother's voice revealed the indignation her mother felt, but Gemma also heard something else in her voice. Fear!

Her mother was trembling. Gemma saw the shame riddled across her face and felt bad she had embarrassed her. "What are you afraid of, Mum?" She went to her mother's side. "He's not here? It's just us talking. He has pitted us against each other all my life." Gemma saw the lines on her mother's face from the years of stress. Her dad never touched either one of them, but he had a way of cutting with his words. "You know what I learned being with Jason? He hit me and it hurt like hell, but the bruises healed every time. The aftermath reminded me of what he did and how wrong he was. I knew he was wrong, Mum. I knew what he did to me was not natural. I became paralyzed in my situation. I knew I should have left him, but I couldn't." Gemma desperately wanted her mother to understand her.

"It was his words that kept me there. He constantly told me you didn't love me and he was all I had. He told me you didn't love me!" She yelled the words this time, hoping her mother could feel her frustration. "I believed him, so Mummy, you see it wasn't the punches that hurt me. They kept me there because I believed as long as he hit me he still loved me. I was afraid if the hitting stopped, he was hitting someone else and didn't love me anymore. You see, I could deal with the physical pain." Gemma dropped to her knees. "His words haunt me even now, Mummy. I'm kneeling here wondering if you will put me out for my hurtful words. I wonder if you can put away your own hurt long enough and hear me; really hear me!"

Gemma watched her mother through her now blurred vision. Her mother's face was expressionless from the years of building her emotional shield that protected her from her personal pain.

Her mother knelt on the floor next to her and hugged her. "I've never not loved you a day in your life, Gemma. You have been in my prayers every night and sometimes all day. There is nothing and no one who could change that." Her mother released her. "How could you have believed him?"

"You never called me or came to see me. He was all I had. Why didn't you call me, Mummy?" Gemma searched her mother's face for the answers she greatly needed. She knew her father forbade her or made her feel that Gemma didn't want to hear from her, but that upset her more because she knew there was nothing and no one that could keep her from her child.

She saw the shame on her mother's face and the shine in her eyes and knew the truth, although her mother may never admit it, was there just below the surface. Gemma rubbed her mother's face and the tears she desperately held back released like mist running slowly down the side of a cold drink. "Mummy, it's okay to cry. I know you have your demons to deal with, too." Gemma drew her mother into her arms and held her while she cried.

She didn't feel her mother was ready for all she had to share with her. There was still so much she needed to learn herself.

During the remainder of her stay, she found herself being polite to her dad. She cringed when he was rude to her mother, but she was careful not to say anything. When he looked for her to co-sign, she took her mother's side; no longer wanting his love at the cost of her mother's hurt.

Her mother was sad when she told her she needed to get back to her place. "Why do you want to go back there? Stay here where we can love on you."

"I'll be back more often," she promised and hugged her mother good-bye. She had intended to stay longer, but she didn't know how much longer she could be silent. "I love you, Mum." She wanted to pack her in her suitcase and take her to protect her, but she knew her mother's changes were totally up to her mother.

The drive home wasn't long. She was thankful Caden let her borrow his car while he was out of the country. Jacque let her stay in the spare bedroom at his place as well. Jason was out now and she was a little frightened he would find her. Although Jacque assured her she could take care of herself, she wasn't ready to face him.

Jacque lived simpler than his brother, in a three-level townhouse, with a basement gym. Gemma found herself in the basement many nights when she couldn't sleep. She felt she needed to spend time there now. Her visit with her parents was much more emotional than expected. Her feelings for her dad had turned to hate. She couldn't stand the way he laughed freely with her and with the same lips was rude to her mother, but most of all she hated the way he bullied her mother.

Jacque wasn't home so she quickly put her things in her room, changed, and made her way to the basement gym. Her favorite was the bag so she punched and kicked until she could no longer lift her legs or arms.

"Dang, girl, you mad at somebody?" Jacque asked from the doorway.

Gemma looked up to find Jacque dressed to work out. She smiled at him, happy he was there. She missed their conversations while she was gone. He had some insight on hurt so he understood where she was in her journey. "Hey, Pretty," she teased. She remembered telling him he spent too much time in the bathroom and she started calling him pretty.

Jacque laughed at her as he made his way across the room to hug her. "You stink," he teased, still hugging her. Gemma pushed him away and they both laughed.

"I'm going for a run. Coming?" Jacque asked.

"I still have something left. Sure."

"Grab your hoodie, it has gotten cooler," he suggested and made his way out the door.

Across the street sat a black truck. Neither noticed its occupants as they prepared for their run.

It was beginning to get dark when Gemma and Jacque returned. The same truck was parked across the street, watching as they entered the house.

"Make sure you stretch before you cool down too much. I am going to kick for a while," Jacque told Gemma.

Jacque entered the small gym and began his workout. His legs felt heavy from the run, but he worked through it. The mixed martial arts competition was coming up and he wanted to stay in shape. After kicking the bag and doing his other exercises, he made his way to the main level.

The fruits in the fridge were cleaned earlier, so he took an apple and threw it in the blender with the protein, water, ice, and spinach. Gemma entered the kitchen and sat on the barstool.

Being with Gemma was relaxing for Jacque. They did a lot together that made him not feel so lonely, which was how he felt most of the time. He liked her, but saw how she looked at Caden and didn't want to cross that line.

"Make some for me?"

Her hair was wet from her shower and she had on her shorts and tank. Although he was accustomed to seeing her in lately, he could still feel the heat rise in him so he looked away. "You want to make it a movie night and you can fill me in on your visit?"

"So long as I get to pick. I refuse to watch another *Kung Fu* movie for at least a month." Imitating him, punching and making fight sounds, made her laugh.

"As long as it's not a girl flick."

"Okay. Let's do adventure," she suggested.

"Deal. We can ride to the box at the drug store and pick out something."

"You stink. I'm not riding with you until you take a shower." She wrinkled her nose.

Jacque came around the counter and smothered her with hugs, wiping his sweat on her. Gemma screamed, trying to get away, but Jacque held onto her as she squirmed and laughed. "Stop! Stop, you're making me stink!" she yelled.

Jacque let her go and ran up the steps to take a shower, forgetting the drink he had not finished on the counter. "You need to change because you aren't going anywhere with me in those booty shorts!" he yelled back down the steps.

Jacque quickly showered and dressed. When he returned downstairs, he saw Gemma had changed into her jeans and oversized shirt with her tank under. She had on flip-flops, which were customary for her as well. She was very earthy and he loved that about her. Her short cut flattered her and lay perfectly, framing her oval-shaped face.

The two walked out and locked the door. "If you're going to wear those things you need to get your feet done," he teased.

Gemma pushed him and looked down at her toes. "My feet are pretty," she said smugly.

The same truck still sat across the street, but this time Jacque noticed it. He didn't look directly at the occupant, but made sure he backed out the driveway slow enough to get the tag number and to try to get a look at the driver without alarming Gemma.

As they drove, he checked his mirrors often. Once he was sure they had not been followed, he relaxed. *Maybe I'm just being paranoid.*

When he reached the store, he told Gemma to go pick out the movie since she didn't like his. He watched her walk into the drug store then picked up his phone to make a call. "Titus, I need a favor. There is a truck outside of my house with a guy sitting in it. I will text you the tag number and make and model. Can you send someone by to check him out and text me afterward?"

"I'll get back to you when we find out something," Titus answered.

Jacque watched everyone who entered the store and nothing looked out of place. He saw Gemma head back to the car with a bag and a smile. He liked that she was now able to smile. She was so frail and timid when he first met her, but he could see where her therapy sessions were helping her to open up and their sparring sessions helped her to relax. He really liked her, but once again, he lost out to his brother's charm. He could feel the jealousy rise up in him, but quickly squashed it, hearing his pastor's words echoing in his ear, *What's for you is for you.*

"I said movie, Gemma." He laughed as she got into the car.

"I thought we needed some movie snacks," she said, smiling back at him.

Jacque looked into the bag and laughed. "I can't eat any of that."

"Why!" She was deflated.

"I'm in training and you shouldn't eat any of that either; they are empty calories."

"Well, don't eat then. More for me," she rebutted. "Don't sneak any either."

Jacque drove a different way home. "You want to get a bite to eat?" he asked, trying to buy time before they went home.

"I could eat," she said.

Jacque drove to Reggae.

Gemma watched Jacque across the table. He was rambling about some upcoming tournament he wanted to enter, but she was thinking about her mother. Gemma felt free from her prison and her mother still lived in one. As happy as she was in the past month, she was sad for her.

"And I entered you to fight in the women's tournament," Jacque was saying.

"What! I'm not ready to fight in any tournament," she argued.

"You were not listening to me. Where were you just now?"

She flopped on the table and sat back up. "Busted," she answered. "I was thinking of my mum and her situation. I tried to tell her a little about my life with Jason, but I didn't want to get too deep with her because I want her to make the decision to get help.

"I'm sitting here so happy in my new life and I really don't know if she's happy. I don't know." She tried not to pout, but she knew she could with Jacque.

"Come on, let's dance. There will be no pouting tonight, woman!" He stood, putting his hands on his hips like he was a super hero.

Gemma took his hand and made her way to the floor behind him. She watched him dance somewhat awkwardly and laughed when she realized he was mocking her. He turned and backed up to her and touched the floor, twerking. Gemma laughed at his silliness and, once again, he was able to bring her back to her happy zone.

Gemma could feel herself falling for him, but was afraid to let anyone that close again. She also wasn't sure how he felt about her. At one point, he would seem interested, but as quickly as she saw it he seemed indifferent. Right now, she liked just having a friend she could be free with and who knew her dirty laundry.

Across the room, the stranger sat in the booth watching the two. He thought he had been made when they left the house. He was turned on by Gemma's laughter and playfulness. She had thickened up since the last time he saw her. She looked perfect.

While eating, Jacque received a text indicating no one was sitting outside of the house and all was clear. He was relieved, but not convinced. On their ride home, he reminded Gemma not to let her guard down.

"Hey. I need you to still be aware of your surroundings when you're out. Jason is out now and I'm sure he's looking for you."

He could see the fear on her face. "Don't be afraid. You're more than ready to defend yourself if it comes down to that. We've done the drills over and over, again, and you're prepared, but I don't want you to take this lightly. Okay?"

"Yes," she answered, but he could see she was tense, again.

Jacque drove slowly down their street until they came to his house. The truck was gone as his text indicated. He opened the garage door and parked inside. He could feel Gemma look at him because he usually didn't park there.

"I need to stay on my toes, too," he said, answering the question on her face.

"What's going on, Jacque?" She wasn't buying his explanation.

"I don't know," he answered truthfully. "Let's just say my spidey senses are up. I'd rather be overly cautious." He looked at her, choosing his words. "You're my friend. I haven't had one of those in a while."

Gemma smiled, twisting his stomach into knots.

"Now let's throw this away," he said, taking her bag of junk and jumping from the car. She was soon in pursuit.

Escape to Anthony's

When Brenda Davidson was around there was never a dull moment. The family sat on the beach under the moon as the kids slept. Mr. Washington laughed at her jokes and quick wit.

"You keep laughing like that and we will have to make this a double wedding," she teased Mr. Washington.

"Momma," Cuyler whispered.

"Girl, you better sit down."

"Your mother is fine, Cuyler," Mr. Washington assured her.

"This was your idea to invite her here," Tashia whispered to Anthony.

He laughed, rocking in the chair, holding her. "You ready to go back to the house?"

"With pleasure."

"We are about to go back to the house," Anthony announced to the group of adults. "We will scoop up the kids and see you tomorrow."

"Leave them be. They can stay for the night. They will be fine," Mr. Washington guaranteed. "Go home and have fun. Make babies!"

"Oh, that one don't need no more kids!" Mrs. Davidson remarked.

Anthony spun Tashia around and pointed her to the brush before she could retaliate. "We have an empty house. You want to stay here with Brenda and argue or leave with me?"

"I want to leave with you after I curse her out!"

"Then you will ruin my mood." He pushed Tashia now leaning back on his chest as they walked through the trees.

They headed to the house to kiss the kids goodnight, but Tashia changed her mind believing she may wake them. "Let's go!"

"You are talking my language, because I got something for you, girl!"

The house was dark when they entered. "Meet me in the pool. I will get us something to drink."

Tashia striped where she was and exited the house through the sliding glass door to the pool. When Anthony joined her, he had a bottle of wine and two glasses and was butt naked, smiling at her as she laughed at his prolific style.

Anthony hit the power button on the remote he held and the music blared from the speakers placed strategically throughout the yard. He adjusted the volume and joined her in the water.

Tashia removed the bottle and glasses from his hands and kissed him. "I am beginning to believe you are beauty and I am the beast. You know how to put out my inner rage."

"Why do you allow your mother to push your buttons?"

"I don't know. I guess because she doesn't know what to say out of her mouth."

"Well since you know that, why do you let her push your buttons?" he asked again.

"I don't want to talk about my mother." Tashia tried to leave the pool, but Anthony pulled her back.

"We don't run from each other, Tashia. We are each other's safe zone." He watched her face soften. "Why do they bother you?"

"I'm not sure."

Anthony saw she was honest about her answer. "Since we are here and no one can run away, the three of you need to get together and talk before the wedding."

"Stop talking. My song is on and I can't talk to them tonight." Tashia put her arms around his neck and pulled him closer. She dropped the bottle and the glasses in the water. Slowly, the bottle dropped to the bottom of the pool.

"You know I love you, right? I can't wait to marry you next week." Leaning back, he took them both under water in the fashion they were used to. When they resurfaced, they were on the other side of the small pool. Anthony pinned her to the side of the pool and grabbed her hair, roughly pulling her head back. She knew him now, but mostly he knew she understood how he liked it. Talking could commence in the morning.

Do You Remember?

Tashia shopped with Annetta and Cuyler over the next few days to find her perfect dress. They visited many stores and were stopped all over to ask if they were Anthony's girl and Preston's wife. Tashia thought it was funny that so many knew them and they had never met before.

They strolled along the main strip until they came to a small shop. Tashia wasn't sure why Annetta brought them there because there didn't seem to be any dresses in the place.

A small Asian woman came from the back of the shop and Tashia recognized her from the party.

"Hello, Tashia." The little Asian woman stepped forward and took her hand. "I am your future Aunt Ming. I am going to show you a few dresses you may like. The girls have been bombarding you with questions over the days to get an idea of what you may like and I have made three dresses for you to look at. So, come to the back with me and I will let you try them on."

Tashia disappeared to the back while Annetta and Cuyler sat and waited. When she came out in the first dress she resembled a mermaid in a beautiful pearl pink dress that flared below her knees. The back was detailed with pink pearl-looking buttons. The middle had a single ribbon around the waist. The sides were see-through mesh and there were knotted balls covering the dress giving an illusion of pearls all over.

"Shia! You look beautiful!" Cuyler went to her sister and circled her. "It complements your small waist and shapely hips. The girls will think you are a mermaid." She laughed, thinking of the girls.

"It is lovely, Shia," Annetta said echoing Cuyler.

Ming stepped forward and pinned a few areas on the gown. "Come. You have two more."

Tashia tried on the last two dresses, but knew her mind was made up after the first. Ming told her she could pick up the dress in three days. The only thing left to get were her shoes and jewelry, but it was getting hot so they decided to go back to the house and to the beach.

When Tashia arrived back to the house the men were gone fishing with the kids. The only person in the house was her mother.

"Hey, Momma." Tashia entered the kitchen flanked by Cuyler and Annetta. "What are you up to?"

"I sat by the pool and read and just came in the house to grab a bite to eat. Cuyler have you eaten?"

"We got something light while we were out."

"Tashia, make sure you don't eat too much. You look like you've packed on a few. Don't no man want no fat woman."

Tashia felt the blood rise to her face. She had always been more hippy than Cuyler and envied her thin, but shapely, build. *Here we go, again.*

Cuyler saw the glare on Tashia's face. She had seen the same look many times from Callia in the past eighteen months. Quickly she changed the subject. "We were going to grab something to drink and head to the beach. Do you want to come with?"

"Come with?"

"Come with us!" Cuyler changed so her mother would understand what she was saying.

"I will come with," her mother said, imitating her.

The women grabbed a few things and something to drink and headed to the shallow group of trees that led them to the circle of chairs at the beach. Brenda walked ahead, while Annetta and Tashia hung back with a slow walking Cuyler.

"Why did you get quiet back there?" Cuyler asked Tashia. "You didn't want her to come?"

"No."

Cuyler was shocked at Tashia's honesty. She looked at her sister and saw she was serious. Cuyler stopped walking. "What's going on?"

Tashia felt ashamed. How would she tell her sister she didn't feel like competing with her? She thought about telling her the truth, but decided she was acting like a bitch. "I just wanted to chill with you and Annetta, is all." Tashia put her arm around her younger sister. "C'mon."

The two walked the rest of the way to the beach, talking about the wedding. When they reached the chairs, Tashia helped her sister sit and put everything close so Cuyler could reach without getting up. She didn't care if her mother could reach. *She wasn't worried if I ate, so I don't care if she drinks.*

"Did you find a dress, Tashia?"

"Yes, Mom."

"Did you like it?"

Tashia thought that had to be one of the stupidest questions she had heard in a while. Why would she choose a dress she didn't like? *"Yes."*

"Are you giving me tone, little girl?"

"No, Mom, that was just a stupid question. Why would I choose a dress I didn't like?" She saw her mother look at her like she did when she and Cuyler were children and Tashia challenged her. They referred to it as the death grip. "I'm sorry."

"What is wrong with you? You got a nice man like Cuyler, someone who can take care of you and your three children. You should count yourself as lucky." Brenda watched her daughter. "Most men don't want a woman with luggage."

Tashia watched her mother stare at her and knew she was baiting her, but she held her tongue no longer. She took a lot from her mother, but calling her children luggage hurt her deeply. "What, Mom? I should feel lucky that someone would want me because I have three children? Or, should I feel lucky that someone would want me because of where I come from? Or, maybe it's because I am not as pretty as Cuyler. Which is it, Mom?"

Brenda sat up in her chair, prepared for the fight. She smiled a warning at Tashia. "Do you have anything else you want to say, little girl?"

"I'm not a little girl!"

"Then stop acting like one!"

Cuyler put her hands in the air to silence the two of them. "You two stop! Look at the water coming in and going out. Look at where we are and enjoy it!"

Tashia took a deep breath, trying to heed her sister's advice. She had already said too much and was afraid of what would come out of her mouth next. She didn't understand what was going on with her lately. She should be happy, but lately she was only happy when with Anthony and the kids.

Cuyler reached for Tashia's hand and held it like she did when she was afraid. Tashia leaned back in her chair and closed her eyes. "I'm sorry, Annetta."

"Oh, I come from a big family and we have our share of fights."

Cuyler tried to change the mood of the conversation. "Annetta! Preston and Anthony are so competitive. Why?"

Annetta threw her head back and laughed. "I think the competition is more on Preston's part. Anthony has never been big in competing. He has always been his own person and has never felt the need to compete. Preston, on the other hand, has to show he is the best at everything he does to Anthony. I don't believe it is competition. I believe it is more he wants Anthony's approval that he is doing well, because Anthony has always excelled at whatever he does."

Cuyler smiled, thinking of her poor husband running behind Anthony. "I used to think he was a mean bully."

"Anthony!" Annetta laughed until she cried. "Of all my brothers, Anthony is the most giving and loving. He would give all he has if you needed. This is why he works with the boys. But, if you are on the outside of the family I can see why you would think that. He can be cold to those outside of the family, or those who he knows are taking advantage of him. He will defend his loved ones to the end. He's a very faithful family man."

Tashia smiled, knowing she could identify with everything Annetta said about him. Suddenly, she missed him and wanted to be with him.

"But there is a dark side to that. A man can't love that hard and not have a wrath to match." Annetta looked at her phone. "They are back, so I am headed back to the house to help with supper."

"I'll come help," Tashia volunteered.

"No. I don't do much because the boys do most of the work. They have to gut and scale the fish."

Tashia felt like a caged animal. She needed to escape. She needed to be with Anthony. She felt vulnerable and insecure.

Annetta disappeared through the shrubbery. Tashia could see her mother adjust in her seat and ready for round two.

Brenda was watching Tashia, now openly challenging her. Tashia was her fiery child, always challenging and testing her. Brenda watched as Tashia smugly smiled wanting to say something, but dared not.

She remembered as a little girl she questioned anyone who entered their home. She wanted to know what they were there for as though she was the gatekeeper. She reminisced about a happier time before she became entangled in drugs and alcohol when she was able to watch them through sober eyes.

She remembered when Tashia's father was killed for disobeying his gang's commander. The vision of him coming to check on them every day, making sure they were fine and holding Tashia until she was sleep each night, then he returned to the brutality of the streets to do the things he did to take care of them.

After he died, she couldn't pay her rent. The landlord came by one day to collect and realized Mateo was no longer around; he wanted to make payment arrangements with her, but they were not the type of arrangements that would stop. She knew that and understood her dilemma.

She found herself pregnant with her second child. When she began showing he told her she would have to move out after the baby was born. He said he needed the money from the place.

They moved to the towers not long after and remained, never able to escape. Brenda started drinking and then graduated to drugs. The girls were seven and five when things reached the ugly reality that she was not able to take care of her children. Most of the time she was either drunk or high.

Tashia became Cuyler's mother, combing her hair, bathing and dressing her, and cooking whatever they had in the house. Brenda knew Tashia's childhood was stolen from her, but she refused to give them up to a system that would probably do worse.

"What you smirking about, Tashia?" Brenda knew she should drop it, but she sensed there was much she wanted to say and probably needed to get off her chest.

"No, Momma. I am not going there with you. I am going to lay here and enjoy the sun, the breeze, and the ocean." Smiling, Tashia closed her eyes.

"I know you don't think much of me. I know I wasn't there for you as a child, but I never handed you over to some strangers or a system that didn't work. I'm here today, but that still isn't enough for you. You went and got your degree and look down on me like you are better, but we the same; two women with luggage, trying to make it through!"

Tashia's eyes opened and the shadows of indignation rose up in her. She could feel Brenda baiting her, but she couldn't stop. "What does today have to do with then? What are you trying to say, Mother? You asking for forgiveness? Well you're too late because I forgave you a long time ago!"

"Then what is your issue, Tashia?"

Tashia closed her eyes. She didn't want this argument, but she could feel her mother needed it, and she refused to oblige her. She could feel Cuyler holding her hand again, encouraging her to be quiet. When they were younger, she did the same. She knew if she could get Tashia to be quiet, the battle would end sooner. It took two to argue.

"Well if you are not going to be woman enough to tell me then you need to shut down this attitude you have with me!"

Pushing Cuyler's hand away, Tashia stood to her feet. "You know my issue with you, Brenda! When I was seven, I cleaned your house, cooked your food, took care of your child....hell, I even took care of you! I wiped your ass when you didn't even know you messed yourself, bathed you when you smelled like piss so our home didn't reek!

"You left us alone to fend for ourselves many nights and when the things that went bump in the night came you weren't there to tell us it was nothing and everything would be okay!"

Cuyler was now standing next to her sister, rubbing her back, but the inner beast was awake, and she couldn't calm it.

"You brought men to our home!" she cried. "Men that I had to fight off of me or protect Cuyler from because she was now my responsibility! I was seven years old!" she yelled, now crying uncontrollably. "At fourteen, I was raped in the basement of our building and you never knew. You never noticed that I had difficulty walking or sitting. You didn't notice the bruises on my face nor were you there to soothe me and tell me I would heal and get better. You didn't even notice I came home in someone else's clothes that day. Where were you?" She now stood above Brenda, looking down at the woman she had long ago disregarded as her mother.

Cuyler was now crying with her sister as she remembered the day Tashia came home bruised and barely able to walk. She remembered crying then, because she knew something was wrong and she wanted to help her sister. She remembered holding her sister at night when she cried and tried to hide her tears from her. Tashia would just say, "I'm okay, Sunshine, go back to sleep. I'm just sad."

"Where were you, Mother? I'll tell you where you were. You were laid up with whoever had your high for the moment not even knowing where we were or whether we were safe.

"I was forced to have a relationship with a drug dealer because he protected me that day and I knew he could protect and feed us. So, when I went out with him and you called me a whore that's what you made me, because no one was going to touch me, again, and I never wanted my sister to experience that hurt!"

Tashia did not hear Anthony and Preston approaching from the bush and continued down the destructive path she had started.

"You were an ungrateful bitch, calling me names and telling me to be more like my sister. She stays out of trouble. She's not laying up with these boys. Cuyler gets good grades, Cuyler is beautiful, Cuyler is my little princess, Cuyler found a man who took her away from here, she's not out here making babies, she's smart and is getting her education. Cuyler is going to make something of herself and all you will ever be is the whore of a gang banger! DO YOU REMEMBER THOSE WORDS!" Tashia screamed, stomping in the sand like a spoiled child having a temper tantrum.

Preston moved forward to console her, but Anthony lifted his hand for him to stop. Since they were children, he always did as his brother said despite his competitive nature.

"I was never his whore. I was your whore and you were my pimp. You threw Cuyler in my face so much I started hating my own child." Tashia stepped forward, one-step away from Cuyler and pointed to her. "SHE *is* MY child. I raised her for fifteen years of her life and everything she became is because I guided her. You don't get to claim any of that success.

"But you tainted our relationship and I was torn between love for my Sunshine and resentment toward her for not experiencing anything I went through and doing everything I wanted to do, but couldn't because of my responsibilities. I always felt like I was in *her* shadow. If I had to hear one more time how beautiful she was I....Even in my own house, Jesus and his boys talked about her. I know it wasn't her fault she's beautiful, but if I heard it one more time.

"I walked out on Jesus because I no longer believed he loved me. I always saw him looking at Cuyler, and your words haunted me. I was just his little whore, so I became pregnant. I know it was stupid, but I was desperate to have something that was truly mine.

"I hear you rave about Callia, Momma. And, yes, I think she is a very bright child, but have you ever considered my son Zander? He is going to be one to reckon with, but never have you told me how bright any of my children are, and they all are. Zane can talk politics to a grown man and hold his own at ten, did you know that? Solana is Cuyler all over again. She is my Sunshine reincarnated and if she turns out to be half the woman my sister is I will be so proud of her."

Tashia was sobbing through her distorted words. "And don't you ever compare me to you. I would die for my children! The only thing you would die for was your next high.

"You tried it. You tried to tear us apart, but you can't. You won't!" Tashia pulled a now hysterically crying Cuyler to her and held her. "Don't cry, Sunshine. The wicked witch, Brenda, will never take you away from me. You will always be my Sunshine."

"I'm sorry I left you alone, Tashia." Cuyler sobbed in her sister's arms, finally understanding her attitude toward her lately.

Tashia palmed both sides of her sister's face as she had done many times when they were children. "I wanted you to go. I didn't want you to stay there in that shithole. You were so smart and I wanted better for you." Tashia pulled her as close as she could with her sister's growing belly between them. "Shhh! Don't cry or you will upset my new baby."

Brenda stood, smiling at her daughters. Tashia didn't understand why she smiled after all the ugly things she had just said. "Now that you have gotten that off your heart and soul, let me tell you a few things." Brenda put her arms around them both. Tashia resisted, but her mother pulled her back in.

"I do know I was a bad mother. Sometimes issues make us what we are. I just know that I did not want you two away from me. I wasn't always that mother. There was a time when I was sober and you were my Sunshine, Tashia, but some things happened and I dealt with them in a bad way." Again, Tashia tried to pull away. "Hold it, little momma. I listened to you and you are going to listen to me.

"I know I was an awful mother! I know I will never be mother of the year. I am proud of both of you. I may not have told you, Tashia, but I tell my grandchildren all the time how special and smart they are.

"When I called you names I was in a bad place. I was jealous of you because you were taking care of what I should have taken care of. I knew something happened to you when I saw the bruises, but I couldn't handle it. I wasn't there to protect you and I needed another high not to think about it.

"You took care of all of us and I stole your life away from you. It's something I can never repay you for, but I am here now and I'm not trying to make up for what I didn't do. I just want to know these two beautiful women.

"I've been pushing your buttons for a while now, Tashia, because I needed you to get this off your chest and I knew if I pushed you would. We cannot build any kind of relationship if you have all this resentment bottled up. I know because that was me.

"You don't owe me anything. I just want to see the real you, because for years I have seen the dutiful daughter Tashia, and I wanted to meet the real Tashia.

"I want you to think about what role you want me to play in your life. I'm not looking for an answer today. I came here because your man loves you and felt we needed to share this moment, 'because we have missed so many others', I believe is how he put it." Brenda wiped the tears from her daughters' faces. "I wanted to set you free to be happy in life and not live in shadows of your past. I wanted you to enjoy the sunshine and know life can be good and you deserve some good in your life for a change.

"I took so much from you and this was the most important thing I could give you." Brenda pulled a reluctant Tashia into her arms and held her as she sobbed. "Now let's sit and enjoy the sun and beach without the shade."

Induction to Fatherhood

Preston and Anthony walked back to the house, allowing the women to have their moment. Preston looked at Anthony, seeing him for the first time through Tashia's eyes. They did not have the same father, but they shared the same dad.

He could remember Anthony watching over them like hawks were going to come down and swoop them up. "Did you feel pressure like that being the eldest?"

Anthony looked at his younger brother by eight years and pushed him. "No."

Preston searched his face to see if he was lying and he saw something there, but he didn't feel Anthony was lying to him. Pressing on he decided to dig further. "Then what was it? Because I always felt you were intense when we were with you."

Anthony stopped and looked at his brother. Seconds ticked by before he answered. "I feared for your safety, but I didn't feel pressured." Reaching out his long arms, Anthony reached around his brother's shoulders, hugging him, and patted him on the back. "Maybe one day I will share that with you, but not today."

The two men walked to the house in silence. Preston jokingly put his hand on Anthony's behind. Anthony shoved him hard and continued to the house with Preston behind, laughing as they walked.

Anthony was on the side of his father's pool when the ladies returned from the beach. Tashia and Cuyler held hands like Solana and Callia. He could see Tashia was at peace with her sister, but he couldn't tell where Brenda fell in the mix.

"Call the other distributor to see if he carries the same mix," he was telling Snow. "When are you flying in?"

Tashia looked his way and he blew her a kiss. She broke off from Cuyler and walked in his direction. He motioned for her to sit in the chair with him and she obliged him, resting her head on his chest.

"How are the new girls working out?...Well, did Myra train her?...Oh Myra, Myra, Myra. Okay we will pick you up from the airport when you get here. Call me if you need me."

Anthony disconnected the call and looked down on Tashia. He lifted her chin to see her face. "You good?"

"I'm good."

"You want to get the kids and take the boat out?"

"Just us?"

"If that's what you want."

"Okay!"

He saw the light in her brighten. "How was the beach?"

Her mood changed. Snuggling her head under his arm, again, she shrugged. "What's wrong?"

"Nothing. We can talk later, but for now, I am mellow. I feel at peace with myself." Turning to her side, she leaned her head back. "How are you, Anthony?"

Her question caught him off guard. He wasn't asked that often. Lightly, he kissed her for being his protector. "I'm always good, if you are. Let's go get our kids and go for a boat ride."

The sea was calm and the sun hot. Zander guided the boat through the waters as his brother stood beside him, complaining it was his turn. Tashia lay in the back with Solana and Callia in her bikini, trying to catch the breeze from the ride.

Anthony took pictures of everyone then returned to the squabbling boys at the helm. "Okay, ease the boat down to a stop like I taught you, Zander, so Zane can drive."

Reluctantly, he brought the boat to a halt and traded places with Zane. "Wait, Zane! You can't just start. You have to go through all your checkpoints first."

Zane started naming the things he was supposed to do out loud and when he would miss one Zander made him restart. Anthony chuckled as he remembered the first time his dad let Preston drive the boat. Preston started off so quickly that he fell in the water. He swore Preston did it on purpose so he stayed under the water as long as he could before resurfacing to a frantic Preston.

"If you are not going to help him, Zander, then take a seat in the back and I will review with him."

Zander rolled his eyes at Zane and sighed. He reviewed all the checkpoints with Zane and made him repeat them back. Once he was able to repeat them, he announced that Zane was about to start the ride.

Solana sat in Anthony's lap and pushed Callia away every time she tried to sit there. Callia was beginning to whine.

"If you do not share, I will put you down and pick her up."

"She has two daddies and I only have one and I don't always want to share. She doesn't."

Anthony smiled at Solana referring to him as her daddy. He wondered when they should tell the kids about Fatimah. "Sometimes you are going to have to share me, Solana, but it won't be all the time. Okay?"

"Okay," Solana answered and tried to push from Anthony's lap, but he held her back and picked Callia up, placing her on his other leg.

Callia lay on Anthony's chest. "Daddy."

"He's not your daddy! He's my daddy!" Solana told a sleepy Callia. Callia cried.

"That wasn't nice, Sunshine," Zander said, lifting her up from Anthony.

"I don't care. Anthony is my daddy. She has two already." Solana began to cry as well.

"Zane! Can you turn the boat slowly around and head back to the shore?" Anthony asked. He made his way back to Tashia who was smiling. "What are you smiling about?"

"You. Bailing so soon?"

"This one is sleepy and missing Caden. That one is sleepy and spoiled," he said, pointing to Solana.

"Give me Callia. You tend to *your* child." She watched him as he took Solana from Zander and helped Zane maneuver the boat. Fun at sea was now officially over.

Anthony watched the boat trailing them in the distance. There was something familiar, but he didn't know what it was.

Back at shore, the boys docked the boat and Tashia took the girls to the house. Callia was on her back and Solana pouted as she walked alongside Tashia. Tashia thought she heard something in the brush.

She stopped, making sure it was not some strange animal or snake, but the sound was gone. Quickening her pace, she hurried to pass the shallow brush in case the animal returned.

Preston saw Tashia walking with Callia in tow with a crying Solana and rushed to help. Callia reached for him the closer he got, but he picked up Solana instead, sending her into convulsions.

"They are tired. This was a bad idea."

"Hahaha! Is this what I am in for?"

Tashia put the girls to bed and met everyone at the pool. She watched Zane struggle as he dozed in his chair. "Zane! You aren't going to miss anything, honey, so go and lay down!" Zane declined.

"Do you have everything ready for the ceremony?" Mr. Washington asked.

"Annetta took care of the catering. My dress will be ready tomorrow. And, Blaine is in charge of music." Tashia thought of everything that needed to be in place. "We meet with the pastor, again, in two days and that's all I can think of right now."

Anthony was asleep in the lounger, which was different because he rarely slept during the day. Tashia ran her hand down his chest then rubbed his baldhead. She let him sleep.

Thinking about the events of the day, she smiled. Her little family had already bonded and now she was ready.

The Ceremony

Guests began arriving over a two-day period. Everyone's house was maxed. Candice and Meagan stayed with Annetta in her home. Blaine and his girl were back for the wedding and stayed with them at Anthony's while Caden was at the main house with Mr. Washington and the rest of their clan.

Tashia sat in her slip as Cuyler did her makeup. The pounding in her head was beginning to subside from their exploits the night before.

"I still can't believe you yanked that girl off the stage and got on the pole last night!" Meagan and Candace laughed, remembering the episode.

"No, the ultimate was Anthony cheering her on with the crowd," Candace added. "Where the hell you learn to do that? You did the damn thing!"

Tashia smiled, remembering the fun they had. After dancing, she was offered a job, but Anthony declined for her.

"Turn your head, Shia," Cuyler fussed.

The cameraman took pictures as she prepared for her day. Callia and Solana sat quietly on the couch, waiting their turn to be dressed. Callia's head was in Solana's lap as Solana listened to the adults.

Annetta walked the house in her robe, making sure everything was flowing. No one could make her stay in the room and relax. She needed to know everything was taken care of.

The door swung open, startling them. Annetta returned to the room with another tall Asian-looking beauty. She carried a small child, who looked to be about two, on her hip, clinging to her, afraid.

The young woman looked around the room shyly as though she was in the wrong place. Annetta was rolling a small suitcase behind her and the beauty quickly took it once inside.

"Everyone this is my sister, Ava."

No one moved. Tashia had heard about the young woman, but not much. Anthony always seemed guarded and protective of her.

Under protest from Cuyler, Tashia got up from her chair and introduced herself to Ava, embracing her. Cuyler followed and then took her to the girls and introducing them.

"Who is this little prince?" Tashia asked, peeping at the baby who clearly did not want to be seen.

"He is Marc Anthony. I named him after his uncle." She shyly looked, away glancing around the room. She walked to the couch were the girls sat and took a seat beside them. Solana looked at the woman and protectively put her arm around her cousin.

Cuyler looked at Tashia and shrugged at the woman's awkwardness. Tashia sat back in the chair so Cuyler could finish her hair.

Meagan and Candace followed Annetta's instructions and left to make sure the rest of the catering had arrived and the boys were seating the guests properly.

From the corner of her eye, Tashia saw Ava watching her, making her feel uneasy.

"Cuyler, you are not going to get it perfect."

"The hell I won't!" Cuyler stepped back and looked at her masterpiece. She pinned the ring portion of Tashia's headpiece under her hair so it wouldn't be seen. The only thing left to do was to put the veil in place around her bun.

"Should we get the girls dressed first?" Tashia questioned.

"They are quiet, so let them remain quiet as long as they will," Annetta interjected.

"She has a point."

Cuyler went to the bathroom to put on her dress, allowing the photographer to take more pictures of Tashia. When she returned, she saw that Annetta had donned her dress in the room. The lacy, two-piece dress showed off her tiny waist and the long skirt accentuated her lengthy, ebony legs.

"You look beautiful, Annetta!"

Annetta smiled and continued to put on her jewelry.

"You ready to put on your dress!" Cuyler was excited. She hugged Tashia and went to get the beautiful gown that hung on the closet.

Tashia stood to step into the stunning gown. Pulling it up over her shoulders, she allowed Cuyler to zip the back of the gown. It fit like a glove.

Cuyler shrieked with excitement and clapped. "Let me get your shoes."

Getting the beautiful silver shoes, Cuyler dropped them on the floor, allowing her sister to step into them.

Tashia looked at her sister. "What?" Cuyler asked. "I can't get my big belly down there or I would have." But Tashia continued to stare. Then Cuyler saw the shine in her eyes.

"I wish I could have been here to help you."

"We can't do this, Tashia, or we are going to mess up our makeup." Cuyler hugged her sister and the photographer snapped.

Everyone was in their places ready for the wedding to commence. Anthony and Preston walked to the front of the chairs and took their positions. Preston whispered to Anthony as they walked, smiling. Caden waited with Tashia ready to escort her to Anthony. Cuyler talked to the girls, preparing them to walk down the aisle. She pointed to Jessica letting them know they were to follow her instructions and handed them their basket of petals. Mr. Washington was seated, awaiting the commencement of the wedding.

When the music began to play, Tashia felt the wave of heat rise in her. She was so excited she thought she would pee her panties. Running down the aisle to Anthony was more her mood.

The procession began with Cuyler, then Annetta and Blaine. Jessica stood with Callia and Solana waiting to give them their cue to walk down the aisle. Under protest, Zane walked to the altar. Zander had been teasing him about being the ring bearer. Once everyone was in place, Jessica let the anxious girls walk down the aisle. Callia dropped one petal at a time so Solana stopped and showed her how to drop more, but stubbornness would not allow her to adjust to Solana's instructions. She continued to drop one petal at a time. The crowd laughed.

Caden stood pensively as he watched his baby girl walk down the aisle. Tashia laid her head on his arm. "You okay?"

Not realizing he was staring, he turned, looked at her, and smiled. "I'm okay. I was just thinking about India and how she never got her day."

"I appreciate you being here for me. I can share this day with India by having you here."

Caden smiled at Tashia and hugged her. "No, this is your day. And I am honored you asked me to give you away."

The music Tashia picked out for her entrance started and Preston began the song. "That's our cue. Are you ready?" asked Caden.

"I was ready when he asked me."

"He said you asked him."

"That's his story." They laughed.

Caden escorted Tashia through the double doors and together they walked slowly through the standing crowd to Anthony. Tashia saw the grin that broke down her walls months ago, waiting for her. She didn't care about the ceremony; she just wanted to be Mrs. Laurent. Once the ceremony began, she saw Anthony cry for the second time in their relationship.

A Bad Feeling

The reception was beautiful. There were many surprises such as the ice carving of a Phoenix, the fountain containing liquor, and the pony and clown for the children.

Tashia was by Anthony's side all evening. She periodically saw Ava watching them together. She looked as though she wanted to approach, but was too shy to do so. Tashia found her strange. Eventually, the peculiar woman made her way to the newlyweds to congratulate them.

"Congratulations, Anthony. Your bride is beautiful."

Anthony turned and lifted his sister in the air. She protested and laughed at the same time. "I heard you were here and was wondering when I was going to see you! I am so glad you came. You said you couldn't make it! How long have you been here?"

"Slow down." Ava looked at Tashia and back to Anthony.

"Oh, this is my beautiful wife, Tashia. Tashia, this is my baby sister, Ava."

"We met earlier," Tashia said hugging Ava.

"Welcome to the family."

"Thank you."

Ava still made her uneasy. She looked at Anthony strangely, almost inappropriately. Tashia stood closer to Anthony as though protecting her territory and him.

Ava turned to Anthony. "I wouldn't have missed your wedding for the world. I haven't been home since I left, but it was time to come back," she said as though in code.

Tashia saw Anthony's demeanor change and he nodded. Grabbing her arm, he looked her over. "Well, you look great. You are as beautiful as you were as a teen and I hear there is a child named after me!"

"Yes! Marc Anthony. He is lying down in your old room asleep. He is beautiful like his uncle and very smart!"

Tashia looked at Anthony for clarification. Why did she name this child after him when he had no contact with her for years?

Anthony appeared uncomfortable with the conversation and hugged her again. "Tomorrow we will have to play catch up and you can tell me more about what you have been up to, but right now we have to make our rounds and greet our guests. Okay?"

Ava looked disappointed, but complied.

Annetta made her way to the couple. "It's time for the dance so come on you two. You and Ava can talk later, Anthony." Annetta grabbed each of their hands and led them to the wooden floor that had been set up on the lawn.

The song they danced to at Preston's house the night of his and Cuyler's Anniversary party, "We are Not Alone" by Demi Grace, was playing. Anthony bowed and asked Tashia to dance with him. Accepting his invite, the two stepped onto the dance floor and danced with the same intensity they had the night of the party. They received the same reaction from the crowd before they joined them on the floor.

Tashia saw Ava standing on the side, openly challenging her. Although not understanding the challenge, Tashia accepted, not wavering from her stare.

The children road the pony until it was time for princess the pony to go home. Zander supervised Solana and Callia while talking to his new island girlfriends who begged him to sing again, so he made his way to the deejay and sang a song, dedicating it to Anthony and Tashia. The girls giggled and fought for his attention when he was finished.

"We're going to make some money off that boy," Blaine announced to Anthony. "He's getting requests and singing on demand. Guaranteed money in the bank."

"Well, we will leave that up to you to make that happen," Tashia joked.

"Hey, gorgeous, come dance with your momma," Brenda joked with Anthony.

"Can you keep up?"

"The question is can you keep up with me!" Brenda pulled Anthony and they were gone.

Tashia stood alone for the first time. She caught a glimpse of Ava coming her way and deliberately walked to where Candace and Meagan stood talking. She didn't know her well enough to feel comfortable with her alone. She saw the woman stop abruptly.

Meagan and Candace both embraced her in a group hug. "You are so beautiful! And that dance! You need to bottle it and sell it as an aphrodisiac!" Meagan said. They all laughed.

Tashia was interrupted by Mr. Washington. "Come on, young lady, and do an old man the honors." He guided her to the wooden floor and they danced. They laughed and hooped for a while with the crowd until Anthony came and claimed her, again.

"Let's go back to the house and change clothes."

Tashia looked down at her beautiful gown. She wasn't sure if she was ready to take it off yet. When would she get the opportunity to wear it again?

Anthony lifted her chin and kissed her lightly. "You can either go with me now or I will take you in the woods in that dress, Mrs. Laurent."

Tashia smiled, daring him. Anthony picked her up, carrying her over his shoulder. When he passed Blaine, he whispered, "No one comes beyond this point. She needs a spanking."

"Oh so now I get a spanking!'

"You're being disobedient and need a spanking. If I don't get you in order now you will continue to disobey me."

Tashia laughed, but did not protest. Anthony took her to the private beach just beyond the brush and softly placed her on the lounge chair. Slowly, he lifted her gown exposing her garter belt and stockings. He unclipped the stockings and pulled them off followed by the belt.

"I've been watching you all day," she whispered in his ear as he breathed her in.

He kissed her neck, still lifting her gown to expose her bronze skin. Ducking his head under her gown, he sniffed. "I've been smelling you all day, thinking of all the lustful things I could do to you." Gently he kissed her there were he lay. "I've wanted to taste you all day. And after I taste I want to drink," he said, now tasting her wine and feeling her contort with each sample.

There was a rustle in the brush and Tashia jumped. "There is someone coming, Anthony!" But, he didn't stop. She threw her head back as the waves vibrated through her body. There it was again! "Anthony, there is someone in the brush!"

"Too bad. This is my wedding day so I have no boundaries," he said from under her gown. He pulled her in closer, snatching her further down the lounge to close the gap created by her movements and continued protest.

Tashia moaned, forgetting about the noises, getting lost in the attention he was giving her. She no longer heard the misplaced sounds being made in the brush nor cared. She thought it was probably the same animal she heard a few days ago after the boat ride.

Anthony wanted to show her that her needs superseded his and he would always take care of her first. This was how it was going to be from here on out. He wanted to prepare her for the rest of the night. He felt her vibrating under him, letting him know he was in the right place. He heard her changing from one language to another as though she was professing her love at the altar of Anthony until her pleasure erupted and she screamed for him to stop and then changing her mind wanting more and begging him not to stop.

He pulled her gown down making sure he put it back the way he found it. Her eyes were still closed as she caught her breath. Moving her gown to the side, he lay next to her, watching her. She was his final destination. He would know no other woman. Before kissing her, he watched the fullness of her lips and her long lashes resting on her cheeks.

She opened her eyes and he kissed her, again, sucking her tongue as though it was a lollipop and was trying to determine the flavor. "Let's go back before someone realizes we are missing."

Anthony helped her to her feet and stuffed her stockings in his pocket with her garter, but her legs were wobbly and he had to catch her. "You did this to me!"

"And I'm going to do much more later." He winked at her.

On the other side of the bush, Blaine was still on guard with Jessica. He was slow dancing with her.

"Were you in the brush?" Anthony asked.

"Do I look like a peeping Tom?" Blaine asked.

"Did you hear anything?"

"No, but I was busy," Blaine answered, dipping Jessica back.

Anthony shrugged it off and the four walked back to the party. When they were closer, he and Tashia made their way to Snow who was there with his new friend.

Anthony embraced the albino then Snow turned his attention to Tashia, lifting her in the air. "You are the beauty who took the beast off the market. There will be some broken hearts and tears shed, young lady." He put her down and looked her over. "You are stunning!"

"Thank you, Snow."

"When is the party over?"

"Probably sometime in the morning. Stay as long as you like. We will be in the guesthouse tonight so you can have the house with Blaine and Jessica. The kids are staying here. Blaine knows he is responsible for getting you back if we leave before you." Anthony hugged Snow again. "I am so glad you could make it. Enjoy yourselves."

"Let's check on the kids," Anthony suggested. They found them in the middle of the yard. Zane was sleeping on the lounger with Solana curled up next to him. Caden sat in the lounger next to the two with Callia asleep in his lap.

"Caden, would you like for us to help you get them in bed?" Tashia asked. "You should be enjoying yourself."

Caden shrugged. "Let them stay here for a while. It is so nice out here, let them breathe in the fresh air."

"Okay, but if you need help let me know."

Caden sat and looked around. There was something wrong and he didn't know what. Before he came, he was led to pray for the family and he didn't know why, but he was obedient. He wanted Callia close to him right now. For now, he would watch.

It was two in the morning and many of the guests were leaving. Cuyler had long since taken Callia, Solana, and Zane and put them to bed against the protest of Caden. She promised she would lay with them until Zander came in.

Caden reluctantly helped her take the kids to the house. She lay down with the girls while Zane lay in the opposite bed. She was exhausted, but was sure Preston had more in him. He remained outside with his father and the two would probably bring up the sun together. Sleep came quickly for Cuyler.

Family Secrets Exposed

*Z*ander walked his final guest to the car with her parents and told her goodnight. The small group had planned a beach day for later in the week.

Zander walked into the house to see if the kids were in bed. When he entered the room, everyone was sound asleep. He closed the door lightly and was startled by a woman in the hall. "Can I help you?" he asked, confused as to why she was there alone.

"I just came from the bathroom." She smiled at him, making him blush.

"Well the next time, there are several portable bathrooms in the yard, because the house is off limits." Zander found her beautiful, but he also found her to be sneaky. The other thing that bothered him was he had not seen her amongst the guests earlier. He took the time and walked her to the door to ensure she left and then latched it. Heading back to the kitchen, he went through the sliding glass door to rejoin the party.

Zander found Anthony and went to sit with him. His mother was sharing a seat with him and she was still wearing her gown.

Zander walked to his parents and hugged them both. "Momma, you were on fleek today!"

"I guess that's good." Tashia smiled at her son. "I see you around here singing to these young ladies. When did you start singing like that?"

Zander laughed at his mom. "Well, you know. I have to give the honeys what they want, Mom."

"The honeys? Boy, take several seats," Tashia told him as the men laughed at his new suave demeanor.

"I'm just kidding, Mom. I'm just having a good time."

"Boy, you sounded great tonight. We gonna work on that," Blaine told him.

"Nah. I'm not that good."

"You're better than most! Just keep practicing with Anthony and we will see."

"Okay Uncle Blaine," he promised. "Where is Pop?"

"Talking to Ava," Anthony said, pointing to his father sitting on a lawn chair across the yard beside Ava. She was holding Marc Anthony in her lap.

"Man, she's still strange as hell," Blaine said.

"She's different and don't talk about your sister," Anthony said.

"She's been through some things, but she's okay," Preston added.

"What type of things?" Zander asked.

Anthony looked hard at Preston and Tashia saw he was silencing him. "Zander, it's late so why don't you go to bed. I believe Pop is going out on the boat tomorrow."

Zander stood to oblige them. He was feeling the effects of the day and thought it a good idea. "Goodnight everyone," he said and hugged them before heading back to the house.

Once Zander was in the house, Tashia turned her attention to Anthony. "What is going on, Anthony? What is up with her? I got bad vibes from her all night?"

Anthony hung his head and, again, Tashia could feel his torment as she had months ago. He was silent for what seemed like minutes and then patted her leg. "Not tonight. Okay?"

Preston excused himself and went to the house. He saw Cuyler snuggled with the girls and Zander was leaving the room. "I am going into the other room with Caden and sleep on the other bed. Zane sleeps too wild." Preston patted him on the back and decided to leave Cuyler there with the girls. He was about to leave and thought he would rather have her with him, but felt selfish for wanting to wake her. Closing the door, he went to his room.

"There are still so many people here, Anthony. Shouldn't we stay a while longer?"

Anthony was about to tell his dad they were leaving and her words hit him. They had the rest of their life so maybe they did need to stay a while. The only person he had to worry about was Snow and he was bunned with his new love interest. "Let's go to our spot then."

She laughed, knowing she would never tell him no. Holding his hand, she led *him* to the path they knew so well and to the lounges on the beach. Turning to him she began to undress him and he her. The day was perfect and exciting. It was a day she would never forget. She would spend the rest of her life with this man who could calm her with a touch or word, and turn her on with a smile.

Tashia was startled by the voice of Ava approaching from behind them. She was now only dressed in her half bra and underwear and Anthony was totally nude.

Anthony scramble for his underwear, but it was too dark to determine where they were. "Ava! What do you want?" he yelled to her, trying to stop her approach, but she continued to come.

Tashia could see her eyes wash over Anthony, even in the darkness of the night. She was watching his nakedness, smiling. Stepping sideways, she moved to cover her husband's nakedness, but she still continued to walk their way.

"Poppa thinks I should leave. What do you think, Anthony? Should I leave?"

"What the hell are you doing, Ava?"

"I'm coming to say my goodbyes, since he doesn't want me here!"

"Well can you say them from a distance? We were busy here."

"Ava! Come from there!" Mr. Washington was standing at the top of the brush.

"No, Poppa. I am saying my goodbyes. I haven't seen Anthony in years and will probably not see him, again, since he has his replacement girl."

Tashia turned and looked at Anthony. Confusion riddled her face. "What is she talking about, Anthony?"

"Tell her, Anthony! Tell her the things we had to do for our mother! The nasty dirty things our beautiful mother made us do for money, so she could live her life!

"You see, Tashia, or should I call you Sh-i-a-a-a, Anthony will never have more than a whore because our mother made sure we were so screwed up we could never accept normal love, because she was screwed up."

Horror was on Tashia's face as she listened to this woman tell her things about a man she had given her life to. She heard Cuyler's words ring in her ears. *Do you really know him?* She began to hyperventilate. The question was there, but she couldn't ask it.

"Ava! That is enough!" Preston was walking down the path toward them.

"Oh, the golden child arrives. You were always father's favorite. Did you know that mother was jealous of you? She let your pet goat go when Poppa ruled against her. Did you know that?"

"Stop this now, Ava! This is a special day. Your brother just got married!" Preston, now close to her, pulled Tashia's dress up around her shoulders. He stood in front of her as though warding off Ava's words.

"Well, it is time to air our dirty laundry. She needs to know that all this here is no more than Neverland. It is fantasy, an illusion." Ava, the girl Tashia thought was shy when they first met, was reeling, and spinning her web, drawing everyone in.

Ava came closer. She looked Tashia up and down. "Sh-i-i-a-a," she hissed at Tashia. "You're a stripper, right? My brother likes the dark side." She spun to observe Mr. Washington who stood quietly. "Oh Poppa! You didn't know Anthony married a stripper?"

"She is a nurse, Ava!" Preston said, defending Tashia.

Ava waved her hand in the air and spun to face him. "Nurse by day, stripper by night, still makes her a stripper."

"You are crazy!" Preston said.

"Why? Because I am the only one willing to tell the truth? I'm not crazy, Preston. I am just tired of not coming around, because I thought you guys knew what she did to us and didn't care.

"But while talking to Poppa earlier, I discovered that you didn't have a clue. I went to live with her because I thought she needed my love and I would get all this attention, because I came with her. Anthony didn't have a choice, but if he had, he would not have chosen her. She used to tell him every day that Poppa didn't love him, that he pitied him. She told him every day that he was probably glad he was gone."

Ava spun and gave her attention back to Anthony. She attempted to walk to him, but Tashia blocked her way. "Maybe you married the right one, Tony."

"Don't call me that!" Anthony was now dressed. Tashia could see the anger and hurt in his face as he stared at Ava.

"Oh yeah. You hate that name." She diverted her attention back to Tashia. "Do you know why he hates that name, Sh-i-i-a-a?"

"That's enough, Ava!" Anthony took a step toward her, but Tashia put her hand out to stop him.

"That was his trick name. When he was a boy our mother tricked him out to pay for passage to come here." She looked at Anthony with pity, but there was no shame in her eyes.

Preston looked at his big brother, waiting for him to deny what she was saying, but he didn't. This was not the mother he knew. He didn't know this woman, Ava, was describing. He turned to look at his father for confirmation or denial, but he was broken.

Tashia, knowing of the one incident, was not caught totally off guard, but she did not know he was used as a pawn. She took his hand to let him know she was true to her word. She would protect him as he would her. He was trembling. "That's enough, Ava! Everyone has heard enough!"

"Oh, but there is more!"

"I'm sure, but so far you have done nothing but tear everyone else down. You have said nothing about yourself. The only thing I've heard from you is you had a mother who didn't love you. You're not the first and won't be the last.

"Tell us about this nasty love thing you have for my husband. You have been eyeing him since you arrived. You named your child after him. You air his dirty laundry in front of us. What did you think? I wouldn't want him anymore? I would leave him and he would be alone, again, and you would have him to yourself?" Tashia wanted to punch her. Anger now replaced shock. "Oh I get it. You didn't believe Daddy loved you, so you are angry because you made the wrong choice and want to rip everyone else apart."

Ava smiled at the now angry Tashia. "You haven't heard the worst."

"Stop this, Ava!"

"No, Anthony. We need to let it out so we can be free! They need to know the real person she was."

"She can't hurt us anymore. Let them have their memories."

"They need to know, Anthony."

"No they don't" he whispered. "No."

Ava turned and looked at her father. "Did you know she pimped me out, too, Poppa?" She began to cry. "China was my name. She was smart. She took me to the tourist area. She knew no man would touch me here because they would have to deal with you.

"I stayed away because I thought you knew and didn't want me. You used to call me your little China doll so I thought you knew and I didn't understand why you never came to get me. I was fourteen years old.

"Anthony didn't know she was doing this. I was too ashamed to tell him, but one day one of the men hurt me really bad. When she brought me home, Anthony saw me and asked me who hurt me." A tearful Ava looked at her father.

"I told him I didn't know him, and that Momma had been taking me to men every night." She hung her head and whispered. "He was so upset. I was so scared. He started looking for his gun and I thought he was going to find the guy and kill him, and then Momma would be mad at me. But, he had something else in mind.

"Don't do this, Ava," Anthony begged, approaching her. "Please."

She looked at Anthony with pity. "It still eats at you, doesn't it? It haunts me knowing that only we know. Don't you want to be free, Anthony? Don't you feel like one day someone will find out and they will never see you the same?" She silently searched his face.

"Don't," he said, barely audible. "Please. Don't."

"Finish, Ava," Preston said. He could see the anguish on his brother's face and knew he needed to be free of this secret once and for all. Preston knew when he received the report years ago there was more to it. Anthony was always the protector.

Preston pulled his father closer to the group, because he felt it was important for him to hear the truth about his wife. He needed to be freed, too.

"Does Tashia know, Anthony?" Ava waited, again, as her brother broke down.

He dropped to his knees and moaned. Tashia dropped with him and held him. "Breathe, Anthony," she whispered. "Let it out. I'm not going anywhere. I told you I would protect you. Hold my hand."

Blaine came through the brush, running to the group. "What is going on? I heard someone yell." Blaine looked around. He couldn't make out what was happening.

"I'm glad you are here, Blaine. I was about to tell a story of family secrets and since you are family." She looked at Blaine. He was so young when everything happened.

"Go on, Ava." Preston wanted this to be done.

"Anthony left the house in a rage. He told me to lock the door and not to open it for anyone. I hid in my room for what seemed to be days, but it was only hours. When he returned I knew something bad had happened.

"Anthony was distraught. He was muddy and he would not look at me. He went straight to the bathroom and bathed. When he came out, he asked me had I bathed. I told him no. He told me to go and fix my bath. When I asked him would I have to go out with Momma that evening, because I hurt down there," she cried. "He said I would never have to do that again. I was safe."

She knelt with Anthony. Lifting his tear-stained face, she ran her hands down both sides and Tashia knocked them away. "And I was safe. But, we both carried the burden of what you did. You are still carrying it and you need to let it go. She was a bad mother, Anthony."

Anthony remembered the night clearly. The events came when he closed his eyes many nights. He told the small group the story.

He remembered his mother arguing with the man, telling him he had to pay her more because she had to take Ava to the doctors. When the man asked her how she would do that without going to jail for prostituting Ava, Pillar told the man she would have Ava say he raped her.

Anthony's anger rekindled when he watched his mother take the additional money from the man. He remembered her taking payment from the men who had done monstrous things to him back in Granada. The dirt he thought he had shed engulfed him again, making him feel nasty and unworthy. As she walked home, he confronted her and she laughed, reminding him there was still a market for him as well. He knew it would continue as long as Ava was with her and if he told his father he would kill her. He knew he had to do something, so he grabbed her by the neck and squeezed until he felt it snap.

"I didn't cry. I carried her to the mud land and dropped her body there hoping the mud would take her, but they found her a week later. For so long I thought I was evil because I felt no remorse for what I did. It was like taking out the trash. I felt relieved she couldn't hurt any of my family again."

"I didn't know or I would have come for you Ava. I would have taken you both. I didn't want you to go with her, neither of you. But, Ava, you ran around always trying to please her. You always wanted to go where she went. I knew what she was when I met her. But, I loved her anyway." Mr. Washington went to Anthony and helped him to his feet. He embraced his son, holding him like a small child. "I am sorry you had to do what I was responsible for. You should not have had to protect your sister. I should have been there to protect her. I could not protect you before you came to me, but you became my son the moment I laid eyes on you and you, too, were my responsibility to protect.

"Anthony, I knew what you had been through, but I did not know it was at the hands of your mother. This was not the story I was told. I am sorry. That should not happen to any child."

"We will not speak of this again. There is no statute of limitation for murder in Antigua. Does everyone understand?" The silence gave him his answer. "Everyone come here."

The small group closed around their father. He first embraced Ava. "I love you and have always. I thought you blamed me for your mother's death as the rumors ran through the town. I would like to be a part of your life again. Please come back and see an old man. I don't have too many years left." Ava lay in her father's arms and cried like a child who had made her way home. The small group all embraced in one big hug.

"I'm sorry," Anthony said, wiping the tears from his face. "I had to stop her from hurting the family."

"Shhh! We will talk of this no more." Mr. Washington embraced his son. "I love you, Anthony, I always have. She lied to you, but no more. Do you understand?" He hugged him again. "You are my son!"

Tashia watched Ava. There was more to this story than she was telling. She enjoyed looking at Anthony, and her look was one of lust.

Anthony helped Tashia fix her dress and they all headed back to the house. A joyful occasion turned emotional very quickly. The night was not done.

Caden's Regrets

Tashia kept Anthony close to her. It was time to go. She went to check in on the kids. Solana was lying across the one bed and Zane slept alone in the other. She didn't peep in on Zander, because she thought it inappropriate to enter the room he shared with Caden.

Moving down the wide hall, she went to Preston's room to see if Cuyler was still awake. She remembered she had problems sleeping at night. She knocked, but there was no answer so she assumed she was asleep. She slightly opened the door and saw no one there. *Maybe she is outside and I missed her.*

Tashia met Anthony back in the living room, talking with Preston. "Have you seen Cuyler and Callia?"

The men looked one to the other. Preston went to his room and Anthony to the kid's room. They were not there. Anthony entered the room where Caden and Zander were, but they still could not be found.

Anthony woke Caden. "Have you seen Cuyler and Callia?"

Caden jumped from the bed and donned his shorts. "No, but I've had a bad feeling all day. They were sleeping with Solana when I went to bed."

The men searched outside and still no trace of the two. Anthony and Tashia went to their home to make sure they did not go there, but they were not there.

Tashia quickly changed out of her gown. She watched Anthony pull a strong box from the bedroom closet and press his fingerprint on the case. It sprung open. He pulled a gun from the box and popped the clip of bullets in the bottom. Sticking the gun in the back of his pants, he looked at her in silence, but she didn't protest. "Let's go find your sister."

The three headed back to the family house, but there was still no sign of the two. Preston stood in the middle of the yard, holding his head as Caden paced. Mr. Williams talked to the guests to see if they saw anything, but no one noticed anything.

Tashia ran inside the house and woke Zander. "Zander!"

"What, Mom!" a startle Zander sat up. "What's going on?"

"I need you to stay in the bedroom with your sister and brother. We can't find Cuyler and Callia and need to go look for them."

Zander was on his feet, getting dressed. "What do you mean can't find?"

"They are not here! We can't find them anywhere!" Tashia could feel her emotions rising, but subdued them.

"I'm going with you. Grandma can watch them."

Tashia agreed that he had a better idea. She went to get Brenda, but she was already in the hall. "What is going on?"

"Cuyler and Callia are missing and we are going to look for them. Can you stay in the room with Solana and Zane, Mom?"

"Of course I can, but where could they be!"

"I don't know, Mom, but we need to go, okay?"

"Go! Go!"

When they returned to the yard, the search had begun. Tashia saw Blaine and Jessica heading for the beach with four other people.

Caden and Preston were headed for the cars. Anthony came to Tashia to let her know the plan. They had divided the island up. They were headed to their assignment.

Zander and his parents headed to their car to cover their portion of the island. It would be light soon and no one knew how long they had been gone.

Caden rode with Preston in silence. His head bowed as he prayed. He asked for direction. He knew he missed it earlier, because he was uneasy all day and he didn't want to miss it again.

The further they went from the house the more he felt they should go back. The feeling was so strong he couldn't breathe. "Go back t0 the house."

"The plan is good," Preston protested.

"Go back to the house. We missed something. She could not have gotten far carrying Callia in her condition and Callia won't go to everyone. We missed something!"

Preston thought about Caden's words and found them to be sound. Quickly, he flipped the car around and headed back to the house.

Preston and Caden went back to the bedroom where the kids were sleeping. Cuyler's flats were still on the floor and the small cover that Callia slept with was gone. Caden walked the room, praying in silence and left.

"Now what?" Preston asked frustrated. "Now what!"

"Let's go to the beach," Caden said, heading that way. Preston was close on his heels.

Caden began to trot through the path. When he got to the other side, he looked around. He couldn't understand why the Holy Spirit sent him that way, but he continued to walk past the semi-circle of chairs down the shoreline. He was sure he saw something on the ground ahead and he began to run.

When he reached the object, he picked it up. Preston was at his side. It was Callia's blanket. He hugged the blanket and dropped to his knees. "Now what, Lord? Now what?"

Epilogue

The old boat propelled through the calm waters, with the moon as its only light and the shore was well behind them. It made no sense to scream; no one would hear her. Besides, Cuyler needed to remain quiet, as she held a sleeping Callia. She hoped her baby girl slept for a while, so she would not be scared. Although Cuyler was terrified, she had to stay calm for her child's sake and to figure out how they were going to get through this.

The mid cabin beneath the helm had no windows, but the moonlight crept through the cracks. It stunk of old furniture. The motor hummed. They were moving slower now. She was tired, but had no time to sleep. They had to escape as soon as possible to ensure their survival.

She knew Preston would be frantic by now and Caden out of his mind. They would be looking for them, but they would not find them. She had dropped Callia's blanket on the beach, hoping someone would find it. The rest was up to them because she did not know the island.

Motion sickness overwhelmed Cuyler from the rocking of the boat. The waters were calmer, thank goodness, or it could have been worse. *The floor is filthy*, she thought, but laughed for thinking of something so trivial. *The last thing I should be thinking about is a dirty floor.*

The baby kicked. Cuyler was hungry. She could feel the tears coming. She cried for fear of what would become of Callia and her unborn child. She was on her own now. Her protectors weren't there to rescue her, as they had all her life. She would have to do it herself.

Diva Dorreen Morgan

Diva Dorreen lives in Southern Maryland with her husband Bernard. *Faith, Hope and Love* is her second novel and the sequel to *Love is Patient Love is Kind,* which is a part of her *Heart Series.*

Dorreen is a new writer who finally put pen to paper. Her first book *Love is Patient Love is Kind* has received great reviews. Readers have said:

"This is an excellent story that comes to life from the first pages! You become easily engrossed in the lives of Cuyler and Caden, and then India and Preston."

"What a wonderful and moving story! I found myself on an emotional roller coaster experiencing each character's highs and lows."

"I found this story to be very captivating from the start. The characters were well developed and their triumphs & tragedies were very believable and could apply to a multitude of individuals who know that faith overcomes all."

"I encourage everyone who reads my work to please write a review on Amazon, Barnes and Nobel and Goodreads! Thank you!"

Follow Diva Dorreen

Instagram – Divadorreen
Facebook – Dorreen Kei Morgan
Twitter – DivaDorreen
Snapchat – DivaDorreen
Website – www.divasdynamics.com

Books by the Author

The Heart Series

Love is Patient Love is Kind: Book 1 (2015)
Faith Hope and Love: Book 2 (2016)
Agape Love: Book 3 (Fall 2019)
UnRaveled (2018)